# Treasure Island

## Robert Louis Stevenson

Illustrations by David Mackintosh

ALMA CLASSICS

ALMA CLASSICS LTD
3 Castle Yard
Richmond
Surrey TW10 6TF
United Kingdom
www.almaclassics.com

*Treasure Island* first published in volume form in 1883
First published (without illustrations) by Alma Classics Ltd
(previously Oneworld Classics Ltd) in 2008
This new edition published by Alma Classics Ltd in 2015
Reprinted 2016, 2017

Text Illustrations © David Mackintosh, 2015

Cover illustration: David Mackintosh, 2015

Extra Material © Alma Classics Ltd

Printed and bound by CPI Group (UK) Ltd, Croydon, CR0 4YY

ISBN: 978-1-84749-486-3

# Contents

*Treasure Island*

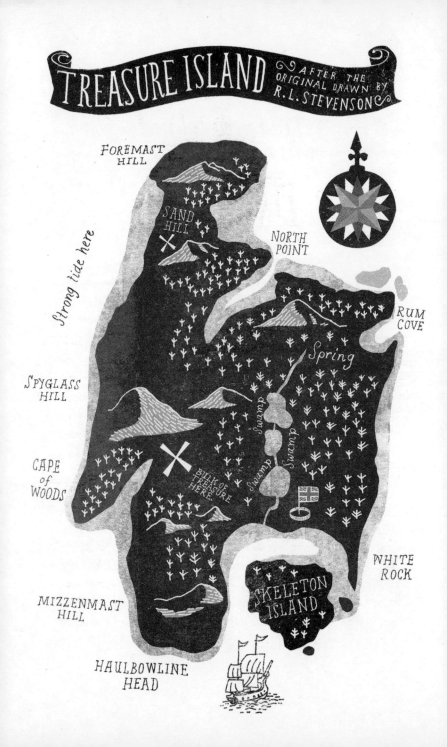

# 1

## *The Old Sea Dog at the "Admiral Benbow"*

SQUIRE TRELAWNEY, DR LIVESEY and the rest of these gentlemen having asked me to write down the whole particulars about Treasure Island, from the beginning to the end, keeping nothing back but the bearings of the island, and that only because there is still treasure not yet lifted, I take up my pen in the year of grace 17–, and go back to the time when my father kept the Admiral Benbow inn, and the brown old seaman, with the sabre cut, first took up his lodging under our roof.

I remember him as if it were yesterday, as he came plodding to the inn door, his sea chest following behind him in a hand-barrow; a tall, strong, heavy, nut-brown man; his tarry pigtail falling over the shoulders of his soiled blue coat; his hands ragged and scarred, with black, broken nails; and the sabre cut across one cheek, a dirty, livid white. I remember him looking round the cove and whistling to himself as he did so, and then breaking out in that old sea song that he sang so often afterwards:

> Fifteen men on the dead man's chest –
> Yo-ho-ho, and a bottle of rum!

in the high, old tottering voice that seemed to have been tuned and broken at the capstan bars. Then he rapped on the door with a bit of stick like a handspike that he carried, and when my father appeared, called roughly for a glass of rum. This, when it was brought to him, he drank slowly, like a connoisseur, lingering on the taste, and still looking about him at the cliffs and up at our signboard.

"This is a handy cove," says he at length, "and a pleasant sit-tyated grog shop. Much company, mate?"

My father told him no, very little company, the more was the pity.

"Well then," said he, "this is the berth for me. Here you, matey," he cried to the man who trundled the barrow, "bring up alongside and help up my chest. I'll stay here a bit," he continued. "I'm a plain man; rum and bacon and eggs is what I want, and that head up there for to watch ships off. What you mought call me? You mought call me Captain. Oh, I see what you're at: there" – and he threw down three or four gold pieces on the threshold. "You can tell me when I've worked through that," says he, looking as fierce as a commander.

And indeed, bad as his clothes were, and coarsely as he spoke, he had none of the appearance of a man who sailed before the mast, but seemed like a mate or skipper,* accustomed to be obeyed or to strike. The man who came with the barrow told us the mail had set him down the morning before at the Royal George; that he had inquired what inns there were along the coast, and hearing ours well spoken of, I suppose, and described as lonely, had chosen it from the others for his place of residence. And that was all we could learn of our guest.

He was a very silent man by custom. All day he hung round the cove, or upon the cliffs, with a brass telescope; all evening he sat in a corner of the parlour next the fire, and drank rum and water very strong. Mostly he would not speak when spoken to; only look up sudden and fierce, and blow through his nose like a foghorn; and we and the people who came about our house soon learnt to let him be. Every day, when he came back from his stroll, he would ask if any seafaring men had gone by along the road. At first we thought it was the want of company of his own kind that made him ask this question; but at last we began to see he was desirous to avoid them. When a seaman put up at the Admiral Benbow (as now and then some did, making by the coast road for Bristol), he would look in at him through the curtained door before he entered the parlour; and he was always sure to be as silent as a mouse when any such was present. For me, at least, there was no secret about the matter; for I was, in a way, a sharer in his alarms. He had taken me aside one day, and promised me a silver fourpenny on the first of every month if I would only keep my "weather eye open for a seafaring man with one leg," and let him know the moment he appeared. Often enough, when the first of the month came round, and I applied to him for my wage, he would only blow through his nose at me, and stare me down; but before the week was out he was sure to think better of it, bring me my fourpenny piece, and repeat his orders to look out for "the seafaring man with one leg."

How that personage haunted my dreams, I need scarcely tell you. On stormy nights, when the wind shook the four corners of the house, and the surf roared along the cove and up the cliffs, I would see him in a thousand forms, and with a thousand diabolical expressions. Now the leg would be cut off at the knee, now at the hip; now he was a monstrous kind of a creature who had never had but the one leg, and that in the middle of his body. To see him leap and run and pursue me over hedge and ditch was the worst of nightmares. And altogether I paid pretty dear for my monthly fourpenny piece, in the shape of these abominable fancies.

But though I was so terrified by the idea of the seafaring man with one leg, I was far less afraid of the captain himself than anybody else who knew him. There were nights when he took a deal more rum and water than his head would carry; and then he would sometimes sit and sing his wicked, old, wild sea songs, minding nobody; but sometimes he would call for glasses round, and force all the trembling company to listen to his stories or bear a chorus to his singing. Often I have heard the house shaking with "Yo-ho-ho, and a bottle of rum," all the neighbours joining in for dear life, with the fear of death upon them, and each singing louder than the other, to avoid remark. For in these fits he was the most overriding companion ever known; he would slap his hand on the table for silence all round; he would fly up in a passion of anger at a question, or sometimes because none was put, and so he judged the company was not following his story. Nor would he allow anyone to leave the inn till he had drunk himself sleepy and reeled off to bed.

His stories were what frightened people worst of all. Dreadful stories they were; about hanging, and walking the plank, and storms at sea, and the Dry Tortugas,* and wild deeds and places on the Spanish Main.* By his own account, he must have lived his life among some of the wickedest men that God ever allowed upon the sea; and the language in which he told these stories shocked our plain country people almost as much as the crimes that he described. My father was always saying the inn would be ruined, for people would soon cease coming there to be tyrannized over and put down, and sent shivering to their beds; but I really believe his presence did us good. People were frightened at the time, but on looking back they rather liked it; it was a fine excitement in a quiet country life; and there was even a party of the younger men who pretended to admire him, calling him a "true sea dog," and a "real old salt," and suchlike names, and saying there was the sort of man that made England terrible at sea.

In one way, indeed, he bade fair to ruin us; for he kept on staying week after week, and at last month after month, so that all the money had been long exhausted, and still my father never plucked up the heart to insist on having more. If ever he mentioned it, the captain blew through his nose so loudly that you might say he roared, and stared my poor father out of the room. I have seen him wringing his hands after such a rebuff, and I am sure the annoyance and the terror he lived in must have greatly hastened his early and unhappy death.

All the time he lived with us, the captain made no change whatever in his dress but to buy some stockings from a hawker. One of the cocks of his hat having fallen down, he let it hang from that day forth, though it was a great annoyance when it blew. I remember the appearance of his coat, which he patched himself upstairs in his room, and which, before the end, was nothing but patches. He never wrote or received a letter, and he never spoke with any but the neighbours, and with these, for the most part, only when drunk on rum. The great sea chest none of us had ever seen open.

He was only once crossed, and that was towards the end, when my poor father was far gone in a decline that took him off.* Dr Livesey came late one afternoon to see the patient, took a bit of dinner from my mother, and went into the parlour to smoke a pipe until his horse should come down from the hamlet, for we had no stabling at the old Benbow. I followed him in, and I remember observing the contrast the neat, bright doctor, with his powder as white as snow, and his bright, black eyes and pleasant manners, made with the coltish country folk, and above all, with that filthy, heavy, bleared scarecrow of a pirate of ours, sitting, far gone in rum, with his arms on the table. Suddenly he – the captain, that is – began to pipe up his eternal song:

Fifteen men on the dead man's chest –
Yo-ho-ho, and a bottle of rum!
Drink and the devil had done for the rest –
Yo-ho-ho, and a bottle of rum!

At first I had supposed "the dead man's chest" to be that identical big box of his upstairs in the front room, and the thought had been mingled in my nightmares with that of the one-legged seafaring man. But by this time we had all long ceased to pay any particular notice to the song; it was new, that night, to nobody but Dr Livesey, and on him I observed it did not produce an agreeable effect, for he looked up for a moment quite angrily before he went on with his talk to old Taylor, the gardener, on a new cure for the rheumatics. In the meantime, the captain gradually brightened up at his own music, and at last flapped his hand upon the table before him in a way we all knew to mean – silence. The voices stopped at once, all but Dr Livesey's; he went on as before, speaking clear and kind, and drawing briskly at his pipe between every word or two. The captain glared at him for a while, flapped his hand again, glared still harder, and at last broke out with a villainous, low oath: "Silence, there, between decks!"

"Were you addressing me, sir?" says the doctor; and when the ruffian had told him, with another oath, that this was so, "I have only one thing to say to you, sir," replies the doctor, "that if you keep on drinking rum, the world will soon be quit of a very dirty scoundrel!"

The old fellow's fury was awful. He sprang to his feet, drew and opened a sailor's clasp knife, and, balancing it open on the palm of his hand, threatened to pin the doctor to the wall.

The doctor never so much as moved. He spoke to him, as before, over his shoulder, and in the same tone of voice; rather high, so that all the room might hear, but perfectly calm and steady:

"If you do not put that knife this instant in your pocket, I promise, upon my honour, you shall hang at the next assizes."

Then followed a battle of looks between them; but the captain soon knuckled under, put up his weapon, and resumed his seat, grumbling like a beaten dog.

"And now, sir," continued the doctor, "since I now know there's such a fellow in my district, you may count I'll have an eye upon you day and night. I'm not a doctor only; I'm a magistrate; and if I catch a breath of complaint against you, if it's only for a piece of incivility like tonight's, I'll take effectual means to have you hunted down and routed out of this. Let that suffice."

Soon after, Dr Livesey's horse came to the door, and he rode away; but the captain held his peace that evening, and for many evenings to come.

## 2

*Black Dog Appears and Disappears*

IT WAS NOT VERY LONG AFTER THIS that there occurred the first of the mysterious events that rid us at last of the captain, though not, as you will see, of his affairs. It was a bitter-cold winter, with long, hard frosts and heavy gales; and it was plain from the first that my poor father was little likely to see the spring. He sank daily, and my mother and I had all the inn upon our hands; and were kept busy enough, without paying much regard to our unpleasant guest.

It was one January morning, very early – a pinching, frosty morning – the cove all grey with hoar frost, the ripple lapping softly on the stones, the sun still low and only touching the hilltops and shining far to seaward. The captain had risen earlier than usual, and set out down the beach, his cutlass swinging under the broad skirts of the old blue coat, his brass telescope under his arm, his hat tilted back upon his head. I remember his breath hanging like smoke in his wake as he strode off, and the last sound I heard of him, as he turned the big rock, was a loud snort of indignation, as though his mind was still running upon Dr Livesey.

Well, mother was upstairs with father; and I was laying the breakfast table against the captain's return, when the parlour door opened, and a man stepped in on whom I had never set my eyes before. He was a pale, tallowy creature, wanting two fingers of the left hand; and, though he wore a cutlass, he did not look much like a fighter. I had always my eye open for seafaring men, with one leg or two, and I remember this one puzzled me. He was not sailorly, and yet he had a smack of the sea about him too.

I asked him what was for his service, and he said he would take rum; but as I was going out of the room to fetch it he sat down upon a table, and motioned me to draw near. I paused where I was with my napkin in my hand.

"Come here, sonny," says he. "Come nearer here."

I took a step nearer.

"Is this here table for my mate, Bill?" he asked, with a kind of leer.

I told him I did not know his mate Bill; and this was for a person who stayed in our house, whom we called the captain.

"Well," said he, "my mate Bill would be called the captain, as like as not. He has a cut on one cheek, and a mighty pleasant way with him, particularly in drink, has my mate, Bill. We'll put it, for argument like, that your captain has a cut on one cheek – and we'll put it, if you like, that that cheek's the right one. Ah, well! I told you. Now, is my mate Bill in this here house?"

I told him he was out walking.

"Which way, sonny? Which way is he gone?"

And when I had pointed out the rock and told him how the captain was likely to return, and how soon, and answered a few other questions, "Ah," said he, "this'll be as good as drink to my mate Bill."

The expression of his face as he said these words was not at all pleasant, and I had my own reasons for thinking that the stranger was mistaken, even supposing he meant what he said. But it was no affair of mine, I thought; and besides, it was difficult to know what to do. The stranger kept hanging about just inside the inn door, peering round the corner like a cat waiting for a mouse. Once I stepped out myself into the road, but he immediately called me back, and as I did not obey quick enough for his fancy, a most horrible change came over his tallowy face, and he ordered me in with an oath that made me jump. As soon as I was back again he returned to his former manner – half-fawning, half-sneering – patted me on the shoulder, told me I was a good boy, and he had taken quite a fancy to me. "I have a son of my own," said he, "as like you as two blocks, and he's all the pride of my 'art. But the great thing for boys is discipline, sonny – discipline. Now, if you had sailed along of Bill, you wouldn't have stood there to be spoke to twice – not you. That was never Bill's way, nor the way of sich as sailed with him. And here, sure enough, is my mate Bill, with a spyglass under his arm, bless his old 'art to be sure. You and me'll just go back into the parlour, sonny, and get behind the door, and we'll give Bill a little surprise – bless his 'art, I say again."

So saying, the stranger backed along with me into the parlour, and put me behind him in the corner, so that we were both hidden by the open door. I was very uneasy and alarmed, as you may fancy, and it rather added to my fears to observe that the stranger was certainly frightened himself. He cleared the hilt of his cutlass and loosened the blade in the sheath; and all the time we were waiting there he kept swallowing as if he felt what we used to call a lump in the throat.

At last in strode the captain, slammed the door behind him, without looking to the right or left, and marched straight across the room to where his breakfast awaited him.

"Bill," said the stranger, in a voice that I thought he had tried to make bold and big.

The captain spun round on his heel and fronted us; all the brown had gone out of his face, and even his nose was blue; he had the look of a man who sees a ghost, or the evil one, or something worse, if anything can be; and, upon my word, I felt sorry to see him, all in a moment, turn so old and sick.

"Come, Bill, you know me; you know an old shipmate, Bill, surely," said the stranger.

The captain made a sort of gasp.

"Black Dog!" said he.

"And who else?" returned the other, getting more at his ease. "Black Dog as ever was, come for to see his old shipmate Billy, at the Admiral Benbow inn. Ah, Bill, Bill, we have seen a sight of times, us two, since I lost them two talons," holding up his mutilated hand.

"Now, look here," said the captain, "you've run me down; here I am; well then speak up: what is it?"

"That's you, Bill," returned Black Dog, "you're in the right of it, Billy. I'll have a glass of rum from this dear child here, as I've took such a liking to; and we'll sit down, if you please, and talk square, like old shipmates."

When I returned with the rum, they were already seated on either side of the captain's breakfast table – Black Dog next to the door, and sitting sideways, so as to have one eye on his old shipmate, and one, as I thought, on his retreat.

He bade me go, and leave the door wide open. "None of your keyholes for me, sonny," he said; and I left them together, and retired into the bar.

"For a long time, though I certainly did my best to listen, I could hear nothing but a low gabbling; but at last the voices began to grow higher, and I could pick up a word or two, mostly oaths, from the captain.

"No, no, no, no; and an end of it!" he cried once. And again, "If it comes to swinging, swing all, say I."

Then all of a sudden there was a tremendous explosion of oaths and other noises – the chair and table went over in a lump, a clash of steel followed, and then a cry of pain, and the next instant I saw Black Dog in full flight, and the captain hotly pursuing, both with drawn cutlasses, and the former streaming blood from the left shoulder. Just at the door, the captain aimed at the fugitive one last tremendous cut, which would certainly have split him to the chine had it not been intercepted by our big signboard of Admiral Benbow. You may see the notch on the lower side of the frame to this day.

That blow was the last of the battle. Once out upon the road, Black Dog, in spite of his wound, showed a wonderful clean pair of heels, and disappeared over the edge of the hill in half a minute. The captain, for his part, stood staring at the signboard like a bewildered man. Then he passed his hand over his eyes several times, and at last turned back into the house.

"Jim," says he, "rum," and as he spoke, he reeled a little, and caught himself with one hand against the wall.

"Are you hurt?" cried I.

"Rum," he repeated. "I must get away from here. Rum! Rum!"

I ran to fetch it; but I was quite unsteadied by all that had fallen out, and I broke one glass and fouled the tap, and while I was still getting in my own way, I heard a loud fall in the parlour, and, running in, beheld the captain lying full length upon the floor. At the same instant my mother, alarmed by the cries and fighting, came running downstairs to help me. Between us we raised his head. He was breathing very loud and hard; but his eyes were closed, and his face a horrible colour.

"Dear, deary me," cried my mother, "what a disgrace upon the house! And your poor father sick!"

In the meantime, we had no idea what to do to help the captain, nor any other thought but that he had got his death-hurt in the scuffle with the stranger. I got the rum, to be sure, and tried to put it down his throat; but his teeth were tightly shut, and his jaws as strong as iron. It was a happy relief for us when the door opened and Doctor Livesey came in, on his visit to my father.

"Oh, Doctor," we cried, "what shall we do? Where is he wounded?"

"Wounded? A fiddlestick's end!"* said the doctor. "No more wounded than you or I. The man has had a stroke, as I warned him. Now, Mrs Hawkins, just you run upstairs to your husband, and tell him, if possible, nothing about it. For my part, I must do my best to save this fellow's trebly worthless life; and Jim, you get me a basin."

When I got back with the basin, the doctor had already ripped up the captain's sleeve, and exposed his great sinewy arm. It was tattooed in several places. "Here's luck", "A fair wind" and "Billy Bones his fancy" were very neatly and clearly executed on the forearm; and up near the shoulder there was a sketch of a gallows and a man hanging from it – done, as I thought, with great spirit.

"Prophetic," said the doctor, touching this picture with his finger. "And now, Master Billy Bones, if that be your name, we'll have a look at the colour of your blood. Jim," he said, "are you afraid of blood?"

"No, sir," said I.

"Well then," said he, "you hold the basin," and with that he took his lancet and opened a vein.

A great deal of blood was taken before the captain opened his eyes and looked mistily about him. First he recognized the doctor with an unmistakable frown; then his glance fell upon me, and he looked relieved. But suddenly his colour changed, and he tried to raise himself, crying:

"Where's Black Dog?"

"There is no Black Dog here," said the doctor, "except what you have on your own back. You have been drinking rum; you have had a stroke, precisely as I told you; and I have just, very much against my own will, dragged you head foremost out of the grave. Now, Mr Bones—"

"That's not my name," he interrupted.

"Much I care," returned the doctor. "It's the name of a buccaneer of my acquaintance; and I call you by it for the sake of shortness, and what I have to say to you is this: one glass of rum won't kill you, but if you take one you'll take another and another, and I stake my wig if you don't break off short, you'll die – do you understand that? – die, and go to your own place, like the man in the Bible.* Come, now, make an effort. I'll help you to your bed for once."

Between us, with much trouble, we managed to hoist him upstairs, and laid him on his bed, where his head fell back on the pillow as if he were almost fainting.

"Now, mind you," said the doctor, "I clear my conscience – the name of rum for you is death."

And with that he went off to see my father, taking me with him by the arm.

"This is nothing," he said, as soon as he had closed the door. "I have drawn blood enough to keep him quiet a while; he should lie for a week where he is – that is the best thing for him and you; but another stroke would settle him."

# 3

## *The Black Spot*

**A**BOUT NOON I STOPPED at the captain's door with some cooling drinks and medicines. He was lying very much as we had left him, only a little higher, and he seemed both weak and excited.

"Jim," he said, "you're the only one here that's worth anything; and you know I've been always good to you. Never a month but I've given you a silver fourpenny for yourself. And now you see, mate, I'm pretty low, and deserted by all; and Jim, you'll bring me one noggin of rum, now, won't you, matey?"

"The doctor—" I began.

But he broke in cursing the doctor, in a feeble voice, but heartily. "Doctors is all swabs," he said, "and that doctor there, why, what do he know about seafaring men? I been in places hot as pitch, and mates dropping round with yellow jack, and the blessed land a-heaving like the sea with earthquakes – what do the doctor know of lands like that? – and I lived on rum, I tell you. It's been meat and drink, and man and wife to me; and if I'm not to have my rum now I'm a poor old hulk on a lee shore, my blood'll be on you, Jim, and that doctor swab," and he ran on again for a while with curses. "Look, Jim, how my fingers fidges," he continued, in the pleading tone. "I can't keep 'em still, not I. I haven't had a drop this blessed day. That doctor's a fool, I tell you. If I don't have a drain o' rum, Jim, I'll have the horrors; I seen some on 'em already. I seen old Flint in the corner there, behind you; as plain as print, I seen him; and if I get the horrors, I'm a man that has lived rough, and I'll raise Cain.* Your doctor hisself said one glass wouldn't hurt me. I'll give you a golden guinea for a noggin, Jim."

He was growing more and more excited, and this alarmed me for my father, who was very low that day and needed quiet; besides, I was reassured by the doctor's words, now quoted to me, and rather offended by the offer of a bribe.

"I want none of your money," said I, "but what you owe my father. I'll get you one glass, and no more."

When I brought it to him, he seized it greedily, and drank it out.

"Ay, ay," said he, "that's some better, sure enough. And now, matey, did that doctor say how long I was to lie here in this old berth?"

"A week at least," said I.

"Thunder!" he cried. "A week! I can't do that: they'd have the black spot on me by then. The lubbers is going about to get the wind of me this blessed moment; lubbers as couldn't keep what they got, and want to nail what is another's. Is that seamanly behaviour, now, I want to know? But I'm a saving soul. I never wasted good money of mine, nor lost it neither; and I'll trick 'em again. I'm not afraid on 'em. I'll shake out another reef, matey, and daddle 'em again."*

As he was thus speaking, he had risen from bed with great difficulty, holding to my shoulder with a grip that almost made me cry out, and moving his legs like so much deadweight. His words, spirited as they were in meaning, contrasted sadly with the weakness of the voice in which they were uttered. He paused when he had got into a sitting position on the edge.

"That doctor's done me," he murmured. "My ears is singing. Lay me back."

Before I could do much to help him, he had fallen back again to his former place, where he lay for a while silent.

"Jim," he said at length, "you saw that seafaring man today?"

"Black Dog?" I asked.

"Ah! Black Dog," says he. "*He's* a bad 'un; but there's worse that put him on. Now, if I can't get away nohow, and they tip me the black spot, mind you, it's my old sea chest they're after; you get on a horse – you can, can't you? Well then you get on a horse, and go to – well, yes, I will! – to that eternal doctor swab, and tell him to pipe all hands* – magistrates and sich – and he'll lay 'em aboard at the Admiral Benbow – all old Flint's crew, man and boy, all on 'em that's left. I was first mate, I was, old Flint's first mate, and I'm the on'y one as knows the place. He gave it me at Savannah, when he lay a-dying, like as if I was to now, you see. But you won't peach unless they get the black spot on me, or unless you see that Black Dog again, or a seafaring man with one leg, Jim – him above all."

"But what is the black spot, Captain?" I asked.

"That's a summons, mate. I'll tell you if they get that. But you keep your weather eye open, Jim, and I'll share with you equals, upon my honour."

He wandered a little longer, his voice growing weaker; but soon after I had given him his medicine, which he took like a child, with the remark, "If ever a seaman wanted drugs, it's me," he fell at last into a heavy, swoon-like sleep, in which I left him. What I should have done, had all gone well, I do not know. Probably I should have told the whole story to the doctor; for I was in mortal fear lest the captain should repent of his confessions and make an end of me. But as things fell out, my poor father died quite suddenly that evening, which put all other matters on one side. Our natural distress, the visits of the neighbours, the arranging of the funeral, and all the work of the inn to be carried on in the meanwhile, kept me so busy that I had scarcely time to think of the captain, far less to be afraid of him.

He got downstairs next morning, to be sure, and had his meals as usual, though he ate little, and had more, I am afraid, than his usual supply of rum, for he helped himself out of the bar, scowling and blowing through his nose, and no one dared to cross him. On the night before the funeral he was as drunk as ever; and it was shocking, in that house of mourning, to hear him singing away at his ugly old sea song; but, weak as he was, we were all in the fear of death for him, and the doctor was suddenly taken up with a case many miles away, and was never near the house after my father's death. I have said the captain was weak; and indeed he seemed rather to grow weaker than regain his strength. He clambered up and downstairs, and went from the parlour to the bar and back again, and sometimes put his nose out of doors to smell the sea, holding on to the walls as he went for support, and breathing hard and fast like a man on a steep mountain. He never particularly addressed me, and it is my belief he had as good as forgotten his confidences; but his temper was more flighty and, allowing for his bodily weakness, more violent than ever. He had an alarming way now when he was drunk of drawing his cutlass and laying it bare before him on the table. But with all that, he minded people less, and seemed shut up in his own thoughts and rather wandering. Once, for instance, to our extreme wonder, he piped up to a different air, a kind of country love song, that he must have learnt in his youth before he had begun to follow the sea.

So things passed until, the day after the funeral, and about three o'clock of a bitter, foggy, frosty afternoon, I was standing at the door for a moment, full of sad thoughts about my father, when I saw someone drawing slowly near along the road. He was plainly blind, for he tapped before him with a stick, and wore a great green shade over his eyes and nose; and he was hunched, as if with age or weakness, and wore a huge old tattered sea cloak with a hood that made him appear positively deformed. I never saw in my life a more dreadful-looking figure. He stopped a little from the inn, and raising his voice in an odd sing-song, addressed the air in front of him:

"Will any kind friend inform a poor blind man, who has lost the precious sight of his eyes in the gracious defence of his native country, England, and God bless King George! – where or in what part of this country he may now be?"

"You are at the Admiral Benbow, Black Hill Cove, my good man," said I.

"I hear a voice," said he, "a young voice. Will you give me your hand, my kind young friend, and lead me in?"

I held out my hand, and the horrible, soft-spoken, eyeless creature gripped it in a moment like a vice. I was so much startled that I struggled to withdraw; but the blind man pulled me close up to him with a single action of his arm.

"Now, boy," he said, "take me in to the captain."

"Sir," said I, "upon my word I dare not."

"Oh," he sneered, "that's it! Take me in straight, or I'll break your arm."

And he gave it, as he spoke, a wrench that made me cry out.

"Sir," said I, "it is for yourself I mean. The captain is not what he used to be. He sits with a drawn cutlass. Another gentleman—"

"Come, now, march," interrupted he; and I never heard a voice so cruel, and cold, and ugly as that blind man's. It cowed me more than the pain; and I began to obey him at once, walking straight in at the door and towards the parlour, where our sick

21

old buccaneer was sitting, dazed with rum. The blind man clung close to me, holding me in one iron fist, and leaning almost more of his weight on me than I could carry. "Lead me straight up to him, and when I'm in view, cry out, 'Here's a friend for you, Bill.' If you don't, I'll do this," and with that he gave me a twitch that I thought would have made me faint. Between this and that, I was so utterly terrified of the blind beggar that I forgot my terror of the captain, and as I opened the parlour door, cried out the words he had ordered in a trembling voice.

The poor captain raised his eyes, and at one look the rum went out of him, and left him staring sober. The expression of his face was not so much of terror as of mortal sickness. He made a movement to rise, but I do not believe he had enough force left in his body.

"Now, Bill, sit where you are," said the beggar. "If I can't see, I can hear a finger stirring. Business is business. Hold out your left hand. Boy, take his left hand by the wrist, and bring it near to my right."

We both obeyed him to the letter, and I saw him pass something from the hollow of the hand that held his stick into the palm of the captain's, which closed upon it instantly.

"And now that's done," said the blind man; and at the words he suddenly left hold of me, and, with incredible accuracy and nimbleness, skipped out of the parlour and into the road, where, as I still stood motionless, I could hear his stick go tap-tap-tapping into the distance.

It was some time before either I or the captain seemed to gather our senses; but at length, and about at the same moment, I released his wrist, which I was still holding, and he drew in his hand and looked sharply into the palm.

"Ten o'clock!" he cried. "Six hours. We'll do them yet," and he sprang to his feet.

# CHAPTER 3

Even as he did so, he reeled, put his hand to his throat, stood swaying for a moment, and then, with a peculiar sound, fell from his whole height face foremost to the floor.

I ran to him at once, calling to my mother. But haste was all in vain. The captain had been struck dead by thundering apoplexy. It is a curious thing to understand, for I had certainly never liked the man, though of late I had begun to pity him, but as soon as I saw that he was dead, I burst into a flood of tears. It was the second death I had known, and the sorrow of the first was still fresh in my heart.

# 4

*The Sea Chest*

I LOST NO TIME, OF COURSE, in telling my mother all that I knew, and perhaps should have told her long before, and we saw ourselves at once in a difficult and dangerous position. Some of the man's money – if he had any – was certainly due to us; but it was not likely that our captain's shipmates, above all the two specimens seen by me, Black Dog and the blind beggar, would be inclined to give up their booty in payment of the dead man's debts. The captain's order to mount at once and ride for Doctor Livesey would have left my mother alone and unprotected, which was not to be thought of. Indeed, it seemed impossible for either of us to remain much longer in the house: the fall of coals in the kitchen grate, the very ticking of the clock, filled us with alarms. The neighbourhood, to our ears, seemed haunted by approaching footsteps; and what between the dead body of the captain on the parlour floor, and the thought of that detestable blind beggar hovering near at hand, and ready to return, there were moments when, as the saying goes, I jumped in my skin for terror. Something must speedily be resolved upon; and

24

it occurred to us at last to go forth together and seek help in the neighbouring hamlet. No sooner said than done. Bare-headed as we were, we ran out at once in the gathering evening and the frosty fog.

The hamlet lay not many hundred yards away though out of view, on the other side of the next cove; and what greatly encouraged me: it was in an opposite direction from that whence the blind man had made his appearance, and whither he had presumably returned. We were not many minutes on the road, though we sometimes stopped to lay hold of each other and hearken. But there was no unusual sound – nothing but the low wash of the ripple and the croaking of the inmates of the wood.

It was already candlelight when we reached the hamlet, and I shall never forget how much I was cheered to see the yellow shine in doors and windows; but that, as it proved, was the best of the help we were likely to get in that quarter. For – you would have thought men would have been ashamed of themselves – no soul would consent to return with us to the Admiral Benbow. The more we told of our troubles, the more – man, woman and child – they clung to the shelter of their houses. The name of Captain Flint, though it was strange to me, was well enough known to some there, and carried a great weight of terror. Some of the men who had been to fieldwork on the far side of the Admiral Benbow remembered, besides, to have seen several strangers on the road, and taking them to be smugglers, to have bolted away; and one at least had seen a little lugger in what we called Kitt's Hole. For that matter, anyone who was a comrade of the captain's was enough to frighten them to death. And the short and the long of the matter was that while we could get several who were willing enough to ride to Dr Livesey's which lay in another direction, not one would help us to defend the inn.

They say cowardice is infectious; but then argument is, on the other hand, a great emboldener; and so when each had said his say, my mother made them a speech. She would not, she declared, lose money that belonged to her fatherless boy, "if none of the rest of you dare," she said, "Jim and I dare. Back we will go, the way we came, and small thanks to you big, hulking, chicken-hearted men. We'll have that chest open if we die for it. And I'll thank you for that bag, Mrs Crossley, to bring back our lawful money in."

Of course, I said I would go with my mother; and of course, they all cried out at our foolhardiness; but even then not a man would go along with us. All they would do was to give me a loaded pistol, lest we were attacked; and to promise to have horses ready saddled, in case we were pursued on our return; while one lad was to ride forwards to the doctor's in search of armed assistance.

My heart was beating finely when we two set forth in the cold night upon this dangerous venture. A full moon was beginning to rise and peered redly through the upper edges of the fog, and this increased our haste, for it was plain, before we came forth again, that all would be as bright as day, and our departure exposed to the eyes of any watchers. We slipped along the hedges, noiseless and swift, nor did we see or hear anything to increase our terrors, till, to our relief, the door of the Admiral Benbow had closed behind us.

I slipped the bolt at once, and we stood and panted for a moment in the dark, alone in the house with the dead captain's body. Then my mother got a candle in the bar, and, holding each other's hands, we advanced into the parlour. He lay as we had left him, on his back, with his eyes open, and one arm stretched out.

"Draw down the blind, Jim," whispered my mother, "they might come and watch outside. And now," said she, when I had done so, "we have to get the key off *that*; and who's to touch it, I should like to know!" and she gave a kind of sob as she said the words.

I went down on my knees at once. On the floor close to his hand there was a little round of paper, blackened on the one side. I could not doubt that this was the "black spot"; and taking it up, I found written on the other side, in a very good, clear hand, this short message: "You have till ten tonight."

"He had till ten, mother," said I; and just as I said it, our old clock began striking. This sudden noise startled us shockingly; but the news was good, for it was only six.

"Now, Jim," she said, "that key."

I felt in his pockets, one after another. A few small coins, a thimble and some thread and big needles, a piece of pigtail tobacco bitten away at the end, his gully with the crooked handle, a pocket compass and a tinderbox were all that they contained, and I began to despair.

"Perhaps it's round his neck," suggested my mother.

Overcoming a strong repugnance, I tore open his shirt at the neck, and there, sure enough, hanging to a bit of tarry string, which I cut with his own gully, we found the key. At this triumph we were filled with hope, and hurried upstairs without delay to the little room where he had slept so long, and where his box had stood since the day of his arrival.

It was like any other seaman's chest on the outside, the initial "B" burnt on the top of it with a hot iron, and the corners somewhat smashed and broken, as by long, rough usage.

"Give me the key," said my mother; and though the lock was very stiff, she had turned it and thrown back the lid in a twinkling.

A strong smell of tobacco and tar rose from the interior, but nothing was to be seen on the top except a suit of very good clothes, carefully brushed and folded. They had never been worn, my mother said. Under that, the miscellany began – a quadrant, a tin canikin, several sticks of tobacco, two brace of very handsome pistols, a piece of bar silver, an old Spanish watch and some

other trinkets of little value and mostly of foreign make, a pair
of compasses mounted with brass, and five or six curious West
Indian shells. I have often wondered since why he should have
carried about these shells with him in his wandering, guilty and
hunted life.

In the meantime, we had found nothing of any value but the
silver and the trinkets, and neither of these were in our way.
Underneath there was an old boat cloak, whitened with sea salt
on many a harbour-bar. My mother pulled it up with impatience,
and there lay before us the last things in the chest: a bundle tied
up in oilcloth, and looking like papers, and a canvas bag, that
gave forth at a touch the jingle of gold.

"I'll show these rogues that I'm an honest woman," said my
mother. "I'll have my dues, and not a farthing over. Hold Mrs
Crossley's bag." And she began to count over the amount of
the captain's score from the sailor's bag into the one that I was
holding.

It was a long, difficult business, for the coins were of all
countries and sizes – doubloons, and louis d'or, and guineas,
and pieces of eight, and I know not what besides, all shaken
together at random. The guineas, too, were about the scarc-
est, and it was with these only that my mother knew how to
make her count.

When we were about halfway through, I suddenly put my
hand upon her arm; for I had heard in the silent, frosty air a
sound that brought my heart into my mouth – the tap-tapping
of the blind man's stick upon the frozen road. It drew nearer
and nearer, while we sat holding our breath. Then it struck
sharp on the inn door, and then we could hear the handle
being turned, and the bolt rattling as the wretched being tried
to enter; and then there was a long time of silence both within
and without. At last the tapping recommenced, and, to our

indescribable joy and gratitude, died slowly away again until it ceased to be heard.

"Mother," said I, "take the whole and let's be going," for I was sure the bolted door must have seemed suspicious, and would bring the whole hornet's nest about our ears; though how thankful I was that I had bolted it, none could tell who had never met that terrible blind man.

But my mother, frightened as she was, would not consent to take a fraction more than was due to her, and was obstinately unwilling to be content with less. It was not yet seven, she said, by a long way; she knew her rights and she would have them; and she was still arguing with me, when a little low whistle sounded a good way off upon the hill. That was enough, and more than enough, for both of us.

"I'll take what I have," she said, jumping to her feet.

"And I'll take this to square the count," said I, picking up the oilskin packet.

Next moment we were both groping downstairs, leaving the candle by the empty chest; and the next we had opened the door and were in full retreat. We had not started a moment too soon. The fog was rapidly dispersing; already the moon shone quite clear on the high ground on either side; and it was only in the exact bottom of the dell and round the tavern door that a thin veil still hung unbroken to conceal the first steps of our escape. Far less than halfway to the hamlet, very little beyond the bottom of the hill, we must come forth into the moonlight. Nor was this all; for the sound of several footsteps running came already to our ears, and as we looked back in their direction, a light tossing to and fro and still rapidly advancing showed that one of the newcomers carried a lantern.

"My dear," said my mother suddenly, "take the money and run on. I am going to faint."

This was certainly the end for both of us, I thought. How I cursed the cowardice of the neighbours; how I blamed my poor mother for her honesty and her greed, for her past foolhardiness and present weakness! We were just at the little bridge, by good fortune; and I helped her, tottering as she was, to the edge of the bank, where sure enough she gave a sigh and fell on my shoulder. I do not know how I found the strength to do it at all, and I am afraid it was roughly done; but I managed to drag her down the bank and a little way under the arch. Further I could not move her, for the bridge was too low to let me do more than crawl below it. So there we had to stay – my mother almost entirely exposed, and both of us within earshot of the inn.

# 5

## *The Last of the Blind Man*

MY CURIOSITY, IN A SENSE, was stronger than my fear;
for I could not remain where I was, but crept back to the
bank again, whence, sheltering my head behind a bush of broom,
I might command the road before our door. I was scarcely in
position ere my enemies began to arrive, seven or eight of them,
running hard, their feet beating out of time along the road, and
the man with the lantern some paces in front. Three men ran
together, hand in hand; and I made out, even through the mist,
that the middle man of this trio was the blind beggar. The next
moment his voice showed me that I was right.

"Down with the door!" he cried.

"Ay, ay, sir!" answered two or three; and a rush was made upon
the Admiral Benbow, the lantern-bearer following; and then I could
see them pause, and hear speeches passed in a lower key, as if they
were surprised to find the door open. But the pause was brief, for
the blind man again issued his commands. His voice sounded
louder and higher, as if he were afire with eagerness and rage.

"In, in, in!" he shouted, and cursed them for their delay.

Four or five of them obeyed at once, two remaining on the road with the formidable beggar. There was a pause, then a cry of surprise, and then a voice shouting from the house:

"Bill's dead!"

But the blind man swore at them again for their delay.

"Search him, some of you shirking lubbers, and the rest of you aloft and get the chest," he cried.

I could hear their feet rattling up our old stairs, so that the house must have shook with it. Promptly afterwards, fresh sounds of astonishment arose; the window of the captain's room was thrown open with a slam and a jingle of broken glass; and a man leant out into the moonlight, head and shoulders, and addressed the blind beggar on the road below him.

"Pew," he cried, "they've been before us. Someone's turned the chest out alow and aloft."

"Is it there?" roared Pew.

"The money's there."

The blind man cursed the money.

"Flint's fist, I mean," he cried.

"We don't see it here nohow," returned the man.

"Here, you below there, is it on Bill?" cried the blind man again.

At that, another fellow, probably him who had remained below to search the captain's body, came to the door of the inn. "Bill's been overhauled a'ready," said he, "nothin' left."

"It's these people of the inn – it's that boy. I wish I had put his eyes out!" cried the blind man, Pew. "They were here no time ago – they had the door bolted when I tried it. Scatter, lads, and find 'em."

"Sure enough, they left their glim here," said the fellow from the window.

"Scatter and find 'em! Rout the house out!"* reiterated Pew, striking with his stick upon the road.

Then there followed a great to-do through all our old inn – heavy feet pounding to and fro, furniture thrown over, doors kicked in, until the very rocks re-echoed, and the men came out again, one after another, on the road, and declared that we were nowhere to be found. And just then the same whistle that had alarmed my mother and myself over the dead captain's money was once more clearly audible through the night, but this time twice repeated. I had thought it to be the blind man's trumpet, so to speak, summoning his crew to the assault; but I now found that it was a signal from the hillside towards the hamlet, and, from its effect upon the buccaneers, a signal to warn them of approaching danger.

"There's Dirk again," said one. "Twice! We'll have to budge, mates."

"Budge, you skulk!" cried Pew. "Dirk was a fool and a coward from the first – you wouldn't mind him. They must be close by; they can't be far; you have your hands on it. Scatter and look for them, dogs! Oh, shiver my soul," he cried, "if I had eyes!"

This appeal seemed to produce some effect, for two of the fellows began to look here and there among the lumber, but half-heartedly, I thought, and with half an eye to their own danger all the time, while the rest stood irresolute on the road.

"You have your hands on thousands, you fools, and you hang a leg!* You'd be as rich as kings if you could find it, and you know it's here, and you stand there skulking. There wasn't one of you dared face Bill, and I did it – a blind man! And I'm to lose my chance for you! I'm to be a poor, crawling beggar, sponging for rum, when I might be rolling in a coach! If you had the pluck of a weevil in a biscuit you would catch them still."

"Hang it, Pew, we've got the doubloons!" grumbled one.

"They might have hid the blessed thing," said another. "Take the Georges, Pew, and don't stand here squalling."

Squalling was the word for it, Pew's anger rose so high at these objections; till at last, his passion completely taking the upper hand, he struck at them right and left in his blindness, and his stick sounded heavily on more than one.

These, in their turn, cursed back at the blind miscreant, threatened him in horrid terms, and tried in vain to catch the stick and wrest it from his grasp.

This quarrel was the saving of us; for while it was still raging, another sound came from the top of the hill on the side of the hamlet – the tramp of horses galloping. Almost at the same time a pistol shot, flash and report came from the hedge side. And that was plainly the last signal of danger; for the buccaneers turned at once and ran, separating in every direction, one seawards along the cove, one slant across the hill, and so on, so that in half a minute not a sign of them remained but Pew. Him they had deserted, whether in sheer panic or out of revenge for his ill words and blows, I know not; but there he remained behind, tapping up and down the road in a frenzy, and groping and calling for his comrades. Finally he took the wrong turn, and ran a few steps past me, towards the hamlet, crying:

"Johnny, Black Dog, Dirk" – and other names – "you won't leave old Pew, mates – not old Pew!"

Just then the noise of horses topped the rise, and four or five riders came in sight in the moonlight, and swept at full gallop down the slope.

At this Pew saw his error, turned with a scream, and ran straight for the ditch, into which he rolled. But he was on his feet again in a second, and made another dash, now utterly bewildered, right under the nearest of the coming horses.

The rider tried to save him, but in vain. Down went Pew with a cry that rang high into the night; and the four hoofs trampled and spurned him and passed by. He fell on his side, then gently collapsed upon his face, and moved no more.

I leapt to my feet and hailed the riders. They were pulling up at any rate, horrified at the accident; and I soon saw what they were. One, tailing out behind the rest, was a lad that had gone from the hamlet to Dr Livesey's; the rest were revenue officers, whom he had met by the way, and with whom he had had the intelligence to return at once. Some news of the lugger in Kitt's Hole had found its way to Supervisor Dance, and set him forth that night in our direction, and to that circumstance my mother and I owed our preservation from death.

Pew was dead, stone dead. As for my mother, when we had carried her up to the hamlet, a little cold water and salts and that soon brought her back again, and she was none the worse for her terror, though she still continued to deplore the balance of the money. In the meantime the supervisor rode on, as fast as he could, to Kitt's Hole; but his men had to dismount and grope down the dingle, leading, and sometimes supporting their horses, and in continual fear of ambushes; so it was no great matter for surprise that when they got down to the hole the lugger was already under way, though still close in. He hailed her. A voice replied, telling him to keep out of the moonlight, or he would get some lead in him,* and at the same time a bullet whistled close by his arm. Soon after, the lugger doubled the point and disappeared. Mr Dance stood there, as he said, "like a fish out of water," and all he could do was to dispatch a man to B— to warn the cutter. "And that," said he, "is just about as good as nothing. They've got off clean, and there's an end. Only," he added, "I'm glad I trod on Master Pew's corns" – for by this time he had heard my story.

I went back with him to the Admiral Benbow, and you cannot imagine a house in such a state of smash; the very clock had been thrown down by these fellows in their furious hunt after my mother and myself; and though nothing had actually been taken away except the captain's money-bag and a little silver from the till, I could see at once that we were ruined. Mr Dance could make nothing of the scene.

"They got the money, you say? Well then, Hawkins, what in fortune were they after? More money, I suppose?"

"No, sir; not money, I think," replied I. "In fact, sir, I believe I have the thing in my breast-pocket; and to tell you the truth, I should like to get it put in safety."

"To be sure, boy; quite right," said he. "I'll take it, if you like."

"I thought, perhaps, Dr Livesey—" I began.

"Perfectly right," he interrupted very cheerily, "perfectly right – a gentleman and a magistrate. And now I come to think of it, I might as well ride round there myself and report to him or squire. Master Pew's dead, when all's done; not that I regret it, but he's dead, you see, and people will make it out against an officer of His Majesty's Revenue, if make it out they can. Now, I'll tell you, Hawkins: if you like, I'll take you along."

I thanked him heartily for the offer, and we walked back to the hamlet where the horses were. By the time I had told mother of my purpose they were all in the saddle.

"Dogger," said Mr Dance, "you have a good horse; take up this lad behind you."

As soon as I was mounted, holding on to Dogger's belt, the supervisor gave the word, and the party struck out at a bouncing trot on the road to Dr Livesey's house.

# 6

## *The Captain's Papers*

WE RODE HARD ALL THE WAY, till we drew up before Dr Livesey's door. The house was all dark to the front.

Mr Dance told me to jump down and knock, and Dogger gave me a stirrup to descend by. The door was opened almost at once by the maid.

"Is Dr Livesey in?" I asked.

No, she said; he had come home in the afternoon, but had gone up to the hall to dine and pass the evening with the squire.

"So there we go, boys," said Mr Dance.

This time, as the distance was short, I did not mount, but ran with Dogger's stirrup-leather to the lodge gates, and up the long, leafless, moonlit avenue to where the white line of the hall buildings looked on either hand on great old gardens. Here Mr Dance dismounted, and, taking me along with him, was admitted at a word into the house.

The servant led us down a matted passage, and showed us at the end into a great library, all lined with bookcases and busts upon the top of them, where the squire and Dr Livesey sat, pipe in hand, on either side of a bright fire.

I had never seen the squire so near at hand. He was a tall man, over six feet high, and broad in proportion, and he had a bluff, rough-and-ready face, all roughened and reddened and lined in his long travels. His eyebrows were very black, and moved readily, and this gave him a look of some temper, not bad, you would say, but quick and high.

"Come in, Mr Dance," says he, very stately and condescending.

"Good evening, Dance," says the doctor with a nod. "And good evening to you, friend Jim. What good wind brings you here?"

The supervisor stood up straight and stiff, and told his story like a lesson; and you should have seen how the two gentlemen leant forwards and looked at each other, and forgot to smoke in their surprise and interest. When they heard how my mother went back to the inn, Dr Livesey fairly slapped his thigh, and the squire cried, "Bravo!" and broke his long pipe against the grate. Long before it was done, Mr Trelawney (that, you will remember, was the squire's name) had got up from his seat, and was striding about the room, and the doctor, as if to hear the better, had taken off his powdered wig, and sat there, looking very strange indeed with his own close-cropped, black poll.

At last Mr Dance finished the story.

"Mr Dance," said the squire, "you are a very noble fellow. And as for riding down that black, atrocious miscreant, I regard it as an act of virtue, sir, like stamping on a cockroach. This lad Hawkins is a trump, I perceive. Hawkins, will you ring that bell? Mr Dance must have some ale."

"And so, Jim," said the doctor, "you have the thing that they were after, have you?"

"Here it is, sir," said I, and gave him the oilskin packet.

The doctor looked it all over, as if his fingers were itching to open it; but instead of doing that, he put it quietly in the pocket of his coat.

"Squire," said he, "when Dance has had his ale he must, of course, be off on His Majesty's service; but I mean to keep Jim Hawkins here to sleep at my house, and with your permission, I propose we should have up the cold pie, and let him sup."

"As you will, Livesey," said the squire, "Hawkins has earned better than cold pie."

So a big pigeon pie was brought in and put on a side table, and I made a hearty supper, for I was as hungry as a hawk, while Mr Dance was further complimented, and at last dismissed.

"And now, squire," said the doctor.

"And now, Livesey," said the squire in the same breath.

"One at a time, one at a time," laughed Dr Livesey. "You have heard of this Flint, I suppose?"

"Heard of him!" cried the squire. "Heard of him, you say! He was the bloodthirstiest buccaneer that sailed. Blackbeard was a child to Flint. The Spaniards were so prodigiously afraid of him that I tell you, sir, I was sometimes proud he was an Englishman. I've seen his top-sails with these eyes, off Trinidad, and the cowardly son of a rum puncheon that I sailed with put back – put back, sir, into Port of Spain."

"Well, I've heard of him myself, in England," said the doctor. "But the point is, had he money?"

"Money!" cried the squire. "Have you heard the story? What were these villains after but money? What do they care for but money? For what would they risk their rascal carcasses but money?"

"That we shall soon know," replied the doctor. "But you are so confoundedly hot-headed and exclamatory that I cannot get a word in. What I want to know is this: Supposing that I have here in my pocket some clue to where Flint buried his treasure, will that treasure amount to much?"

"Amount, sir!" cried the squire. "It will amount to this; if we have the clue you talk about, I fit out a ship in Bristol dock, and take you and Hawkins here along, and I'll have that treasure if I search a year."

"Very well," said the doctor. "Now then, if Jim is agreeable, we'll open the packet," and he laid it before him on the table.

The bundle was sewn together, and the doctor had to get out his instrument-case, and cut the stitches with his medical scissors. It contained two things – a book and a sealed paper.

"First of all we'll try the book," observed the doctor.

The squire and I were both peering over his shoulder as he opened it, for Dr Livesey had kindly motioned me to come round from the side table, where I had been eating, to enjoy the sport of the search. On the first page there were only some scraps of writing, such as a man with a pen in his hand might make for idleness or practice. One was the same as the tattoo mark, "Billy Bones his fancy", then there was "Mr W. Bones, mate", "No more rum", "Off Palm Key he got itt", and some other snatches, mostly single words and unintelligible. I could not help wondering who it was that had "got itt", and what "itt" was that he got. A knife in his back as like as not.

"Not much instruction there," said Dr Livesey as he passed on.

The next ten or twelve pages were filled with a curious series of entries. There was a date at one end of the line and at the other a sum of money, as in common account books; but instead of explanatory writing, only a varying number of crosses between the two. On the 12th of June, 1745, for instance, a sum of seventy pounds had plainly become due to someone, and there was nothing but six crosses to explain the cause. In a few cases, to be sure, the name of a place would be added, as "Offe Caraccas", or a mere entry of latitude and longitude, as "62° 17′ 20″, 19° 2′ 40″".

The record lasted over nearly twenty years, the amount of the separate entries growing larger as time went on, and at the end a grand total had been made out after five or six wrong additions, and these words appended: "Bones, his pile".

"I can't make head or tail of this," said Dr Livesey.

"The thing is as clear as noonday," cried the squire. "This is the black-hearted hound's account book. These crosses stand for the names of ships or towns that they sank or plundered. The sums are the scoundrel's share, and where he feared an ambiguity, you see he added something clearer. "Offe Caraccas", now; you see, here was some unhappy vessel boarded off that coast. God help the poor souls that manned her – coral long ago."*

"Right!" said the doctor. "See what it is to be a traveller. Right! And the amounts increase, you see, as he rose in rank."

There was little else in the volume but a few bearings of places noted in the blank leaves towards the end, and a table for reducing French, English and Spanish moneys to a common value.

"Thrifty man!" cried the doctor. "He wasn't the one to be cheated."

"And now," said the squire, "for the other."

The paper had been sealed in several places with a thimble by way of seal; the very thimble, perhaps, that I had found in the captain's pocket. The doctor opened the seals with great care, and there fell out the map of an island, with latitude and longitude, soundings, names of hills and bays and inlets, and every particular that would be needed to bring a ship to a safe anchorage upon its shores. It was about nine miles long and five across, shaped, you might say, like a fat dragon standing up, and had two fine landlocked harbours, and a hill in the centre part marked "The Spyglass". There were several additions of a later date; but above all, three crosses of red ink – two on the north part of the island, one in the south-west, and beside this last, in the same red ink, and in a small, neat hand, very different from the captain's tottery characters, these words: "Bulk of treasure here."

Over on the back the same hand had written this further information:

> *Tall tree, Spyglass shoulder, bearing a point to the N of NNE.*
> *Skeleton Island ESE and by E.*
> *Ten feet.*
> *The bar silver is in the north cache; you can find it by the trend of the east hummock, ten fathoms south of the black crag with the face on it.*
> *The arms are easy found, in the sand hill, N point of north inlet cape, bearing E and a quarter N.*
>
> *J.F.*

That was all; but brief as it was, and to me incomprehensible, it filled the squire and Dr Livesey with delight.

"Livesey," said the squire, "you will give up this wretched practice at once. Tomorrow I start for Bristol. In three weeks' time – three weeks! – two weeks – ten days – we'll have the best ship, sir, and the choicest crew in England. Hawkins shall come as cabin boy. You'll make a famous cabin boy, Hawkins. You, Livesey, are ship's doctor; I am admiral. We'll take Redruth, Joyce and Hunter. We'll have favourable winds, a quick passage and not the least difficulty in finding the spot, and money to eat – to roll in – to play duck and drake with ever after."

"Trelawney," said the doctor, "I'll go with you; and I'll go bail for it, so will Jim, and be a credit to the undertaking. There's only one man I'm afraid of."

"And who's that?" cried the squire. "Name the dog, sir!"

"You," replied the doctor, "for you cannot hold your tongue. We are not the only men who know of this paper. These fellows who attacked the inn tonight – bold, desperate blades, for sure – and the rest who stayed aboard that lugger, and more, I dare say, not far off, are one and all, through thick and thin, bound that they'll get that money. We must none of us go alone till we get to sea. Jim and I shall stick together in the meanwhile; you'll take Joyce and Hunter when you ride to Bristol, and from first to last, not one of us must breathe a word of what we've found."

"Livesey," returned the squire, "you are always in the right of it. I'll be as silent as the grave."

# 7

## *I Go to Bristol*

I T WAS LONGER THAN the squire imagined ere we were
ready for the sea, and none of our first plans – not even
Dr Livesey's, of keeping me beside him – could be carried out
as we intended. The doctor had to go to London for a phy-
sician to take charge of his practice; the squire was hard at
work at Bristol; and I lived on at the hall under the charge of
old Redruth, the gamekeeper, almost a prisoner, but full of
sea dreams and the most charming anticipations of strange
islands and adventures. I brooded by the hour together over
the map, all the details of which I well remembered. Sitting by
the fire in the housekeeper's room, I approached that island in
my fancy from every possible direction; I explored every acre
of its surface; I climbed a thousand times to that tall hill they
call the "Spyglass", and from the top enjoyed the most wonderful and changing prospects. Sometimes the isle was thick with
savages, with whom we fought; sometimes full of dangerous
animals that hunted us; but in all my fancies nothing occurred
to me so strange and tragic as our actual adventures.

So the weeks passed on, till one fine day there came a letter addressed to Dr Livesey, with this addition: "To be opened, in the case of his absence, by Tom Redruth, or young Hawkins." Obeying this order, we found, or rather, I found – for the gamekeeper was a poor hand at reading anything but print – the following important news:

*Old Anchor Inn, Bristol,*
*March 1, 17–.*
*Dear Livesey,*

*As I do not know whether you are at the hall or still in London, I send this in double to both places.*

*The ship is bought and fitted. She lies at anchor, ready for sea. You never imagined a sweeter schooner – a child might sail her – two hundred tons; name,* Hispaniola.

*I got her through my old friend, Blandly, who has proved himself throughout the most surprising trump. The admirable fellow literally slaved in my interest, and so, I may say, did everyone in Bristol, as soon as they got wind of the port we sailed for – treasure, I mean.*

"Redruth," said I, interrupting the letter, "Doctor Livesey will not like that. The squire has been talking, after all."

"Well, who's a better right?" growled the gamekeeper. "A pretty rum go if squire ain't to talk for Doctor Livesey, I should think."

At that I gave up all attempt at commentary, and read straight on:

*Blandly himself found the* Hispaniola, *and by the most admirable management got her for the merest trifle. There is a class of men in Bristol monstrously prejudiced against Blandly. They go the length of declaring that this honest creature would do any-thing for money, that the* Hispaniola *belonged to him, and that he sold it me absurdly high – the most transparent calumnies. None of them dare, however, to deny the merits of the ship.*

*So far there was not a hitch. The workpeople, to be sure – riggers and what not – were most annoyingly slow; but time cured that. It was the crew that troubled me.*

*I wished a round score of men – in case of natives, buccaneers or the odious French – and I had the worry of the deuce itself to find so much as half a dozen, till the most remarkable stroke of fortune brought me the very man that I required.*

*I was standing on the dock, when by the merest accident, I fell in talk with him. I found he was an old sailor, kept a public house, knew all the seafaring men in Bristol, had lost his health ashore, and wanted a good berth as cook to get to sea again. He had hobbled down there that morning, he said, to get a smell of the salt.*

*I was monstrously touched – so would you have been – and, out of pure pity, I engaged him on the spot to be ship's cook. Long John Silver, he is called, and has lost a leg; but that I regarded as a recommendation, since he lost it in his country's service, under the immortal Hawke.\* He has no pension, Livesey. Imagine the abominable age we live in!*

*Well, sir, I thought I had only found a cook, but it was a crew I had discovered. Between Silver and myself we got together in a few days a company of the toughest old salts imaginable – not pretty to look at, but fellows, by their faces, of the most indomitable spirit. I declare we could fight a frigate.*

*Long John even got rid of two out of the six or seven I had already engaged. He showed me in a moment that they were just the sort of freshwater swabs we had to fear in an adventure of importance.*

*I am in the most magnificent health and spirits, eating like a bull, sleeping like a tree, yet I shall not enjoy a moment till I hear my old tarpaulins tramping round the capstan. Seaward ho! Hang the treasure! It's the glory of the sea that has turned my head. So now, Livesey, come post; do not lose an hour, if you respect me.*

*Let young Hawkins go at once to see his mother, with Redruth for a guard, and then both come full speed to Bristol.*

John Trelawney.

*Postscript: I did not tell you that Blandly, who, by the way, is to send a consort after us if we don't turn up by the end of August, had found an admirable fellow for sailing master – a stiff man, which I regret, but in all other respects, a treasure. Long John Silver unearthed a very competent man for a mate, a man named Arrow. I have a boatswain who pipes, Livesey; so things shall go man-o'-war fashion on board the good ship* Hispaniola.

*I forgot to tell you that Silver is a man of substance; I know of my own knowledge that he has a banker's account, which has never been overdrawn. He leaves his wife to manage the inn; and as she is a woman of colour, a pair of old bachelors like you and I may be excused for guessing that it is the wife, quite as much as the health, that sends him back to roving.*

J.T.

*PPS: Hawkins may stay one night with his mother.*

J.T.

You can fancy the excitement into which that letter put me. I was half beside myself with glee; and if ever I despised a man, it was old Tom Redruth, who could do nothing but grumble and lament. Any of the under-gamekeepers would gladly have changed places with him; but such was not the squire's pleasure, and the squire's pleasure was like law among them all. Nobody but old Redruth would have dared so much as even to grumble.

The next morning he and I set out on foot for the Admiral Benbow, and there I found my mother in good health and spirits. The captain, who had so long been a cause of so much discomfort, was gone where the wicked cease from troubling.* The squire had had everything repaired, and the public rooms and the sign repainted, and had added some furniture – above all a beautiful armchair for mother in the bar. He had found her a boy as an apprentice also, so that she should not want help while I was gone.

It was on seeing that boy that I understood, for the first time, my situation. I had thought up to that moment of the adventures before me, not at all of the home that I was leaving; and now, at the sight of this clumsy stranger, who was to stay here in my place beside my mother, I had my first attack of tears. I am afraid I led that boy a dog's life; for as he was new to the work, I had a hundred opportunities of setting him right and putting him down, and I was not slow to profit by them.

The night passed, and the next day, after dinner, Redruth and I were afoot again, and on the road. I said goodbye to mother and the cove where I had lived since I was born, and the dear old Admiral Benbow – since he was repainted, no longer quite so dear. One of my last thoughts was of the captain, who had so often strode along the beach with his cocked hat, his sabre-cut cheek and his old brass telescope. Next moment we had turned the corner, and my home was out of sight.

The mail picked us up about dusk at the Royal George on the heath. I was wedged in between Redruth and a stout old gentle-man, and in spite of the swift motion and the cold night air, I must have dozed a great deal from the very first, and then slept like a log up hill and down dale through stage after stage; for when I was awakened, at last, it was by a punch in the ribs, and I opened my eyes to find that we were standing still before a large building in a city street, and that the day had already broken a long time.

"Where are we?" I asked.

"Bristol," said Tom. "Get down."

Mr Trelawney had taken up his residence at an inn far down the docks, to superintend the work upon the schooner. Thither we had now to walk, and our way, to my great delight, lay along the quays and beside the great multitude of ships of all sizes and rigs and nations. In one, sailors were singing at their work; in another, there were men aloft, high over my head, hanging to threads that seemed no thicker than a spider's. Though I had lived by the shore all my life, I seemed never to have been near the sea till then. The smell of tar and salt was something new. I saw the most wonderful figureheads that had all been far over the ocean. I saw, besides, many old sailors, with rings in their ears, and whiskers curled in ringlets, and tarry pigtails, and their swaggering, clumsy sea walk; and if I had seen as many kings or archbishops I could not have been more delighted.

And I was going to sea myself; to sea in a schooner, with a piping boatswain, and pigtailed singing seamen; to sea, bound for an unknown island, and to seek for buried treasures!

While I was still in this delightful dream, we came suddenly in front of a large inn, and met Squire Trelawney, all dressed out like a sea officer in stout blue cloth, coming out of the door with a smile on his face, and a capital imitation of a sailor's walk.

"Here you are," he cried, "and the doctor came last night from London. Bravo! the ship's company complete!"

"Oh, sir," cried I, "when do we sail?"

"Sail!" says he. "We sail tomorrow!"

# 8

## *At the Sign of the "Spyglass"*

WHEN I HAD DONE BREAKFASTING, the squire gave me a note addressed to John Silver, at the sign of the "Spyglass", and told me I should easily find the place by following the line of the docks, and keeping a bright lookout for a little tavern with a large brass telescope for sign. I set off, overjoyed at this opportunity to see some more of the ships and seamen, and picked my way among a great crowd of people and carts and bales, for the dock was now at its busiest, until I found the tavern in question.

It was a bright enough little place of entertainment. The sign was newly painted; the windows had neat red curtains; the floor was cleanly sanded. There was a street on each side, and an open door on both, which made the large, low room pretty clear to see in, in spite of clouds of tobacco smoke.

The customers were mostly seafaring men; and they talked so loudly that I hung at the door, almost afraid to enter.

As I was waiting, a man came out of a side room, and at a glance, I was sure he must be Long John. His left leg was cut off close by the hip, and under the left shoulder he carried a crutch, which he managed with wonderful dexterity, hopping about upon it like a bird. He was very tall and strong, with a face as big as a ham – plain and pale, but intelligent and smiling. Indeed, he seemed in the most cheerful spirits, whistling as he moved about among the tables, with a merry word or a slap on the shoulder for the more favoured of his guests.

Now to tell you the truth, from the very first mention of Long John in Squire Trelawney's letter, I had taken a fear in my mind that he might prove to be the very one-legged sailor whom I had watched for so long at the old Benbow. But one look at the man before me was enough. I had seen the captain, and Black Dog, and the blind man Pew, and I thought I knew what a buccaneer was like – a very different creature, according to me, from this clean and pleasant-tempered landlord.

I plucked up courage at once, crossed the threshold, and walked right up to the man where he stood, propped on his crutch, talking to a customer.

"Mr Silver, sir?" I asked, holding out the note.

"Yes, my lad," said he, "such is my name, to be sure. And who may you be?" And then, as he saw the squire's letter, he seemed to me to give something almost like a start.

"Oh!" said he, quite loud, and offering his hand, "I see. You are our new cabin boy; pleased I am to see you."

And he took my hand in his large firm grasp.

Just then one of the customers at the far side rose suddenly and made for the door. It was close by him, and he was out in the street in a moment. But his hurry had attracted my notice, and I recognized him at a glance. It was the tallow-faced man, wanting two fingers, who had come first to the Admiral Benbow.

"Oh," I cried, "stop him! It's Black Dog!"

"I don't care two coppers who he is," cried Silver. "But he hasn't paid his score. Harry, run and catch him."

One of the others who was nearest the door leapt up, and started in pursuit.

"If he were Admiral Hawke he shall pay his score," cried Silver; and then, relinquishing my hand, "Who did you say he was?" he asked. "Black what?"

"Dog, sir," said I. "Has Mr Trelawney not told you of the buccaneers? He was one of them."

"So?" cried Silver. "In my house! Ben, run and help Harry. One of those swabs, was he? Was that you drinking with him, Morgan? Step up here."

The man whom he called Morgan – an old, grey-haired, mahogany-faced sailor – came forwards pretty sheepishly, rolling his quid.

"Now, Morgan," said Long John very sternly, "you never clapped your eyes on that Black – Black Dog before, did you now?"

"Not I, sir," said Morgan, with a salute.

"You didn't know his name, did you?"

"No, sir."

"By the powers, Tom Morgan, it's as good for you!" exclaimed the landlord. "If you had been mixed up with the like of that, you would never have put another foot in my house, you may lay to that. And what was he saying to you?"

"I don't rightly know, sir," answered Morgan.

"Do you call that a head on your shoulders, or a blessed dead-eye?" cried Long John. "Don't rightly know, don't you! Perhaps you don't happen to rightly know who you was speaking to, perhaps? Come now, what was he jawing – v'yages, cap'ns, ships? Pipe up! What was it?"

"We was a-talkin' of keelhauling," answered Morgan.

"Keelhauling, was you? and a mighty suitable thing, too, and you may lay to that. Get back to your place for a lubber, Tom."

And then, as Morgan rolled back to his seat, Silver added to me in a confidential whisper that was very flattering, as I thought:

"He's quite an honest man, Tom Morgan, on'y stupid. And now," he ran on again, aloud, "let's see – Black Dog? No, I don't know the name, not I. Yet I kind of think I've – yes, I've seen the swab. He used to come here with a blind beggar, he used."

"That he did, you may be sure," said I. "I knew that blind man, too. His name was Pew."

"It was!" cried Silver, now quite excited. "Pew! That were his name for certain. Ah, he looked a shark, he did! If we run down this Black Dog, now, there'll be news for Cap'n Trelawney! Ben's a good runner; few seamen run better than Ben. He should run him down, hand over hand, by the powers! He talked o' keelhauling, did he? *I'll* keelhaul him!"

All the time he was jerking out these phrases, he was stumping up and down the tavern on his crutch, slapping tables with his hand, and giving such a show of excitement as would have convinced an Old Bailey Judge or a Bow Street Runner.* My suspicions had been thoroughly reawakened on finding Black Dog at the Spyglass, and I watched the cook narrowly. But he was too deep, and too ready, and too clever for me, and by the time the two men had come back out of breath, and confessed that they had lost the track in a crowd, and been scolded like thieves, I would have gone bail for the innocence of Long John Silver.

"See here, now, Hawkins," said he, "here's a blessed hard thing on a man like me, now, ain't it? There's Cap'n Trelawney – what's he to think? Here I have this confounded son of a Dutchman sitting in my own house, drinking of my own rum! Here you comes and tells me of it plain; and here I let him give us all the slip before my blessed deadlights! Now, Hawkins, you do me justice with the cap'n. You're a lad, you are, but you're as smart as paint. I see that when you first came in. Now here it is: What could I do, with this old timber I hobble on? When I was an AB master mariner I'd have come up alongside of him, hand over hand, and broached him to in a brace of old shakes, I would; but now…"

And then all of a sudden he stopped, and his jaw dropped as though he had remembered something.

"The score!" he burst out. "Three goes o' rum! Why, shiver my timbers, if I hadn't forgotten my score!"

And falling on a bench, he laughed until the tears ran down his cheeks. I could not help joining; and we laughed together, peal after peal, until the tavern rang again.

"Why, what a precious old sea calf I am!" he said at last, wiping his cheeks. "You and me should get on well, Hawkins, for I'll take my davy I should be rated ship's boy. But come now, stand by to go about. This won't do. Dooty is dooty, messmates. I'll put on my old cocked hat, and step along of you to Cap'n Trelawney, and report this here affair. For mind you, it's serious, young Hawkins; and neither you nor me's come out of it with what I should make so bold as to call credit. Nor you neither, says you; not smart – none of the pair of us smart. But dash my buttons! that was a good 'un about my score."

And he began to laugh again, and that so heartily, that though I did not see the joke as he did, I was again obliged to join him in his mirth.

On our little walk along the quays, he made himself the most interesting companion, telling me about the different ships that we passed by, their rig, tonnage and nationality, explaining the work that was going forwards – how one was discharging, another taking in cargo and a third making ready for sea; and every now and then telling me some little anecdote of ships or seamen, or repeating a nautical phrase till I had learnt it perfectly. I began to see that here was one of the best of possible shipmates.

When we got to the inn, the squire and Dr Livesey were seated together, finishing a quart of ale with a toast in it, before they should go aboard the schooner on a visit of inspection.

Long John told the story from first to last, with a great deal of spirit and the most perfect truth. "That was how it were, now, weren't it, Hawkins?" he would say, now and again, and I could always bear him entirely out.

The two gentlemen regretted that Black Dog had got away; but we all agreed there was nothing to be done, and after he had been complimented, Long John took up his crutch and departed.

"All hands aboard by four this afternoon," shouted the squire after him.

"Ay, ay, sir," cried the cook in the passage.

"Well, squire," said Dr Livesey, "I don't put much faith in your discoveries, as a general thing; but I will say this, John Silver suits me."

"The man's a perfect trump," declared the squire.

"And now," added the doctor, "Jim may come on board with us, may he not?"

"To be sure he may," says squire. "Take your hat, Hawkins, and we'll see the ship."

# 9

## Powder and Arms

THE *HISPANIOLA* LAY SOME WAY OUT, and we went under the figureheads and round the sterns of many other ships, and their cables sometimes grated underneath our keel, and sometimes swung above us. At last, however, we got alongside, and were met and saluted as we stepped aboard by the mate, Mr Arrow, a brown old sailor, with earrings in his ears and a squint. He and the squire were very thick and friendly, but I soon observed that things were not the same between Mr Trelawney and the captain.

This last was a sharp-looking man, who seemed angry with everything on board, and was soon to tell us why, for we had hardly got down into the cabin when a sailor followed us.

"Captain Smollett, sir, axing to speak with you," said he.

"I am always at the captain's order. Show him in," said the squire.

The captain, who was close behind his messenger, entered at once, and shut the door behind him.

"Well, Captain Smollett, what have you to say? All well, I hope; all shipshape and seaworthy?"

"Well, sir," said the captain, "better speak plain, I believe, even at the risk of offence. I don't like this cruise; I don't like the men; and I don't like my officer. That's short and sweet."

"Perhaps, sir, you don't like the ship?" enquired the squire, very angry, as I could see.

"I can't speak as to that, sir, not having seen her tried," said the captain. "She seems a clever craft; more I can't say."

"Possibly, sir, you may not like your employer either?" says the squire.

But here Dr Livesey cut in.

"Stay a bit," said he, "stay a bit. No use of such questions as that but to produce ill feeling. The captain has said too much or he has said too little, and I'm bound to say that I require an explanation of his words. You don't, you say, like this cruise. Now, why?"

"I was engaged, sir, on what we call sealed orders, to sail this ship for that gentleman where he should bid me," said the captain. "So far so good. But now I find that every man before the mast knows more than I do. I don't call that fair, now, do you?"

"No," said Dr Livesey, "I don't."

"Next," said the captain, "I learn we are going after treasure – hear it from my own hands, mind you. Now, treasure is ticklish work; I don't like treasure voyages on any account; and I don't like them, above all, when they are secret, and when (begging your pardon, Mr Trelawney) the secret has been told to the parrot."

"Silver's parrot?" asked the squire.

"It's a way of speaking," said the captain. "Blabbed, I mean. It's my belief neither of you gentlemen know what you are about; but I'll tell you my way of it – life or death, and a close run."

"That is all clear, and I dare say, true enough," replied Dr Livesey. "We take the risk; but we are not so ignorant as you believe us. Next, you say you don't like the crew. Are they not good seamen?"

"I don't like them, sir," returned Captain Smollett. "And I think I should have had the choosing of my own hands, if you go to that."

"Perhaps you should," replied the doctor. "My friend should, perhaps, have taken you along with him; but the slight, if there be one, was unintentional. And you don't like Mr Arrow?"

"I don't, sir. I believe he's a good seaman; but he's too free with the crew to be a good officer. A mate should keep himself to himself – shouldn't drink with the men before the mast!"

"Do you mean he drinks?" cried the squire.

"No, sir," replied the captain, "only that he's too familiar."

"Well now, and the short and long of it, captain?" asked the doctor. "Tell us what you want."

"Well, gentlemen, are you determined to go on this cruise?"

"Like iron," answered the squire.

"Very good," said the captain. "Then, as you've heard me very patiently, saying things that I could not prove, hear me a few words more. They are putting the powder and the arms in the forehold. Now, you have a good place under the cabin; why not put them there? – first point. Then you are bringing four of your own people with you, and they tell me some of them are to be berthed forwards. Why not give them the berths here beside the cabin? – second point."

"Any more?" asked Mr Trelawney.

"One more," said the captain. "There's been too much blabbing already."

"Far too much," agreed the doctor.

"I'll tell you what I've heard myself," continued Captain Smollett: "that you have a map of an island; that there's crosses on the map to show where treasure is; and that the island lies…" And then he named the latitude and longitude exactly.

"I never told that," cried the squire, "to a soul!"

"The hands know it, sir," returned the captain.

"Livesey, that must have been you or Hawkins," cried the squire.

"It doesn't much matter who it was," replied the doctor. And I could see that neither he nor the captain paid much regard to Mr Trelawney's protestations. Neither did I, to be sure – he was so loose a talker; yet in this case I believe he was really right, and that nobody had told the situation of the island.

"Well, gentlemen," continued the captain, "I don't know who has this map; but I make it a point: it shall be kept secret even from me and Mr Arrow. Otherwise I would ask you to let me resign."

"I see," said the doctor. "You wish us to keep this matter dark, and to make a garrison of the stern part of the ship, manned with my friend's own people, and provided with all the arms and powder on board. In other words, you fear a mutiny."

"Sir," said Captain Smollett, "with no intention to take offence, I deny your right to put words into my mouth. No captain, sir, would be justified in going to sea at all if he had ground enough to say that. As for Mr Arrow, I believe him thoroughly honest; some of the men are the same; all may be for what I know. But I am responsible for the ship's safety and the life of every man jack* aboard of her. I see things going, as I think, not quite right. And I ask you to take certain precautions, or let me resign my berth. And that's all."

"Captain Smollett," began the doctor, with a smile, "did ever you hear the fable of the mountain and the mouse?* You'll excuse me, I dare say, but you remind me of that fable. When you came in here, I'll stake my wig you meant more than this."

"Doctor," said the captain, "you are smart. When I came in here I meant to get discharged. I had no thought that Mr Trelawney would hear a word."

"No more I would," cried the squire. "Had Livesey not been here I should have seen you to the deuce. As it is, I have heard you. I will do as you desire; but I think the worse of you."

"That's as you please, sir," said the captain. "You'll find I do my duty."

And with that he took his leave.

"Trelawney," said the doctor, "contrary to all my notions, I believe you have managed to get two honest men on board with you – that man and John Silver."

"Silver, if you like," cried the squire, "but as for that intolerable humbug, I declare I think his conduct unmanly, unsailorly and downright un-English."

"Well," says the doctor, "we shall see."

When we came on deck, the men had begun already to take out the arms and powder, yo-ho-ing at their work, while the captain and Mr Arrow stood by superintending.

The new arrangement was quite to my liking. The whole schooner had been overhauled; six berths had been made astern, out of what had been the after-part of the main hold; and this set of cabins was only joined to the galley and forecastle by a sparred passage on the port side. It had been originally meant that the captain, Mr Arrow, Hunter, Joyce, the doctor and the squire were to occupy these six berths. Now Redruth and I were to get two of them, and Mr Arrow and the captain were to sleep on deck in the companion, which had been enlarged on each side till you might almost have called it a roundhouse. Very low it was still, of course; but there was room to swing two hammocks, and even the mate seemed pleased with the arrangement. Even he, perhaps, had been doubtful as to the crew, but that is only guess; for as you shall hear, we had not long the benefit of his opinion.

We were all hard at work, changing the powder and the berths, when the last man or two, and Long John along with them, came off in a shore-boat.

The cook came up the side like a monkey for cleverness, and as soon as he saw what was doing, "So ho, mates!" says he, "what's this?"

"We're a-changing of the powder, Jack," answers one.

"Why, by the powers," cried Long John, "if we do, we'll miss the morning tide!"

"My orders!" said the captain shortly. "You may go below, my man. Hands will want supper."

"Ay, ay, sir," answered the cook, and, touching his forelock, he disappeared at once in the direction of his galley.

"That's a good man, captain," said the doctor.

"Very likely sir," replied Captain Smollett. "Easy with that, men – easy," he ran on, to the fellows who were shifting the powder; and then, suddenly observing me examining the swivel we carried amidships, a long brass nine: "Here, you ship's boy," he cried, "out o' that! Off with you to the cook and get some work."

And then, as I was hurrying off, I heard him say quite loudly to the doctor:

"I'll have no favourites on my ship."

I assure you, I was quite of the squire's way of thinking, and hated the captain deeply.

# 10

## *The Voyage*

ALL THAT NIGHT WE WERE in a great bustle getting things stowed in their place, and boatfuls of the squire's friends, Mr Blandly and the like, coming off to wish him a good voyage and a safe return. We never had a night at the Admiral Benbow when I had half the work; and I was dog-tired when, a little before dawn, the boatswain sounded his pipe, and the crew began to man the capstan bars. I might have been twice as weary, yet I would not have left the deck; all was so new and interesting to me – the brief commands, the shrill note of the whistle, the men bustling to their places in the glimmer of the ship's lanterns.

"Now, Barbecue, tip us a stave,"* cried one voice.

"The old one," cried another.

"Ay, ay, mates," said Long John, who was standing by, with his crutch under his arm, and at once broke out in the air and words I knew so well:

"Fifteen men on the dead man's chest –"

And then the whole crew bore chorus:

"Yo-ho-ho, and a bottle of rum!"

And at the third "ho!" drove the bars before them with a will.

Even at that exciting moment it carried me back to the old Admiral Benbow in a second; and I seemed to hear the voice of the captain piping in the chorus. But soon the anchor was short up; soon it was hanging dripping at the bows; soon the sails began to draw, and the land and shipping to flit by on either side; and before I could lie down to snatch an hour of slumber, the *Hispaniola* had begun her voyage to the isle of treasure.

I am not going to relate that voyage in detail. It was fairly prosperous. The ship proved to be a good ship, the crew were capable seamen, and the captain thoroughly understood his business. But before we came the length of Treasure Island, two or three things had happened which require to be known.

Mr Arrow, first of all, turned out even worse than the captain had feared. He had no command among the men, and people did what they pleased with him. But that was by no means the worst of it; for after a day or two at sea he began to appear on deck with hazy eye, red cheeks, stuttering tongue and other marks of drunkenness. Time after time he was ordered below in disgrace. Sometimes he fell and cut himself; sometimes he lay all day long in his little bunk at one side of the companion; sometimes for a day or two he would be almost sober and attend to his work at least passably.

In the meantime, we could never make out where he got the drink. That was the ship's mystery. Watch him as we pleased, we could do nothing to solve it; and when we asked him to his face, he would only laugh, if he were drunk, and if he were sober, deny solemnly that he ever tasted anything but water.

He was not only useless as an officer, and a bad influence amongst the men, but it was plain that at this rate he must soon kill himself outright; so nobody was much surprised, nor very sorry, when one dark night with a head sea, he disappeared entirely and was seen no more.

"Overboard!" said the captain. "Well, gentlemen, that saves the trouble of putting him in irons."

But there we were, without a mate; and it was necessary, of course, to advance one of the men. The boatswain, Job Anderson, was the likeliest man aboard, and though he kept his old title, he served in a way as mate. Mr Trelawney had followed the sea, and his knowledge made him very useful, for he often took a watch himself in easy weather. And the coxswain, Israel Hands, was a careful, wily, old, experienced seaman, who could be trusted at a pinch with almost anything.

He was a great confidant of Long John Silver, and so the mention of his name leads me on to speak of our ship's cook – "Barbecue", as the men called him.

Aboard ship he carried his crutch by a lanyard round his neck, to have both hands as free as possible. It was something to see him wedge the foot of the crutch against a bulkhead, and, propped against it, yielding to every movement of the ship, get on with his cooking like someone safe ashore. Still more strange was it to see him in the heaviest of weather cross the deck. He had a line or two rigged up to help him across the widest spaces – Long John's earrings, they were called; and he would hand himself from one place to another, now using the crutch, now trailing it alongside by the lanyard, as quickly as another man could walk. Yet some of the men who had sailed with him before expressed their pity to see him so reduced.

"He's no common man, Barbecue," said the coxswain to me. "He had good schooling in his young days, and can speak like a book when so minded; and brave – a lion's nothing alongside of Long John! I seen him grapple four, and knock their heads together – him unarmed."

All the crew respected and even obeyed him. He had a way of talking to each, and doing everybody some particular service. To me he was unweariedly kind; and always glad to see me in the galley, which he kept as clean as a new pin; the dishes hanging up burnished, and his parrot in a cage in one corner.

"Come away, Hawkins," he would say, "come and have a yarn with John. Nobody more welcome than yourself, my son. Sit you down and hear the news. Here's Cap'n Flint – I calls my parrot Cap'n Flint, after the famous buccaneer – here's Cap'n Flint predicting success to our v'yage. Wasn't you, Cap'n?"

And the parrot would say, with great rapidity, "Pieces of eight! Pieces of eight! Pieces of eight!" till you wondered that it was not out of breath, or till John threw his handkerchief over the cage.

"Now, that bird," he would say, "is maybe two hundred years old, Hawkins – they lives for ever mostly; and if anybody's seen more wickedness, it must be the Devil himself. She's sailed with England, the great Cap'n England, the pirate. She's been at Madagascar, and at Malabar,* and Surinam, and Providence, and Portobello. She was at the fishing up of the wrecked plate ships. It's there she learnt "Pieces of eight", and little wonder; three hundred and fifty thousand of 'em, Hawkins! She was at the boarding of the Viceroy of the Indies out of Goa, she was; and to look at her you would think she was a babby. But you smelt powder – didn't you, Cap'n?"

"Stand by to go about," the parrot would scream.

"Ah, she's a handsome craft, she is," the cook would say, and give her sugar from his pocket, and then the bird would peck at the bars and swear straight on, passing belief for wickedness. "There," John would add, "you can't touch pitch and not be mucked, lad. Here's this poor old innocent bird o' mine swearing blue fire, and none the wiser, you may lay to that. She would swear the same, in a manner of speaking, before, chaplain." And John would touch his forelock with a solemn way he had, that made me think he was the best of men.

In the meantime, the squire and Captain Smollett were still on pretty distant terms with one another. The squire made no bones about the matter; he despised the captain. The captain, on his part, never spoke but when he was spoken to, and then sharp and short and dry, and not a word wasted. He owned, when driven into a corner, that he seemed to have been wrong about the crew, that some of them were as brisk as he wanted to see, and all had behaved fairly well. As for the ship, he had taken a downright fancy to her. "She'll lie a point nearer the wind than a man has a right to expect of his own married wife, sir. But," he would add, "all I say is we're not home again, and I don't like the cruise."

The squire, at this, would turn away and march up and down the deck, chin in air.

"A trifle more of that man," he would say, "and I shall explode."

We had some heavy weather, which only proved the qualities of the *Hispaniola*. Every man on board seemed well content, and they must have been hard to please if they had been otherwise; for it is my belief there was never a ship's company so spoilt since Noah put to sea. Double grog was going on the least excuse; there was duff on odd days, as, for instance, if the squire heard it was any man's birthday; and always a barrel of apples standing broached in the waist, for anyone to help himself that had a fancy.

"Never knew good come of it yet," the captain said to Dr Livesey. "Spoil foc's'le hands, make devils. That's my belief."

But good did come of the apple barrel, as you shall hear; for if it had not been for that, we should have had no note of warning, and might all have perished by the hand of treachery.

This was how it came about.

We had run up the trades to get the wind of the island we were after – I am not allowed to be more plain – and now we were running down for it with a bright lookout day and night. It was about the last day of our outward voyage, by the largest computation; some time that night, or at latest, before noon of the morrow, we should sight the Treasure Island. We were heading SSW, and had a steady breeze abeam and a quiet sea. The *Hispaniola* rolled steadily, dipping her bowsprit now and then with a whiff of spray. All was drawing alow and aloft; everyone was in the bravest spirits, because we were now so near an end of the first part of our adventure.

Now just after sundown, when all my work was over, and I was on my way to my berth, it occurred to me that I should like an apple. I ran on deck. The watch was all forwards, looking out for the island. The man at the helm was watching the luff of the sail, and whistling away gently to himself; and that was the only sound excepting the swish of the sea against the bows and around the sides of the ship.

In I got bodily into the apple barrel, and found there was scarce an apple left; but sitting down there in the dark, what with the sound of the waters and the rocking movement of the ship, I had either fallen asleep, or was on the point of doing so, when a heavy man sat down with rather a clash close by. The barrel shook as he leant his shoulders against it, and I was just about to jump up when the man began to speak. It was Silver's voice, and before I had heard a dozen words, I would not have shown myself for all the world, but lay there, trembling and listening, in the extreme of fear and curiosity; for from these dozen words I understood that the lives of all the honest men aboard depended upon me alone.

# 11

## *What I Heard in the Apple Barrel*

"Nᴏ, ɴᴏᴛ ɪ," ꜱᴀɪᴅ ꜱɪʟᴠᴇʀ. "Flint was cap'n; I was quarter-master, along of my timber leg. The same broadside I lost my leg, old Pew lost his deadlights. It was a master surgeon, him that ampytated me – out of college and all – Latin by the bucket, and what not; but he was hanged like a dog, and sun-dried like the rest, at Corso Castle. That was Roberts' men, that was, and comed of changing names to their ships – *Royal Fortune* and so on. Now, what a ship was christened, so let her stay, I says. So it was with the *Cassandra*, as brought us all safe home from Malabar, after England took the Viceroy of the Indies; so it was with the old *Walrus*, Flint's old ship, as I've seen a-muck with the red blood and fit to sink with gold."

"Ah!" cried another voice, that of the youngest hand on board, and evidently full of admiration, "he was the flower of the flock, was Flint!"

"Davis was a man, too, by all accounts," said Silver. "I never sailed along of him; first with England, then with Flint, that's my story; and now here on my own account, in a manner of speaking.

I laid by nine hundred safe, from England, and two thousand after Flint. That ain't bad for a man before the mast – all safe in bank. 'Tain't earning now, it's saving does it, you may lay to that. Where's all England's men now? I dunno. Where's Flint's? Why, most on 'em aboard here, and glad to get the duff – been begging before that, some on 'em. Old Pew, as had lost his sight, and might have thought shame, spends twelve hundred pound in a year, like a lord in Parliament. Where is he now? Well, he's dead now and under hatches; but for two year before that, shiver my timbers! the man was starving. He begged, and he stole, and he cut throats, and starved at that, by the powers!"

"Well, it ain't much use, after all," said the young seaman.

"'Tain't much use for fools, you may lay to it – that, nor nothing," cried Silver. "But now, you look here: you're young, you are, but you're as smart as paint. I see that when I set my eyes on you, and I'll talk to you like a man."

You may imagine how I felt when I heard this abominable old rogue addressing another in the very same words of flattery as he had used to myself. I think, if I had been able, that I would have killed him through the barrel. Meantime, he ran on, little supposing he was overheard.

"Here it is about gentlemen of fortune. They lives rough, and they risk swinging, but they eat and drink like fighting cocks, and when a cruise is done, why, it's hundreds of pounds instead of hundreds of farthings in their pockets. Now, the most goes for rum and a good fling, and to sea again in their shirts. But that's not the course I lay. I puts it all away, some here, some there, and none too much anywheres, by reason of suspicion. I'm fifty, mark you; once back from this cruise, I set up gentleman in earnest. Time enough, too, says you. Ah, but I've lived easy in the meantime; never denied myself o' nothing heart desires, and slep' soft and ate dainty all my days, but when at sea. And how did I begin? Before the mast, like you!"

"Well," said the other, "but all the other money's gone now, ain't it? You daren't show face in Bristol after this."

"Why, where might you suppose it was?" asked Silver derisively.

"At Bristol, in banks and places," answered his companion.

"It were," said the cook, "it were when we weighed anchor. But my old missis has it all by now. And the Spyglass is sold, lease and goodwill and rigging; and the old girl's off to meet me. I would tell you where, for I trust you; but it 'ud make jealousy among the mates."

"And can you trust your missis?" asked the other.

"Gentlemen of fortune," returned the cook, "usually trusts little among themselves, and right they are, you may lay to it. But I have a way with me, I have. When a mate brings a slip on his cable – one as knows me, I mean – it won't be in the same world with old John. There was some that was feared of Pew, and some that was feared of Flint; but Flint his own self was feared of me. Feared he was, and proud. They was the roughest crew afloat, was Flint's; the Devil himself would have been feared to go to sea with them. Well now, I tell you, I'm not a boasting man, and you seen yourself how easy I keep company; but when I was quartermaster, 'lambs' wasn't the word for Flint's old buccaneers. Ah, you may be sure of yourself in old John's ship."

"Well, I tell you now," replied the lad, "I didn't half a quarter like the job till I had this talk with you, John; but there's my hand on it now."

"And a brave lad you were, and smart, too," answered Silver, shaking hands so heartily that all the barrel shook, "and a finer figurehead for a gentleman of fortune I never clapped my eyes on."

By this time I had begun to understand the meaning of their terms. By a "gentleman of fortune" they plainly meant neither more nor less than a common pirate, and the little scene that I had overheard was the last act in the corruption of one of the honest hands – perhaps of the last one left aboard. But on this point I was soon to be relieved, for Silver giving a little whistle, a third man strolled up and sat down by the party.

"Dick's square," said Silver.

"Oh, I know'd Dick was square," returned the voice of the coxswain, Israel Hands. "He's no fool, is Dick." And he turned his quid and spat. "But look here," he went on, "here's what I want to know, Barbecue: how long are we a-going to stand off and on like a blessed bumboat? I've had a'most enough o' Cap'n Smollett; he's hazed me long enough, by thunder! I want to go into that cabin, I do. I want their pickles and wines, and that."

"Israel," said Silver, "your head ain't much account, nor ever was. But you're able to hear, I reckon; leastways, your ears is big enough. Now, here's what I say: you'll berth forwards, and you'll live hard, and you'll speak soft, and you'll keep sober, till I give the word; and you may lay to that, my son."

"Well, I don't say no, do I?" growled the coxswain. "What I say is, when? That's what I say."

"When! by the powers!" cried Silver. "Well now, if you want to know, I'll tell you when. The last moment I can manage; and that's when. Here's a first-rate seaman, Cap'n Smollett, sails the blessed ship for us. Here's this squire and doctor with a map and such – I don't know where it is, do I? No more do you, says you. Well then, I mean this squire and doctor shall find the stuff, and help us to get it aboard, by the powers. Then we'll see. If I was sure of you all, sons of double Dutchmen, I'd have Cap'n Smollett navigate us halfway back again before I struck."

"Why, we're all seamen aboard here, I should think," said the lad Dick.

"We're all foc's'le hands, you mean," snapped Silver. "We can steer a course, but who's to set one? That's what all you gentlemen split on, first and last. If I had my way, I'd have Cap'n Smollett work us back into the trades at least; then we'd have no blessed

71

miscalculations and a spoonful of water a day. But I know the sort you are. I'll finish with 'em at the island, as soon's the blunt's on board, and a pity it is. But you're never happy till you're drunk. Split my sides, I've a sick heart to sail with the likes of you!"

"Easy all, Long John," cried Israel. "Who's a-crossin' of you?"

"Why, how many tall ships, think ye now, have I seen laid aboard? and how many brisk lads drying in the sun at Execution Dock?"* cried Silver, "and all for this same hurry and hurry and hurry. You hear me? I seen a thing or two at sea, I have. If you would on'y lay your course, and a p'int to windwards, you would ride in carriages, you would. But not you! I know you. You'll have your mouthful of rum tomorrow, and go hang."

"Everybody know'd you was a kind of a chapling, John; but there's others as could hand and steer as well as you," said Israel. "They liked a bit o' fun, they did. They wasn't so high and dry, nohow, but took their fling, like jolly companions every one."

"So?" says Silver. "Well, and where are they now? Pew was that sort, and he died a beggar-man. Flint was, and he died of rum at Savannah. Ah, they was a sweet crew, they was! on'y, where are they?"

"But," asked Dick, "when we do lay 'em athwart, what are we to do with 'em, anyhow?"

"There's the man for me!" cried the cook admiringly. "That's what I call business. Well, what would you think? Put 'em ashore like maroons? That would have been England's way. Or cut 'em down like that much pork? That would have been Flint's or Billy Bones's."

"Billy was the man for that," said Israel. "'Dead men don't bite,' says he. Well, he's dead now hisself; he knows the long and short on it now; and if ever a rough hand come to port, it was Billy."

"Right you are," said Silver, "rough and ready. But mark you here: I'm an easy man – I'm quite the gentleman, says you; but this time it's serious. Dooty is dooty, mates. I give my vote – death. When I'm in Parlyment, and riding in my coach, I don't want none of these sea lawyers in the cabin a-coming home unlooked for, like the Devil at prayers. Wait is what I say; but when the time comes, why let her rip!"

"John," cries the coxswain, "you're a man!"

"You'll say so, Israel, when you see," said Silver. "Only one thing I claim – I claim Trelawney. I'll wring his calf's head off his body with these hands. Dick!" he added, breaking off, "you just jump up, like a sweet lad, and get me an apple, to wet my pipe like."

You may fancy the terror I was in! I should have leapt out and run for it, if I had found the strength; but my limbs and heart alike misgave me. I heard Dick begin to rise, and then someone seemingly stopped him, and the voice of Hands exclaimed:

"Oh, stow that! Don't you get sucking of that bilge, John. Let's have a go of the rum."

"Dick," said Silver, "I trust you. I've a gauge on the keg, mind. There's the key; you fill a pannikin and bring it up."

Terrified as I was, I could not help thinking to myself that this must have been how Mr Arrow got the strong waters that destroyed him.

Dick was gone but a little while, and during his absence Israel spoke straight on in the cook's ear. It was but a word or two that I could catch, and yet I gathered some important news; for besides other scraps that tended to the same purpose, this whole clause was audible: "Not another man of them'll jine." Hence there were still faithful men on board.

When Dick returned, one after another of the trio took the pannikin and drank – one "To luck" – another with a "Here's to old Flint" – and Silver himself saying, in a kind of song, "Here's to ourselves, and hold your luff, plenty of prizes and plenty of duff."

Just then a sort of brightness fell upon me in the barrel, and looking up, I found the moon had risen, and was silvering the mizzen-top and shining white on the luff of the foresail; and almost at the same time the voice of the lookout shouted, "Land ho!"

# 12

## Council of War

THERE WAS A GREAT RUSH OF FEET across the deck. I could hear people tumbling up from the cabin and the foc's'le; and slipping in an instant outside my barrel, I dived behind the foresail, made a double towards the stern, and came out upon the open deck in time to join Hunter and Dr Livesey in the rush for the weather-bow.

There all hands were already congregated. A belt of fog had lifted almost simultaneously with the appearance of the moon. Away to the south-west of us we saw two low hills, about a couple of miles apart, and rising behind one of them a third and higher hill, whose peak was still buried in the fog. All three seemed sharp and conical in figure.

So much I saw almost in a dream, for I had not yet recovered from my horrid fear of a minute or two before. And then I heard the voice of Captain Smollett issuing orders. The *Hispaniola* was laid a couple of points nearer the wind, and now sailed a course that would just clear the island on the east.

"And now, men," said the captain, when all was sheeted home, "has any one of you ever seen that land ahead?"

"I have, sir," said Silver. "I've watered there with a trader I was cook in."

"The anchorage is on the south, behind an islet, I fancy?" asked the captain.

"Yes, sir; Skeleton Island they calls it. It were a main place for pirates once, and a hand we had on board knowed all their names for it. That hill to the nor'ard they calls the Foremast Hill; there are three hills in a row running south'ard – fore, main and mizzen, sir. But the main – that's the big 'un, with the cloud on it – they usually calls the Spyglass, by reason of a lookout they kept when they was in the anchorage cleaning; for it's there they cleaned their ships, sir, asking your pardon."

"I have a chart here," says Captain Smollett. "See if that's the place."

Long John's eyes burnt in his head as he took the chart; but, by the fresh look of the paper, I knew he was doomed to disappointment. This was not the map we found in Billy Bones's chest, but an accurate copy, complete in all things – names and heights and soundings – with the single exception of the red crosses and the written notes. Sharp as must have been his annoyance, Silver had the strength of mind to hide it.

"Yes, sir," said he, "this is the spot to be sure; and very prettily drawed out. Who might have done that, I wonder? The pirates were too ignorant, I reckon. Ay, here it is: 'Capt. Kidd's Anchorage' – just the name my shipmate called it. There's a strong current runs along the south, and then away nor'ard up the west coast. Right you was, sir," says he, "to haul your wind and keep the weather of the island. Leastways, if such was your intention as to enter and careen, and there ain't no better place for that in these waters."

"Thank you, my man," says Captain Smollett. "I'll ask you later on to give us a help. You may go."

I was surprised at the coolness with which John avowed his knowledge of the island; and I own I was half-frightened when I saw him drawing nearer to myself. He did not know, to be sure, that I had overheard his council from the apple barrel, and yet I had by this time taken such a horror of his cruelty, duplicity and power, that I could scarce conceal a shudder when he laid his hand upon my arm.

"Ah," says he, "this here is a sweet spot, this island – a sweet spot for a lad to get ashore on. You'll bathe, and you'll climb trees, and you'll hunt goats, you will; and you'll get aloft on them hills like a goat yourself. Why, it makes me young again. I was going to forget my timber leg, I was. It's a pleasant thing to be young, and have ten toes, and you may lay to that. When you want to go a bit of exploring, you just ask old John, and he'll put up a snack for you to take along."

And clapping me in the friendliest way upon the shoulder, he hobbled off forwards and went below.

Captain Smollett, the squire and Dr Livesey were talking together on the quarterdeck, and, anxious as I was to tell them my story, I durst not interrupt them openly. While I was still casting about in my thoughts to find some probable excuse, Dr Livesey called me to his side. He had left his pipe below, and being a slave to tobacco, had meant that I should fetch it; but as soon as I was near enough to speak and not to be overheard, I broke out immediately: "Doctor, let me speak. Get the captain and squire down to the cabin, and then make some pretence to send for me. I have terrible news."

The doctor changed countenance a little, but next moment he was master of himself.

"Thank you, Jim," said he quite loudly, "that was all I wanted to know," as if he had asked me a question.

And with that he turned on his heel and rejoined the other two. They spoke together for a little, and though none of them started, or raised his voice, or so much as whistled, it was plain enough that Dr Livesey had communicated my request; for the next thing that I heard was the captain giving an order to Job Anderson, and all hands were piped on deck.

"My lads," said Captain Smollett, "I've a word to say to you. This land that we have sighted is the place we have been sailing for. Mr Trelawney, being a very open-handed gentleman, as we all know, has just asked me a word or two, and as I was able to tell him that every man on board had done his duty, alow and aloft, as I never ask to see it done better, why, he and I and the doctor are going below to the cabin to drink *your* health and luck, and you'll have grog served out for you to drink *our* health and luck. I'll tell you what I think of this: I think it handsome. And if you think as I do, you'll give a good sea cheer for the gentleman that does it."

The cheer followed – that was a matter of course; but it rang out so full and hearty, that I confess I could hardly believe these same men were plotting for our blood.

"One more cheer for Cap'n Smollett," cried Long John, when the first had subsided.

And this also was given with a will.

On the top of that the three gentlemen went below, and not long after, word was sent forwards that Jim Hawkins was wanted in the cabin.

I found them all three seated round the table, a bottle of Spanish wine and some raisins before them, and the doctor smoking away, with his wig on his lap, and that, I knew, was a sign that he was agitated. The stern window was open, for it was a warm night, and you could see the moon shining behind on the ship's wake.

"Now, Hawkins," said the squire, "you have something to say. Speak up."

I did as I was bid, and as short as I could make it, told the whole details of Silver's conversation. Nobody interrupted me till I was done, nor did any one of the three of them make so much as a movement, but they kept their eyes upon my face from first to last.

"Jim," said Dr Livesey, "take a seat."

And they made me sit down at table beside them, poured me out a glass of wine, filled my hands with raisins, and all three, one after the other, and each with a bow, drank my good health, and their service to me for my luck and courage.

"Now, captain," said the squire, "you were right, and I was wrong. I own myself an ass, and I await your orders."

"No more an ass than I, sir," returned the captain. "I never heard of a crew that meant to mutiny but what showed signs before, for any man that had an eye in his head to see the mischief and take steps according. But this crew," he added, "beats me."

"Captain," said the doctor, "with your permission, that's Silver. A very remarkable man."

"He'd look remarkably well from a yardarm, sir," returned the captain. "But this is talk; this don't lead to anything. I see three or four points, and with Mr Trelawney's permission, I'll name them."

"You, sir, are the captain. It is for you to speak," says Mr Trelawney grandly.

"First point," began Mr Smollett. "We must go on, because we can't turn back. If I gave the word to go about, they would rise at once. Second point, we have time before us – at least, until this treasure's found. Third point, there are faithful hands. Now, sir, it's got to come to blows sooner or later; and what I propose is to take time by the forelock, as the saying is, and come to blows some fine day when they least expect it. We can count, I take it, on your own home servants, Mr Trelawney?"

"As upon myself," declared the squire.

"Three," reckoned the captain, "ourselves make seven, counting Hawkins here. Now, about the honest hands?"

"Most likely Trelawney's own men," said the doctor, "those he had picked up for himself, before he lit on Silver."

"Nay," replied the squire, "Hands was one of mine."

"I did think I could have trusted Hands," added the captain.

"And to think that they're all Englishmen!" broke out the squire. "Sir, I could find it in my heart to blow the ship up."

"Well, gentlemen," said the captain, "the best that I can say is not much. We must lay to, if you please, and keep a bright lookout. It's trying on a man, I know. It would be pleasanter to come to blows. But there's no help for it till we know our men. Lay to, and whistle for a wind, that's my view."

"Jim here," said the doctor, "can help us more than anyone. The men are not shy with him, and Jim is a noticing lad."

"Hawkins, I put prodigious faith in you," added the squire.

I began to feel pretty desperate at this, for I felt altogether helpless; and yet, by an odd train of circumstances, it was indeed through me that safety came. In the meantime, talk as we pleased, there were only seven out of the twenty-six on whom we knew we could rely; and out of these seven, one was a boy, so that the grown men on our side were six to their nineteen.

# 13

## *How My Shore Adventure Began*

THE APPEARANCE OF THE ISLAND when I came on deck next morning was altogether changed. Although the breeze had now utterly ceased, we had made a great deal of way during the night, and were now lying becalmed about half a mile to the south-east of the low eastern coast. Grey-coloured woods covered a large part of the surface. This even tint was indeed broken up by streaks of yellow sandbreak in the lower lands, and by many tall trees of the pine family, out-topping the others – some singly, some in clumps; but the general colouring was uniform and sad. The hills ran up clear above the vegetation in spires of naked rock. All were strangely shaped, and the Spyglass, which was by three or four hundred feet the tallest on the island, was likewise the strangest in configuration, running up sheer from almost every side, then suddenly cut off at the top like a pedestal to put a statue on.

The *Hispaniola* was rolling scuppers under in the ocean swell. The booms were tearing at the blocks, the rudder was banging to and fro, and the whole ship creaking, groaning and jumping like a manufactory. I had to cling tight to the backstay, and the world turned giddily before my eyes; for though I was a good enough sailor when there was way on, this standing still and being rolled about like a bottle was a thing I never learnt to stand without a qualm or so, above all in the morning on an empty stomach.

Perhaps it was this – perhaps it was the look of the island, with its grey, melancholy woods, and wild stone spires, and the surf that we could both see and hear foaming and thundering on the steep beach – at least, although the sun shone bright and hot, and the shore birds were fishing and crying all around us, and you would have thought anyone would have been glad to get to land after being so long at sea, my heart sank, as the saying is, into my boots; and from that first look onwards, I hated the very thought of Treasure Island.

We had a dreary morning's work before us, for there was no sign of any wind, and the boats had to be got out and manned, and the ship warped three or four miles round the corner of the island, and up the narrow passage to the haven behind Skeleton Island. I volunteered for one of the boats, where I had, of course, no business. The heat was sweltering, and the men grumbled fiercely over their work. Anderson was in command of my boat, and instead of keeping the crew in order, he grumbled as loud as the worst.

"Well," he said, with an oath, "it's not for ever."

I thought this was a very bad sign; for up to that day, the men had gone briskly and willingly about their business; but the very sight of the island had relaxed the cords of discipline.

All the way in, Long John stood by the steersman and conned the ship. He knew the passage like the palm of his hand; and though the man in the chains got everywhere more water than was down in the chart, John never hesitated once.

"There's a strong scour with the ebb," he said, "and this here passage has been dug out, in a manner of speaking, with a spade."

We brought up just where the anchor was in the chart, about a third of a mile from each shore, the mainland on one side, and Skeleton Island on the other. The bottom was clean sand. The plunge of our anchor sent up clouds of birds wheeling and crying over the woods; but in less than a minute they were down again, and all was once more silent.

The place was entirely landlocked, buried in woods, the trees coming right down to high water mark, the shores mostly flat, and the hilltops standing round at a distance in a sort of amphitheatre, one here, one there. Two little rivers, or rather, two swamps, emptied out into this pond, as you might call it; and the foliage round that part of the shore had a kind of poisonous brightness. From the ship, we could see nothing of the house or stockade, for they were quite buried among trees; and if it had not been for the chart on the companion, we might have been the first that had ever anchored there since the island arose out of the seas.

There was not a breath of air moving, nor a sound but that of the surf booming half a mile away along the beaches and against the rocks outside. A peculiar stagnant smell hung over the anchorage – a smell of sodden leaves and rotting tree trunks. I observed the doctor sniffing and sniffing, like someone tasting a bad egg.

"I don't know about treasure," he said, "but I'll stake my wig there's fever here."

If the conduct of the men had been alarming in the boat, it became truly threatening when they had come aboard. They lay about the deck growling together in talk. The slightest order was received with a black look, and grudgingly and carelessly obeyed. Even the honest hands must have caught the infection, for there was not one man aboard to mend another. Mutiny, it was plain, hung over us like a thundercloud.

And it was not only we of the cabin party who perceived the danger. Long John was hard at work going from group to group, spending himself in good advice, and as for example, no man could have shown a better. He fairly outstripped himself in willingness and civility; he was all smiles to everyone. If an order were given, John would be on his crutch in an instant, with the cheeriest "Ay, ay, sir!" in the world; and when there was nothing else to do, he kept up one song after another, as if to conceal the discontent of the rest.

Of all the gloomy features of that gloomy afternoon, this obvious anxiety on the part of Long John appeared the worst.

We held a council in the cabin.

"Sir," said the captain, "if I risk another order, the whole ship'll come about our ears by the run. You see, sir, here it is. I get a rough answer, do I not? Well, if I speak back, pikes will be going in two shakes; if I don't, Silver will see there's something under that, and the game's up. Now, we've only one man to rely on."

"And who is that?" asked the squire.

"Silver, sir," returned the captain, "he's as anxious as you and I to smother things up. This is a tiff; he'd soon talk 'em out of it if he had the chance, and what I propose to do is to give him the chance. Let's allow the men an afternoon ashore. If they all go, why, we'll fight the ship. If they none of them go, well, then we hold the cabin, and God defend the right. If some go, you mark my words, sir, Silver'll bring 'em aboard again as mild as lambs."

It was so decided; loaded pistols were served out to all the sure men; Hunter, Joyce and Redruth were taken into our confidence, and received the news with less surprise and a better spirit than we had looked for, and then the captain went on deck and addressed the crew.

"My lads," said he, "we've had a hot day, and are all tired and out of sorts. A turn ashore'll hurt nobody – the boats are still in the water; you can take the gigs, and as many as please may go ashore for the afternoon. I'll fire a gun half an hour before sundown."

I believe the silly fellows must have thought they would break their shins over treasure as soon as they were landed; for they all came out of their sulks in a moment, and gave a cheer that started the echo in a faraway hill, and sent the birds once more flying and squalling round the anchorage.

The captain was too bright to be in the way. He whipped out of sight in a moment, leaving Silver to arrange the party; and I fancy it was as well he did so. Had he been on deck, he could no longer so much as have pretended not to understand the situation. It was as plain as day. Silver was the captain, and a mighty rebellious crew he had of it. The honest hands – and I was soon to see it proved that there were such on board – must have been stupid fellows. Or rather, I suppose the truth was this, that all hands were disaffected by the example of the ringleaders – only some more, some less: and a few, being good fellows in the main, could neither be led nor driven any further. It is one thing to be idle and skulk, and quite another to take a ship and murder a number of innocent men.

At last, however, the party was made up. Six fellows were to stay on board, and the remaining thirteen, including Silver, began to embark.

Then it was that there came into my head the first of the mad notions that contributed so much to save our lives. If six men were left by Silver, it was plain our party could not take and fight the ship; and since only six were left, it was equally plain that the cabin party had no present need of my assistance. It occurred to me at once to go ashore. In a jiffy I had slipped over the side, and curled up in the foresheets of the nearest boat, and almost at the same moment she shoved off.

No one took notice of me, only the bow oar saying, "Is that you, Jim? Keep your head down." But Silver, from the other boat, looked sharply over and called out to know if that were me; and from that moment I began to regret what I had done.

The crews raced for the beach; but the boat I was in, having some start, and being at once the lighter and the better-manned, shot far ahead of her consort, and the bow had struck among the shoreside trees, and I had caught a branch and swung myself out, and plunged into the nearest thicket, while Silver and the rest were still a hundred yards behind.

"Jim, Jim!" I heard him shouting.

But you may suppose I paid no heed; jumping, ducking and breaking through, I ran straight before my nose, till I could run no longer.

# 14

## *The First Blow*

I WAS SO PLEASED AT HAVING given the slip to Long John, that I began to enjoy myself and look around me with some interest on the strange land that I was in.

I had crossed a marshy tract full of willows, bulrushes and odd, outlandish, swampy trees; and I had now come out upon the skirts of an open piece of undulating, sandy country, about a mile long, dotted with a few pines, and a great number of contorted trees, not unlike the oak in growth, but pale in the foliage, like willows. On the far side of the open stood one of the hills, with two quaint, craggy peaks, shining vividly in the sun.

I now felt for the first time the joy of exploration. The isle was uninhabited; my shipmates I had left behind, and nothing lived in front of me but dumb brutes and fowls. I turned hither and thither among the trees. Here and there were flowering plants, unknown to me; here and there I saw snakes, and one raised his head from a ledge of rock and hissed at me with a noise not unlike the spinning of a top. Little did I suppose that he was a deadly enemy, and that the noise was the famous rattle.

Then I came to a long thicket of these oak-like trees – live, or evergreen oaks, I heard afterwards they should be called – which grew low along the sand like brambles, the boughs curiously twisted, the foliage compact, like thatch. The thicket stretched down from the top of one of the sandy knolls, spreading and growing taller as it went, until it reached the margin of the broad, reedy fen, through which the nearest of the little rivers soaked its way into the anchorage. The marsh was steaming in the strong sun, and the outline of the Spyglass trembled through the haze.

All at once there began to go a sort of bustle among the bulrushes; a wild duck flew up with a quack, another followed, and soon over the whole surface of the marsh a great cloud of birds hung screaming and circling in the air. I judged at once that some of my shipmates must be drawing near along the borders of the fen. Nor was I deceived; for soon I heard the very distant and low tones of a human voice, which, as I continued to give ear, grew steadily louder and nearer.

This put me in a great fear, and I crawled under cover of the nearest live oak, and squatted there, hearkening, as silent as a mouse.

Another voice answered; and then the first voice, which I now recognized to be Silver's, once more took up the story, and ran on for a long while in a stream, only now and again interrupted by the other. By the sound they must have been talking earnestly, and almost fiercely; but no distinct word came to my hearing.

At last the speakers seemed to have paused, and perhaps to have sat down; for not only did they cease to draw any nearer, but the birds themselves began to grow more quiet, and to settle again to their places in the swamp.

And now I began to feel that I was neglecting my business; that since I had been so foolhardy as to come ashore with these desperadoes, the least I could do was to overhear them at their councils; and that my plain and obvious duty was to draw as close as I could manage, under the favourable ambush of the crouching trees.

I could tell the direction of the speakers pretty exactly, not only by the sound of their voices, but by the behaviour of the few birds that still hung in alarm above the heads of the intruders.

Crawling on all fours, I made steadily but slowly towards them; till at last, raising my head to an aperture among the leaves, I could see clear down into a little green dell beside the marsh, and closely set about with trees, where Long John Silver and another of the crew stood face to face in conversation.

The sun beat full upon them. Silver had thrown his hat beside him on the ground, and his great, smooth, blond face, all shining with heat, was lifted to the other man's in a kind of appeal.

"Mate," he was saying, "it's because I thinks gold dust of you – gold dust, and you may lay to that! If I hadn't took to you like pitch, do you think I'd have been here a-warning of you? All's up – you can't make nor mend; it's to save your neck that I'm a-speaking, and if one of the wild 'uns knew it, where 'ud I be, Tom – now, tell me, where 'ud I be?"

"Silver," said the other man – and I observed he was not only red in the face, but spoke as hoarse as a crow, and his voice shook, too, like a taut rope – "Silver," says he, "you're old, and you're honest, or has the name for it; and you've money, too, which lots of poor sailors hasn't; and you're brave, or I'm mistook. And will you tell me you'll let yourself be led away with that kind of a mess of swabs? not you! As sure as God sees me, I'd sooner lose my hand. If I turn agin my dooty—"

And then all of a sudden he was interrupted by a noise. I had found one of the honest hands – well, here, at that same moment, came news of another. Far away out in the marsh there arose, all of a sudden, a sound like the cry of anger, then another on the back of it; and then one horrid, long-drawn scream. The rocks of the Spyglass re-echoed it a score of times; the whole troop of marsh-birds rose again, darkening heaven, with a simultaneous whirr; and long after that death yell was still ringing in my brain, silence had re-established its empire, and only the rustle of the redescending birds and the boom of the distant surges disturbed the languor of the afternoon.

Tom had leapt at the sound, like a horse at the spur, but Silver had not winked an eye. He stood where he was, resting lightly on his crutch, watching his companion like a snake about to spring.

"John!" said the sailor, stretching out his hand.

"Hands off!" cried Silver, leaping back a yard, as it seemed to me, with the speed and security of a trained gymnast.

"Hands off, if you like, John Silver," said the other. "It's a black conscience that can make you feared of me. But, in heaven's name, tell me what was that?"

"That?" returned Silver, smiling away, but warier than ever, his eye a mere pinpoint in his big face, but gleaming like a crumb of glass. "That? Oh, I reckon that'll be Alan."

And at this poor Tom flashed out like a hero.

"Alan!" he cried. "Then rest his soul for a true seaman! And as for you, John Silver, long you've been a mate of mine, but you're mate of mine no more. If I die like a dog, I'll die in my dooty. You've killed Alan, have you? Kill me, too, if you can. But I defies you."

And with that, this brave fellow turned his back directly on the cook, and set off walking for the beach. But he was not destined to go far. With a cry, John seized the branch of a tree, whipped the crutch out of his armpit, and sent that uncouth missile hurtling through the air. It struck poor Tom, point foremost and with stunning violence, right between the shoulders in the middle of his back. His hands flew up, he gave a sort of gasp, and fell.

Whether he were injured much or little, none could ever tell. Like enough, to judge from the sound, his back was broken on the spot. But he had no time given him to recover. Silver, agile as a monkey, even without leg or crutch, was on the top of him next moment, and had twice buried his knife up to the hilt in that defenceless body. From my place of ambush, I could hear him pant aloud as he struck the blows.

I do not know what it rightly is to faint, but I do know that for the next little while the whole world swam away from before me in a whirling mist; Silver and the birds, and the tall Spyglass hilltop, going round and round and topsy-turvy before my eyes, and all manner of bells ringing and distant voices shouting in my ear.

When I came again to myself, the monster had pulled himself together, his crutch under his arm, his hat upon his head. Just before him Tom lay motionless upon the sward; but the murderer minded him not a whit, cleansing his bloodstained knife the while upon a wisp of grass. Everything else was unchanged, the sun still shining mercilessly on the steaming marsh and the tall pinnacle of the mountain, and I could scarce persuade myself that murder had been actually done, and a human life cruelly cut short a moment since before my eyes.

But now John put his hand into his pocket, brought out a whistle, and blew upon it several modulated blasts, that rang far across the heated air. I could not tell, of course, the meaning of the signal; but it instantly awoke my fears. More men would be coming. I might be discovered. They had already slain two of the honest people; after Tom and Alan, might not I come next?

Instantly I began to extricate myself and crawl back again, with what speed and silence I could manage, to the more open portion of the wood. As I did so, I could hear hails coming and going between the old buccaneer and his comrades, and this sound of danger lent me wings. As soon as I was clear of the thicket, I ran as I never ran before, scarce minding the direction of my flight, so long as it led me from the murderers; and as I ran, fear grew and grew upon me, until it turned into a kind of frenzy.

Indeed, could anyone be more entirely lost than I? When the gun fired, how should I dare to go down to the boats among those fiends, still smoking from their crime? Would not the first of them who saw me wring my neck like a snipe's? Would not my absence itself be an evidence to them of my alarm, and therefore of my fatal knowledge? It was all over, I thought. Goodbye to the *Hispaniola*; goodbye to the squire, the doctor and the captain! There was nothing left for me but death by starvation, or death by the hands of the mutineers.

All this while, as I say, I was still running, and, without taking any notice, I had drawn near to the foot of the little hill with the two peaks, and had got into a part of the island where the live oaks grew more widely apart, and seemed more like forest trees in their bearing and dimensions. Mingled with these were a few scattered pines, some fifty, some nearer seventy feet high. The air, too, smelt more freshly than down beside the marsh.

And here a fresh alarm brought me to a standstill with a thumping heart.

# 15

## The Man of the Island

F ROM THE SIDE OF THE HILL, which was here steep and
stony, a spout of gravel was dislodged, and fell rattling and
bounding through the trees. My eyes turned instinctively in that
direction, and I saw a figure leap with great rapidity behind the
trunk of a pine. What it was, whether bear or man or monkey,
I could in no wise tell. It seemed dark and shaggy; more I knew
not. But the terror of this new apparition brought me to a stand.

I was now, it seemed, cut off upon both sides; behind me the
murderers, before me this lurking nondescript. And immediately
I began to prefer the dangers that I knew to those I knew not.
Silver himself appeared less terrible in contrast with this creature
of the woods, and I turned on my heel, and, looking sharply
behind me over my shoulder, began to retrace my steps in the
direction of the boats.

Instantly the figure reappeared, and, making a wide circuit,
began to head me off. I was tired, at any rate; but had I been as
fresh as when I rose, I could see it was in vain for me to contend
in speed with such an adversary. From trunk to trunk the creature

flitted like a deer, running manlike on two legs, but unlike any man that I had ever seen, stooping almost double as it ran. Yet a man it was, I could no longer be in doubt about that.

I began to recall what I had heard of cannibals. I was within an ace of calling for help. But the mere fact that he was a man, however wild, had somewhat reassured me, and my fear of Silver began to revive in proportion. I stood still, therefore, and cast about for some method of escape; and as I was so thinking, the recollection of my pistol flashed into my mind. As soon as I remembered I was not defenceless, courage glowed again in my heart; and I set my face resolutely for this man of the island, and walked briskly towards him.

He was concealed by this time behind another tree trunk; but he must have been watching me closely, for as soon as I began to move in his direction he reappeared and took a step to meet me. Then he hesitated, drew back, came forwards again, and at last, to my wonder and confusion, threw himself on his knees and held out his clasped hands in supplication.

At that I once more stopped.

"Who are you?" I asked.

"Ben Gunn," he answered, and his voice sounded hoarse and awkward, like a rusty lock. "I'm poor Ben Gunn, I am; and I haven't spoke with a Christian these three years."

I could now see that he was a white man like myself, and that his features were even pleasing. His skin, wherever it was exposed, was burnt by the sun; even his lips were black; and his fair eyes looked quite startling in so dark a face. Of all the beggar-men that I had seen or fancied, he was the chief for raggedness. He was clothed with tatters of old ship's canvas and old sea cloth; and this extraordinary patchwork was all held together by a system of the most various and incongruous fastenings, brass buttons, bits of stick, and loops of tarry gaskin. About his waist he wore an old brass-buckled leather belt, which was the one thing solid in his whole accoutrement.

"Three years!" I cried. "Were you shipwrecked?"

"Nay, mate," said he, "marooned."

I had heard the word, and I knew it stood for a horrible kind of punishment common enough among the buccaneers, in which the offender is put ashore with a little powder and shot, and left behind on some desolate and distant island.

"Marooned three years agone," he continued, "and lived on goats since then, and berries, and oysters. Wherever a man is, says I, a man can do for himself. But mate, my heart is sore for Christian diet. You mightn't happen to have a piece of cheese about you, now? No? Well, many's the long night I've dreamt of cheese – toasted, mostly – and woke up again, and here I were."

"If ever I can get aboard again," said I, "you shall have cheese by the stone."

All this time he had been feeling the stuff of my jacket, smoothing my hands, looking at my boots, and generally, in the intervals of his speech, showing a childish pleasure in the presence of a fellow-creature. But at my last words he perked up into a kind of startled slyness.

"If ever you can get aboard again, says you?" he repeated. "Why, now, who's to hinder you?"

"Not you, I know," was my reply.

"And right you was," he cried. "Now you – what do you call yourself, mate?"

"Jim," I told him.

"Jim, Jim," says he, quite pleased apparently. "Well now, Jim, I've lived that rough as you'd be ashamed to hear of. Now, for instance, you wouldn't think I had had a pious mother – to look at me?" he asked.

"Why, no, not in particular," I answered.

"Ah, well," said he, "but I had – remarkable pious. And I was a civil, pious boy, and could rattle off my catechism that fast, as you couldn't tell one word from another. And here's what it come to, Jim, and it begun with chuck-farthen on the blessed gravestones! That's what it begun with, but it went further'n that; and so my mother told me, and predicked the whole, she did, the pious woman! But it were Providence that put me here. I've thought it all out in this here lonely island, and I'm back on piety. You don't catch me tasting rum so much; but just a thimbleful for luck, of course, the first chance I have. I'm bound I'll be good, and I see the way to. And, Jim" – looking all round him, and lowering his voice to a whisper – "I'm rich."

I now felt sure that the poor fellow had gone crazy in his solitude, and I suppose I must have shown the feeling in my face, for he repeated the statement hotly:

"Rich! rich! I says. And I'll tell you what: I'll make a man of you, Jim. Ah, Jim, you'll bless your stars, you will, you was the first that found me!"

And at this there came suddenly a lowering shadow over his face; and he tightened his grasp upon my hand, and raised a forefinger threateningly before my eyes.

"Now, Jim, you tell me true: that ain't Flint's ship?" he asked.

At this I had a happy inspiration. I began to believe that I had found an ally, and I answered him at once.

"It's not Flint's ship, and Flint is dead; but I'll tell you true, as you ask me – there are some of Flint's hands aboard; worse luck for the rest of us."

"Not a man – with one – leg?" he gasped.

"Silver?" I asked.

"Ah, Silver!" says he, "that were his name."

"He's the cook; and the ringleader, too."

He was still holding me by the wrist, and at that he gave it quite a wring.

"If you was sent by Long John," he said, "I'm as good as pork, and I know it. But where was you, do you suppose?"

I had made my mind up in a moment, and by way of answer told him the whole story of our voyage, and the predicament in which we found ourselves. He heard me with the keenest interest, and when I had done he patted me on the head.

"You're a good lad, Jim," he said, "and you're all in a clove hitch, ain't you? Well, you just put your trust in Ben Gunn – Ben Gunn's the man to do it. Would you think it likely, now, that your squire would prove a liberal-minded one in case of help – him being in a clove hitch, as you remark?"

I told him the squire was the most liberal of men.

"Ay, but you see," returned Ben Gunn, "I didn't mean giving me a gate to keep, and a shuit of livery clothes, and such; that's not my mark, Jim. What I mean is, would he be likely to come down to the toon of, say one thousand pounds out of money that's as good as a man's own already?"

"I am sure he would," said I. "As it was, all hands were to share."

"*And* a passage home?" he added, with a look of great shrewdness.

"Why," I cried, "the squire's a gentleman. And besides, if we got rid of the others, we should want you to help work the vessel home."

"Ah," said he, "so you would." And he seemed very much relieved.

"Now, I'll tell you what," he went on. "So much I'll tell you, and no more. I were in Flint's ship when he buried the treasure; he and six along – six strong seamen. They were ashore nigh on a week, and us standing off and on in the old *Walrus*. One fine day up went the signal, and here come Flint by himself in a little boat, and his head done up in a blue scarf. The sun was getting up, and mortal white he looked about the cutwater. But there he was, you mind, and the six all dead – dead and buried. How he done it, not a man aboard us could make out. It was battle, murder and sudden death, leastways – him against six. Billy Bones was the mate; Long John, he was quartermaster; and they asked him where the treasure was. 'Ah,' says he, 'you can go ashore, if you like, and stay,' he says, 'but as for the ship, she'll beat up for more, by thunder!' That's what he said.

"Well, I was in another ship three years back, and we sighted this island. 'Boys,' said I, 'here's Flint's treasure; let's land and find it.' The cap'n was displeased at that; but my messmates were all of a mind, and landed. Twelve days they looked for it, and every day they had the worse word for me, until one fine morning all hands went aboard. 'As for you, Benjamin Gunn,' says they, 'here's a musket,' they says, 'and a spade, and pickaxe. You can stay here, and find Flint's money for yourself,' they says.

"Well, Jim, three years have I been here, and not a bite of Christian diet from that day to this. But now, you look here; look at me. Do I look like a man before the mast? No, says you. Nor I weren't, neither, I says."

And with that he winked and pinched me hard.

"Just you mention them words to your squire, Jim" – he went on – "Nor he weren't, neither – that's the words. Three years he were the man of this island, light and dark, fair and rain; and sometimes he would, maybe, think upon a prayer (says you), and sometimes he would, maybe, think of his old mother, so be as she's alive (you'll say); but the most part of Gunn's time (this is what you'll say) – the most part of his time was took up with another matter. And then you'll give him a nip, like I do."

And he pinched me again in the most confidential manner.

"Then," he continued, "then you'll up, and you'll say this: Gunn is a good man (you'll say), and he puts a precious sight more confidence – a precious sight, mind that – in a gen'leman born than in these gen'lemen of fortune, having been one hisself."

"Well," I said, "I don't understand one word that you've been saying. But that's neither here nor there; for how am I to get on board?"

"Ah," said he, "that's the hitch, for sure. Well, there's my boat, that I made with my two hands. I keep her under the white rock. If the worst come to the worst, we might try that after dark. Hi!" he broke out, "what's that?"

For just then, although the sun had still an hour or two to run, all the echoes of the island awoke and bellowed to the thunder of a cannon.

"They have begun to fight!" I cried. "Follow me."

And I began to run towards the anchorage, my terrors all forgotten; while, close at my side, the marooned man in his goatskins trotted easily and lightly.

"Left, left," says he, "keep to your left hand, mate Jim! Under the trees with you! Theer's where I killed my first goat. They don't come down here now; they're all mastheaded on them mountings for the fear of Benjamin Gunn. Ah! and there's the cetemery" – cemetery, he must have meant – "You see the mounds? I come here and prayed, nows and thens, when I thought maybe a Sunday would be about doo. It weren't quite a chapel, but it seemed more solemn-like; and then, says you, Ben Gunn was short-handed – no chapling, nor so much as a Bible and a flag, you says."

So he kept talking as I ran, neither expecting nor receiving any answer.

The cannon shot was followed, after a considerable interval, by a volley of small arms.

Another pause, and then, not a quarter of a mile in front of me, I beheld the Union Jack flutter in the air above a wood.

# 16

*Narrative Continued by the Doctor:*
*How the Ship Was Abandoned*

I T WAS ABOUT HALF-PAST ONE – three bells in the sea
phrase – that the two boats went ashore from the *Hispaniola*.
The captain, the squire and I were talking matters over in the
cabin. Had there been a breath of wind we should have fallen
on the six mutineers who were left aboard with us, slipped
our cable, and away to sea. But the wind was wanting; and to
complete our helplessness, down came Hunter with the news
that Jim Hawkins had slipped into a boat and gone ashore
with the rest.

It never occurred to us to doubt Jim Hawkins; but we were
alarmed for his safety. With the men in the temper they were
in, it seemed an even chance if we should see the lad again. We
ran on deck. The pitch was bubbling in the seams; the nasty
stench of the place turned me sick; if ever a man smelt fever
and dysentery, it was in that abominable anchorage. The six
scoundrels were sitting grumbling under a sail in the forecastle;
ashore we could see the gigs made fast, and a man sitting in

each, hard by where the river runs in. One of them was whistling 'Lillibullero'.*

Waiting was a strain; and it was decided that Hunter and I should go ashore with the jolly boat, in quest of information. The gigs had leant to their right; but Hunter and I pulled straight in, in the direction of the stockade upon the chart. The two who were left guarding their boats seemed in a bustle at our appearance, 'Lillibullero' stopped off, and I could see the pair discussing what they ought to do. Had they gone and told Silver, all might have turned out differently; but they had their orders, I suppose, and decided to sit quietly where they were and hark back again to 'Lillibullero'.

There was a slight bend in the coast, and I steered so as to put it between us; even before we landed we had thus lost sight of the gigs. I jumped out, and came as near running as I durst, with a big silk handkerchief under my hat for coolness' sake, and a brace of pistols ready primed for safety.

I had not gone a hundred yards when I reached the stockade.

This was how it was: a spring of clear water rose almost at the top of a knoll. Well, on the knoll, and enclosing the spring, they had clapped a stout log house, fit to hold two score of people on a pinch, and loopholed for musketry on every side. All round this they had cleared a wide space, and then the thing was completed by a paling six feet high, without door or opening, too strong to pull down without time and labour, and too open to shelter the besiegers. The people in the log house had them in every way; they stood quiet in shelter and shot the others like partridges. All they wanted was a good watch and food; for short of a complete surprise, they might have held the place against a regiment.

What particularly took my fancy was the spring. For, though we had a good enough place of it in the cabin of the *Hispaniola*, with plenty of arms and ammunition, and things to eat, and excellent wines, there had been one thing overlooked – we had no water. I was thinking this over, when there came ringing over the island the cry of a man at the point of death. I was not new to violent death – I have served his Royal Highness the Duke of Cumberland, and got a wound myself at Fontenoy – but I know my pulse went dot and carry one.* "Jim Hawkins is gone," was my first thought.

It is something to have been an old soldier, but more still to have been a doctor. There is no time to dilly-dally in our work. And so now I made up my mind instantly, and with no time lost returned to the shore, and jumped on board the jolly boat.

By good fortune Hunter pulled a good oar. We made the water fly; and the boat was soon alongside, and I aboard the schooner.

I found them all shaken, as was natural. The squire was sitting down, as white as a sheet, thinking of the harm he had led us to, the good soul! and one of the six forecastle hands was little better.

"There's a man," says Captain Smollett, nodding towards him, "new to this work. He came nigh hand fainting, Doctor, when he heard the cry. Another touch of the rudder and that man would join us."

I told my plan to the captain, and between us we settled on the details of its accomplishment.

We put old Redruth in the gallery between the cabin and the forecastle, with three or four loaded muskets and a mattress for protection. Hunter brought the boat round under the stern-port, and Joyce and I set to work loading her with powder tins, muskets, bags of biscuits, kegs of pork, a cask of cognac and my invaluable medicine chest.

In the meantime, the squire and the captain stayed on deck, and the latter hailed the coxswain, who was the principal man aboard.

"Mr Hands," he said, "here are two of us with a brace of pistols each. If any one of you six make a signal of any description, that man's dead."

They were a good deal taken aback; and after a little consultation, one and all tumbled down the fore-companion, thinking, no doubt, to take us on the rear. But when they saw Redruth waiting for them in the sparred gallery, they went about ship at once, and a head popped out again on deck.

"Down, dog!" cries the captain.

And the head popped back again; and we heard no more, for the time, of these six very faint-hearted seamen.

By this time, tumbling things in as they came, we had the jolly boat loaded as much as we dared. Joyce and I got out through the stern-port, and we made for shore again, as fast as oars could take us.

This second trip fairly aroused the watchers alongshore. 'Lillibullero' was dropped again; and just before we lost sight of them behind the little point, one of them whipped ashore and disappeared. I had half a mind to change my plan and destroy their boats, but I feared that Silver and the others might be close at hand, and all might very well be lost by trying for too much.

We had soon touched land in the same place as before, and set to provision the blockhouse. All three made the first journey, heavily laden, and tossed our stores over the palisade. Then, leaving Joyce to guard them – one man, to be sure, but with half a dozen muskets – Hunter and I returned to the jolly boat, and loaded ourselves once more. So we proceeded without pausing to take breath, till the whole cargo was bestowed, when the two servants took up their position in the blockhouse, and I, with all my power, sculled back to the *Hispaniola*.

That we should have risked a second boat-load seems more daring than it really was. They had the advantage of numbers, of course, but we had the advantage of arms. Not one of the men ashore had a musket, and before they could get within range for pistol shooting, we flattered ourselves we should be able to give a good account of* a half-dozen at least.

The squire was waiting for me at the stern window, all his faintness gone from him. He caught the painter and made it fast, and we fell to loading the boat for our very lives. Pork, powder and biscuit was the cargo, with only a musket and a cutlass apiece for the squire and me and Redruth and the captain. The rest of the arms and powder we dropped over-board in two fathoms and a half of water, so that we could see the bright steel shining far below us in the sun on the clean, sandy bottom.

By this time the tide was beginning to ebb, and the ship was swinging round to her anchor. Voices were heard faintly halloo-ing in the direction of the two gigs; and though this reassured us for Joyce and Hunter, who were well to the eastwards, it warned our party to be off.

Redruth retreated from his place in the gallery, and dropped into the boat, which we then brought round to the ship's counter, to be handier for Captain Smollett.

"Now men," said he, "do you hear me?"

There was no answer from the forecastle.

"It's to you, Abraham Gray – it's to you I am speaking."

Still no reply.

"Gray," resumed Mr Smollett, a little louder, "I am leaving this ship, and I order you to follow your captain. I know you are a good man at bottom, and I dare say not one of the lot of you's as bad as he makes out. I have my watch here in my hand; I give you thirty seconds to join me in."

There was a pause.

"Come, my fine fellow," continued the captain, "don't hang so long in stays. I'm risking my life, and the lives of these good gentlemen every second."

There was a sudden scuffle, a sound of blows, and out burst Abraham Gray with a knife-cut on the side of the cheek, and came running to the captain, like a dog to the whistle.

"I'm with you, sir," said he.

And the next moment he and the captain had dropped aboard of us, and we had shoved off and given way.

We were clear out of the ship; but not yet ashore in our stockade.

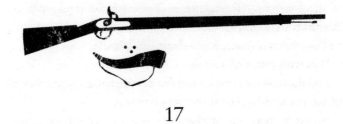

## 17

*Narrative Continued by the Doctor:*
*The Jolly Boat's Last Trip*

T HIS FIFTH TRIP WAS QUITE DIFFERENT from any of the others. In the first place, the little gallipot of a boat that we were in was gravely overloaded. Five grown men, and three of them – Trelawney, Redruth and the captain – over six feet high, was already more than she was meant to carry. Add to that the powder, pork and bread-bags. The gunwale was lipping astern. Several times we shipped a little water, and my breeches and the tails of my coat were all soaking wet before we had gone a hundred yards.

The captain made us trim the boat, and we got her to lie a little more evenly. All the same, we were afraid to breathe.

In the second place, the ebb was now making a strong rippling current running westwards through the basin, and then south'ards and seawards down the straits by which we had entered in the morning. Even the ripples were a danger to our overloaded craft; but the worst of it was that we were swept out of our true course, and away from our proper landing place behind the point. If we let the current have its way, we should come ashore beside the gigs, where the pirates might appear at any moment.

"I cannot keep her head for the stockade, sir," said I to the captain. I was steering, while he and Redruth, two fresh men, were at the oars. "The tide keeps washing her down. Could you pull a little stronger?"

"Not without swamping the boat," said he. "You must bear up, sir, if you please – bear up until you see you're gaining."

I tried, and found by experiment that the tide kept sweeping us westwards until I had laid her head due east, or just about right angles to the way we ought to go.

"We'll never get ashore at this rate," said I.

"If it's the only course that we can lie, sir, we must even lie it," returned the captain. "We must keep upstream. You see, sir," he went on, "if once we dropped to leewards of the landing place, it's hard to say where we should get ashore, besides the chance of being boarded by the gigs; whereas, the way we go the current must slacken, and then we can dodge back along the shore."

"The current's less a'ready, sir," said the man Gray, who was sitting in the foresheets, "you can ease her off a bit."

"Thank you, my man," said I, quite as if nothing had happened; for we had all quietly made up our minds to treat him like one of ourselves.

Suddenly the captain spoke up again, and I thought his voice was a little changed.

"The gun!" said he.

"I have thought of that," said I, for I made sure he was thinking of a bombardment of the fort. "They could never get the gun ashore, and if they did, they could never haul it through the woods."

"Look astern, Doctor," replied the captain.

We had entirely forgotten the long nine; and there, to our horror, were the five rogues busy about her, getting off her jacket, as they called the stout tarpaulin cover under which she sailed. Not only that, but it flashed into my mind at the same moment that the round shot and the powder for the gun had been left behind, and a stroke with an axe would put it all into the possession of the evil ones aboard.

"Israel was Flint's gunner," said Gray hoarsely.

At any risk, we put the boat's head direct for the landing place. By this time we had got so far out of the run of the current that we kept steerage way even at our necessarily gentle rate of rowing, and I could keep her steady for the goal. But the worst of it was that with the course I now held, we turned our broadside instead of our stern to the *Hispaniola*, and offered a target like a barn door.

I could hear, as well as see, that brandy-faced rascal, Israel Hands, plumping down a round shot on the deck.

"Who's the best shot?" asked the captain.

"Mr Trelawney, out and away," said I.

"Mr Trelawney, will you please pick me off one of these men, sir? Hands, if possible," said the captain.

Trelawney was as cool as steel. He looked to the priming of his gun.

"Now," cried the captain, "easy with that gun, sir, or you'll swamp the boat. All hands stand by to trim her when he aims."

The squire raised his gun, the rowing ceased, and we leant over to the other side to keep the balance, and all was so nicely contrived that we did not ship a drop.

They had the gun, by this time, slewed round upon the swivel, and Hands, who was at the muzzle with the rammer, was in consequence the most exposed. However, we had no luck; for just as Trelawney fired, down he stooped, the ball whistled over him, and it was one of the other four who fell.

The cry he gave was echoed not only by his companions on board, but by a great number of voices from the shore, and looking in that direction I saw the other pirates trooping out from among the trees and tumbling into their places in the boats.

"Here come the gigs, sir," said I.

"Give way then," cried the captain. "We mustn't mind if we swamp her now. If we can't get ashore, all's up."

"Only one of the gigs is being manned, sir," I added, "the crew of the other most likely going round by shore to cut us off."

"They'll have a hot run, sir," returned the captain. "Jack ashore, you know. It's not them I mind; it's the round shot. Carpet bowls!* My lady's maid couldn't miss. Tell us, squire, when you see the match, and we'll hold water."*

In the meanwhile we had been making headway at a good pace for a boat so overloaded, and we had shipped but little water in the process. We were now close in; thirty or forty strokes and we should beach her; for the ebb had already disclosed a narrow belt of sand below the clustering trees. The gig was no longer to be feared; the little point had already concealed it from our eyes. The ebb tide, which had so cruelly delayed us, was now making reparation, and delaying our assailants. The one source of danger was the gun.

"If I durst," said the captain, "I'd stop and pick off another man."

But it was plain that they meant nothing should delay their shot. They had never so much as looked at their fallen comrade, though he was not dead, and I could see him trying to crawl away.

"Ready!" cried the squire.

"Hold!" cried the captain, quick as an echo.

And he and Redruth backed with a great heave that sent her stern bodily underwater. The report fell in at the same instant of time. This was the first that Jim heard, the sound of the squire's shot not having reached him. Where the ball passed, not one of us precisely knew; but I fancy it must have been over our heads, and that the wind of it may have contributed to our disaster.

At any rate, the boat sank by the stern, quite gently, in three feet of water, leaving the captain and myself facing each other on our feet. The other three took complete headers, and came up again, drenched and bubbling.

So far there was no great harm. No lives were lost, and we could wade ashore in safety. But there were all our stores at the bottom, and to make things worse, only two guns out of five remained in a state for service. Mine I had snatched from my knees and held over my head by a sort of instinct. As for the captain, he had carried his over his shoulder by a bandolier, and, like a wise man, lock uppermost. The other three had gone down with the boat.

To add to our concern, we heard voices already drawing near us in the woods alongshore; and we had not only the danger of being cut off from the stockade in our half-crippled state, but the fear before us whether, if Hunter and Joyce were attacked by half a dozen, they would have the sense and conduct to stand firm. Hunter was steady, that we knew; Joyce was a doubtful case – a pleasant, polite man for a valet, and to brush one's clothes, but not entirely fitted for a man-o'-war.

With all this in our minds, we waded ashore as fast as we could, leaving behind us the poor jolly boat, and a good half of all our powder and provisions.

# 18

*Narrative Continued by the Doctor:*
*End of the First Day's Fighting*

WE MADE OUR BEST SPEED across the strip of wood that now divided us from the stockade; and at every step we took, the voices of the buccaneers rang nearer. Soon we could hear their footfalls as they ran, and the cracking of the branches as they breasted across a bit of thicket.

I began to see we should have a brush for it in earnest, and looked to my priming.

"Captain," said I, "Trelawney is the dead shot. Give him your gun; his own is useless."

They exchanged guns, and Trelawney, silent and cool as he had been since the beginning of the bustle, hung a moment on his heel to see that all was fit for service. At the same time, observing Gray to be unarmed, I handed him my cutlass. It did all our hearts good to see him spit in his hand, knit his brows, and make the blade sing through the air. It was plain from every line of his body that our new hand was worth his salt.

Forty paces further we came to the edge of the wood and saw the stockade in front of us. We struck the enclosure about the middle of the south side, and, almost at the same time, seven mutineers – Job Anderson, the boatswain, at their head – appeared in full cry at the south-western corner.

They paused, as if taken aback; and before they recovered, not only the squire and I, but Hunter and Joyce from the blockhouse, had time to fire. The four shots came in rather a scattering volley; but they did the business: one of the enemy actually fell, and the rest, without hesitation, turned and plunged into the trees.

After reloading, we walked down the outside of the palisade to see the fallen enemy. He was stone-dead – shot through the heart.

We began to rejoice over our good success, when just at that moment a pistol cracked in the bush, a ball whistled close past my ear, and poor Tom Redruth stumbled and fell his length on the ground. Both the squire and I returned the shot; but as we had nothing to aim at, it is probable we only wasted powder. Then we reloaded, and turned our attention to poor Tom.

The captain and Gray were already examining him; and I saw with half an eye that all was over.

I believe the readiness of our return volley had scattered the mutineers once more, for we were suffered without further molestation to get the poor old gamekeeper hoisted over the stockade, and carried, groaning and bleeding, into the log house.

Poor old fellow, he had not uttered one word of surprise, complaint, fear or even acquiescence, from the very beginning of our troubles till now, when we had laid him down in the log house to die. He had lain like a Trojan behind his mattress in the gallery; he had followed every order silently, doggedly and well; he was the oldest of our party by a score of years; and now, sullen, old, serviceable servant, it was he that was to die.

The squire dropped down beside him on his knees and kissed his hand, crying like a child.

"Be I going, Doctor?" he asked.

"Tom, my man," said I, "you're going home."

"I wish I had had a lick at them with the gun first," he replied.

"Tom," said the squire, "say you forgive me, won't you?"

"Would that be respectful like, from me to you, squire?" was the answer. "Howsoever, so be it, amen!"

After a little while of silence, he said he thought some-body might read a prayer. "It's the custom, sir," he added apologetically. And not long after, without another word, he passed away.

In the meantime the captain, whom I had observed to be won-derfully swollen about the chest and pockets, had turned out a great many various stores – the British colours, a Bible, a coil of stoutish rope, pen, ink, the logbook and pounds of tobacco. He had found a longish fir tree lying felled and trimmed in the enclosure, and, with the help of Hunter, he had set it up at the corner of the log house where the trunks crossed and made an angle. Then, climbing on the roof, he had with his own hand bent and run up the colours.

This seemed mightily to relieve him. He re-entered the log house, and set about counting up the stores, as if nothing else existed. But he had an eye on Tom's passage for all that; and as soon as all was over, came forwards with another flag, and reverently spread it on the body.

"Don't you take on, sir," he said, shaking the squire's hand. "All's well with him; no fear for a hand that's been shot down in his duty to captain and owner. It mayn't be good divinity, but it's a fact."

Then he pulled me aside.

"Dr Livesey," he said, "in how many weeks do you and squire expect the consort?"

I told him it was a question not of weeks, but of months; that if we were not back by the end of August, Blandly was to send to find us; but neither sooner nor later. "You can calculate for yourself," I said.

"Why, yes," returned the captain, scratching his head, "and making a large allowance, sir, for all the gifts of Providence, I should say we were pretty close hauled."

"How do you mean?" I asked.

"It's a pity, sir, we lost that second load. That's what I mean," replied the captain. "As for powder and shot, we'll do. But the rations are short, very short – so short, Dr Livesey, that we're perhaps as well without that extra mouth."

And he pointed to the dead body under the flag.

Just then, with a roar and a whistle, a round shot passed high above the roof of the log house and plumped far beyond us in the wood.

"Oho!" said the captain. "Blaze away! You've little enough powder already my lads."

At the second trial, the aim was better, and the ball descended inside the stockade, scattering a cloud of sand, but doing no further damage.

"Captain," said the squire, "the house is quite invisible from the ship. It must be the flag they are aiming at. Would it not be wiser to take it in?"

"Strike my colours!" cried the captain. "No, sir, not I" – and as soon as he had said the words, I think we all agreed with him. For it was not only a piece of stout, seamanly good feeling; it was good policy besides, and showed our enemies that we despised their cannonade.

All through the evening they kept thundering away. Ball after ball flew over or fell short, or kicked up the sand in the enclosure, but they had to fire so high that the shot fell dead and buried itself in the soft sand. We had no ricochet to fear, and though one popped in through the roof of the log house and out again through the floor, we soon got used to that sort of horseplay, and minded it no more than cricket.

"There is one thing good about all this," observed the captain, "the wood in front of us is likely clear. The ebb has made a good while; our stores should be uncovered. Volunteers to go and bring in pork."

Gray and Hunter were the first to come forwards. Well-armed, they stole out of the stockade; but it proved a useless mission. The mutineers were bolder than we fancied, or they put more trust in Israel's gunnery. For four or five of them were busy carrying off our stores, and wading out with them to one of the gigs that lay close by, pulling an oar or so to hold her steady against the current. Silver was in the stern-sheets in command; and every man of them was now provided with a musket from some secret magazine of their own.

The captain sat down to his log, and here is the beginning of the entry:

*Alexander Smollett, master; David Livesey, ship's doctor; Abraham Gray, carpenter's mate; John Trelawney, owner; John Hunter and Richard Joyce, owner's servants, landsmen – being all that is left faithful of the ship's company – with stores for ten days at short rations, came ashore this day, and flew British colours on the log house in Treasure Island. Thomas Redruth, owner's servant, landsman, shot by the mutineers; James Hawkins, cabin boy—*

And at the same time I was wondering over poor Jim Hawkins's fate.

A hail on the land side.

"Somebody hailing us," said Hunter, who was on guard.

"Doctor! Squire! Captain! Hullo, Hunter, is that you?" came the cries.

And I ran to the door in time to see Jim Hawkins, safe and sound, come climbing over the stockade.

# 19

*Narrative Resumed by Jim Hawkins:*
*The Garrison in the Stockade*

A S SOON AS BENN GUNN SAW THE COLOURS, he came to a halt, stopped me by the arm, and sat down.

"Now," said he, "there's your friends, sure enough."

"Far more likely it's the mutineers," I answered.

"That!" he cried. "Why, in a place like this, where nobody puts in but gen'lemen of fortune, Silver would fly the Jolly Roger, you don't make no doubt of that. No; that's your friends. There's been blows, too, and I reckon your friends has had the best of it; and here they are ashore in the old stockade, as was made years and years ago by Flint. Ah, he was the man to have a headpiece, was Flint! Barring rum, his match were never seen. He were afraid of none, not he; on'y Silver – Silver was that genteel."

"Well," said I, "that may be so, and so be it; all the more reason that I should hurry on and join my friends."

"Nay, mate," returned Ben, "not you. You're a good boy, or I'm mistook; but you're on'y a boy, all told. Now, Ben Gunn is fly. Rum wouldn't bring me there, where you're going – not rum wouldn't, till I see your born gen'leman, and gets it on his word of honour. And you won't forget my words: 'A precious sight (that's what you'll say), a precious sight more confidence' – and then nips him."

And he pinched me the third time with the same air of cleverness.

"And when Ben Gunn is wanted, you know where to find him, Jim. Just where you found him today. And him that comes is to have a white thing in his hand: and he's to come alone. Oh! and you'll say this: 'Ben Gunn,' says you, 'has reasons of his own.'"

"Well," said I, "I believe I understand. You have something to propose, and you wish to see the squire or the doctor; and you're to be found where I found you. Is that all?"

"And 'when?' says you," he added. "Why, from about noon observation to about six bells."

"Good," said I, "and now may I go?"

"You won't forget?" he enquired anxiously. "Precious sight, and reasons of his own, says you. Reasons of his own; that's the mainstay; as between man and man. Well, then" – still holding me – "I reckon you can go, Jim. And, Jim, if you was to see Silver, you wouldn't go for to sell Ben Gunn? Wild horses wouldn't draw it from you? No, says you. And if them pirates camp ashore, Jim, what would you say but there'd be widders in the morning?"

Here he was interrupted by a loud report, and a cannon ball came tearing through the trees and pitched in the sand, not a hundred yards from where we two were talking. The next moment, each of us had taken to his heels in a different direction.

For a good hour to come, frequent reports shook the island, and balls kept crashing through the woods. I moved from hiding place to hiding place, always pursued, or so it seemed to me, by these terrifying missiles. But towards the end of the bombardment, though still I durst not venture in the direction of the stockade, where the balls fell oftenest, I had begun, in a manner, to pluck up my heart again; and after a long detour to the east, crept down among the shoreside trees.

The sun had just set, the sea breeze was rustling and tumbling in the woods, and ruffling the grey surface of the anchorage; the tide, too, was far out, and great tracts of sand lay uncovered; the air, after the heat of the day, chilled me through my jacket.

The *Hispaniola* still lay where she had anchored; but, sure enough, there was the Jolly Roger – the black flag of piracy – flying from her peak. Even as I looked, there came another red flash and another report that sent the echoes clattering, and one more round shot whistled through the air. It was the last of the cannonade.

I lay for some time, watching the bustle which succeeded the attack. Men were demolishing something with axes on the beach near the stockade; the poor jolly boat, I afterwards discovered. Away, near the mouth of the river, a great fire was glowing among the trees, and between that point and the ship one of the gigs kept coming and going; the men, whom I had seen so gloomy, shouting at the oars like children. But there was a sound in their voices which suggested rum.

At length I thought I might return towards the stockade. I was pretty far down on the low, sandy spit that encloses the anchorage to the east, and is joined at half-water to Skeleton Island; and now, as I rose to my feet, I saw, some distance further down the spit, and rising from among low bushes, an isolated rock, pretty high, and peculiarly white in colour. It occurred to me that this might be the white rock of which Ben Gunn had spoken, and that some day or other a boat might be wanted, and I should know where to look for one.

Then I skirted among the woods until I had regained the rear, or shoreward side of the stockade, and was soon warmly welcomed by the faithful party.

I had soon told my story, and began to look about me. The log house was made of unsquared trunks of pine – roof, walls and floor. The latter stood in several places as much as a foot or a foot and a half above the surface of the sand. There was a porch at the door, and under this porch the little spring welled up into an artificial basin of a rather odd kind – no other than a great ship's kettle of iron, with the bottom knocked out, and sunk "to her bearings," as the captain said, among the sand.

Little had been left beside the framework of the house; but in one corner there was a stone slab laid down by way of hearth, and an old rusty iron basket to contain the fire.

The slopes of the knoll and all the inside of the stockade had been cleared of timber to build the house, and we could see by the stumps what a fine and lofty grove had been destroyed. Most of the soil had been washed away or buried in drift after the removal of the trees; only where the streamlet ran down from the kettle a thick bed of moss and some ferns and little creeping bushes were still green among the sand. Very close around the stockade – too close for defence, they said – the wood still flourished high and dense, all of fir on the land side, but towards the sea with a large admixture of live oaks.

The cold evening breeze, of which I have spoken, whistled through every chink of the rude building, and sprinkled the floor with a continual rain of fine sand. There was sand in our eyes, sand in our teeth, sand in our suppers, sand dancing in the spring at the bottom of the kettle, for all the world like porridge beginning to boil. Our chimney was a square hole in the roof; it was but a little part of the smoke that found its way out, and the rest eddied about the house, and kept us coughing and piping the eye.

Add to this that Gray, the new man, had his face tied up in a bandage for a cut he had got in breaking away from the mutineers; and that poor old Tom Redruth, still unburied, lay along the wall, stiff and stark, under the Union Jack.

If we had been allowed to sit idle, we should all have fallen in the blues, but Captain Smollett was never the man for that. All hands were called up before him, and he divided us into watches. The doctor and Gray and I, for one; the squire, Hunter, and Joyce, upon the other. Tired though we all were, two were sent out for firewood; two more were set to dig a grave for Redruth; the doctor was named cook; I was put sentry at the door; and the captain himself went from one to another, keeping up our spirits and lending a hand wherever it was wanted.

From time to time the doctor came to the door for a little air and to rest his eyes, which were almost smoked out of his head; and whenever he did so, he had a word for me.

"That man Smollett," he said once, "is a better man than I am. And when I say that it means a deal, Jim."

Another time he came and was silent for a while. Then he put his head on one side, and looked at me.

"Is this Ben Gunn a man?" he asked.

"I do not know, sir," said I. "I am not very sure whether he's sane."

"If there's any doubt about the matter, he is," returned the doctor. "A man who has been three years biting his nails on a desert island, Jim, can't expect to appear as sane as you or me. It doesn't lie in human nature. Was it cheese you said he had a fancy for?"

"Yes, sir, cheese," I answered.

"Well, Jim," says he, "just see the good that comes of being dainty in your food. You've seen my snuffbox, haven't you? And you never saw me take snuff; the reason being that in my snuffbox I carry a piece of Parmesan cheese – a cheese made in Italy, very nutritious. Well, that's for Ben Gunn!"

Before supper was eaten we buried old Tom in the sand, and stood round him for a while, bare-headed in the breeze. A good deal of firewood had been got in, but not enough for the captain's fancy; and he shook his head over it, and told us we "must get back to this tomorrow rather livelier." Then, when we had eaten our pork, and each had a good stiff glass of brandy grog, the three chiefs got together in a corner to discuss our prospects.

It appears they were at their wits' end what to do, the stores being so low that we must have been starved into surrender long before help came. But our best hope, it was decided, was to kill off the buccaneers until they either hauled down their flag or ran away with the *Hispaniola*. From nineteen they were already reduced to fifteen, two others were wounded, and one, at least – the man shot beside the gun – severely wounded, if he were not dead. Every time we had a crack at them, we were to take it, saving our own lives, with the extremest care. And, besides that, we had two able allies – rum and the climate.

As for the first, though we were about half a mile away, we could hear them roaring and singing late into the night; and as for the second, the doctor staked his wig that, camped where they were in the marsh, and unprovided with remedies, the half of them would be on their backs before a week.

"So," he added, "if we are not all shot down first they'll be glad to be packing in the schooner. It's always a ship, and they can get to buccaneering again, I suppose."

"First ship that ever I lost," said Captain Smollett.

I was dead tired, as you may fancy, and when I got to sleep, which was not till after a great deal of tossing, I slept like a log of wood.

The rest had long been up, and had already breakfasted and increased the pile of firewood by about half as much again, when I was wakened by a bustle and the sound of voices.

"Flag of truce!" I heard someone say; and then, immediately after, with a cry of surprise, "Silver himself!"

And at that, up I jumped, and rubbing my eyes, ran to a loophole in the wall.

# 20

## Silver's Embassy

SURE ENOUGH, THERE WERE TWO MEN just outside the stockade, one of them waving a white cloth; the other, no less a person than Silver himself, standing placidly by.

It was still quite early, and the coldest morning that I think I ever was abroad in; a chill that pierced into the marrow. The sky was bright and cloudless overhead, and the tops of the trees shone rosily in the sun. But where Silver stood with his lieutenant all was still in shadow, and they waded knee-deep in a low, white vapour that had crawled during the night out of the morass. The chill and the vapour taken together told a poor tale of the island. It was plainly a damp, feverish, unhealthy spot.

"Keep indoors, men," said the captain. "Ten to one this is a trick."

Then he hailed the buccaneer.

"Who goes? Stand, or we fire."

"Flag of truce," cried Silver.

The captain was in the porch, keeping himself carefully out of the way of a treacherous shot should any be intended. He turned and spoke to us:

"Doctor's watch on the lookout. Dr Livesey take the north side, if you please; Jim, the east; Gray, west. The watch below, all hands to load muskets. Lively, men, and careful."

And then he turned again to the mutineers.

"And what do you want with your flag of truce?" he cried.

This time it was the other man who replied.

"Cap'n Silver, sir, to come on board and make terms," he shouted.

"Cap'n Silver! Don't know him. Who's he?" cried the captain. And we could hear him adding to himself: "Cap'n, is it? My heart, and here's promotion!"

Long John answered for himself.

"Me, sir. These poor lads have chosen me cap'n, after your desertion, sir" – laying a particular emphasis upon the word "desertion" – "We're willing to submit, if we can come to terms, and no bones about it. All I ask is your word, Cap'n Smollett, to let me safe and sound out of this here stockade, and one minute to get out o' shot before a gun is fired."

"My man," said Captain Smollett, "I have not the slightest desire to talk to you. If you wish to talk to me, you can come, that's all. If there's any treachery, it'll be on your side, and the Lord help you."

"That's enough, Cap'n," shouted Long John cheerily. "A word from you's enough. I know a gentleman, and you may lay to that."

We could see the man who carried the flag of truce attempting to hold Silver back. Nor was that wonderful, seeing how cavalier had been the captain's answer. But Silver laughed at him aloud, and slapped him on the back, as if the idea of alarm had been absurd. Then he advanced to the stockade, threw over his crutch, got a leg up, and with great vigour and skill succeeded in surmounting the fence and dropping safely to the other side.

I will confess that I was far too much taken up with what was going on to be of the slightest use as sentry; indeed, I had already deserted my eastern loophole, and crept up behind the captain, who had now seated himself on the threshold, with his elbows on his knees, his head in his hands, and his eyes fixed on the water, as it bubbled out of the old iron kettle in the sand. He was whistling to himself 'Come, Lasses and Lads'.*

Silver had terrible hard work getting up the knoll. What with the steepness of the incline, the thick tree stumps and the soft sand, he and his crutch were as helpless as a ship in stays. But he stuck to it like a man in silence, and at last arrived before the captain, whom he saluted in the handsomest style. He was tricked out in his best; an immense blue coat, thick with brass buttons, hung as low as to his knees, and a fine laced hat was set on the back of his head.

"Here you are, my man," said the captain, raising his head. "You had better sit down."

"You ain't a-going to let me inside, Cap'n?" complained Long John. "It's a main cold morning, to be sure, sir, to sit outside upon the sand."

"Why, Silver," said the captain, "if you had pleased to be an honest man, you might have been sitting in your galley. It's your own doing. You're either my ship's cook – and then you were treated handsome – or Cap'n Silver, a common mutineer and pirate, and then you can go hang!"

"Well, well, Cap'n," returned the sea cook, sitting down as he was bidden on the sand, "you'll have to give me a hand up again, that's all. A sweet pretty place you have of it here. Ah, there's Jim! The top of the morning to you, Jim. Doctor, here's my service. Why, there you all are together like a happy family, in a manner of speaking."

"If you have anything to say, my man, better say it," said the captain.

"Right you were, Cap'n Smollett," replied Silver. "Dooty is dooty, to be sure. Well now, you look here, that was a good lay of yours last night. I don't deny it was a good lay. Some of you pretty handy with a handspike-end. And I'll not deny neither but what some of my people was shook – maybe all was shook; maybe I was shook myself; maybe that's why I'm here for terms. But you mark me, Cap'n, it won't do twice, by thunder! We'll have to do sentry-go, and ease off a point or so on the rum. Maybe you think we were all a sheet in the wind's eye. But I'll tell you I was sober; I was on'y dog tired; and if I'd awoke a second sooner I'd a' caught you at the act, I would. He wasn't dead when I got round to him, not he."

"Well?" says Captain Smollett, as cool as can be.

All that Silver said was a riddle to him, but you would never have guessed it from his tone. As for me, I began to have an ink-ling. Ben Gunn's last words came back to my mind. I began to suppose that he had paid the buccaneers a visit while they all lay drunk together round their fire, and I reckoned up with glee that we had only fourteen enemies to deal with.

"Well, here it is," said Silver. "We want that treasure, and we'll have it – that's our point! You would just as soon save your lives, I reckon; and that's yours. You have a chart, haven't you?"

"That's as may be," replied the captain.

"Oh, well, you have, I know that," returned Long John. "You needn't be so husky with a man; there ain't a particle of service in that, and you may lay to it. What I mean is, we want your chart. Now, I never meant you no harm, myself."

"That won't do with me, my man," interrupted the captain. "We know exactly what you meant to do, and we don't care; for now, you see, you can't do it."

And the captain looked at him calmly, and proceeded to fill a pipe.

"If Abe Gray—" Silver broke out.

"Avast there!" cried Mr Smollett. "Gray told me nothing, and I asked him nothing; and what's more I would see you and him and this whole island blown clean out of the water into blazes first. So there's my mind for you, my man, on that."

This little whiff of temper seemed to cool Silver down. He had been growing nettled before, but now he pulled himself together.

"Like enough," said he. "I would set no limits to what gentlemen might consider shipshape, or might not, as the case were. And, seein' as how you are about to take a pipe, Cap'n, I'll make so free as do likewise."

And he filled a pipe and lit it; and the two men sat silently smoking for quite a while, now looking each other in the face, now stopping their tobacco, now leaning forwards to spit. It was as good as the play to see them.

"Now," resumed Silver, "here it is. You give us the chart to get the treasure by, and drop shooting poor seamen, and stoving of their heads in while asleep. You do that, and we'll offer you a choice. Either you come aboard along of us, once the treasure shipped, and then I'll give you my affy-davy, upon my word of honour, to clap you somewhere safe ashore. Or if that ain't to your fancy, some of my hands being rough, and having old scores, on account of hazing, then you can stay here, you can. We'll divide stores with you, man for man; and I'll give my affy-davy, as before, to speak the first ship I sight, and send 'em here to pick you up. Now you'll own that's talking. Handsomer you couldn't look to get, not you. And I hope" – raising his voice – "that all hands in this here blockhouse will overhaul my words, for what is spoke to one is spoke to all."

Captain Smollett rose from his seat, and knocked out the ashes of his pipe in the palm of his left hand.

"Is that all?" he asked.

"Every last word, by thunder!" answered John. "Refuse that, and you've seen the last of me but musket balls."

"Very good," said the captain. "Now you'll hear me. If you'll come up one by one, unarmed, I'll engage to clap you all in irons, and take you home to a fair trial in England. If you won't, my name is Alexander Smollett, I've flown my sovereign's colours, and I'll see you all to Davy Jones. You can't find the treasure. You can't sail the ship – there's not a man among you fit to sail the ship. You can't fight us – Gray, there, got away from five of you. Your ship's in irons, Master Silver; you're on a lee shore, and so you'll find. I stand here and tell you so; and they're the last good words you'll get from me; for in the name of Heaven, I'll put a bullet in your back when next I meet you. Tramp, my lad. Bundle out of this, please, hand over hand, and double quick."

Silver's face was a picture; his eyes started in his head with wrath. He shook the fire out of his pipe.

"Give me a hand up!" he cried.

"Not I," returned the captain.

"Who'll give me a hand up?" he roared.

Not a man among us moved. Growling the foulest imprecations, he crawled along the sand till he got hold of the porch and could hoist himself again upon his crutch. Then he spat into the spring.

"There!" he cried, "that's what I think of ye. Before an hour's out, I'll stove in your old blockhouse like a rum puncheon. Laugh, by thunder, laugh! Before an hour's out, ye'll laugh upon the other side. Them that die'll be the lucky ones."

And with a dreadful oath he stumbled off, ploughed down the sand, was helped across the stockade, after four or five failures, by the man with the flag of truce, and disappeared in an instant afterwards among the trees.

# 21

## *The Attack*

As soon as Silver disappeared, the captain, who had been closely watching him, turned towards the interior of the house, and found not a man of us at his post but Gray. It was the first time we had ever seen him angry.

"Quarters!" he roared. And then, as we all slunk back to our places, "Gray," he said, "I'll put your name in the log; you've stood by your duty like a seaman. Mr Trelawney, I'm surprised at you, sir. Doctor, I thought you had worn the king's coat! If that was how you served at Fontenoy, sir, you'd have been better in your berth."

The doctor's watch were all back at their loopholes, the rest were busy loading the spare muskets, and every one with a red face, you may be certain, and a flea in his ear, as the saying is.

The captain looked on for a while in silence. Then he spoke.

"My lads," said he, "I've given Silver a broadside. I pitched it in red-hot on purpose; and before the hour's out, as he said, we shall be boarded. We're outnumbered, I needn't tell you that, but we fight in shelter; and a minute ago, I should have said we fought with discipline. I've no manner of doubt that we can drub them, if you choose."

Then he went the rounds, and saw, as he said, that all was clear.

On the two short sides of the house, east and west, there were only two loopholes; on the south side where the porch was, two again; and on the north side, five. There was a round score of muskets for the seven of us; the firewood had been built into four piles – tables, you might say – one about the middle of each side, and on each of these tables some ammunition and four loaded muskets were laid ready to the hand of the defenders. In the middle, the cutlasses lay ranged.

"Toss out the fire," said the captain, "the chill is past, and we mustn't have smoke in our eyes."

The iron fire-basket was carried bodily out by Mr Trelawney, and the embers smothered among sand.

"Hawkins hasn't had his breakfast. Hawkins, help yourself, and back to your post to eat it," continued Captain Smollett. "Lively, now, my lad; you'll want it before you've done. Hunter, serve out a round of brandy to all hands."

And while this was going on, the captain completed, in his own mind, the plan of the defence.

"Doctor, you will take the door," he resumed. "See, and don't expose yourself; keep within, and fire through the porch. Hunter, take the east side, there. Joyce, you stand by the west, my man. Mr Trelawney, you are the best shot – you and Gray will take this long north side, with the five loopholes; it's there the danger is. If they can get up to it, and fire in upon us through our own ports, things would begin to look dirty. Hawkins, neither you nor I are much account at the shooting; we'll stand by to load and bear a hand."

As the captain had said, the chill was past. As soon as the sun had climbed above our girdle of trees, it fell with all its force upon the clearing, and drank up the vapours at a draught. Soon the sand was baking, and the resin melting in the logs of the blockhouse. Jackets and coats were flung aside; shirts thrown open at the neck, and rolled up to the shoulders; and we stood there, each at his post, in a fever of heat and anxiety.

An hour passed away.

"Hang them!" said the captain. "This is as dull as the doldrums. Gray, whistle for a wind."

And just at that moment came the first news of the attack.

"If you please, sir," said Joyce, "if I see anyone am I to fire?"

"I told you so!" cried the captain.

"Thank you, sir," returned Joyce, with the same quiet civility.

Nothing followed for a time, but the remark had set us all on the alert, straining ears and eyes – the musketeers with their pieces balanced in their hands, the captain out in the middle of the blockhouse, with his mouth very tight and a frown on his face.

So some seconds passed, till suddenly Joyce whipped up his musket and fired. The report had scarcely died away ere it was repeated and repeated from without in a scattering volley, shot behind shot, like a string of geese, from every side of the enclosure. Several bullets struck the log house, but not one entered; and as the smoke cleared away and vanished, the stockade and the woods around it looked as quiet and empty as before. Not a bough waved, not the gleam of a musket-barrel betrayed the presence of our foes.

"Did you hit your man?" asked the captain.

"No, sir," replied Joyce. "I believe not, sir."

"Next best thing to tell the truth," muttered Captain Smollett. "Load his gun, Hawkins. How many should you say there were on your side, Doctor?"

"I know precisely," said Dr Livesey. "Three shots were fired on this side. I saw the three flashes – two close together – one further to the west."

"Three!" repeated the captain. "And how many on yours, Mr Trelawney?"

But this was not so easily answered. There had come many from the north – seven, by the squire's computation; eight or nine, according to Gray. From the east and west only a single shot had been fired. It was plain, therefore, that the attack would be developed from the north, and that on the other three sides we were only to be annoyed by a show of hostilities. But Captain Smollett made no change in his arrangements. If the mutineers succeeded in crossing the stockade, he argued, they would take possession of any unprotected loophole, and shoot us down like rats in our own stronghold.

Nor had we much time left to us for thought. Suddenly, with a loud huzzah, a little cloud of pirates leapt from the woods on the north side, and ran straight on the stockade. At the same moment, the fire was once more opened from the woods, and a rifle-ball sang through the doorway, and knocked the doctor's musket into bits.

The boarders swarmed over the fence like monkeys. Squire and Gray fired again and yet again; three men fell, one forwards into the enclosure, two back on the outside. But of these, one was evidently more frightened than hurt, for he was on his feet again in a crack, and instantly disappeared among the trees.

Two had bit the dust, one had fled, four had made good their footing inside our defences; while from the shelter of the woods, seven or eight men, each evidently supplied with several muskets, kept up a hot though useless fire on the log house.

The four who had boarded made straight before them for the building, shouting as they ran, and the men among the trees shouted back to encourage them. Several shots were fired; but, such was the hurry of the marksmen, that not one appeared to have taken effect. In a moment, the four pirates had swarmed up the mound and were upon us.

The head of Job Anderson, the boatswain, appeared at the middle loophole.

"At 'em, all hands – all hands!" he roared, in a voice of thunder.

At the same moment, another pirate grasped Hunter's musket by the muzzle, wrenched it from his hands, plucked it through the loophole, and with one stunning blow, laid the poor fellow senseless on the floor. Meanwhile a third, running unharmed all round the house, appeared suddenly in the doorway, and fell with his cutlass on the doctor.

Our position was utterly reversed. A moment since we were firing, under cover, at an exposed enemy; now it was we who lay uncovered, and could not return a blow.

The log house was full of smoke, to which we owed our comparative safety. Cries and confusion, the flashes and reports of pistol shots, and one loud groan, rang in my ears.

"Out, lads, out, and fight 'em in the open! Cutlasses!" cried the captain.

I snatched a cutlass from the pile, and someone, at the same time snatching another, gave me a cut across the knuckles which I hardly felt. I dashed out of the door into the clear sunlight. Someone was close behind, I knew not whom. Right in front, the doctor was pursuing his assailant down the hill, and just as my eyes fell upon him, beat down his guard, and sent him sprawling on his back with a great slash across the face.

"Round the house, lads! Round the house!" cried the captain; and even in the hurly-burly I perceived a change in his voice.

Mechanically I obeyed, turned eastwards, and with my cutlass raised, ran round the corner of the house. Next moment I was face to face with Anderson. He roared aloud, and his hanger went up above his head, flashing in the sunlight. I had not time to be afraid, but, as the blow still hung impending, leapt in a trice upon one side, and missing my foot in the soft sand, rolled headlong down the slope.

When I had first sallied from the door, the other mutineers had been already swarming up the palisade to make an end of us. One man, in a red nightcap, with his cutlass in his mouth, had even got upon the top and thrown a leg across. Well, so short had been the interval, that when I found my feet again all was in the same posture, the fellow with the red nightcap still halfway over, another still just showing his head above the top of the stockade. And yet, in this breath of time, the fight was over, and the victory was ours.

Gray, following close behind me, had cut down the big boatswain ere he had time to recover from his lost blow. Another had been shot at a loophole in the very act of firing into the house, and now lay in agony, the pistol still smoking in his hand. A third, as I had seen, the doctor had disposed of at a blow. Of the four who had scaled the palisade, one only remained unaccounted for, and he, having left his cutlass on the field, was now clambering out again with the fear of death upon him.

"Fire – fire from the house!" cried the doctor. "And you, lads, back into cover."

But his words were unheeded, no shot was fired, and the last boarder made good his escape, and disappeared with the rest into the wood. In three seconds nothing remained of the attacking party but the five who had fallen, four on the inside, and one on the outside of the palisade.

The doctor and Gray and I ran full speed for shelter. The survivors would soon be back where they had left their muskets, and at any moment the fire might recommence.

The house was by this time somewhat cleared of smoke, and we saw at a glance the price we had paid for victory. Hunter lay beside his loophole, stunned; Joyce by his, shot through the head, never to move again; while right in the centre, the squire was supporting the captain, one as pale as the other.

"The captain's wounded," said Mr Trelawney.

"Have they run?" asked Mr Smollett.

"All that could, you may be bound," returned the doctor, "but there's five of them will never run again."

"Five!" cried the captain. "Come, that's better. Five against three leaves us four to nine. That's better odds than we had at starting. We were seven to nineteen then, or thought we were, and that's as bad to bear."*

# 22

## *How My Sea Adventure Began*

THERE WAS NO RETURN OF THE MUTINEERS – not so much as another shot out of the woods. They had "got their rations for that day," as the captain put it, and we had the place to ourselves and a quiet time to overhaul the wounded and get dinner. Squire and I cooked outside in spite of the danger, and even outside we could hardly tell what we were at, for horror of the loud groans that reached us from the doctor's patients.

Out of the eight men who had fallen in the action, only three still breathed – that one of the pirates who had been shot at the loophole, Hunter and Captain Smollett; and of these the first two were as good as dead; the mutineer indeed died under the doctor's knife, and Hunter, do what we could, never recovered consciousness in this world. He lingered all day, breathing loudly like the old buccaneer at home in his apoplectic fit; but the bones of his chest had been crushed by the blow and his skull fractured in falling, and some time in the following night, without sign or sound, he went to his Maker.

As for the captain, his wounds were grievous indeed, but not dangerous. No organ was fatally injured. Anderson's ball – for it was Job that shot him first – had broken his shoulder blade and touched the lung, not badly; the second had only torn and displaced some muscles in the calf. He was sure to recover, the doctor said, but in the meantime and for weeks to come, he must not walk nor move his arm, nor so much as speak when he could help it.

My own accidental cut across the knuckles was a flea-bite. Dr Livesey patched it up with plaster, and pulled my ears for me into the bargain.

After dinner the squire and the doctor sat by the captain's side awhile in consultation; and when they had talked to their heart's content, it being then a little past noon, the doctor took up his hat and pistols, girt on a cutlass, put the chart in his pocket, and with a musket over his shoulder, crossed the palisade on the north side, and set off briskly through the trees.

Gray and I were sitting together at the far end of the blockhouse, to be out of earshot of our officers consulting; and Gray took his pipe out of his mouth and fairly forgot to put it back again, so thunderstruck he was at this occurrence.

"Why, in the name of Davy Jones," said he, "is Dr Livesey mad?"

"Why, no," says I. "He's about the last of this crew for that, I take it."

"Well, shipmate," said Gray, "mad he may not be; but if *he's* not, you mark my words, *I* am."

"I take it," replied I, "the doctor has his idea; and if I am right, he's going now to see Ben Gunn."

I was right, as appeared later; but in the meantime, the house being stifling hot, and the little patch of sand inside the palisade ablaze with midday sun, I began to get another thought into my head, which was not by any means so right. What I began to do was to envy the doctor, walking in the cool shadow of the woods, with the birds about him, and the pleasant smell of the pines, while I sat grilling, with my clothes stuck to the hot resin, and so much blood about me, and so many poor dead bodies lying all around, that I took a disgust of the place that was almost as strong as fear.

All the time I was washing out the blockhouse, and then washing up the things from dinner, this disgust and envy kept growing stronger and stronger, till at last, being near a bread-bag, and no one then observing me, I took the first step towards my escapade, and filled both pockets of my coat with biscuit.

I was a fool, if you like, and certainly I was going to do a foolish, overbold act; but I was determined to do it with all the precautions in my power. These biscuits, should anything befall me, would keep me, at least, from starving till far on in the next day.

The next thing I laid hold of was a brace of pistols, and as I already had a powder-horn and bullets, I felt myself well-supplied with arms.

As for the scheme I had in my head, it was not a bad one in itself. I was to go down the sandy spit that divides the anchorage on the east from the open sea, find the white rock I had observed last evening, and ascertain whether it was there or not that Ben Gunn had hidden his boat; a thing quite worth doing, as I still believe. But as I was certain I should not be allowed to leave the enclosure, my only plan was to take French leave, and slip out when nobody was watching; and that was so bad a way of doing it as made the thing itself wrong. But I was only a boy, and I had made my mind up.

Well, as things at last fell out, I found an admirable opportunity. The squire and Gray were busy helping the captain with his bandages; the coast was clear; I made a bolt for it over the stockade and into the thickest of the trees, and before my absence was observed I was out of cry of my companions.

This was my second folly, far worse than the first, as I left but two sound men to guard the house; but like the first, it was a help towards saving all of us.

I took my way straight for the east coast of the island, for I was determined to go down the sea side of the spit to avoid all chance of observation from the anchorage. It was already late in the afternoon, although still warm and sunny. As I continued to thread the tall woods I could hear from far before me not only the continuous thunder of the surf, but a certain tossing of foliage and grinding of boughs which showed me the sea breeze had set in higher than usual. Soon cool draughts of air began to reach me; and a few steps further I came forth into the open borders of the grove, and saw the sea lying blue and sunny to the horizon, and the surf tumbling and tossing its foam along the beach.

I have never seen the sea quiet round Treasure Island. The sun might blaze overhead, the air be without a breath, the surface smooth and blue, but still these great rollers would be running along all the external coast, thundering and thundering by day and night; and I scarce believe there is one spot in the island where a man would be out of earshot of their noise.

I walked along beside the surf with great enjoyment, till, thinking I was now got far enough to the south, I took the cover of some thick bushes, and crept warily up to the ridge of the spit.

Behind me was the sea, in front the anchorage. The sea breeze, as though it had the sooner blown itself out by its unusual violence, was already at an end; it had been succeeded by light, variable airs from the south and south-east, carrying great banks of fog; and the anchorage, under lee of Skeleton Island, lay still and leaden as when first we entered it. The *Hispaniola*, in that unbroken mirror, was exactly portrayed from the truck to the waterline, the Jolly Roger hanging from her peak.

Alongside lay one of the gigs, Silver in the stern-sheets – him I could always recognize – while a couple of men were leaning over the stern bulwarks, one of them with a red cap – the very rogue that I had seen some hours before stride-legs upon the palisade. Apparently they were talking and laughing, though at that distance – upwards of a mile – I could, of course, hear no word of what was said. All at once, there began the most horrid, unearthly screaming, which at first startled me badly, though I had soon remembered the voice of Captain Flint, and even thought I could make out the bird by her bright plumage as she sat perched upon her master's wrist.

Soon after the jolly boat shoved off and pulled for shore, and the man with the red cap and his comrade went below by the cabin-companion.

Just about the same time the sun had gone down behind the Spyglass, and as the fog was collecting rapidly, it began to grow dark in earnest. I saw I must lose no time if I were to find the boat that evening.

The white rock, visible enough above the brush, was still some eighth of a mile further down the spit, and it took me a goodish while to get up with it, crawling, often on all-fours, among the scrub. Night had almost come when I laid my hand on its rough sides. Right below it there was an exceedingly small hollow of green turf, hidden by banks and a thick underwood about knee-deep, that grew there very plentifully; and in the centre of the dell, sure enough, a little tent of goatskins, like what the Gypsies carry about with them in England.

I dropped into the hollow, lifted the side of the tent, and there was Ben Gunn's boat – home-made if ever anything was home-made: a rude, lopsided framework of tough wood, and stretched upon that a covering of goatskin, with the hair inside. The thing was extremely small, even for me, and I can hardly imagine that it could have floated with a full-sized man. There was one thwart set as low as possible, a kind of stretcher in the bows, and a double paddle for propulsion.

I had not then seen a coracle, such as the ancient Britons made, but I have seen one since, and I can give you no fairer idea of Ben Gunn's boat than by saying it was like the first and the worst coracle ever made by man. But the great advantage of the coracle it certainly possessed, for it was exceedingly light and portable.

Well, now that I had found the boat, you would have thought I had had enough of truantry for once; but in the meantime, I had taken another notion, and became so obstinately fond of it, that I would have carried it out, I believe, in the teeth of Captain Smollett himself. This was to slip out under cover of the night, cut the *Hispaniola* adrift, and let her go ashore where she fancied. I had quite made up my mind that the mutineers, after their repulse of the morning, had nothing nearer their hearts than to up-anchor and away to sea; this, I thought, it would be a fine thing to prevent, and now that I had seen how they left their watchmen unprovided with a boat, I thought it might be done with little risk.

Down I sat to wait for darkness, and made a hearty meal of biscuit. It was a night out of ten thousand for my purpose. The fog had now buried all heaven. As the last rays of daylight dwindled and disappeared, absolute blackness settled down on Treasure Island. And when, at last, I shouldered the coracle, and groped my way stumblingly out of the hollow where I had supped, there were but two points visible on the whole anchorage.

One was the great fire onshore, by which the defeated pirates lay carousing in the swamp. The other, a mere blur of light upon the darkness, indicated the position of the anchored ship. She had swung round to the ebb – her bow was now towards me – the only lights on board were in the cabin, and what I saw was merely a reflection on the fog of the strong rays that flowed from the stern window.

The ebb had already run some time, and I had to wade through a long belt of swampy sand, where I sank several times above the ankle, before I came to the edge of the retreating water, and wading a little way in, with some strength and dexterity, set my coracle, keel downwards, on the surface.

## 23

### *The Ebb Tide Runs*

THE CORACLE – as I had ample reason to know before I was done with her – was a very safe boat for a person of my height and weight, both buoyant and clever in a seaway; but she was the most cross-grained lopsided craft to manage. Do as you please, she always made more leeway than anything else, and turning round and round was the manoeuvre she was best at. Even Ben Gunn himself has admitted that she was "queer to handle till you knew her way."

Certainly I did not know her way. She turned in every direction but the one I was bound to go; the most part of the time we were broadside on, and I am very sure I never should have made the ship at all but for the tide. By good fortune, paddle as I pleased, the tide was still sweeping me down; and there lay the *Hispaniola* right in the fairway, hardly to be missed.

First she loomed before me like a blot of something yet blacker than darkness, then her spars and hull began to take shape, and the next moment, as it seemed (for the further I went, the brisker grew the current of the ebb), I was alongside of her hawser, and had laid hold.

The hawser was as taut as a bowstring, and the current so strong she pulled upon her anchor. All round the hull, in the blackness, the rippling current bubbled and chattered like a little mountain stream. One cut with my sea gully, and the *Hispaniola* would go humming down the tide.

So far so good, but it next occurred to my recollection that a taut hawser, suddenly cut, is a thing as dangerous as a kicking horse. Ten to one, if I were so foolhardy as to cut the *Hispaniola* from her anchor, I and the coracle would be knocked clean out of the water.

This brought me to a full stop, and if fortune had not again particularly favoured me, I should have had to abandon my design. But the light airs which had begun blowing from the south-east and south had hauled round after nightfall into the south-west. Just while I was meditating, a puff came, caught the *Hispaniola*, and forced her up into the current; and to my great joy, I felt the hawser slacken in my grasp, and the hand by which I held it dip for a second underwater.

With that I made my mind up, took out my gully, opened it with my teeth, and cut one strand after another, till the vessel swung only by two. Then I lay quiet, waiting to sever these last when the strain should be once more lightened by a breath of wind.

All this time I had heard the sound of loud voices from the cabin; but, to say truth, my mind had been so entirely taken up with other thoughts that I had scarcely given ear. Now, however, when I had nothing else to do, I began to pay more heed.

One I recognized for the coxswain's, Israel Hands, that had been Flint's gunner in former days. The other was, of course, my friend of the red nightcap. Both men were plainly the worse of drink, and they were still drinking; for, even while I was listening, one of them, with a drunken cry, opened the stern window and threw out something, which I divined to be an empty bottle. But they were not only tipsy; it was plain that they were furiously angry. Oaths flew like hailstones, and every now and then there came forth such an explosion as I thought was sure to end in blows. But each time the quarrel passed off, and the voices grumbled lower for a while, until the next crisis came, and, in its turn, passed away without result.

Onshore, I could see the glow of the great campfire burning warmly through the shoreside trees. Someone was singing, a dull, old, droning sailor's song, with a droop and a quaver at the end of every verse, and seemingly no end to it at all but the patience of the singer. I had heard it on the voyage more than once, and remembered these words:

> But one man of her crew alive,
> What put to sea with seventy-five.

And I thought it was a ditty rather too dolefully appropriate for a company that had met such cruel losses in the morning. But indeed from what I saw, all these buccaneers were as callous as the sea they sailed on.

At last the breeze came; the schooner sidled and drew nearer in the dark; I felt the hawser slacken once more, and with a good, tough effort, cut the last fibres through.

The breeze had but little action on the coracle, and I was almost instantly swept against the bows of the *Hispaniola*. At the same time the schooner began to turn upon her heel, spinning slowly, end for end, across the current.

I wrought like a fiend, for I expected every moment to be swamped; and since I found I could not push the coracle directly off, I now shoved straight astern. At length I was clear of my dangerous neighbour; and just as I gave the last impulsion, my hands came across a light cord that was trailing overboard across the stern bulwarks. Instantly I grasped it.

Why I should have done so I can hardly say. It was at first mere instinct; but once I had it in my hands and found it fast, curiosity began to get the upper hand, and I determined I should have one look through the cabin window.

I pulled in hand over hand on the cord, and when I judged myself near enough, rose at infinite risk to about half my height, and thus commanded the roof and a slice of the interior of the cabin.

By this time the schooner and her little consort were gliding pretty swiftly through the water; indeed, we had already fetched up level with the campfire. The ship was talking, as sailors say, loudly, treading the innumerable ripples with an incessant weltering splash; and until I got my eye above the window sill I could not comprehend why the watchmen had taken no alarm. One glance, however, was sufficient; and it was only one glance that I durst take from that unsteady skiff. It showed me Hands and his companion locked together in deadly wrestle, each with a hand upon the other's throat.

I dropped upon the thwart again, none too soon, for I was near-overboard. I could see nothing for the moment but these two furious, encrimsoned faces, swaying together under the smoky lamp; and I shut my eyes to let them grow once more familiar with the darkness.

The endless ballad had come to an end at last, and the whole diminished company about the campfire had broken into the chorus I had heard so often:

> "Fifteen men on the dead man's chest –
> Yo-ho-ho, and a bottle of rum!

Drink and the devil had done for the rest –
Yo-ho-ho, and a bottle of rum!"

I was just thinking how busy drink and the Devil were at that very moment in the cabin of the *Hispaniola*, when I was surprised by a sudden lurch of the coracle. At the same moment she yawed sharply and seemed to change her course. The speed in the meantime had strangely increased.

I opened my eyes at once. All round me were little ripples, combing over with a sharp, bristling sound and slightly phosphorescent. The *Hispaniola* herself, a few yards in whose wake I was still being whirled along, seemed to stagger in her course, and I saw her spars toss a little against the blackness of the night; nay, as I looked longer, I made sure she also was wheeling to the southward.

I glanced over my shoulder, and my heart jumped against my ribs. There, right behind me, was the glow of the campfire. The current had turned at right angles, sweeping round along with it the tall schooner and the little dancing coracle; ever quickening, ever bubbling higher, ever muttering louder, it went spinning through the narrows for the open sea.

Suddenly the schooner in front of me gave a violent yaw, turning, perhaps, through twenty degrees; and almost at the same moment one shout followed another from on board; I could hear feet pounding on the companion-ladder; and I knew that the two drunkards had at last been interrupted in their quarrel and awakened to a sense of their disaster.

I lay down flat in the bottom of that wretched skiff, and devoutly recommended my spirit to its Maker. At the end of the straits, I made sure we must fall into some bar of raging breakers, where all my troubles would be ended speedily; and though I could, perhaps, bear to die, I could not bear to look upon my fate as it approached.

So I must have lain for hours, continually beaten to and fro upon the billows, now and again wetted with flying sprays, and never ceasing to expect death at the next plunge. Gradually weariness grew upon me; a numbness, an occasional stupor, fell upon my mind even in the midst of my terrors; until sleep at last supervened, and in my sea-tossed coracle I lay and dreamt of home and the old Admiral Benbow.

# 24

## The Cruise of the Coracle

I T WAS BROAD DAY WHEN I AWOKE, and found myself tossing at the south-west end of Treasure Island. The sun was up, but was still hid from me behind the great bulk of the Spyglass, which on this side descended almost to the sea in formidable cliffs.

Haulbowline Head and Mizzenmast Hill were at my elbow; the hill bare and dark, the head bound with cliffs forty or fifty feet high, and fringed with great masses of fallen rock. I was scarce a quarter of a mile to seaward, and it was my first thought to paddle in and land.

That notion was soon given over. Among the fallen rocks the breakers spouted and bellowed; loud reverberations, heavy sprays flying and falling, succeeded one another from second to second; and I saw myself, if I ventured nearer, dashed to death upon the rough shore, or spending my strength in vain to scale the beetling crags.

Nor was that all; for crawling together on flat tables of rock, or letting themselves drop into the sea with loud reports, I beheld huge slimy monsters – soft snails as it were, of incredible bigness

– two or three score of them together, making the rocks to echo with their barkings.

I have understood since that they were sea lions, and entirely harmless. But the look of them, added to the difficulty of the shore and the high running of the surf, was more than enough to disgust me of that landing place. I felt willing rather to starve at sea than to confront such perils.

In the meantime I had a better chance, as I supposed, before me. North of Haulbowline Head, the land runs in a long way, leaving, at low tide, a long stretch of yellow sand. To the north of that, again, there comes another cape – Cape of the Woods, as it was marked upon the chart – buried in tall green pines, which descended to the margin of the sea.

I remembered what Silver had said about the current that sets northwards along the whole west coast of Treasure Island; and seeing from my position that I was already under its influence, I preferred to leave Haulbowline Head behind me, and reserve my strength for an attempt to land upon the kindlier-looking Cape of the Woods.

There was a great, smooth swell upon the sea. The wind blowing steady and gentle from the south, there was no contrariety between that and the current, and the billows rose and fell unbroken.

Had it been otherwise, I must long ago have perished; but as it was, it is surprising how easily and securely my little and light boat could ride. Often, as I still lay at the bottom, and kept no more than an eye above the gunwale, I would see a big blue summit heaving close above me; yet the coracle would but bounce a little, dance as if on springs, and subside on the other side into the trough as lightly as a bird.

I began after a little to grow very bold, and sat up to try my skill at paddling. But even a small change in the disposition of the weight will produce violent changes in the behaviour of a coracle. And I had hardly moved before the boat, giving up at once her gentle dancing movement, ran straight down a slope of water so steep that it made me giddy, and struck her nose, with a spout of spray, deep into the side of the next wave.

I was drenched and terrified, and fell instantly back into my old position, whereupon the coracle seemed to find her head again, and led me as softly as before among the billows. It was plain she was not to be interfered with, and at that rate, since I could in no way influence her course, what hope had I left of reaching land?

I began to be horribly frightened, but I kept my head, for all that. First, moving with all care, I gradually baled out the coracle with my sea cap; then getting my eye once more above the gunwale, I set myself to study how it was she managed to slip so quietly through the rollers.

I found each wave, instead of the big, smooth glossy mountain it looks from shore, or from a vessel's deck, was for all the world like any range of hills on the dry land, full of peaks and smooth places and valleys. The coracle, left to herself, turning from side to side, threaded, so to speak, her way through these lower parts, and avoided the steep slopes and higher toppling summits of the wave.

"Well now," thought I to myself, "it is plain I must lie where I am, and not disturb the balance; but it is plain, also, that I can put the paddle over the side, and from time to time, in smooth places, give her a shove or two towards land." No sooner thought upon than done. There I lay on my elbows, in the most trying attitude, and every now and again gave a weak stroke or two to turn her head to shore.

It was very tiring, and slow work, yet I did visibly gain ground; and as we drew near the Cape of the Woods, though I saw I must infallibly miss that point, I had still made some hundred yards of easting. I was indeed close in. I could see the cool, green treetops swaying together in the breeze, and I felt sure I should make the next promontory without fail.

It was high time, for I now began to be tortured with thirst. The glow of the sun from above, its thousandfold reflection from the waves, the sea water that fell and dried upon me, caking my very lips with salt, combined to make my throat burn and my brain ache. The sight of the trees so near at hand had almost made me sick with longing; but the current had soon carried me past the point; and as the next reach of sea opened out, I beheld a sight that changed the nature of my thoughts.

Right in front of me, not half a mile away, I beheld the *Hispaniola* under sail. I made sure, of course, that I should be taken; but I was so distressed for want of water, that I scarce knew whether to be glad or sorry at the thought; and long before I had come to a conclusion, surprise had taken entire possession of my mind, and I could do nothing but stare and wonder.

The *Hispaniola* was under her mainsail and two jibs, and the beautiful white canvas shone in the sun like snow or silver. When I first sighted her, all her sails were drawing; she was lying a course about north-west, and I presumed the men on board were going round the island on their way back to the anchorage. Presently she began to fetch more and more to the westward, so that I thought they had sighted me and were going about in chase. At last, however, she fell right into the wind's eye, was taken dead aback, and stood there awhile helpless, with her sails shivering.

"Clumsy fellows," said I, "they must still be drunk as owls." And I thought how Captain Smollett would have set them skipping.

Meanwhile, the schooner gradually fell off, and filled again upon another tack, sailed swiftly for a minute or so, and brought up once more dead in the wind's eye. Again and again was this repeated. To and fro, up and down, north, south, east and west, the *Hispaniola* sailed by swoops and dashes, and at each repetition ended as she had begun, with idly flapping canvas. It became plain to me that nobody was steering. And if so, where were the men? Either they were dead drunk, or had deserted her, I thought, and perhaps if I could get on board, I might return the vessel to her captain.

The current was bearing coracle and schooner southwards at an equal rate. As for the latter's sailing, it was so wild and intermittent, and she hung each time so long in irons, that she certainly gained nothing, if she did not even lose. If only I dared to sit up and paddle, I made sure that I could overhaul her. The scheme had an air of adventure that inspired me, and the thought of the water-breaker beside the fore-companion doubled my growing courage.

Up I got, was welcomed almost instantly by another cloud of spray, but this time stuck to my purpose; and set myself, with all my strength and caution, to paddle after the unsteered *Hispaniola*. Once I shipped a sea so heavy that I had to stop and bale, with my heart fluttering like a bird; but gradually I got into the way of the thing, and guided my coracle among the waves, with only now and then a blow upon her bows and a dash of foam in my face.

I was now gaining rapidly on the schooner; I could see the brass glisten on the tiller as it banged about; and still no soul appeared upon her decks. I could not choose but suppose she was deserted. If not, the men were lying drunk below, where I might batten them down, perhaps, and do what I chose with the ship.

For some time she had been doing the worst thing possible for me – standing still. She headed nearly due south, yawing, of course, all the time. Each time she fell off her sails partly filled, and these brought her, in a moment, right to the wind again. I have said this was the worst thing possible for me; for helpless as she looked in this situation, with the canvas cracking like cannon, and the blocks trundling and banging on the deck, she still continued to run away from me, not only with the speed of the current, but by the whole amount of her leeway, which was naturally great.

But now at last I had my chance. The breeze fell for some seconds very low, and the current gradually turning her, the *Hispaniola* revolved slowly round her centre, and at last presented me her stern, with the cabin window still gaping open, and the lamp over the table still burning on into the day. The mainsail hung drooped like a banner. She was stock-still, but for the current.

For the last little while I had even lost; but now, redoubling my efforts, I began once more to overhaul the chase.

I was not a hundred yards from her when the wind came again in a clap; she filled on the port tack, and was off again, stooping and skimming like a swallow.

My first impulse was one of despair, but my second was towards joy. Round she came, till she was broadside on to me – round still, till she had covered a half, and then two-thirds, and then three-quarters of the distance that separated us. I could see the waves boiling white under her forefoot. Immensely tall she looked to me from my low station in the coracle.

And then, of a sudden, I began to comprehend. I had scarce time to think – scarce time to act and save myself. I was on the summit of one swell when the schooner came stooping over the next. The bowsprit was over my head. I sprang to my feet, and leapt, stamping the coracle underwater. With one hand I caught the jib-boom, while my foot was lodged between the stay and the brace; and as I still clung there panting, a dull blow told me that the schooner had charged down upon and struck the coracle, and that I was left without retreat on the *Hispaniola*.

# 25

## *I Strike the Jolly Roger*

I HAD SCARCE GAINED A POSITION on the bowsprit, when the
flying jib flapped and filled upon the other tack, with a report
like a gun. The schooner trembled to her keel under the reverse;
but next moment, the other sails still drawing, the jib flapped
back again, and hung idle.

This had nearly tossed me off into the sea; and now I lost no
time, crawled back along the bowsprit, and tumbled head foremost on the deck.

I was on the lee side of the forecastle, and the mainsail, which was
still drawing, concealed from me a certain portion of the afterdeck.
Not a soul was to be seen. The planks, which had not been swabbed
since the mutiny, bore the print of many feet; and an empty bottle,
broken by the neck, tumbled to and fro like a live thing in the scuppers.

Suddenly the *Hispaniola* came right into the wind. The jibs
behind me cracked aloud; the rudder slammed to; the whole ship
gave a sickening heave and shudder, and at the same moment the
main-boom swung inboard, the sheet groaning in the blocks, and
showed me the lee afterdeck.

There were the two watchmen, sure enough: red-cap on his back, as stiff as a handspike, with his arms stretched out like those of a crucifix, and his teeth showing through his open lips; Israel Hands propped against the bulwarks, his chin on his chest, his hands lying open before him on the deck, his face as white, under its tan, as a tallow candle.

For a while the ship kept bucking and sidling like a vicious horse, the sails filling, now on one tack, now on another, and the boom swinging to and fro till the mast groaned aloud under the strain. Now and again, too, there would come a cloud of light sprays over the bulwark, and a heavy blow of the ship's bows against the swell: so much heavier weather was made of it by this great rigged ship than by my home-made, lopsided coracle, now gone to the bottom of the sea.

At every jump of the schooner, red-cap slipped to and fro; but – what was ghastly to behold – neither his attitude nor his fixed teeth-disclosing grin was anyway disturbed by this rough usage. At every jump, too, Hands appeared still more to sink into himself and settle down upon the deck, his feet sliding ever the further out, and the whole body canting towards the stern, so that his face became, little by little, hid from me; and at last I could see nothing beyond his ear and the frayed ringlet of one whisker.

At the same time, I observed, around both of them, splashes of dark blood upon the planks, and began to feel sure that they had killed each other in their drunken wrath.

While I was thus looking and wondering, in a calm moment, when the ship was still, Israel Hands turned partly round, and with a low moan, writhed himself back to the position in which I had seen him first. The moan, which told of pain and deadly weakness, and the way in which his jaw hung open, went right to my heart. But when I remembered the talk I had overheard from the apple barrel, all pity left me.

I walked aft until I reached the mainmast.

"Come aboard, Mr Hands," I said ironically.

He rolled his eyes round heavily; but he was too far gone to express surprise. All he could do was to utter one word, "Brandy."

It occurred to me there was no time to lose; and dodging the boom as it once more lurched across the deck, I slipped aft, and down the companion-stairs into the cabin.

It was such a scene of confusion as you can hardly fancy. All the lock-fast places had been broken open in quest of the chart. The floor was thick with mud, where ruffians had sat down to drink or consult after wading in the marshes round their camp. The bulkheads, all painted in clear white, and beaded round with gilt, bore a pattern of dirty hands. Dozens of empty bottles clinked together in corners to the rolling of the ship. One of the doctor's medical books lay open on the table, half of the leaves gutted out, I suppose for pipe-lights. In the midst of all this the lamp still cast a smoky glow, obscure and brown as umber.

I went into the cellar; all the barrels were gone, and of the bottles a most surprising number had been drunk out and thrown away. Certainly since the mutiny began, not a man of them could ever have been sober.

Foraging about, I found a bottle with some brandy left, for Hands; and for myself I routed out some biscuits, some pickled fruits, a great bunch of raisins, and a piece of cheese. With these I came on deck, put down my own stock behind the rudder-head, and well out of the coxswain's reach, went forwards to the water-breaker, and had a good, deep drink of water, and then, and not till then, gave Hands the brandy.

He must have drunk a gill before he took the bottle from his mouth.

"Ay," said he, "by thunder, but I wanted some o' that!"

I had sat down already in my own corner and begun to eat.

"Much hurt?" I asked him.

He grunted, or rather I might say, he barked.

"If that doctor was aboard," he said, "I'd be right enough in a couple of turns; but I don't have no manner of luck, you see, and that's what's the matter with me. As for that swab, he's good and dead, he is," he added, indicating the man with the red cap. "He warn't no seaman, anyhow. And where mought you have come from?"

"Well," said I, "I've come aboard to take possession of this ship, Mr Hands; and you'll please regard me as your captain until further notice."

He looked at me sourly enough, but said nothing. Some of the colour had come back into his cheeks, though he still looked very sick, and still continued to slip out and settle down as the ship banged about.

"By the by," I continued, "I can't have these colours, Mr Hands; and by your leave, I'll strike 'em. Better none than these."

And, again dodging the boom, I ran to the colour lines, handed down their cursed black flag, and chucked it overboard.

"God save the king!" said I, waving my cap, "and there's an end to Captain Silver!"

He watched me keenly and slyly, his chin all the while on his breast.

"I reckon," he said at last, "I reckon, Cap'n Hawkins, you'll kind of want to get ashore, now. S'pose we talks."

"Why, yes," says I, "with all my heart, Mr Hands. Say on." And I went back to my meal with a good appetite.

"This man," he began, nodding feebly at the corpse, "O'Brien were his name – a rank Irelander – this man and me got the canvas on her, meaning for to sail her back. Well, *he's* dead now, he is – as dead as bilge; and who's to sail this ship, I don't see. Without I gives you a hint, you ain't that man, as far's I can tell. Now, look here, you gives me food and drink, and a old scarf or ankecher to tie my wound up, you do; and I'll tell you how to sail her; and that's about square all round, I take it."

"I'll tell you one thing," says I: "I'm not going back to Captain Kidd's anchorage. I mean to get into North Inlet, and beach her quietly there."

"To be sure you did," he cried. "Why, I ain't sich an infernal lubber, after all. I can see, can't I? I've tried my fling, I have, and I've lost, and it's you has the wind of me. North Inlet? Why, I haven't no ch'ice, not I! I'd help you sail her up to Execution Dock, by thunder! so I would."

Well, as it seemed to me, there was some sense in this. We struck our bargain on the spot. In three minutes I had the *Hispaniola* sailing easily before the wind along the coast of Treasure Island, with good hopes of turning the northern point ere noon, and beating down again as far as North Inlet before high water, when we might beach her safely, and wait till the subsiding tide permitted us to land.

Then I lashed the tiller and went below to my own chest, where I got a soft silk handkerchief of my mother's. With this, and with my aid, Hands bound up the great bleeding stab he had received in the thigh, and after he had eaten a little and had a swallow or two more of the brandy, he began to pick up visibly, sat straighter up, spoke louder and clearer, and looked in every way another man.

The breeze served us admirably. We skimmed before it like a bird, the coast of the island flashing by, and the view changing every minute. Soon we were past the high lands and bowling beside low, sandy country, sparsely dotted with dwarf pines, and soon we were beyond that again, and had turned the corner of the rocky hill that ends the island on the north.

I was greatly elated with my new command, and pleased with the bright, sunshiny weather and these different prospects of the coast. I had now plenty of water and good things to eat, and my conscience, which had smitten me hard for my desertion, was quieted by the great conquest I had made. I should, I think, have had nothing left me to desire but for the eyes of the coxswain as they followed me derisively about the deck, and the odd smile that appeared continually on his face. It was a smile that had in it something both of pain and weakness – a haggard, old man's smile; but there was, besides that, a grain of derision, a shadow of treachery, in his expression as he craftily watched, and watched, and watched me at my work.

# 26

*Israel Hands*

THE WIND, SERVING US TO A DESIRE, now hauled into the west. We could run so much the easier from the north-east corner of the island to the mouth of the North Inlet. Only, as we had no power to anchor, and dared not beach her till the tide had flowed a good deal further, time hung on our hands. The coxswain told me how to lay the ship to; after a good many trials I succeeded, and we both sat in silence over another meal.

"Cap'n," said he, at length, with that same uncomfortable smile, "here's my old shipmate, O'Brien; s'pose you was to heave him overboard. I ain't partic'lar as a rule, and I don't take no blame for settling his hash;* but I don't reckon him ornamental, now, do you?"

"I'm not strong enough, and I don't like the job; and there he lies, for me," said I.

"This here's an unlucky ship – this *Hispaniola*, Jim," he went on, blinking. "There's a power of men been killed in this *Hispaniola* – a sight o' poor seamen dead and gone since you and me took ship to Bristol. I never seen sich dirty luck, not I. There was this here O'Brien, now – he's dead, ain't he? Well now, I'm no scholar, and you're a lad as can read and figure; and, to put it straight, do you take it as a dead man is dead for good, or do he come alive again?"

"You can kill the body, Mr Hands, but not the spirit; you must know that already," I replied. "O'Brien there is in another world, and maybe watching us."

"Ah!" says he. "Well, that's unfort'nate – appears as if killing parties was a waste of time. Howsomever, sperrits don't reckon for much, by what I've seen. I'll chance it with the sperrits, Jim. And now, you've spoke up free, and I'll take it kind if you'd step down into that there cabin and get me a… well, a… shiver my timbers! I can't hit the name on't; well, you get me a bottle of wine, Jim – this here brandy's too strong for my head."

Now, the coxswain's hesitation seemed to be unnatural; and as for the notion of his preferring wine to brandy, I entirely disbelieved it. The whole story was a pretext. He wanted me to leave the deck – so much was plain; but with what purpose I could in no way imagine. His eyes never met mine; they kept wandering to and fro, up and down, now with a look to the sky, now with a flitting glance upon the dead O'Brien. All the time he kept smiling, and putting his tongue out in the most guilty, embarrassed manner, so that a child could have told that he was bent on some deception. I was prompt with my answer, however, for I saw where my advantage lay; and that with a fellow so densely stupid I could easily conceal my suspicions to the end.

"Some wine?" I said. "Far better. Will you have white or red?"

"Well, I reckon it's about the blessed same to me, shipmate," he replied, "so it's strong, and plenty of it, what's the odds?"

"All right," I answered. "I'll bring you port, Mr Hands. But I'll have to dig for it."

With that I scuttled down the companion with all the noise I could, slipped off my shoes, ran quietly along the sparred gallery, mounted the forecastle ladder, and popped my head out of the fore-companion. I knew he would not expect to see me there; yet I took every precaution possible; and certainly the worst of my suspicions proved too true.

He had risen from his position to his hands and knees; and, though his leg obviously hurt him pretty sharply when he moved – for I could hear him stifle a groan – yet it was at a good, rattling rate that he trailed himself across the deck. In half a minute he had reached the port scuppers, and picked out of a coil of rope a long knife, or rather a short dirk, discoloured to the hilt with blood. He looked upon it for a moment, thrusting forth his under-jaw, tried the point upon his hand, and then, hastily concealing it in the bosom of his jacket, trundled back again into his old place against the bulwark.

This was all that I required to know. Israel could move about; he was now armed; and if he had been at so much trouble to get rid of me, it was plain that I was meant to be the victim. What he would do afterwards – whether he would try to crawl right across the island from North Inlet to the camp among the swamps, or whether he would fire Long Tom, trusting that his own comrades might come first to help him, was, of course, more than I could say.

Yet I felt sure that I could trust him in one point, since in that our interests jumped together, and that was in the disposition of the schooner. We both desired to have her stranded safe enough, in a sheltered place, and so that when the time came she could be got off again with as little labour and danger as might be; and until that was done I considered that my life would certainly be spared.

While I was thus turning the business over in my mind, I had not been idle with my body. I had stolen back to the cabin, slipped once more into my shoes, and laid my hand at random on a bottle of wine, and now with this for an excuse, I made my reappearance on the deck.

Hands lay as I had left him, all fallen together in a bundle, and with his eyelids lowered, as though he were too weak to bear the light. He looked up, however, at my coming, knocked the neck off the bottle, like a man who had done the same thing often, and took a good swig, with his favourite toast of "Here's luck!" Then he lay quiet for a little, and then, pulling out a stick of tobacco, begged me to cut him a quid.

"Cut me a junk o' that," says he, "for I haven't no knife, and hardly strength enough, so be as I had. Ah, Jim, Jim, I reckon I've missed stays! Cut me a quid, as'll likely be the last, lad; for I'm for my long home, and no mistake."

"Well," said I, "I'll cut you some tobacco; but if I was you and thought myself so badly, I would go to my prayers like a Christian man."

"Why?" said he. "Now, you tell me why."

"Why?" I cried. "You were asking me just now about the dead. You've broken your trust; you've lived in sin and lies and blood; there's a man you killed lying at your feet this moment; and you ask me why! For God's mercy, Mr Hands, that's why."

I spoke with a little heat, thinking of the bloody dirk he had hidden in his pocket, and designed, in his ill thoughts, to end me with. He, for his part, took a great draught of the wine, and spoke with the most unusual solemnity.

"For thirty years," he said, "I've sailed the seas, and seen good and bad, better and worse, fair weather and foul, provisions running out, knives going, and what not. Well, now I tell you, I never seen good come o' goodness yet. Him as strikes first is my fancy; dead men don't bite; them's my views – amen, so be it. And now, you look here," he added, suddenly changing his tone, "we've had about enough of this foolery. The tide's made good enough by now. You just take my orders, Cap'n Hawkins, and we'll sail slap in and be done with it."

All told, we had scarce two miles to run; but the navigation was delicate, the entrance to this northern anchorage was not only narrow and shoal, but lay east and west, so that the schooner must be nicely handled to be got in. I think I was a good, prompt subaltern, and I am very sure that Hands was an excellent pilot; for we went about and about, and dodged in, shaving the banks, with a certainty and a neatness that were a pleasure to behold.

Scarcely had we passed the heads before the land closed around us. The shores of North Inlet were as thickly wooded as those of the southern anchorage; but the space was longer and narrower, and more like what in truth it was: the estuary of a river. Right before us, at the southern end, we saw the wreck of a ship in the last stages of dilapidation. It had been a great vessel of three masts, but had lain so long exposed to the injuries of the weather that it was hung about with great webs of dripping seaweed, and on the deck of it, shore-bushes had taken root, and now flourished thick with flowers. It was a sad sight, but it showed us that the anchorage was calm.

"Now," said Hands, "look there; there's a pet bit for to beach a ship in. Fine flat sand, never a cat's paw, trees all around of it, and flowers a-blowing like a garding on that old ship."

"And once beached," I enquired, "how shall we get her off again?"

"Why, so," he replied: "you take a line ashore there on the other side at low water: take a turn about one o' them big pines; bring it back, take a turn round the capstan, and lie-to for the tide. Come high water, all hands take a pull upon the line, and off she comes as sweet as natur'. And now, boy, you stand by. We're near the bit now, and she's too much way on her. Starboard a little – so – steady – starboard – larboard a little – steady – steady!"

So he issued his commands, which I breathlessly obeyed; till all of a sudden he cried, "Now, my hearty, luff!" And I put the helm hard up, and the *Hispaniola* swung round rapidly, and ran stem on for the low wooded shore.

The excitement of these last manoeuvres had somewhat interfered with the watch I had kept hitherto, sharply enough, upon the coxswain. Even then I was still so much interested, waiting for the ship to touch, that I had quite forgot the peril that hung over my head, and stood craning over the starboard bulwarks and watching the ripples spreading wide before the bows. I might have fallen without a struggle for my life, had not a sudden disquietude seized upon me, and made me turn my head. Perhaps I had heard a creak, or seen his shadow moving with the tail of my eye; perhaps it was an instinct like a cat's; but, sure enough, when I looked round, there was Hands, already halfway towards me, with the dirk in his right hand.

We must both have cried out aloud when our eyes met; but while mine was the shrill cry of terror, his was a roar of fury like a charging bull's. At the same instant he threw himself forwards, and I leapt sideways towards the bows. As I did so, I let go of the tiller, which sprang sharp to leeward; and I think this saved my life, for it struck Hands across the chest, and stopped him, for the moment, dead.

Before he could recover, I was safe out of the corner where he had me trapped, with all the deck to dodge about. Just forwards of the mainmast I stopped, drew a pistol from my pocket, took a cool aim, though he had already turned and was once more coming directly after me, and drew the trigger. The hammer fell, but there followed neither flash nor sound; the priming was useless with sea water. I cursed myself for my neglect. Why had not I, long before, reprimed and reloaded my only weapons? Then I should not have been as now, a mere fleeing sheep before this butcher.

Wounded as he was, it was wonderful how fast he could move, his grizzled hair tumbling over his face, and his face itself as red as a red ensign with his haste and fury. I had no time to try my other pistol, nor indeed much inclination, for I was sure it would be useless. One thing I saw plainly: I must not simply retreat before him, or he would speedily hold me boxed into the bows, as a moment since he had so nearly boxed me in the stern. Once so caught, and nine or ten inches of the bloodstained dirk would be my last experience on this side of eternity. I placed my palms against the mainmast, which was of a goodish bigness, and waited, every nerve upon the stretch.

Seeing that I meant to dodge, he also paused; and a moment or two passed in feints on his part, and corresponding movements upon mine. It was such a game as I had often played at home about the rocks of Black Hill Cove; but never before, you may be sure, with such a wildly beating heart as now. Still, as I say, it was a boy's game, and I thought I could hold my own at it against an elderly seaman with a wounded thigh. Indeed, my courage had begun to rise so high, that I allowed myself a few darting thoughts on what would be the end of the affair; and while I saw certainly that I could spin it out for long, I saw no hope of any ultimate escape.

Well, while things stood thus, suddenly the *Hispaniola* struck, staggered, ground for an instant in the sand, and then, swift as a blow, canted over to the port side, till the deck stood at an angle of forty-five degrees, and about a puncheon of water splashed into the scupper holes, and lay in a pool, between the deck and bulwark.

We were both of us capsized in a second, and both of us rolled, almost together, into the scuppers; the dead red-cap, with his arms still spread out, tumbling stiffly after us. So near were we indeed, that my head came against the coxswain's foot with a crack that made my teeth rattle. Blow and all, I was the first afoot again; for Hands had got involved with the dead body. The sudden canting of the ship had made the deck no place for running on; I had to find some new way of escape, and that upon the instant, for my foe was almost touching me. Quick as thought, I sprang into the mizzen shrouds, rattled up hand over hand, and did not draw a breath till I was seated on the crosstrees.

I had been saved by being prompt; the dirk had struck not half a foot below me as I pursued my upwards flight; and there stood Israel Hands with his mouth open and his face upturned to mine, a perfect statue of surprise and disappointment.

Now that I had a moment to myself, I lost no time in changing the priming of my pistol, and then, having one ready for service, and to make assurance doubly sure, I proceeded to draw the load of the other, and recharge it afresh from the beginning.

My new employment struck Hands all of a heap; he began to see the dice going against him; and after an obvious hesitation, he also hauled himself heavily into the shrouds, and, with the dirk in his teeth, began slowly and painfully to mount. It cost him no end of time and groans to haul his wounded leg behind him; and I had quietly finished my arrangements before he was much more than a third of the way up. Then, with a pistol in either hand, I addressed him.

"One more step, Mr Hands," said I, "and I'll blow your brains out! Dead men don't bite, you know," I added, with a chuckle.

He stopped instantly. I could see by the working of his face that he was trying to think, and the process was so slow and laborious that, in my new-found security, I laughed aloud. At last, with a swallow or two, he spoke, his face still wearing the same expression of extreme perplexity. In order to speak he had to take the dagger from his mouth, but in all else, he remained unmoved.

"Jim," says he, "I reckon we're fouled, you and me, and we'll have to sign articles. I'd have had you but for that there lurch: but I don't have no luck, not I; and I reckon I'll have to strike, which comes hard, you see, for a master mariner to a ship's younker like you, Jim."

I was drinking in his words and smiling away, as conceited as a cock upon a wall, when, all in a breath, back went his right hand over his shoulder. Something sang like an arrow through the air; I felt a blow and then a sharp pang, and there I was pinned by the shoulder to the mast. In the horrid pain and surprise of the moment – I scarce can say it was by my own volition, and I am sure it was without a conscious aim – both my pistols went off, and both escaped out of my hands. They did not fall alone; with a choked cry, the coxswain loosed his grasp upon the shrouds, and plunged head first into the water.

# 27

## *"Pieces of Eight"*

OWING TO THE CANT OF THE VESSEL, the masts hung far out over the water, and from my perch on the crosstrees I had nothing below me but the surface of the bay. Hands, who was not so far up, was in consequence nearer to the ship, and fell between me and the bulwarks. He rose once to the surface in a lather of foam and blood, and then sank again for good. As the water settled, I could see him lying huddled together on the clean, bright sand in the shadow of the vessel's sides. A fish or two whipped past his body. Sometimes, by the quivering of the water, he appeared to move a little, as if he were trying to rise. But he was dead enough, for all that, being both shot and drowned, and was food for fish in the very place where he had designed my slaughter.

I was no sooner certain of this than I began to feel sick, faint and terrified. The hot blood was running over my back and chest. The dirk, where it had pinned my shoulder to the mast, seemed to burn like a hot iron; yet it was not so much these real sufferings that distressed me, for these, it seemed to me, I could bear without a murmur; it was the horror I had upon my mind of falling from the crosstrees into that still green water beside the body of the coxswain.

I clung with both hands till my nails ached, and I shut my eyes as if to cover up the peril. Gradually my mind came back again, my pulses quieted down to a more natural time, and I was once more in possession of myself.

It was my first thought to pluck forth the dirk; but either it stuck too hard or my nerve failed me; and I desisted with a violent shudder. Oddly enough, that very shudder did the business. The knife, in fact, had come the nearest in the world to missing me altogether; it held me by a mere pinch of skin, and this the shudder tore away. The blood ran down the faster, to be sure; but I was my own master again, and only tacked to the mast by my coat and shirt.

These last I broke through with a sudden jerk, and then regained the deck by the starboard shrouds. For nothing in the world would I have again ventured, shaken as I was, upon the overhanging port shrouds, from which Israel had so lately fallen.

I went below, and did what I could for my wound; it pained me a good deal, and still bled freely; but it was neither deep nor dangerous, nor did it greatly gall me when I used my arm. Then I looked around me, and as the ship was now, in a sense, my own, I began to think of clearing it from its last passenger – the dead man, O'Brien.

He had pitched, as I have said, against the bulwarks, where he lay like some horrible, ungainly sort of puppet; life-sized indeed, but how different from life's colour or life's comeliness! In that position, I could easily have my way with him; and as the habit of tragical adventures had worn off almost all my terror for the dead, I took him by the waist as if he had been a sack of bran, and, with one good heave, tumbled him overboard. He went in with a sounding plunge; the red cap came off, and remained floating on the surface; and as soon as the splash subsided, I could see him and Israel lying side by side, both wavering with the tremulous movement of the water. O'Brien, though still quite a young man, was very bald. There he lay, with that bald head across the knees of the man who had killed him, and the quick fishes steering to and fro over both.

I was now alone upon the ship; the tide had just turned. The sun was within so few degrees of setting that already the shadow of the pines upon the western shore began to reach right across the anchorage, and fall in patterns on the deck. The evening breeze had sprung up, and though it was well warded off by the hill with the two peaks upon the east, the cordage had begun to sing a little softly to itself and the idle sails to rattle to and fro.

I began to see a danger to the ship. The jibs I speedily doused and brought tumbling to the deck; but the mainsail was a harder matter. Of course, when the schooner canted over, the boom had swung outboard, and the cap of it and a foot or two of sail hung even underwater. I thought this made it still more dangerous; yet the strain was so heavy that I half-feared to meddle. At last, I got my knife and cut the halyards. The peak dropped instantly, a great belly of loose canvas floated broad upon the water; and since, pull as I liked, I could not budge the downhaul; that was the extent of what I could accomplish. For the rest, the *Hispaniola* must trust to luck, like myself.

By this time the whole anchorage had fallen into shadow – the last rays, I remember, falling through a glade of the wood, and shining bright as jewels on the flowery mantle of the wreck. It began to be chill; the tide was rapidly fleeting seawards, the schooner settling more and more on her beam-ends.

I scrambled forwards and looked over. It seemed shallow enough, and holding the cut hawser in both hands for a last security, I let myself drop softly overboard. The water scarcely reached my waist; the sand was firm and covered with ripple marks, and I waded ashore in great spirits, leaving the *Hispaniola* on her side, with her mainsail trailing wide upon the surface of the bay. About the same time the sun went fairly down, and the breeze whistled low in the dusk among the tossing pines.

At least, and at last, I was off the sea, nor had I returned thence empty-handed. There lay the schooner, clear at last from buccaneers and ready for our own men to board and get to sea again. I had nothing nearer my fancy than to get home to the stockade and boast of my achievements. Possibly I might be blamed a bit for my truantry, but the recapture of the *Hispaniola* was a clenching answer, and I hoped that even Captain Smollett would confess I had not lost my time.

So thinking, and in famous spirits, I began to set my face homewards for the blockhouse and my companions. I remembered that the most easterly of the rivers which drain into Captain Kidd's anchorage ran from the two-peaked hill upon my left; and I bent my course in that direction that I might pass the stream while it was small. The wood was pretty open, and keeping along the lower spurs, I had soon turned the corner of that hill, and not long after waded to the mid-calf across the watercourse.

This brought me near to where I had encountered Ben Gunn, the maroon; and I walked more circumspectly, keeping an eye on every side. The dusk had come nigh hand completely, and, as I opened out the cleft between the two peaks, I became aware of a wavering glow against the sky, where, as I judged, the man of the island was cooking his supper before a roaring fire. And yet I wondered, in my heart, that he should show himself so careless. For if I could see this radiance, might it not reach the eyes of Silver himself where he camped upon the shore among the marshes?

Gradually the night fell blacker; it was all I could do to guide myself even roughly towards my destination; the double hill behind me and the Spyglass on my right hand loomed faint and fainter; the stars were few and pale; and in the low ground where I wandered I kept tripping among bushes and rolling into sandy pits.

Suddenly a kind of brightness fell about me. I looked up; a pale glimmer of moonbeams had alighted on the summit of the Spyglass, and soon after I saw something broad and silvery moving low down behind the trees, and knew the moon had risen.

With this to help me, I passed rapidly over what remained to me of my journey; and, sometimes walking, sometimes running, impatiently drew near to the stockade. Yet, as I began to thread the grove that lies before it, I was not so thoughtless but that I slacked my pace and went a trifle warily. It would have been a poor end of my adventures to get shot down by my own party in mistake.

The moon was climbing higher and higher; its light began to fall here and there in masses through the more open districts of the wood; and right in front of me a glow of a different colour appeared among the trees. It was red and hot, and now and again it was a little darkened – as it were the embers of a bonfire smouldering.

For the life of me, I could not think what it might be.

At last I came right down upon the borders of the clearing. The western end was already steeped in moonshine; the rest, and the blockhouse itself, still lay in a black shadow, chequered with long, silvery streaks of light. On the other side of the house an immense fire had burnt itself into clear embers and shed a steady, red reverberation, contrasted strongly with the mellow paleness of the moon. There was not a soul stirring, nor a sound beside the noises of the breeze.

I stopped, with much wonder in my heart, and perhaps a little terror also. It had not been our way to build great fires; we were, indeed by the captain's orders, somewhat niggardly of firewood; and I began to fear that something had gone wrong while I was absent.

I stole round by the eastern end, keeping close in shadow, and at a convenient place, where the darkness was thickest, crossed the palisade.

To make assurance surer, I got upon my hands and knees, and crawled, without a sound, towards the corner of the house. As I drew nearer, my heart was suddenly and greatly lightened. It is not a pleasant noise in itself, and I have often complained of it at other times; but just then it was like music to hear my friends snoring together so loud and peaceful in their sleep. The sea cry of the watch, that beautiful "All's well", never fell more reassuringly on my ear.

In the meantime, there was no doubt of one thing; they kept an infamous bad watch. If it had been Silver and his lads that were now creeping in on them, not a soul would have seen daybreak. That was what it was, thought I, to have the captain wounded; and again I blamed myself sharply for leaving them in that danger with so few to mount guard.

By this time I had got to the door and stood up. All was dark within, so that I could distinguish nothing by the eye. As for sounds, there was the steady drone of the snorers, and a small occasional noise, a flickering or pecking that I could in no way account for.

With my arms before me I walked steadily in. I should lie down in my own place (I thought, with a silent chuckle) and enjoy their faces when they found me in the morning.

My foot struck something yielding – it was a sleeper's leg; and he turned and groaned, but without awaking.

And then, all of a sudden, a shrill voice broke forth out of the darkness:

"Pieces of eight! Pieces of eight! Pieces of eight! Pieces of eight! Pieces of eight!" and so forth, without pause or change, like the clacking of a tiny mill.

Silver's green parrot, Captain Flint! It was she whom I had heard pecking at a piece of bark; it was she, keeping better watch than any human being, who thus announced my arrival with her wearisome refrain.

I had no time left me to recover. At the sharp, clipping tone of the parrot, the sleepers awoke and sprang up; and with a mighty oath, the voice of Silver cried:

"Who goes?"

I turned to run, struck violently against one person, recoiled, and ran full into the arms of a second, who for his part closed upon and held me tight.

"Bring a torch, Dick," said Silver, when my capture was thus assured.

And one of the men left the log house, and presently returned with a lit brand.

## 28

*In the Enemy's Camp*

THE RED GLARE OF THE TORCH, lighting up the interior of the blockhouse, showed me the worst of my apprehensions realized. The pirates were in possession of the house and stores: there was the cask of cognac, there were the pork and bread, as before; and, what tenfold increased my horror, not a sign of any prisoner. I could only judge that all had perished, and my heart smote me sorely that I had not been there to perish with them.

There were six of the buccaneers, all told; not another man was left alive. Five of them were on their feet, flushed and swollen, suddenly called out of the first sleep of drunkenness. The sixth had only risen upon his elbow: he was deadly pale, and the bloodstained bandage round his head told that he had recently been wounded, and still more recently dressed. I remembered the man who had been shot and had run back among the woods in the great attack, and doubted not that this was he.

The parrot sat, preening her plumage, on Long John's shoulder. He himself, I thought, looked somewhat paler and more stern than I was used to. He still wore the fine broadcloth suit in which he

175

had fulfilled his mission, but it was bitterly the worse for wear, daubed with clay, and torn with the sharp briers of the wood.

"So," said he, "here's Jim Hawkins, shiver my timbers! dropped in, like, eh? Well, come, I take that friendly."

And thereupon he sat down across the brandy cask, and began to fill a pipe.

"Give me a loan of the link, Dick," said he; and then, when he had a good light, "that'll do, lad," he added, "stick the glim in the wood heap; and you, gentlemen, bring yourselves to! – you needn't stand up for Mr Hawkins; *he'll* excuse you, you may lay to that. And so, Jim" – stopping the tobacco – "here you were, and quite a pleasant surprise for poor old John. I see you were smart when first I set my eyes on you; but this here gets away from me clean, it do."

To all this, as may be well-supposed, I made no answer. They had set me with my back against the wall; and I stood there, looking Silver in the face pluckily enough, I hope, to all outward appearance, but with black despair in my heart.

Silver took a whiff or two of his pipe with great composure, and then ran on again.

"Now, you see, Jim, so be as you *are* here," says he, "I'll give you a piece of my mind. I've always liked you, I have, for a lad of spirit, and the picter of my own self when I was young and handsome. I always wanted you to jine and take your share, and die a gentleman, and now, my cock, you've got to. Cap'n Smollett's a fine seaman, as I'll own up to any day, but stiff on discipline. 'Dooty is dooty,' says he, and right he is. Just you keep clear of the cap'n. The doctor himself is gone dead again you – 'ungrateful scamp' was what he said; and the short and the long of the whole story is about here: you can't go back to your own lot, for they won't have you; and, without you start a third ship's company all by yourself, which might be lonely, you'll have to jine with Cap'n Silver."

So far so good. My friends, then, were still alive, and though I partly believed the truth of Silver's statement that the cabin party were incensed at me for my desertion, I was more relieved than distressed by what I heard.

"I don't say nothing as to your being in our hands," continued Silver, "though there you are, and you may lay to it. I'm all for argyment; I never seen good come out o' threatening. If you like the service, well, you'll jine; and if you don't, Jim, why, you're free to answer no – free and welcome, shipmate; and if fairer can be said by mortal seaman, shiver my sides!"

"Am I to answer, then?" I asked, with a very tremulous voice. Through all this sneering talk, I was made to feel the threat of death that overhung me, and my cheeks burnt and my heart beat painfully in my breast.

"Lad," said Silver, "no one's a-pressing of you. Take your bearings. None of us won't hurry you, mate; time goes so pleasant in your company, you see."

"Well," says I, growing a bit bolder, "if I'm to choose, I declare I have a right to know what's what, and why you're here, and where my friends are."

"Wot's wot?" repeated one of the buccaneers, in a deep growl. "Ah, he'd be a lucky one as knowed that!"

"You'll, perhaps, batten down your hatches till you're spoke to, my friend," cried Silver truculently to this speaker. And then, in his first gracious tones, he replied to me: "Yesterday morning, Mr Hawkins," said he, "in the dogwatch, down came Doctor Livesey with a flag of truce. Says he, 'Cap'n Silver, you're sold out. Ship's gone.' Well, maybe we'd been taking a glass and a song to help it round. I won't say no. Leastways, none of us had looked out. We looked out, and by thunder! the old ship was gone. I never seen a pack o' fools look fishier; and you may lay to that, if I tells you that looked the fishiest. 'Well,' says the doctor, 'let's bargain.' We bargained, him and I, and here we are: stores, brandy, blockhouse, the firewood you was thoughtful enough to cut, and in a manner of speaking, the whole blessed boat, from crosstrees to keelson. As for them, they've tramped; I don't know where's they are."

He drew again quietly at his pipe.

"And lest you should take it into that head of yours," he went on, "that you was included in the treaty, here's the last word that was said: 'How many are you,' says I, 'to leave?' 'Four,' says he, 'four, and one of us wounded. As for that boy, I don't know where he is, confound him,' says he, 'nor I don't much care. We're about sick of him.' These was his words."

"Is that all?" I asked.

"Well, it's all that you're to hear, my son," returned Silver.

"And now I am to choose?"

"And now you are to choose, and you may lay to that," said Silver.

"Well," said I, "I am not such a fool but I know pretty well what I have to look for. Let the worst come to the worst, it's little I care. I've seen too many die since I fell in with you. But there's a thing or two I have to tell you," I said, and by this time I was quite excited, "and the first is this: here you are in a bad way: ship lost, treasure lost, men lost; your whole business gone to wreck; and if you want to know who did it – it was I! I was in the apple barrel the night we sighted land, and I heard you, John, and you, Dick Johnson, and Hands, who is now at the bottom of the sea, and told every word you said before the hour was out. And as for the schooner, it was I who cut her cable, and it was I that killed the men you had aboard of her, and it was I who brought her where you'll never see her more, not one of you. The laugh's on my side; I've had the top of this business from the first; I no more fear you than I fear a fly. Kill me, if you please, or spare me. But one thing I'll say, and no more; if you spare me, bygones are bygones, and when you fellows are in court for piracy, I'll save you all I can. It is for you to choose. Kill another and do yourselves no good, or spare me and keep a witness to save you from the gallows."

I stopped, for I tell you I was out of breath, and to my wonder, not a man of them moved, but all sat staring at me like as many sheep. And while they were still staring, I broke out again:

"And now, Mr Silver," I said, "I believe you're the best man here, and if things go to the worst, I'll take it kind of you to let the doctor know the way I took it."

"I'll bear it in mind," said Silver, with an accent so curious that I could not, for the life of me, decide whether he were laughing at my request, or had been favourably affected by my courage.

"I'll put one to that," cried the old mahogany-faced seaman – Morgan by name – whom I had seen in Long John's public house upon the quays of Bristol. "It was him that knowed Black Dog."

"Well, and see here," added the sea cook. "I'll put another again to that, by thunder! for it was this same boy that faked the chart from Billy Bones. First and last, we've split upon Jim Hawkins!"

"Then here goes!" said Morgan, with an oath.

And he sprang up, drawing his knife as if he had been twenty.

"Avast, there!" cried Silver. "Who are you, Tom Morgan? Maybe you thought you was cap'n here, perhaps. By the powers, but I'll teach you better! Cross me, and you'll go where many a good man's gone before you, first and last, these thirty year back – some to the yardarm, shiver my timbers! and some by the board, and all to feed the fishes. There's never a man looked me between the eyes and seen a good day a'terwards, Tom Morgan, you may lay to that."

Morgan paused; but a hoarse murmur rose from the others.

"Tom's right," said one.

"I stood hazing long enough from one," added another. "I'll be hanged if I'll be hazed by you, John Silver."

"Did any of you gentlemen want to have it out with *me*?" roared Silver, bending far forwards from his position on the keg, with his pipe still glowing in his right hand. "Put a name on what you're at; you ain't dumb, I reckon. Him that wants shall get it. Have I lived this many years, and a son of a rum puncheon cock his hat athwart my hawse at the latter end of it? You know the way; you're all gentlemen o' fortune, by your account. Well, I'm ready. Take a cutlass, him that dares, and I'll see the colour of his inside, crutch and all, before that pipe's empty."

Not a man stirred; not a man answered.

"That's your sort, is it?" he added, returning his pipe to his mouth. "Well, you're a gay lot to look at, anyway. Not much worth to fight, you ain't. P'r'aps you can understand King George's English. I'm cap'n here by 'lection. I'm cap'n here because I'm the best man by a long sea mile. You won't fight, as gentlemen o' fortune should; then, by thunder, you'll obey, and you may lay to it! I like that boy, now; I never seen a better boy than that. He's more a man than any pair of rats of you in this here house, and what I say is this: let me see him that'll lay a hand on him – that's what I say, and you may lay to it."

There was a long pause after this. I stood straight up against the wall, my heart still going like a sledgehammer, but with a ray of hope now shining in my bosom. Silver leant back against the wall, his arms crossed, his pipe in the corner of his mouth, as calm as though he had been in church; yet his eye kept wandering furtively, and he kept the tail of it on his unruly followers. They, on their part, drew gradually together towards the far end of the blockhouse, and the low hiss of their whispering sounded in my ear continuously, like a stream. One after another, they would look up, and the red light of the torch would fall for a second on their nervous faces; but it was not towards me, it was towards Silver that they turned their eyes.

"You seem to have a lot to say," remarked Silver, spitting far into the air. "Pipe up and let me hear it, or lay to."

"Ax your pardon, sir," returned one of the men, "you're pretty free with some of the rules; maybe you'll kindly keep an eye upon the rest. This crew's dissatisfied; this crew don't vally bullying a marlinspike;* this crew has its rights like other crews, I'll make so free as that; and by your own rules, I take it we can talk together. I ax your pardon, sir, acknowledging you for to be capting at this present; but I claim my right, and steps outside for a council."

And with an elaborate sea salute, this fellow, a long, ill-looking, yellow-eyed man of five-and-thirty, stepped coolly towards the door and disappeared out of the house. One after another, the rest followed his example; each making a salute as he passed; each adding some apology. "According to rules," said one. "Fo'c's'le council," said Morgan. And so with one remark or another, all marched out, and left Silver and me alone with the torch.

The sea cook instantly removed his pipe.

"Now, look you here, Jim Hawkins," he said, in a steady whisper that was no more than audible, "you're within half a plank of death, and what's a long sight worse, of torture. They're going to throw me off. But, you mark, I stand by you through thick and thin. I didn't mean to; no, not till you spoke up. I was about desperate to lose that much blunt, and be hanged into the bargain. But I see you was the right sort. I says to myself: you stand by Hawkins, John, and Hawkins'll stand by you. You're his last card, and by the living thunder, John, he's yours! Back to back, says I. You save your witness, and he'll save your neck!"

I began dimly to understand.

"You mean all's lost?" I asked.

"Ay, by gum, I do!" he answered. "Ship gone, neck gone – that's the size of it. Once I looked into that bay, Jim Hawkins, and seen no schooner – well, I'm tough, but I gave out. As for that lot and their council, mark me, they're outright fools and cowards. I'll save your life – if so be as I can – from them. But see here, Jim – tit for tat – you save Long John from swinging."

I was bewildered; it seemed a thing so hopeless he was asking – he, the old buccaneer, the ringleader throughout.

"What I can do, that I'll do," I said.

"It's a bargain!" cried Long John. "You speak up plucky, and by thunder! I've a chance."

He hobbled to the torch, where it stood propped among the firewood, and took a fresh light to his pipe.

"Understand me, Jim," he said, returning. "I've a head on my shoulders, I have. I'm on squire's side now. I know you've got that ship safe somewheres. How you done it, I don't know, but safe it is. I guess Hands and O'Brien turned soft. I never much believed in neither of *them*. Now you mark me. I ask no questions, nor I won't let others. I know when a game's up, I do; and I know a lad that's staunch. Ah, you that's young – you and me might have done a power of good together!"

He drew some cognac from the cask into a tin cannikin. "Will you taste, messmate?" he asked; and when I had refused: "Well, I'll take a drain myself, Jim," said he. "I need a caulker, for there's trouble on hand. And, talking o' trouble, why did that doctor give me the chart, Jim?"

My face expressed a wonder so unaffected that he saw the needlessness of further questions.

"Ah well, he did, though," said he. "And there's something under that, no doubt – something surely under that, Jim – bad or good."

And he took another swallow of the brandy, shaking his great fair head like a man who looks forward to the worst.

# 29

## *The Black Spot Again*

T HE COUNCIL OF THE BUCCANEERS had lasted some time, when one of them re-entered the house, and with a repetition of the same salute, which had in my eyes an ironical air, begged for a moment's loan of the torch. Silver briefly agreed; and this emissary retired again, leaving us together in the dark.

"There's a breeze coming, Jim," said Silver, who had by this time adopted quite a friendly and familiar tone.

I turned to the loophole nearest me and looked out. The embers of the great fire had so far burnt themselves out, and now glowed so low and duskily, that I understood why these conspirators desired a torch. About halfway down the slope to the stockade, they were collected in a group; one held the light; another was on his knees in their midst, and I saw the blade of an open knife shine in his hand with varying colours in the moon and torchlight. The rest were all somewhat stooping, as though watching the manoeuvres of this last. I could just make out that he had a book as well as a knife in his hand; and was still wondering how anything so incongruous had come in their possession, when the kneeling figure rose once more to his feet, and the whole party began to move together towards the house.

"Here they come," said I; and I returned to my former position, for it seemed beneath my dignity that they should find me watching them.

"Well, let 'em come, lad – let 'em come," said Silver cheerily. "I've still a shot in my locker."

The door opened, and the five men, standing huddled together just inside, pushed one of their number forwards. In any other circumstances it would have been comical to see his slow advance, hesitating as he set down each foot, but holding his closed right hand in front of him.

"Step up, lad," cried Silver. "I won't eat you. Hand it over, lubber. I know the rules, I do; I won't hurt a depytation."

Thus encouraged, the buccaneer stepped forth more briskly, and having passed something to Silver from hand to hand, slipped yet more smartly back again to his companions.

The sea cook looked at what had been given him.

"The black spot! I thought so," he observed. "Where might you have got the paper? Why, hillo! look here now: this ain't lucky! You've gone and cut this out of a Bible. What fool's cut a Bible?"

"Ah, there!" said Morgan, "There! Wot did I say? No good'll come o' that, I said."

"Well, you've about fixed it now, among you," continued Silver. "You'll all swing now, I reckon. What soft-headed lubber had a Bible?"

"It was Dick," said one.

"Dick, was it? Then Dick can get to prayers," said Silver. "He's seen his slice of luck, has Dick, and you may lay to that."

But here the long man with the yellow eyes struck in.

"Belay that talk, John Silver," he said. "This crew has tipped you the black spot in full council, as in dooty bound; just you turn it over, as in dooty bound, and see what's wrote there. Then you can talk."

"Thanky, George," replied the sea cook. "You always was brisk for business, and has the rules by heart, George, as I'm pleased to see. Well, what is it anyway? Ah! 'Deposed' – that's it, is it? Very pretty wrote, to be sure; like print, I swear. Your hand o' write, George? Why, you was gettin' quite a leadin' man in this here crew. You'll be cap'n next, I shouldn't wonder. Just oblige me with that torch again, will you? This pipe don't draw."

"Come, now," said George, "you don't fool this crew no more. You're a funny man, by your account; but you're over now, and you'll maybe step down off that barrel, and help vote."

"I thought you said you knowed the rules," returned Silver contemptuously. "Leastways, if you don't, I do; and I wait here – and I'm still your cap'n, mind – till you outs with your grievances, and I reply, in the meantime, your black spot ain't worth a biscuit. After that, we'll see."

"Oh," replied George, "you don't be under no kind of apprehension; *we're* all square, we are. First, you've made a hash of this cruise – you'll be a bold man to say no to that. Second, you let the enemy out o' this here trap for nothing. Why did they want out? I dunno; but it's pretty plain they wanted it. Third, you wouldn't let us go at them upon the march. Oh, we see through you, John Silver; you want to play booty, that's what's wrong with you. And then, fourth, there's this here boy."

"Is that all?" asked Silver quietly.

"Enough, too," retorted George. "We'll all swing and sundry for your bungling."

"Well now, look here, I'll answer these four p'ints; one after another I'll answer 'em. I made a hash o' this cruise, did I? Well now, you all know what I wanted; and you all know, if that had been done, that we'd 'a' been aboard the *Hispaniola* this night as ever was, every man of us alive, and fit, and full of good plum duff, and the treasure in the hold of her, by thunder! Well, who crossed me? Who forced my hand, as was the lawful cap'n? Who tipped me the black spot the day we landed, and began this dance? Ah, it's a fine dance – I'm with you there – and looks mighty like a hornpipe in a rope's end at Execution Dock by London town, it does. But who done it? Why, it was Anderson, and Hands, and you, George Merry! And you're the last above-board of that same meddling crew; and you have the Davy Jones's insolence to up and stand for cap'n over me – you, that sank the lot of us! By the powers! but this tops the stiffest yarn to nothing."

Silver paused, and I could see by the faces of George and his late comrades that these words had not been said in vain.

"That's for number one," cried the accused, wiping the sweat from his brow, for he had been talking with a vehemence that shook the house. "Why, I give you my word, I'm sick to speak to you. You've neither sense nor memory, and I leave it to fancy where your mothers was that let you come to sea. Sea! Gentlemen o' fortune! I reckon tailors is your trade."

"Go on, John," said Morgan. "Speak up to the others."

"Ah, the others!" returned John. "They're a nice lot, ain't they? You say this cruise is bungled. Ah! by gum, if you could understand how bad it's bungled, you would see! We're that near the gibbet that my neck's stiff with thinking on it. You've seen 'em, maybe, hanged in chains, birds about 'em, seamen p'inting 'em out as they go down with the tide. 'Who's that?' says one. 'That! Why, that's John Silver. I knowed him well,' says another. And you can hear the chains a-jangle as you go about and reach for the other buoy. Now that's about where we are, every mother's son of us, thanks to him, and Hands, and Anderson, and other ruination fools of you. And if you want to know about number four, and that boy, why, shiver my timbers! isn't he a hostage? Are we a-going to waste a hostage? No, not us; he might be our last chance, and I shouldn't wonder. Kill that boy? not me, mates! And number three? Ah, well, there's a deal to say to number three. Maybe you don't count it nothing to have a real college doctor come to see you every day – you, John, with your head broke – or you, George Merry, that had the ague shakes upon you not six hours agone, and has your eyes the colour of lemon peel to this same moment on the clock? And maybe, perhaps, you didn't know there was a consort coming, either? But there is; and not so long till then; and we'll see who'll be glad to have a hostage when it comes to that. And as for number two, and why I made a bargain – well, you came crawling on your knees to me to make it – on your knees you came, you was that downhearted – and you'd have starved, too, if I hadn't – but that's a trifle! you look there – that's why!"

And he cast down upon the floor a paper that I instantly recognized – none other than the chart on yellow paper, with the three red crosses, that I had found in the oilcloth at the bottom of the captain's chest. Why the doctor had given it to him was more than I could fancy.

But if it were inexplicable to me, the appearance of the chart was incredible to the surviving mutineers. They leapt upon it like cats upon a mouse. It went from hand to hand, one tearing it from another; and by the oaths and the cries and the childish laughter with which they accompanied their examination, you would have thought, not only they were fingering the very gold, but were at sea with it, besides, in safety.

"Yes," said one, "that's Flint, sure enough. J.F., and a score below, with a clove hitch to it; so he done ever."

"Mighty pretty," said George. "But how are we to get away with it, and us no ship?"

Silver suddenly sprang up, and supporting himself with a hand against the wall: "Now I give you warning, George," he cried. "One more word of your sauce, and I'll call you down and fight you. How? Why, how do I know? You had ought to tell me that – you and the rest, that lost me my schooner with your interference, burn you! But not you, you can't; you hain't got the invention of a cockroach. But civil you can speak, and shall, George Merry, you may lay to that."

"That's fair enow," said the old man Morgan.

"Fair! I reckon so," said the sea cook. "You lost the ship; I found the treasure. Who's the better man at that? And now I resign, by thunder! Elect whom you please to be your cap'n now; I'm done with it."

"Silver!" they cried. "Barbecue for ever! Barbecue for cap'n!"

"So that's the toon, is it?" cried the cook. "George, I reckon you'll have to wait another turn, friend; and lucky for you as I'm not a revengeful man. But that was never my way. And now, shipmates, this black spot? 'Tain't much good now, is it? Dick's crossed his luck and spoilt his Bible, and that's about all."

"It'll do to kiss the book on still, won't it?" growled Dick, who was evidently uneasy at the curse he had brought upon himself.

"A Bible with a bit cut out!" returned Silver derisively. "Not it. It don't bind no more 'n a ballad-book."

"Don't it, though?" cried Dick, with a sort of joy. "Well, I reckon that's worth having, too."

"Here, Jim – here's a cur'osity for you," said Silver; and he tossed me the paper.

It was a round about the size of a crown piece. One side was blank, for it had been the last leaf; the other contained a verse or two of Revelation – these words among the rest, which struck sharply home upon my mind: "Without are dogs and murderers." The printed side had been blackened with wood ash, which already began to come off and soil my fingers; on the blank side had been written with the same material the one word "Depposed". I have that curiosity beside me at this moment; but not a trace of writing now remains beyond a single scratch, such as a man might make with his thumbnail.

That was the end of the night's business. Soon after, with a drink all round, we lay down to sleep, and the outside of Silver's vengeance was to put George Merry up for sentinel, and threaten him with death if he should prove unfaithful.

It was long ere I could close an eye, and Heaven knows I had matter enough for thought in the man whom I had slain that afternoon, in my own most perilous position, and above all, in the remarkable game that I saw Silver now engaged upon – keeping the mutineers together with one hand, and grasping, with the other, after every means, possible and impossible, to make his peace and save his miserable life. He himself slept peacefully, and snored aloud; yet my heart was sore for him, wicked as he was, to think on the dark perils that environed, and the shameful gibbet that awaited him.

# 30

## *On Parole*

I WAS WAKENED – INDEED, we were all wakened, for I could see even the sentinel shake himself together from where he had fallen against the doorpost – by a clear, hearty voice hailing us from the margin of the wood:

"Blockhouse, ahoy!" it cried. "Here's the doctor."

And the doctor it was. Although I was glad to hear the sound, yet my gladness was not without admixture. I remembered with confusion my insubordinate and stealthy conduct; and when I saw where it had brought me – among what companions and surrounded by what dangers – I felt ashamed to look him in the face.

He must have risen in the dark, for the day had hardly come; and when I ran to a loophole and looked out, I saw him standing, like Silver once before, up to the mid-leg in creeping vapour.

"You, Doctor! Top o' the morning to you, sir!" cried Silver, broad awake and beaming with good nature in a moment. "Bright and early, to be sure; and it's the early bird, as the saying goes, that gets the rations. George, shake up your timbers, son, and help Dr Livesey over the ship's side. All a-doin' well, your patients was – all well and merry."

So he pattered on, standing on the hilltop, with his crutch under his elbow, and one hand upon the side of the log house – quite the old John in voice, manner and expression.

"We've quite a surprise for you, too, sir," he continued. "We've a little stranger here – he! he! A noo boarder and lodger, sir, and looking fit and taut as a fiddle; slep' like a supercargo, he did, right alongside of John – stem to stem we was, all night."

Dr Livesey was by this time across the stockade and pretty near the cook; and I could hear the alteration in his voice as he said:

"Not Jim?"

"The very same Jim as ever was," says Silver.

The doctor stopped outright, although he did not speak, and it was some seconds before he seemed able to move on.

"Well, well," he said, at last, "duty first and pleasure afterwards, as you might have said yourself, Silver. Let us overhaul these patients of yours."

A moment afterwards he had entered the blockhouse, and with one grim nod to me, proceeded with his work among the sick. He seemed under no apprehension, though he must have known that his life, among these treacherous demons, depended on a hair; and he rattled on to his patients as if he were paying an ordinary professional visit in a quiet English family. His manner, I suppose, reacted on the men; for they behaved to him as if nothing had occurred – as if he were still ship's doctor, and they still faithful hands before the mast.

"You're doing well, my friend," he said to the fellow with the bandaged head, "and if ever any person had a close shave, it was you; your head must be as hard as iron. Well, George, how goes it? You're a pretty colour, certainly; why, your liver, man, is upside down. Did you take that medicine? Did he take that medicine, men?"

"Ay, ay, sir, he took it, sure enough," returned Morgan.

"Because, you see, since I am mutineers' doctor, or prison doctor, as I prefer to call it," says Dr Livesey in his pleasantest way, "I make it a point of honour not to lose a man for King George (God bless him!) and the gallows."

The rogues looked at each other, but swallowed the home-thrust in silence.

"Dick don't feel well, sir," said one.

"Don't he?" replied the doctor. "Well, step up here, Dick, and let me see your tongue. No, I should be surprised if he did! The man's tongue is fit to frighten the French. Another fever."

"Ah, there," said Morgan, "that comed of sp'iling Bibles."

"That comed – as you call it – of being arrant asses," retorted the doctor, "and not having sense enough to know honest air from poison, and the dry land from a vile, pestiferous slough. I think it most probable – though, of course, it's only an opinion – that you'll all have the deuce to pay before you get that malaria out of your systems. Camp in a bog, would you? Silver, I'm surprised at you. You're less of a fool than many, take you all round; but you don't appear to me to have the rudiments of a notion of the rules of health."

"Well," he added, after he had dosed them round, and they had taken his prescriptions, with really laughable humility, more like charity schoolchildren than blood-guilty mutineers and pirates, "well, that's done for today. And now I should wish to have a talk with that boy, please."

And he nodded his head in my direction carelessly.

George Merry was at the door, spitting and spluttering over some bad-tasted medicine; but at the first word of the doctor's proposal he swung round with a deep flush, and cried "No!" and swore.

Silver struck the barrel with his open hand.

"Si-lence!" he roared, and looked about him positively like a lion. "Doctor," he went on, in his usual tones, "I was a-thinking of that, knowing as how you had a fancy for the boy. We're all humbly grateful for your kindness, and as you see, puts faith in you, and takes the drugs down like that much grog. And I take it I've found a way as'll suit all. Hawkins, will you give me your word of honour as a young gentleman – for a young gentleman you are, although poor born – your word of honour not to slip your cable?"

I readily gave the pledge required.

"Then, Doctor," said Silver, "you just step outside o' that stockade, and once you're there, I'll the bring the boy down on the inside, and I reckon you can yarn through the spars. Good day to you, sir, and all our dooties to the squire and Cap'n Smollett."

The explosion of disapproval, which nothing but Silver's black looks had restrained, broke out immediately the doctor had left the house. Silver was roundly accused of playing double – of trying to make a separate peace for himself – of sacrificing the interests of his accomplices and victims; and in one word, of the identical, exact thing that he was doing. It seemed to me so obvious, in this case, that I could not imagine how he was to turn their anger. But he was twice the man the rest were; and his last night's victory had given him a huge preponderance on their minds. He called them all the fools and dolts you can imagine, said it was necessary I should talk to the doctor, fluttered the chart in their faces, asked them if they could afford to break the treaty the very day they were bound a-treasure-hunting.

"No, by thunder!" he cried, "it's us must break the treaty when the time comes; and till then I'll gammon that doctor, if I have to ile his boots with brandy."

And then he bade them get the fire lit, and stalked out upon his crutch, with his hand on my shoulder, leaving them in a disarray, and silenced by his volubility rather than convinced.

"Slow, lad, slow," he said. "They might round upon us in a twinkle of an eye, if we was seen to hurry."

Very deliberately, then, did we advance across the sand to where the doctor awaited us on the other side of the stockade, and as soon as we were within easy speaking distance, Silver stopped.

"You'll make a note of this here also, Doctor," says he, "and the boy'll tell you how I saved his life, and were deposed for it, too, and you may lay to that. Doctor, when a man's steering as near the wind as me – playing chuck-farthing with the last breath in his body, like – you wouldn't think it too much, mayhap, to give him one good word? You'll please bear in mind it's not my life only now – it's that boy's into the bargain; and you'll speak me fair, Doctor, and give me a bit o' hope to go on, for the sake of mercy."

Silver was a changed man, once he was out there and had his back to his friends and the blockhouse; his cheeks seemed to have fallen in, his voice trembled; never was a soul more dead in earnest.

"Why, John, you're not afraid?" asked Dr Livesey.

"Doctor, I'm no coward; no, not I – not *so* much!" and he snapped his fingers. "If I was I wouldn't say it. But I'll own up fairly, I've the shakes upon me for the gallows. You're a good man and a true; I never seen a better man! And you'll not forget what I done good, not any more than you'll forget the bad, I know. And I step aside – see here – and leave you and Jim alone. And you'll put that down for me, too, for it's a long stretch, is that!"

So saying, he stepped back a little way, till he was out of earshot, and there sat down upon a tree stump and began to whistle; spinning round now and again upon his seat so as to command a sight, sometimes of me and the doctor, and sometimes of his unruly ruffians as they went to and fro in the sand, between the fire – which they were busy rekindling – and the house, from which they brought forth pork and bread to make the breakfast.

"So, Jim," said the doctor sadly, "here you are. As you have brewed, so shall you drink, my boy. Heaven knows, I cannot find it in my heart to blame you; but this much I will say, be it kind or unkind: when Captain Smollett was well, you dared not have gone off; and when he was ill, and couldn't help it, by George, it was downright cowardly!"

I will own that I here began to weep. "Doctor," I said, "you might spare me. I have blamed myself enough; my life's forfeit anyway, and I should have been dead by now, if Silver hadn't stood for me; and Doctor, believe this, I can die – and I dare say I deserve it – but what I fear is torture. If they come to torture me—"

"Jim," the doctor interrupted, and his voice was quite changed, "Jim I can't have this. Whip over, and we'll run for it."

"Doctor," said I, "I passed my word."

"I know, I know," he cried. "We can't help that, Jim, now. I'll take it on my shoulders, holus-bolus, blame and shame, my boy; but stay here, I cannot let you. Jump! One jump, and you're out, and we'll run for it like antelopes."

"No," I replied, "you know right well you wouldn't do the thing yourself; neither you, nor squire, nor captain; and no more will I. Silver trusted me; I passed my word, and back I go. But, Doctor, you did not let me finish. If they come to torture me, I might let slip a word of where the ship is; for I got the ship, part by luck and part by risking, and she lies in North Inlet, on the southern beach, and just below high water. At half-tide she must be high and dry."

"The ship!" exclaimed the doctor.

Rapidly I described to him my adventures, and he heard me out in silence.

"There is a kind of fate in this," he observed, when I had done. "Every step, it's you that saves our lives; and do you suppose by any chance that we are going to let you lose yours? That would be a poor return, my boy. You found out the plot; you found Ben Gunn – the best deed that ever you did, or will do, though you live to ninety. Oh, by Jupiter, and talking of Ben Gunn! why, this is the mischief in person. Silver!" he cried, "Silver! – I'll give you a piece of advice," he continued, as the cook drew near again, "don't you be in any great hurry after that treasure."

"Why, sir, I do my possible, which that ain't," said Silver. "I can only, asking your pardon, save my life and the boy's by seeking for that treasure; and you may lay to that."

"Well, Silver," replied the doctor, "if that is so, I'll go one step further: look out for squalls when you find it."

"Sir," said Silver, "as between man and man, that's too much and too little. What you're after, why you left the blockhouse, why you given me that there chart, I don't know, now, do I? And yet I done your bidding with my eyes shut and never a word of hope! But no, this here's too much. If you won't tell me what you mean plain out, just say so, and I'll leave the helm."

"No," said the doctor musingly, "I've no right to say more; it's not my secret, you see, Silver, or, I give you my word, I'd tell it you. But I'll go as far with you as I dare go, and a step beyond; for I'll have my wig sorted by the captain or I'm mistaken! And, first, I'll give you a bit of hope: Silver, if we both get alive out of this wolf-trap, I'll do my best to save you, short of perjury."

Silver's face was radiant. "You couldn't say more, I'm sure, sir, not if you was my mother," he cried.

"Well, that's my first concession," added the doctor. "My second is a piece of advice: Keep the boy close beside you, and when you need help, halloo. I'm off to seek it for you, and that itself will show you if I speak at random. Goodbye, Jim."

And Dr Livesey shook hands with me through the stockade, nodded to Silver, and set off at a brisk pace into the wood.

# 31

### *The Treasure Hunt – Flint's Pointer*

"JIM," SAID SILVER, when we were alone, "if I saved your life, you saved mine; and I'll not forget it. I seen the doctor waving you to run for it – with the tail of my eye, I did; and I seen you say no, as plain as hearing. Jim, that's one to you. This is the first glint of hope I had since the attack failed, and I owe it you. And now, Jim, we're to go in for this here treasure-hunting, with sealed orders, too, and I don't like it; and you and me must stick close, back to back like, and we'll save our necks in spite o' fate and fortune."

Just then a man hailed us from the fire that breakfast was ready, and we were soon seated here and there about the sand over biscuit and fried junk. They had lit a fire fit to roast an ox; and it was now grown so hot that they could only approach it from the windwards, and even there not without precaution. In the same wasteful spirit, they had cooked, I suppose, three times more than we could eat; and one of them, with an empty laugh, threw what was left into the fire, which blazed and roared again over this unusual fuel. I never in my life saw men so careless of the morrow; hand to mouth is the only word that can describe their way of doing; and what with wasted food and sleeping sentries, though they were bold enough for a brush and be done with it, I could see their entire unfitness for anything like a prolonged campaign.

Even Silver, eating away, with Captain Flint upon his shoulder, had not a word of blame for their recklessness. And this the more surprised me, for I thought he had never shown himself so cunning as he did then.

"Ay, mates," said he, "it's lucky you have Barbecue to think for you with this here head. I got what I wanted, I did. Sure enough, they have the ship. Where they have it, I don't know yet; but once we hit the treasure, we'll have to jump about and find out. And then, mates, us that has the boats, I reckon, has the upper hand."

Thus he kept running on, with his mouth full of the hot bacon: thus he restored their hope and confidence, and, I more than suspect, repaired his own at the same time.

"As for hostage," he continued, "that's his last talk, I guess, with them he loves so dear. I've got my piece o' news, and thanky to him for that; but it's over and done. I'll take him in a line when we go treasure-hunting, for we'll keep him like so much gold, in case of accidents, you mark, and in the meantime. Once we got the ship and treasure both, and off to sea like jolly companions, why, then we'll talk Mr Hawkins over, we will, and we'll give him his share, to be sure, for all his kindness."

It was no wonder the men were in a good humour now. For my part, I was horribly cast down. Should the scheme he had now sketched prove feasible, Silver, already doubly a traitor, would not hesitate to adopt it. He had still a foot in either camp, and there was no doubt he would prefer wealth and freedom with the pirates to a bare escape from hanging, which was the best he had to hope on our side.

Nay, and even if things so fell out that he was forced to keep his faith with Dr Livesey, even then what danger lay before us! What a moment that would be when the suspicions of his followers turned to certainty, and he and I should have to fight for dear life – he, a cripple, and I, a boy – against five strong and active seamen!

Add to this double apprehension the mystery that still hung over the behaviour of my friends; their unexplained desertion of the stockade; their inexplicable cession of the chart; or harder still to understand, the doctor's last warning to Silver, "Look out for squalls when you find it," and you will readily believe how little taste I found in my breakfast, and with how uneasy a heart I set forth behind my captors on the quest for treasure.

We made a curious figure, had anyone been there to see us; all in soiled sailor clothes, and all but me armed to the teeth. Silver had two guns slung about him – one before and one behind – besides the great cutlass at his waist, and a pistol in each pocket of his square-tailed coat. To complete his strange appearance, Captain Flint sat perched upon his shoulder and gabbling odds and ends of purposeless sea talk. I had a line about my waist, and followed obediently after the sea cook, who held the loose end of the rope now in his free hand, now between his powerful teeth. For all the world, I was led like a dancing bear.

The other men were variously burdened; some carrying picks and shovels – for that had been the very first necessary they brought ashore from the *Hispaniola* – others laden with pork, bread and brandy for the midday meal. All the stores, I observed, came from our stock; and I could see the truth of Silver's words the night before. Had he not struck a bargain with the doctor, he and his mutineers, deserted by the ship, must have been driven to subsist on clear water and the proceeds of their hunting. Water would have been little to their taste; a sailor is not usually a good shot;

and besides all that, when they were so short of eatables, it was not likely they would be very flush of powder.

Well, thus equipped, we all set out – even the fellow with the broken head, who should certainly have kept in shadow – and straggled one after another to the beach, where the two gigs awaited us. Even these bore trace of the drunken folly of the pirates, one in a broken thwart, and both in their muddy and unbailed condition. Both were to be carried along with us, for the sake of safety; and so, with our numbers divided between them, we set forth upon the bosom of the anchorage.

As we pulled over, there was some discussion on the chart. The red cross was, of course, far too large to be a guide; and the terms of the note on the back, as you will hear, admitted of some ambiguity. They ran, the reader may remember, thus:

*Tall tree, Spyglass shoulder, bearing a point to the N of NNE.*
*Skeleton Island ESE and by E.*
*Ten feet.*

A tall tree was thus the principal mark. Now, right before us, the anchorage was bounded by a plateau from two to three hundred feet high, adjoining on the north the sloping southern shoulder of the Spyglass, and rising again towards the south into the rough, cliffy eminence called the Mizzenmast Hill. The top of the plateau was dotted thickly with pine trees of varying height. Every here and there, one of a different species rose forty or fifty feet clear above its neighbours, and which of these was the particular "tall tree" of Captain Flint could only be decided on the spot, and by the readings of the compass.

Yet, although that was the case, every man on board the boats had picked a favourite of his own ere we were halfway over, Long

John alone shrugging his shoulders and bidding them wait till they were there.

We pulled easily, by Silver's directions, not to weary the hands prematurely; and after quite a long passage, landed at the mouth of the second river – that which runs down a woody cleft of the Spyglass. Thence, bending to our left, we began to ascend the slope towards the plateau.

At the first outset, heavy, miry ground and a matted, marish vegetation greatly delayed our progress; but by little and little the hill began to steepen and become stony underfoot, and the wood to change its character and to grow in a more open order. It was indeed a most pleasant portion of the island that we were now approaching. A heavy-scented broom and many flowering shrubs had almost taken the place of grass. Thickets of green nutmeg trees were dotted here and there with the red columns and the broad shadow of the pines; and the first mingled their spice with the aroma of the others. The air, besides, was fresh and stirring, and this, under the sheer sunbeams, was a wonderful refreshment to our senses.

The party spread itself abroad in a fan shape, shouting and leaping to and fro. About the centre, and a good way behind the rest, Silver and I followed – I tethered by my rope, he ploughing, with deep pants, among the sliding gravel. From time to time indeed I had to lend him a hand, or he must have missed his footing and fallen backwards down the hill.

We had thus proceeded for about half a mile, and were approaching the brow of the plateau, when the man upon the furthest left began to cry aloud as if in terror. Shout after shout came from him, and the others began to run in his direction.

"He can't 'a' found the treasure," said old Morgan, hurrying past us from the right, "for that's clean a-top."

Indeed, as we found when we also reached the spot, it was something very different. At the foot of a pretty big pine, and involved in a green creeper, which had even partly lifted some of the smaller bones, a human skeleton lay, with a few shreds of clothing, on the ground. I believe a chill struck for a moment to every heart.

"He was a seaman," said George Merry, who, bolder than the rest, had gone up close, and was examining the rags of clothing. "Leastways, this is good sea cloth."

"Ay, ay," said Silver, "like enough; you wouldn't look to find a bishop here, I reckon. But what sort of a way is that for bones to lie? 'Tain't in natur'."

Indeed, on a second glance, it seemed impossible to fancy that the body was in a natural position. But for some disarray (the work, perhaps, of the birds that had fed upon him, or of the slow-growing creeper that had gradually enveloped his remains) the man lay perfectly straight – his feet pointing in one direction, his hands, raised above his head like a diver's, pointing directly in the opposite.

"I've taken a notion into my old numskull," observed Silver. "Here's the compass; there's the tip-top p'int o' Skeleton Island, stickin' out like a tooth. Just take a bearing, will you, along the line of them bones."

It was done. The body pointed straight in the direction of the island, and the compass read duly ESE and by E.

"I thought so," cried the cook, "this here is a p'inter. Right up there is our line for the Pole Star and the jolly dollars. But, by thunder! if it don't make me cold inside to think of Flint. This is one of *his* jokes, and no mistake. Him and these six was alone here; he killed 'em, every man; and this one he hauled here and laid down by compass, shiver my timbers! They're long bones, and the hair's been yellow. Ay, that would be Allardyce. You mind Allardyce, Tom Morgan?"

"Ay, ay," returned Morgan, "I mind him; he owed me money, he did, and took my knife ashore with him."

"Speaking of knives," said another, "why don't we find his 'n lying round? Flint warn't the man to pick a seaman's pocket; and the birds, I guess, would leave it be."

"By the powers, and that's true!" cried Silver.

"There ain't a thing left here," said Merry, still feeling round among the bones, "not a copper doit nor a baccy box. It don't look nat'ral to me."

"No, by gum, it don't," agreed Silver, "not nat'ral, nor not nice, says you. Great guns! messmates, but if Flint was living, this would be a hot spot for you and me. Six they were, and six are we; and bones is what they are now."

"I saw him dead with these here deadlights," said Morgan. "Billy took me in. There he laid, with penny pieces on his eyes."

"Dead – ay, sure enough he's dead and gone below," said the fellow with the bandage, "but if ever sperrit walked, it would be Flint's. Dear heart, but he died bad, did Flint!"

"Ay, that he did," observed another, "now he raged, and now he hollered for the rum, and now he sang. 'Fifteen Men' were his only song, mates; and I tell you true, I never rightly liked to hear it since. It was main hot, and the windy was open, and I hear that old song comin' out as clear as clear – and the death-haul on the man already."

"Come, come," said Silver, "stow this talk. He's dead, and he don't walk, that I know; leastways, he won't walk by day, and you may lay to that. Care killed a cat. Fetch ahead for the doubloons."

We started, certainly; but in spite of the hot sun and the staring daylight, the pirates no longer ran separate and shouting through the wood, but kept side by side and spoke with bated breath. The terror of the dead buccaneer had fallen on their spirits.

## 32

*The Treasure Hunt – The Voice among the Trees*

PARTLY FROM THE DAMPING INFLUENCE of this alarm, partly to rest Silver and the sick folk, the whole party sat down as soon as they had gained the brow of the ascent.

The plateau being somewhat tilted towards the west, this spot on which we had paused commanded a wide prospect on either hand. Before us, over the treetops, we beheld the Cape of the Woods fringed with surf; behind, we not only looked down upon the anchorage and Skeleton Island, but saw – clear across the spit and the eastern lowlands – a great field of open sea upon the east. Sheer above us rose the Spyglass, here dotted with single pines, there black with precipices. There was no sound but that of the distant breakers mounting from all round, and the chirp of countless insects in the brush. Not a man, not a sail upon the sea; the very largeness of the view increased the sense of solitude.

Silver, as he sat, took certain bearings with his compass.

"There are three 'tall trees'" said he, "about in the right line from Skeleton Island. 'Spyglass Shoulder', I take it, means that lower p'int there. It's child's play to find the stuff now. I've half a mind to dine first."

"I don't feel sharp," growled Morgan. "Thinkin' o' Flint – I think it were – as done me."

"Ah, well, my son, you praise your stars he's dead," said Silver.

"He were an ugly devil," cried a third pirate, with a shudder, "that blue in the face, too!"

"That was how the rum took him," added Merry. "Blue! Well, I reckon he was blue. That's a true word."

Ever since they had found the skeleton and got upon this train of thought, they had spoken lower and lower, and they had almost got to whispering by now, so that the sound of their talk hardly interrupted the silence of the wood. All of a sudden, out of the middle of the trees in front of us, a thin, high, trembling voice struck up the well-known air and words:

"Fifteen men on the dead man's chest –
Yo-ho-ho, and a bottle of rum!"

I never have seen men more dreadfully affected than the pirates. The colour went from their six faces like enchantment; some leapt to their feet, some clawed hold of others; Morgan grovelled on the ground.

"It's Flint, by—!" cried Merry.

The song had stopped as suddenly as it began – broken off, you would have said, in the middle of a note, as though someone had laid his hand upon the singer's mouth. Coming so far through the clear, sunny atmosphere among the green treetops, I thought it had sounded airily and sweetly; and the effect on my companions was the stranger.

"Come," said Silver, struggling with his ashen lips to get the word out, "this won't do. Stand by to go about. This is a rum start, and I can't name the voice: but it's someone skylarking – someone that's flesh and blood, and you may lay to that."

His courage had come back as he spoke, and some of the colour to his face along with it. Already the others had begun to lend an ear to this encouragement, and were coming a little to themselves, when the same voice broke out again – not this time singing, but in a faint distant hail, that echoed yet fainter among the clefts of the Spyglass.

"Darby M'Graw," it wailed – for that is the word that best describes the sound: "Darby M'Graw! Darby M'Graw!" again and again and again; and then rising a little higher, and with an oath that I leave out, "Fetch aft the rum, Darby!"

The buccaneers remained rooted to the ground, their eyes starting from their heads. Long after the voice had died away they still stared in silence, dreadfully, before them.

"That fixes it!" gasped one. "Let's go."

"They was his last words," moaned Morgan, "his last words above-board."

Dick had his Bible out, and was praying volubly. He had been well brought up, had Dick, before he came to sea and fell among bad companions.

Still, Silver was unconquered. I could hear his teeth rattle in his head; but he had not yet surrendered.

"Nobody in this here island ever heard of Darby," he muttered, "not one but us that's here." And then, making a great effort, "Shipmates," he cried, "I'm here to get that stuff, and I'll not be beat by man nor devil. I never was feared of Flint in his life, and by the powers, I'll face him dead. There's seven hundred thousand pound not a quarter of a mile from here. When did ever a gentleman o' fortune show his stern to that much dollars, for a boozy old seaman with a blue mug – and him dead, too?"

But there was no sign of reawakening courage in his followers; rather indeed of growing terror at the irreverence of his words.

"Belay there, John!" said Merry. "Don't you cross a sperrit."

And the rest were all too terrified to reply. They would have run away severally had they dared; but fear kept them together, and kept them close by John, as if his daring helped them. He, on this part, had pretty well fought his weakness down.

"Sperrit? Well, maybe," he said. "But there's one thing not clear to me. There was an echo. Now, no man ever seen a sperrit with a shadow; well then what's he doing with an echo to him, I should like to know? That ain't in natur', surely?"

This argument seemed weak enough to me. But you can never tell what will affect the superstitious, and to my wonder, George Merry was greatly relieved.

"Well, that's so," he said. "You've a head upon your shoulders, John, and no mistake. 'Bout ship, mates! This here crew is on a wrong tack, I do believe. And come to think on it, it was like Flint's voice, I grant you, but not just so clear-away like it, after all. It was liker somebody else's voice now – it was liker—"

"By the powers, Ben Gunn!" roared Silver.

"Ay, and so it were," cried Morgan, springing on his knees. "Ben Gunn it were!"

"It don't make much odds, do it now?" asked Dick. "Ben Gunn's not here in the body any more 'n Flint."

But the older hands greeted this remark with scorn.

"Why, nobody minds Ben Gunn," cried Merry, "dead or alive, nobody minds him."

It was extraordinary how their spirits had returned, and how the natural colour had revived in their faces. Soon they were chatting together, with intervals of listening; and not long after, hearing no further sound, they shouldered the tools and set forth again, Merry walking first with Silver's compass to keep them on the right line with Skeleton Island. He had said the truth: dead or alive, nobody minded Ben Gunn.

Dick alone still held his Bible, and looked around him as he went, with fearful glances; but he found no sympathy, and Silver even joked him on his precautions.

"I told you," said he, "I told you, you had sp'iled your Bible. If it ain't no good to swear by, what do you suppose a sperrit would give for it? Not that!" and he snapped his big fingers, halting a moment on his crutch.

But Dick was not to be comforted; indeed, it was soon plain to me that the lad was falling sick; hastened by heat, exhaustion and the shock of his alarm, the fever, predicted by Doctor Livesey, was evidently growing swiftly higher.

It was fine open walking, here upon the summit; our way lay a little downhill, for as I have said, the plateau tilted towards the west. The pines, great and small, grew wide apart; and even between the clumps of nutmeg and azalea, wide-open spaces baked in the hot sunshine. Striking, as we did, pretty near north-west across the island, we drew on the one hand ever nearer under the shoulders of the Spyglass, and on the other, looked ever wider over that western bay where I had once tossed and trembled in the coracle.

The first of the tall trees was reached, and by the bearing, proved the wrong one. So with the second. The third rose nearly two hundred feet into the air above a clump of underwood; a giant of a vegetable, with a red column as big as a cottage, and a wide shadow around in which a company could have manoeuvred. It was conspicuous far to sea both on the east and west, and might have been entered as a sailing mark upon the chart.

But it was not its size that now impressed my companions; it was the knowledge that seven hundred thousand pounds in gold lay somewhere buried below its spreading shadow. The thought of the money, as they drew nearer, swallowed up their previous terrors. Their eyes burnt in their heads; their feet grew speedier and lighter; their whole soul was bound up in that fortune, that whole lifetime of extravagance and pleasure, that lay waiting there for each of them.

Silver hobbled, grunting, on his crutch; his nostrils stood out and quivered; he cursed like a madman when the flies settled on his hot and shiny countenance; he plucked furiously at the line that held me to him, and from time to time, turned his eyes upon me with a deadly look. Certainly he took no pains to hide his thoughts; and certainly I read them like print. In the immediate nearness of the gold, all else had been forgotten; his promise and the doctor's warning were both things of the past; and I could not doubt that he hoped to seize upon the treasure, find and board the *Hispaniola* under cover of night, cut every honest throat about that island, and sail away as he had at first intended, laden with crimes and riches.

Shaken as I was with these alarms, it was hard for me to keep up with the rapid pace of the treasure-hunters. Now and again I stumbled; and it was then that Silver plucked so roughly at the rope and launched at me his murderous glances. Dick, who had dropped behind us, and now brought up the rear, was babbling to himself both prayers and curses, as his fever kept rising. This also added to my wretchedness, and to crown all, I was haunted by the thought of the tragedy that had once been acted on that plateau, when that ungodly buccaneer with the blue face – he who died at Savannah, singing and shouting for drink – had there, with his own hand, cut down his six accomplices. This grove, that was now so peaceful, must then have rung with cries,

I thought; and even with the thought I could believe I heard it ringing still.

We were now at the margin of the thicket.

"Huzzah, mates, altogether!" shouted Merry; and the foremost broke into a run.

And suddenly, not ten yards further, we beheld them stop. A low cry arose. Silver doubled his pace, digging away with the foot of his crutch like one possessed; and next moment he and I had come also to a dead halt.

Before us was a great excavation, not very recent, for the sides had fallen in and grass had sprouted on the bottom. In this were the shaft of a pick broken in two and the boards of several packing cases strewn around. On one of these boards I saw, branded with a hot iron, the name *Walrus* – the name of Flint's ship.

All was clear to probation. The cache had been found and rifled: the seven hundred thousand pounds were gone!

# 33

## *The Fall of a Chieftain*

THERE NEVER WAS SUCH AN OVERTURN in this world. Each of these six men was as though he had been struck. But with Silver the blow passed almost instantly. Every thought of his soul had been set full stretch, like a racer, on that money; well, he was brought up in a single second, dead; and he kept his head, found his temper, and changed his plan before the others had had time to realize the disappointment.

"Jim," he whispered, "take that, and stand by for trouble."

And he passed me a double-barrelled pistol.

At the same time he began quietly moving northwards, and in a few steps had put the hollow between us two and the other five. Then he looked at me and nodded, as much as to say, "Here is a narrow corner," as indeed I thought it was. His looks were now quite friendly; and I was so revolted at these constant changes, that I could not forbear whispering, "So you've changed sides again."

There was no time left for him to answer in. The buccaneers, with oaths and cries, began to leap one after another into the pit, and to dig with their fingers, throwing the boards aside as they did so. Morgan found a piece of gold. He held it up with a perfect spout of oaths. It was a two-guinea piece, and it went from hand to hand among them for a quarter of a minute.

"Two guineas!" roared Merry, shaking it at Silver. "That's your seven hundred thousand pounds, is it? You're the man for bargains, ain't you? You're him that never bungled nothing, you wooden-headed lubber!"

"Dig away, boys," said Silver, with the coolest insolence, "you'll find some pignuts and I shouldn't wonder."

"Pignuts!" repeated Merry, in a scream. "Mates, do you hear that? I tell you now, that man there knew it all along. Look in the face of him, and you'll see it wrote there."

"Ah, Merry," remarked Silver, "standing for cap'n again? You're a pushing lad, to be sure."

But this time everyone was entirely in Merry's favour. They began to scramble out of the excavation, darting furious glances behind them. One thing I observed, which looked well for us: they all got out upon the opposite side from Silver.

Well, there we stood, two on one side, five on the other, the pit between us, and nobody screwed up high enough to offer the first blow. Silver never moved; he watched them, very upright on his crutch, and looked as cool as ever I saw him. He was brave, and no mistake.

At last, Merry seemed to think a speech might help matters.

"Mates," says he, "there's two of them alone there; one's the old cripple that brought us all here and blundered us down to this; the other's that cub that I mean to have the heart of. Now, mates—"

He was raising his arm and his voice, and plainly meant to lead a charge. But just then – crack! crack! crack! – three musket-shots flashed out of the thicket. Merry tumbled head foremost into the excavation; the man with the bandage spun round like a teetotum, and fell all his length upon his side, where he lay dead, but still twitching; and the other three turned and ran for it with all their might.

Before you could wink, Long John had fired two barrels of a pistol into the struggling Merry; and as the man rolled up his eyes at him in the last agony, "George," said he, "I reckon I settled you."

At the same moment the doctor, Gray and Ben Gunn joined us, with smoking muskets, from among the nutmeg trees.

"Forwards!" cried the doctor. "Double quick, my lads. We must head 'em off the boats."

And we set off at a great pace, sometimes plunging through the bushes to the chest.

I tell you, but Silver was anxious to keep up with us. The work that man went through, leaping on his crutch till the muscles of his chest were fit to burst, was work no sound man ever equalled; and so thinks the doctor. As it was, he was already thirty yards behind us, and on the verge of strangling, when we reached the brow of the slope.

"Doctor," he hailed, "see there! no hurry!"

Sure enough there was no hurry. In a more open part of the plateau, we could see the three survivors still running in the same direction as they had started, right for Mizzenmast Hill. We were already between them and the boats; and so we four sat down to breathe, while Long John, mopping his face, came slowly up with us.

"Thank ye kindly, Doctor," says he. "You came in in about the nick, I guess, for me and Hawkins. And so it's you, Ben Gunn!" he added. "Well, you're a nice one to be sure."

"I'm Ben Gunn, I am," replied the maroon, wriggling like an eel in his embarrassment. "And," he added, after a long pause, "how do, Mr Silver? Pretty well, I thank ye, says you."

"Ben, Ben," murmured Silver, "to think as you've done me!"

The doctor sent back Gray for one of the pickaxes, deserted, in their flight, by the mutineers; and then as we proceeded leisurely downhill to where the boats were lying, related in a few words what had taken place. It was a story that profoundly interested Silver; and Ben Gunn, the half-idiot maroon, was the hero from beginning to end.

Ben, in his long, lonely wanderings about the island, had found the skeleton – it was he that had rifled it; he had found the treasure; he had dug it up (it was the haft of his pickaxe that lay broken in the excavation); he had carried it on his back, in many weary journeys, from the foot of the tall pine to a cave he had on the two-pointed hill at the north-east angle of the island, and there it had lain stored in safety since two months before the arrival of the *Hispaniola*.

When the doctor had wormed this secret from him on the afternoon of the attack, and when next morning he saw the anchorage deserted, he had gone to Silver, given him the chart, which was now useless – given him the stores, for Ben Gunn's cave was well-supplied with goats' meat salted by himself – given anything and everything to get a chance of moving in safety from the stockade to the two-pointed hill, there to be clear of malaria and keep a guard upon the money.

"As for you, Jim," he said, "it went against my heart, but I did what I thought best for those who had stood by their duty; and if you were not one of these, whose fault was it?"

That morning, finding that I was to be involved in the horrid disappointment he had prepared for the mutineers, he had run all the way to the cave, and leaving the squire to guard the captain, had taken Gray and the maroon, and started making the diagonal across the island, to be at hand beside the pine. Soon, however, he saw that our party had the start of him; and Ben Gunn, being fleet of foot, had been dispatched in front to do his best alone. Then it had occurred to him to work upon the superstitions of his former shipmates; and he was so far successful that Gray and the doctor had come up and were already ambushed before the arrival of the treasure-hunters.

"Ah," said Silver, "it were fortunate for me that I had Hawkins here. You would have let old John be cut to bits, and never given it a thought, Doctor."

"Not a thought," replied Doctor Livesey cheerily.

And by this time we had reached the gigs. The doctor with the pickaxe demolished one of them, and then we all got aboard the other, and set out to go round by sea for North Inlet.

This was a run of eight or nine miles. Silver, though he was almost killed already with fatigue, was set to an oar, like the rest of us, and we were soon skimming swiftly over a smooth sea. Soon we passed out of the straits and doubled the south-east corner of the island, round which, four days ago, we had towed the *Hispaniola*.

As we passed the two-pointed hill, we could see the black mouth of Ben Gunn's cave, and a figure standing by it, leaning on a musket. It was the squire; and we waved a handkerchief and gave him three cheers, in which the voice of Silver joined as heartily as any.

Three miles further, just inside the mouth of North Inlet, what should we meet but the *Hispaniola*, cruising by herself? The last flood had lifted her; and had there been much wind, or a strong tide current, as in the southern anchorage, we should never have found her more, or found her stranded beyond help. As it was, there was little amiss, beyond the wreck of the mainsail. Another anchor was got ready, and dropped in a fathom and a half of water. We all pulled round again to Rum Cove, the nearest point for Ben Gunn's treasure-house; and then Gray, single-handed, returned with the gig to the *Hispaniola*, where he was to pass the night on guard.

A gentle slope ran up from the beach to the entrance of the cave. At the top, the squire met us. To me he was cordial and kind, saying nothing of my escapade, either in the way of blame or praise. At Silver's polite salute he somewhat flushed.

"John Silver," he said, "you're a prodigious villain and impostor – a monstrous impostor, sir. I am told I am not to prosecute you. Well then I will not. But the dead men, sir, hang about your neck like millstones."

"Thank you kindly, sir," replied Long John, again saluting.

"I dare you to thank me!" cried the squire. "It is a gross dereliction of my duty. Stand back."

And thereupon we all entered the cave. It was a large, airy place, with a little spring and a pool of clear water, overhung with ferns. The floor was sand. Before a big fire lay Captain Smollett; and in a far corner, only duskily flickered over by the blaze, I beheld great heaps of coin and quadrilaterals built of bars of gold. That was Flint's treasure that we had come so far to seek, and that had cost already the lives of seventeen men from the *Hispaniola*. How many it had cost in the amassing, what blood and sorrow, what good ships scuttled on the deep, what brave men walking the plank blindfold, what shot of cannon, what shame and lies and cruelty, perhaps no man alive could tell. Yet there were still three upon that island – Silver, and old Morgan, and Ben Gunn – who had each taken his share in these crimes, as each had hoped in vain to share in the reward.

"Come in, Jim," said the captain. "You're a good boy in your line, Jim, but I don't think you and me'll go to sea again. You're too much of the born favourite for me. Is that you, John Silver? What brings you here, man?"

"Come back to my dooty, sir," returned Silver.

"Ah!" said the captain; and that was all he said.

What a supper I had of it that night, with all my friends around me; and what a meal it was, with Ben Gunn's salted goat, and some delicacies and a bottle of old wine from the *Hispaniola*. Never, I am sure, were people gayer or happier. And there was Silver, sitting back almost out of the firelight, but eating heartily, prompt to spring forwards when anything was wanted, even joining quietly in our laughter – the same bland, polite, obsequious seaman of the voyage out.

# 34

## *And Last*

THE NEXT MORNING WE FELL EARLY to work, for the transportation of this great mass of gold near a mile by land to the beach, and thence three miles by boat to the *Hispaniola*, was a considerable task for so small a number of workmen. The three fellows still abroad upon the island did not greatly trouble us; a single sentry on the shoulder of the hill was sufficient to insure us against any sudden onslaught, and we thought, besides, they had had more than enough of fighting.

Therefore the work was pushed on briskly. Gray and Ben Gunn came and went with the boat, while the rest, during their absences, piled treasure on the beach. Two of the bars, slung in a rope's end, made a good load for a grown man – one that he was glad to walk slowly with. For my part, as I was not much use at carrying, I was kept busy all day in the cave packing the minted money into bread-bags.

It was a strange collection, like Billy Bones's hoard for the diversity of coinage, but so much larger and so much more varied that I think I never had more pleasure than in sorting them. English,

French, Spanish, Portuguese, Georges and Louises, doubloons and double guineas and moidores and sequins, the pictures of all the kings of Europe for the last hundred years, strange Oriental pieces stamped with what looked like wisps of string or bits of spider's web, round pieces and square pieces, and pieces bored through the middle, as if to wear them round your neck – nearly every variety of money in the world must, I think, have found a place in that collection; and for number, I am sure they were like autumn leaves, so that my back ached with stooping and my fingers with sorting them out.

Day after day this work went on; by every evening a fortune had been stowed aboard, but there was another fortune waiting for the morrow; and all this time we heard nothing of the three surviving mutineers.

At last – I think it was on the third night – the doctor and I were strolling on the shoulder of the hill where it overlooks the lowlands of the isle, when from out the thick darkness below the wind brought us a noise between shrieking and singing. It was only a snatch that reached our ears, followed by the former silence.

"Heaven forgive them," said the doctor, "'tis the mutineers!"

"All drunk, sir," struck in the voice of Silver from behind us.

Silver, I should say, was allowed his entire liberty, and in spite of daily rebuffs, seemed to regard himself once more as quite a privileged and friendly dependant. Indeed it was remarkable how well he bore these slights, and with what unwearying politeness he kept on trying to ingratiate himself with all. Yet I think none treated him better than a dog; unless it was Ben Gunn, who was still terribly afraid of his old quartermaster, or myself, who had really something to thank him for; although for that matter, I suppose, I had reason to think even worse of him than anybody else, for I had seen him meditating a fresh treachery upon the plateau. Accordingly, it was pretty gruffly that the doctor answered him.

"Drunk or raving," said he.

"Right you were, sir," replied Silver, "and precious little odds which, to you and me."

"I suppose you would hardly ask me to call you a humane man," returned the doctor, with a sneer, "and so my feelings may surprise you, Master Silver. But if I were sure they were raving – as I am morally certain one at least of them is down with fever – I should leave this camp, and at whatever risk to my own carcass, take them the assistance of my skill."

"Ask your pardon, sir, you would be very wrong," quoth Silver. "You would lose your precious life, and you may lay to that. I'm on your side now, hand and glove; and I shouldn't wish for to see the party weakened, let alone yourself, seeing as I know what I owes you. But these men down there, they couldn't keep their word – no, not supposing they wished to; and what's more, they couldn't believe as you could."

"No," said the doctor. "You're the man to keep your word, we know that."

Well, that was about the last news we had of the three pirates. Only once we heard a gunshot a great way off, and supposed them to be hunting. A council was held, and it was decided that we must desert them on the island – to the huge glee, I must say, of Ben Gunn, and with the strong approval of Gray. We left a good stock of powder and shot, the bulk of the salt goat, a few medicines and some other necessaries: tools, clothing, a spare sail, a fathom or two of rope and by the particular desire of the doctor, a handsome present of tobacco.

That was about our last doing on the island. Before that, we had got the treasure stowed, and had shipped enough water and the remainder of the goat meat, in case of any distress; and at last, one fine morning, we weighed anchor, which was about all that we could manage, and stood out of North Inlet, the same colours flying that the captain had flown and fought under at the palisade.

The three fellows must have been watching us closer than we thought for, as we soon had proved. For, coming through the narrows, we had to lie very near the southern point, and there we saw all three of them kneeling together on a spit of sand, with their arms raised in supplication. It went to all our hearts, I think, to leave them in that wretched state; but we could not risk another mutiny; and to take them home for the gibbet would have been a cruel sort of kindness. The doctor hailed them and told them of the stores we had left, and where they were to find them. But they continued to call us by name, and appeal to us, for God's sake, to be merciful, and not leave them to die in such a place.

At last, seeing the ship still bore on her course, and was now swiftly drawing out of earshot, one of them – I know not which it was – leapt to his feet with a hoarse cry, whipped his musket to his shoulder, and sent a shot whistling over Silver's head and through the mainsail.

After that, we kept under cover of the bulwarks, and when next I looked out they had disappeared from the spit, and the spit itself had almost melted out of sight in the growing distance. That was, at least, the end of that; and before noon, to my inexpressible joy, the highest rock of Treasure Island had sunk into the blue round of sea.

We were so short of men that everyone on board had to bear a hand – only the captain lying on a mattress in the stern and giving his orders; for, though greatly recovered, he was still in want of quiet. We laid her head for the nearest port in Spanish America, for we could not risk the voyage home without fresh hands; and as it was, what with baffling winds and a couple of fresh gales, we were all worn out before we reached it.

It was just at sundown when we cast anchor in a most beautiful landlocked gulf, and were immediately surrounded by shore-boats full of negroes, and Mexican Indians, and half-bloods, selling fruits and vegetables, and offering to dive for bits of money. The sight of so many good-humoured faces (especially the blacks), the taste of the tropical fruits, and above all, the lights that began to shine in the town, made a most charming contrast to our dark and bloody sojourn on the island; and the doctor and the squire, taking me along with them, went ashore to pass the early part of the night. Here they met the captain of an English man-o'-war, fell in talk with him, went on board his ship, and in short had so agreeable a time, that day was breaking when we came alongside the *Hispaniola*.

Ben Gunn was on deck alone, and as soon as we came on board, he began, with wonderful contortions, to make us a confession. Silver was gone. The maroon had connived at his escape in a shore-boat some hours ago, and he now assured us he had only done so to preserve our lives, which would certainly have been forfeit if "that man with the one leg had stayed aboard." But this was not all. The sea cook had not gone empty-handed. He had cut through a bulkhead unobserved, and had removed one of the sacks of coin, worth perhaps three or four hundred guineas, to help him on his further wanderings.

I think we were all pleased to be so cheaply quit of him.

Well, to make a long story short, we got a few hands on board, made a good cruise home, and the *Hispaniola* reached Bristol just as Mr Blandly was beginning to think of fitting out her consort. Five men only of those who had sailed returned with her. "Drink and the devil had done for the rest," with a vengeance; although to be sure we were not quite in so bad a case as that other ship they sang about:

"With one man of her crew alive,
What put to sea with seventy-five."

All of us had an ample share of the treasure, and used it wisely or foolishly, according to our natures. Captain Smollett is now retired from the sea. Gray not only saved his money, but being suddenly smit with the desire to rise, also studied his profession; and he is now mate and part owner of a fine full-rigged ship; married besides, and the father of a family. As for Ben Gunn, he got a thousand pounds, which he spent or lost in three weeks, or to be more exact in nineteen days, for he was back begging on the twentieth. Then he was given a lodge to keep, exactly as he had feared upon the island; and he still lives, a great favourite, though something of a butt, with the country boys, and a notable singer in church on Sundays and saints' days.

Of Silver we have heard no more. That formidable seafaring man with one leg has at last gone clean out of my life; but I dare say he met his old Negress, and perhaps still lives in comfort with her and Captain Flint. It is to be hoped so, I suppose, for his chances of comfort in another world are very small.

The bar silver and the arms still lie, for all that I know, where Flint buried them; and certainly they shall lie there for me. Oxen and wain ropes would not bring me back again to that accursed island; and the worst dreams that ever I have are when I hear the surf booming about its coasts, or start upright in bed, with the sharp voice of Captain Flint still ringing in my ears: "Pieces of eight! Pieces of eight!"

# Note on the Text

The text in the present edition is based on the first edition, published in 1883. The spelling and punctuation have been modernized, standardized and made consistent throughout.

# Notes

p. 4, *none of the appearance... skipper*: This suggests that the Captain looked like he belonged to the upper rather than the lower ranks.

p. 6, *Dry Tortugas*: A small group of islands in the Gulf of Mexico, Florida.

p. 6, *Spanish Main*: At the time, Spain owned the coastline around the Caribbean and the Gulf of Mexico – the whole area was known as the Spanish Main.

p. 7, *decline that took him off*: Ill health, of which he died.

p. 15, *A fiddlestick's end*: An archaism: the equivalent of "nonsense!"

p. 16, *die, and go to your own place, like the man in the Bible*: A reference to Judas – see Acts 1:25.

p. 18, *Cain*: Cain was the first murderer in the Bible and is used to describe those causing uproar – see Genesis 4.

p. 18, *I'll shake out another reef... daddle 'em again*: A nautical term which refers to the spreading out of a sail, used to imply that he can outwit, or "daddle", his opponents.

p. 19, *pipe all hands*: Summon men to the deck to work.

p. 32, *Rout the house out*: "To rout" means "to find", so this is an order to the men to search the house thoroughly for Jim and his mother.

p. 33, *hang a leg*: Hesitate; hang back.

p. 35, *get some lead in him*: Be shot.

p. 41, *coral long ago*: The men were sunk with their ship and have become part of the seabed.

p. 46, *Hawke*: Baron Edward Hawke (1705–81), an English Admiral, famous for his victory over the French at the Battle of Quiberon Bay in 1759.

p. 48, *where the wicked cease from troubling*: A direct quote from Job 3:17, which describes the comfort of the grave.

p. 53, *Bow Street Runner*: Forerunners of the modern British police force.

p. 59, *every man jack*: Every single person.

p. 59, *the fable of the mountain and the mouse*: A reference to a fable written by Ambrose Bierce (1842–1914), the American writer best known for *The Devil's Dictionary* (1906).

p. 62, *tip us a stave*: "Sing us a song".

p. 65, *Cap'n England… Malabar*: The pirate Edward England was said to have been involved in raids in the areas of Madagascar and Malabar.

p. 72, *Execution Dock*: The name of a site in Wapping on the banks of the Thames, where pirates were hung for more than four centuries.

p. 100, *Lillibullero*: A satirical ballad directed against the Catholic supporters of King James II, written in around 1688.

p. 101, *dot and carry one*: An old-fashioned term for someone with a limp – as though the heart had a limp: in this instance it's equivalent to "my heart missed a beat".

p. 103, *give a good account of*: Kill.

p. 108, *Carpet bowls*: The meaning here is that shooting the small boat with the cannon would be as easy as playing indoor bowls.

p. 108, *Tell us, squire… water*: Tell us when you've fixed on your target, and we'll stay still and stop rowing.

p. 123, *Come, Lasses and Lads*: A traditional song, dating from around 1670.

p. 133, *Five against… to bear*: The mutineers were soon only eight in number, for the man shot by Mr Trelawney on board the schooner died that same evening of his wound. But this was, of course, not known till after by the faithful party. (STEVENSON'S NOTE)

p. 159, *settling his hash*: Killing him.

p. 181, *vally bullying a marlinspike*: This probably means "value [appreciate] bullying at all" – a marlinspike is a small pointed metal tool used by sailors to separate strands of rope or wire.

# APPENDIX

# My First Book: Treasure Island

*Stevenson's essay on* Treasure Island *was published in* The Idler, *VI (August 1894)*

I T WAS FAR INDEED FROM BEING my first book, for I am not a novelist alone. But I am well aware that my paymaster, the great public, regards what else I have written with indifference, if not aversion; if it call upon me at all, it calls on me in the familiar and indelible character; and when I am asked to talk of my first book, no question in the world but what is meant is my first novel.

Sooner or later, somehow, anyhow, I was bound to write a novel. It seems vain to ask why. Men are born with various manias: from my earliest childhood, it was mine to make a plaything of imaginary series of events; and as soon as I was able to write, I became a good friend to the paper-makers. Reams upon reams must have gone to the making of 'Rathillet', 'The Pentland Rising', 'The King's Pardon' (otherwise 'Park Whitehead'), 'Edward Daven', 'A Country Dance' and 'A Vendetta in the West'; and it is consolatory to remember that these reams are now all ashes, and have been received again into the soil. I have named but a few of my ill-fated efforts, only such indeed as came to a fair bulk ere they were desisted from; and even so they cover a long vista of years. 'Rathillet' was attempted before fifteen, 'The Vendetta' at twenty-nine, and the succession of defeats lasted unbroken till I was thirty-one. By that time, I had written little books and little essays and

short stories; and had got patted on the back and paid for them –
though not enough to live upon. I had quite a reputation, I was the
successful man; I passed my days in toil, the futility of which would
sometimes make my cheek to burn – that I should spend a man's
energy upon this business, and yet could not earn a livelihood: and
still there shone ahead of me an unattained ideal: although I had
attempted the thing with vigour not less than ten or twelve times,
I had not yet written a novel. All – all my pretty ones – had gone
for a little, and then stopped inexorably like a schoolboy's watch.
I might be compared to a cricketer of many years' standing who
should never have made a run. Anybody can write a short story – a
bad one, I mean – who has industry and paper and time enough;
but not everyone may hope to write even a bad novel. It is the length
that kills. The accepted novelist may take his novel up and put it
down, spend days upon it in vain, and write not any more than
he makes haste to blot. Not so the beginner. Human nature has
certain rights; instinct – the instinct of self-preservation – forbids
that any man (cheered and supported by the consciousness of no
previous victory) should endure the miseries of unsuccessful literary toil beyond a period to be measured in weeks. There must be
something for hope to feed upon. The beginner must have a slant
of wind, a lucky vein must be running, he must be in one of those
hours when the words come and the phrases balance of themselves
– *even to begin*. And having begun, what a dread looking forward
is that until the book shall be accomplished! For so long a time,
the slant is to continue unchanged, the vein to keep running, for
so long a time you must keep at command the same quality of
style: for so long a time your puppets are to be always vital, always
consistent, always vigorous! I remember I used to look, in those
days, upon every three-volume novel with a sort of veneration, as
a feat – not possibly of literature – but at least of physical and
moral endurance and the courage of Ajax.

In the fated year I came to live with my father and mother at Kinnaird, above Pitlochry. Then I walked on the red moors and by the side of the golden burn; the rude, pure air of our mountains inspirited, if it did not inspire us, and my wife and I projected a joint volume of bogey stories, for which she wrote 'The Shadow on the Bed', and I turned out 'Thrawn Janet' and a first draft of 'The Merry Men'. I love my native air, but it does not love me; and the end of this delightful period was a cold, a fly-blister, and a migration by Strathairdle and Glenshee to the Castelton of Braemar. There it blew a good deal and rained in a proportion; my native air was more unkind than man's ingratitude, and I must consent to pass a good deal of my time between four walls in a house lugubriously known as the "late Miss McGregor's cottage". And now admire the finger of predestination. There was a schoolboy in the "late Miss McGregor's cottage" home for the holidays, and much in want of "something craggy to break his mind upon." He had no thought of literature; it was the art of Raphael that received his fleeting suffrages; and with the aid of pen and ink and a shilling box of watercolours, he had soon turned one of the rooms into a picture gallery. My more immediate duty towards the gallery was to be showman; but I would sometimes unbend a little, join the artist (so to speak) at the easel, and pass the afternoon with him in a generous emulation, making coloured drawings. On one of these occasions, I made the map of an island; it was elaborately and (I thought) beautifully coloured; the shape of it took my fancy beyond expression; it contained harbours that pleased me like sonnets; and with the unconsciousness of the predestined, I ticketed my performance "Treasure Island". I am told there are people who do not care for maps, and find it hard to believe. The names, the shapes of the woodlands, the courses of the roads and rivers, the prehistoric footsteps of man still distinctly traceable uphill and down dale, the mills and the ruins, the ponds and the ferries, perhaps the standing stone or the druidic circle on the heath; here is an inexhaustible fund of interest for any man with eyes to see or twopenceworth of imagination to understand with! No child but must remember laying his head in the grass, staring into the infinitesimal forest and seeing it grow populous with fairy armies. Somewhat in this way, as I paused upon my map of "Treasure Island", the future character of the book began to appear there visibly among imaginary woods; and their brown faces and bright weapons peeped out upon me from unexpected quarters as they passed to and fro, fighting and hunting treasure, on these few square inches of a flat projection. The next thing I knew I had some papers before me and was writing out a list of chapters. How often have I done so, and the thing gone no further! But there seemed elements of success about this enterprise. It was to be a story for boys; no need of psychology or fine writing; and I had a boy at hand to be a touchstone. Women were excluded. I was unable to handle a brig (which the *Hispaniola* should have been), but I thought I could make shift to sail her as a schooner without public shame. And then I had an idea for John Silver from which I promised myself funds of entertainment; to take an admired friend of mine (whom the reader very likely knows and admires as much as I do), to deprive him of all his finer qualities and higher graces of temperament, to leave him with nothing but his strength, his courage, his quickness and his magnificent geniality, and to try to express these in terms of the culture of a raw tarpaulin. Such psychical surgery is, I think, a common way of "making character"; perhaps it is indeed the only way. We can put in the quaint figure that spoke a hundred words with us yesterday by the wayside; but do we know him? Our friend, with his infinite variety and flexibility, we know – but can we put him in? Upon the first, we must engraft secondary and imaginary qualities, possibly all wrong; from the second, knife in hand, we must cut away and deduct the needless arborescence of his nature, but the trunk and the few branches that remain we may at least be fairly sure of.

On a chill September morning, by the cheek of a brisk fire, and the rain drumming on the window, I began *The Sea Cook*, for that was the original title. I have begun (and finished) a number of other books, but I cannot remember to have sat down to one of them with more complacency. It is not to be wondered at, for stolen waters are proverbially sweet. I am now upon a painful chapter. No doubt the parrot once belonged to Robinson Crusoe. No doubt the skeleton is conveyed from Poe. I think little of these, they are trifles and details; and no man can hope to have a monopoly of skeletons or make a corner in talking birds. The stockade, I am told, is from *Masterman Ready*. It may be, I care not a jot. These useful writers had fulfilled the poet's saying: departing, they had left behind them footprints on the sands of time, footprints which perhaps another – and I was the other! It is my debt to Washington Irving that exercises my conscience, and justly so, for I believe plagiarism was rarely carried further. I chanced to pick up the *Tales of a Traveller* some years ago with a view to an anthology of prose narrative, and the book flew up and struck me: Billy Bones, his chest, the company in the parlour, the whole inner spirit and a good deal of the material detail of my first chapters – all were there, all were the property of Washington Irving. But I had no guess of it then as I sat writing by the fireside, in what seemed the springtides of a somewhat pedestrian inspiration; nor yet day by day, after lunch, as I read aloud my morning's work to the family. It seemed to me original as sin; it seemed to belong to me like my right eye. I had counted on one boy, I found I had two in my audience. My father caught fire at once with all the romance and childishness of his original nature. His own stories, that every night of his life he put himself to sleep with, dealt perpetually with ships, roadside inns, robbers, old sailors and commercial travellers before the era of steam. He never finished one of these romances; the lucky man did not require to! But in *Treasure Island* he recognized something kindred to his own imagination; it was *his* kind of picturesque; and he not only heard with delight the daily chapter, but set himself acting to collaborate. When the time came for Billy Bones's chest to be ransacked, he must have passed the better part of a day preparing, on the back of a legal envelope, an inventory of its contents, which I exactly followed; and the name of "Flint's old ship" – the *Walrus* – was given at his particular request. And now who should come dropping in, *ex machina*, but Dr Japp, like the disguised prince who is to bring down the curtain upon peace and happiness in the last act; for he carried in his pocket, not a horn or a talisman, but a publisher – had in fact been charged by my old friend, Mr Henderson, to unearth new writers for *Young Folks*. Even the ruthlessness of a united family recoiled before the extreme measure of inflicting on our guest the mutilated members of *The Sea Cook*; at the same time, we would by no means stop our readings; and accordingly the tale was begun again at the beginning, and solemnly redelivered for the benefit of Dr Japp. From that moment on, I have thought highly of his critical faculty; for when he left us, he carried away the manuscript in his portmanteau.

Here then was everything to keep me up: sympathy, help, and now a positive engagement. I had chosen besides a very easy style. Compare it with the almost contemporary *Merry Men*; one reader may prefer the one style, one the other: 'tis an affair of character, perhaps of mood; but no expert can fail to see that the one is much more difficult, and the other much easier to maintain. It seems as though a full-grown experienced man of letters might engage to turn out *Treasure Island* at so many pages a day, and keep his pipe alight. But alas! this was not my case. Fifteen days I stuck to it, and turned out fifteen chapters; and then, in the early paragraphs of the sixteenth, ignominiously lost hold. My mouth was empty; there was not one word of *Treasure Island* in my bosom; and here were the proofs of the beginning already waiting me at the "Hand and Spear"! Then I corrected them, living for the most part alone, walking on the heath at Weybridge in dewy autumn mornings, a good deal pleased with what I had done, and more appalled than I can depict to you in words at what remained for me to do. I was thirty one; I was the head of a family; I had lost my health; I had never yet paid my way, never yet made £200 a year; my father had quite recently bought back and cancelled a book that was judged a failure: was this to be another and last fiasco? I was indeed very close on despair; but I shut my mouth hard, and during the journey to Davos, where I was to pass the winter, had the resolution to think of other things and bury myself in the novels of M. de Boisgobey. Arrived at my destination, down I sat one morning to the unfinished tale; and behold! it flowed from me like small talk; and in a second tide of delighted industry, and again at a rate of a chapter a day, I finished *Treasure Island*. It had to be transcribed almost exactly; my wife was ill; the schoolboy remained alone of the faithful; and John Addington Symonds (to whom I timidly mentioned what I was engaged on) looked on me askance. He was at that time very eager I should write on *The Characters* of Theophrastus: so far out may be the judgements of the wisest men. But Symonds (to be sure) was scarce the confidant to go to for sympathy on a boy's story. He was large-minded, "a full man", if there was one; but the very name of my enterprise would suggest to him only capitulations of sincerity and solecisms of style. Well! he was not far wrong.

*Treasure Island* – it was Mr Henderson who deleted the first title, *The Sea Cook* – appeared duly in the story paper, where it figured in the ignoble midst, without woodcuts, and attracted not the least attention. I did not care. I liked the tale myself, for much the same reason as my father liked the beginning: it was my kind of picturesque. I was not a little proud of John Silver, also; and to this day rather admire that smooth and formidable adventurer. What was infinitely more exhilarating, I had passed a landmark; I had finished a tale, and written "The End" upon my manuscript, as I had not done since 'The Pentland Rising', when I was a boy of sixteen not yet at college. In truth it was so by a set of lucky accidents; had not Dr Japp come on his visit, had not the tale flowed from me with singular ease, it must have been laid aside like its predecessors, and found a circuitous and unlamented way to the fire. Purists may suggest it would have been better so. I am not of that mind. The tale seems to have given much pleasure, and it brought (or was the means of bringing) fire and food and wine to a deserving family in which I took an interest. I need scarcely say I mean my own.

But the adventures of *Treasure Island* are not yet quite at an end. I had written it up to the map. The map was the chief part of my plot. For instance, I had called an islet "Skeleton Island", not knowing what I meant, seeking only for the immediate pictur- esque, and it was to justify this name that I broke into the gallery of Mr Poe and stole Flint's pointer. And in the same way, it was because I had made two harbours that the *Hispaniola* was sent on her wanderings with Israel Hands. The time came when it was decided to republish, and I sent in my manuscript, and the map along with it, to Messrs Cassell. The proofs came, they were cor- rected, but I heard nothing of the map. I wrote and asked; was told it had never been received, and sat aghast. It is one thing to draw a map at random, set a scale in one corner of it at a venture, and write up a story to the measurements. It is quite another to have to examine a whole book, make an inventory of all the allusions contained in it, and with a pair of compasses painfully design a map to suit the data. I did it; and the map was drawn again in my father's office, with embellishments of blowing whales and

sailing ships, and my father himself brought into service a knack
he had of various writing, and elaborately *forged* the signature
of Captain Flint, and the sailing directions of Billy Bones. But
somehow it was never "Treasure Island" to me.

I have said the map was the most of the plot. I might almost
say it was the whole. A few reminiscences of Poe, Defoe and
Washington Irving, a copy of Johnson's *Buccaneers*, the name
of the dead man's chest from Kingsley's *At Last*, some recollec-
tions of canoeing on the high seas, and the map itself, with its
infinite, eloquent suggestion, made up the whole of my materials.
It is, perhaps, not often that a map figures so largely in a tale, yet
it is always important. The author must know his countryside,
whether real or imaginary, like his hand; the distances, the points
of the compass, the place of the sun's rising, the behaviour of
the moon, should all be beyond cavil. And how troublesome the
moon is! I have come to grief over the moon in *Prince Otto*, and
so soon as that was pointed out to me, adopted a precaution
which I recommend to other men – I never write now without an
almanac. With an almanac, and the map of the country, and the
plan of every house, either actually plotted on paper or already
and immediately apprehended in the mind, a man may hope to
avoid some of the grossest possible blunders. With the map before
him, he will scarce allow the sun to set in the east, as it does in
*The Antiquary*. With the almanac at hand, he will scarce allow
two horsemen, journeying on the most urgent affair, to employ six
days, from three of the Monday morning till late in the Saturday
night, upon a journey of, say, ninety or a hundred miles, and before
the week is out, and still on the same nags, to cover fifty in one
day, as may be read at length in the inimitable novel of *Rob Roy*.
And it is certainly well, though far from necessary, to avoid such
"croppers." But it is my contention – my superstition, if you like
– that who is faithful to his map, and consults it, and draws from

it his inspiration daily and hourly, gains positive support, and not mere negative immunity from accident. The tale has a root there; it grows in that soil; it has a spine of its own behind the words. Better if the country be real, and he has walked every foot of it and knows every milestone. But even with imaginary places, he will do well in the beginning to provide a map; as he studies it, relations will appear that he had not thought upon; he will discover obvious, though unsuspected, short cuts and footprints for his messengers; and even when a map is not all the plot, as it was in *Treasure Island*, it will be found to be a mine of suggestion.

# The Persons of the Tale

*This interlude to the action of* Treasure Island *was published posthumously in* Longman's Magazine *in 1895, and collected together with other stories in* Fables *in 1896.*

AFTER THE 32ND CHAPTER of *Treasure Island*, two of the puppets strolled out to have a pipe before business should begin again, and met in an open place not far from the story.

"Good morning, Cap'n," said the first, with a man-o'-war salute and a beaming countenance.

"Ah, Silver!" grunted the other. "You're in a bad way, Silver."

"Now, Cap'n Smollett," remonstrated Silver, "dooty is dooty, as I knows, and none better; but we're off dooty now; and I can't see no call to keep up the morality business."

"You're a damned rogue, my man," said the Captain.

"Come, come, Cap'n, be just," returned the other. "There's no call to be angry with me in earnest. I'm on'y a chara'ter in a sea story. I don't really exist."

"Well, I don't really exist either," says the Captain, "which seems to meet that."

"I wouldn't set no limits to what a virtuous chara'ter might consider argument," responded Silver. "But I'm the villain of this tale, I am; and speaking as one seafaring man to another, what I want to know is, what's the odds?"

"Were you never taught your catechism?" said the Captain. "Don't you know there's such a thing as an Author?"

"Such a thing as a Author?" returned John derisively. "And who better'n me? And the p'int is, if the Author made you, he made Long John, and he made Hands, and Pew, and George Merry – not that George is up to much, for he's little more'n a name; and he made Flint, what there is of him; and he made this here mutiny, you keep such a work about; and he had Tom Redruth shot; and – well, if that's an Author, give me Pew!"

"Don't you believe in a future state?" said Smollett. "Do you think there's nothing but the present story-paper?"

"I don't rightly know for that," said Silver, "and I don't see what it's got to do with it anyway. What I know is this: if there is sich a thing as a Author, I'm his favourite chara'ter. He does me fathoms better'n he does you – fathoms, he does. And he likes doing me. He keeps me on deck mostly all the time, crutch and all; and he leaves you measling in the hold, where nobody can't see you, nor wants to, and you may lay to that! If there is an Author, by thunder, but he's on my side, and you may lay to it!"

"I see he's giving you a long rope," said the Captain. "But that can't change a man's convictions. I know the author respects me; I feel it in my bones; when you and I had that talk at the blockhouse door, who do you think he was for, my man?"

"And don't he respect me?" cried Silver. "Ah, you should 'a' heard me putting down my mutiny, George Merry and Morgan and that lot, no longer ago'n last chapter; you'd 'a' heard something then! You'd 'a' seen what the Author thinks o' me! But come now, do you consider yourself a virtuous chara'ter clean through?"

"God forbid!" said Captain Smollett solemnly. "I am a man that tries to do his duty, and makes a mess of it as often as not. I'm not a very popular man at home, Silver, I'm afraid," and the Captain sighed.

"Ah," says Silver. "Then how about this sequel of yours? Are you to be Cap'n Smollett just the same as ever, and not very popular at home, says you! And if so, why it's *Treasure Island* over again, by thunder; and I'll be Long John, and Pew'll be Pew; and we'll have another mutiny, as like as not. Or are you to be somebody else? And if so, why, what the better are you? And what the worse am I?"

"Why, look here, my man," returned the Captain, "I can't understand how this story comes about at all, can I? I can't see how you and I, who don't exist, should get to speaking here, and smoke our pipes, for all the world like reality? Very well, then, who am I to pipe up with my opinions? I know the Author's on the side of good; he tells me so, it runs out of his pen as he writes. Well, that's all I need to know; I'll take my chance upon the rest."

"It's a fact he seemed to be against George Merry," Silver admitted musingly. "But George is little more'n a name at the best of it," he added, brightening. "And to get into soundings for once. What is this good? I made a mutiny, and I been a gentleman o' fortune; well, but by all stories, you ain't no such saint. I'm a man that keeps company very easy; even by your own account, you ain't, and to my certain knowledge, you're a devil to haze. Which is which? Which is good, and which bad? Ah, you tell me that! Here we are in stays, and you may lay to it!"

"We're none of us perfect," replied the Captain. "That's a fact of religion, my man. All I can say is, I try to do my duty; and if you try to do yours, I can't compliment you on your success."

"And so you was the judge, was you?" said Silver derisively.

"I would be both judge and hangman for you, my man, and never turn a hair," returned the Captain. "But I get beyond that: it mayn't be sound theology, but it's common sense that what is good is useful too – or there and thereabout, for I don't set up to be a thinker. Now, where would a story go to, if there were no virtuous characters?"

"If you go to that," replied Silver, "where would a story begin, if there wasn't no villains?"

"Well, that's pretty much my thought," said Captain Smollett. "The author has to get a story; that's what he wants; and to get a story, and to have a man like the doctor (say) given a proper chance, he has to put in men like you and Hands. But he's on the right side; and you mind your eye! You're not through this story yet; there's trouble coming for you."

"What'll you bet?" asked John.

"Much I care if there ain't," returned the Captain. "I'm glad enough to be Alexander Smollett, bad as he is; and I thank my stars upon my knees that I'm not Silver. But there's the ink bottle opening. To quarters!"

And indeed the author was just then beginning to write the words:

Chapter 33

# EXTRA MATERIAL
## FOR YOUNG READERS

# THE WRITER

Robert Louis Stevenson was born on 13th November 1850 in
Edinburgh. His full name at birth was Robert *Lewis* Balfour
Stevenson, but when he was eighteen he changed the spelling to
Louis, and a few years later he dropped the Balfour. His was a
comfortable, upper-middle-class childhood, based in the grand
eighteenth-century town houses of Edinburgh's New Town area.
His grandfather, Robert Stevenson, had been a renowned lighthouse engineer whose three sons also became highly respected
lighthouse engineers – including Thomas Stevenson, Robert's
father. Robert's mother, Margaret Balfour (whose grandfather, by
coincidence, was also a lighthouse engineer), was of the gentry –
the daughter of a minister in the Church of Scotland in the nearby
suburb of Colinton. Robert spent long holidays staying with this
grandfather throughout his childhood.

Robert often suffered from poor health. Both his mother and
his maternal grandfather had weak chests that made them prone
to coughs, colds and fevers, and Robert was just the same. The
cold and damp Edinburgh winters often affected him badly – no
one is sure which ailment he suffered from, but it was likely to
have been something like tuberculosis or bronchiectasis. Whatever
it was, it blighted him with poor health for the rest of his life.

He was sent to several local schools during his childhood, but
often not for very long, because he would fall ill. This meant
that much of his childhood education was received at home from

private tutors. When he was bed-bound, his fiercely religious nanny, known as Cummy, would read to him from the Bible and from John Bunyan's religious work, *Pilgrim's Progress*. Being confined to bed when young often leads to a love of reading and writing, and Robert showed great promise from a very early age, writing stories throughout his childhood. His father took great pride in these stories, even paying for the publication of one of them when Robert was sixteen.

Robert's health improved for a short spell around 1864, and he spent a few years at a private school in Edinburgh until 1867, when he went to Edinburgh University to study Engineering – he was supposed to become yet another Stevenson lighthouse engineer. Throughout his studies, however, he devoted far more time and energy to his interests in the arts. His father could not have been very surprised when, in 1871, after spending four years as a very poor engineering student, Robert informed him that he intended to construct stories, not lighthouses. Because writing is a precarious profession, Robert agreed to study Law as a back-up. But, as with his engineering studies, he spent more time writing and travelling than studying. He did manage to graduate as a lawyer, however, in 1875. His father proudly attached a brass plaque to the family home – "R.L. Stevenson, Advocate". It probably wasn't polished very often, as Robert, true to form, never practised his profession. He was far too busy writing and making literary connections on his many travels.

Travelling was a great passion of his, which he would indulge in throughout his university holidays – travels with his father, visiting family-built lighthouses across the Scottish coastline, travels to France in pursuit of a better climate for his weak chest, visits to London to seek out like-minded writers. As he gained more experience of less conventional kinds of people – artists' colonies in France, literary hustlers in London – he became less conventional himself, wearing his hair long and ignoring the rigid etiquette of, for example, formal dress at dinner. He was beginning to find out who he was.

Around 1873, while still a law student, Robert was paid for the first time for a piece of writing – an essay called 'Roads' in a journal called *Portfolio*. He was writing many short pieces during this time, and one of them, published in the prestigious *Cornhill Magazine*, was titled 'On Falling in Love'. This article came about following a canoe trip across Belgium and France (which was to be written about five years later in his first book-length work, *An Inland Voyage*), where he met Fanny Van de Grift Osbourne at the artists' colony of Grez, fifty miles south of Paris. Ten years older than Robert – American, married and the mother of three children – Fanny was separated from her husband because of his affairs with other women. It seems that Robert fell in love with her at their first meeting, though they didn't see each other again until 1877, when they finally got together. They spent much of the next year together, to the great disapproval of Robert's parents. Finally, Fanny returned to her husband in America.

To help him come to terms with Fanny's departure, Robert embarked on a solo hiking trip through the impoverished areas of the Cévennes mountains in south-west France, an adventure which led to his book *Travels with a Donkey in the Cévennes*. But a year later, without telling his parents, he set off to America to be near her. Travelling second-class, and then travelling over land by train from New York to California, the journey broke his fragile health, and he was completely incapacitated when he finally arrived. Fanny was still with her husband, and so Robert endured a difficult year alone – writing on demand for very little reward – at the end of which his health broke again, and he was close to death. By this time, Fanny was divorced. She came to see him, nursed him and, in May 1880, when he was still "a mere complication of cough and bones", they married. In August they travelled with one of Fanny's sons to Britain, where his parents came to accept the marriage and Fanny.

The first seven years of his marriage produced the classic novels that Robert Louis Stevenson is most revered and remembered for: *Treasure Island*, *Kidnapped* and *Strange Case of Dr Jekyll and Mr Hyde*. The success of these books made him a wealthy man. Also during this period came other important works, such as *The Black Arrow* and two volumes of poetry. He settled wherever he thought the climate or the air might benefit his health – Bournemouth, France, Switzerland – but didn't venture further afield until his father died in 1888. His doctor then prescribed a complete change of climate. Robert and his family, together with his mother, set sail for America and spent the winter in the Adirondack Mountains, in the state of New York.

The next years saw some of his most far-flung travels – all with his family in tow. He chartered yachts, the first being the *Casco*, and spent three years sailing the Pacific, often stopping for long stays on different islands – the Hawaiian Islands, Tahiti, the Gilbert Islands, the Samoan Islands – all the time writing fiction, non-fiction and poetry, including the travel book *In the South Seas* and the novel *The Master of Ballantrae*. The party also visited Australia and New Zealand.

In April 1890, Robert made his final long voyage, travelling from Sydney in Australia to the Samoan Islands once more. Here, on the island of Upolu, he purchased a large tract of land near the village of Vailima and built a house. He was given the Samoan name Tusitala, meaning "teller of tales", and was a popular figure, becoming a champion of the Samoan people and getting involved in island politics. During this time he exhausted himself, but – as usual – completed many literary works. None of them were his best work, however, and he worried that his spark of genius had gone out. Then he began writing a novel, *The Weir of Hermiston*. He thought of it as his masterpiece, and many commentators today agree. However, it was never completed. On 3rd December 1894, chatting to Fanny while opening a bottle of wine, he collapsed. Within a few hours he was dead. He was only forty-four years old.

## THE BOOK

*Treasure Island*, a rumbustious adventure story for children (though much enjoyed by adults too) about cut-throat pirates and buried treasure, is set in an unspecified period of the 1700s. At first glance, the story may seem overly fantastical, but in the early 1700s piracy had been rampant on the high seas. Thousands of pirates were plundering the mercantile ships setting sail between the great powers. Real-life pirates mentioned in *Treasure Island* include William Kidd, Blackbeard and Edward England. Kidd was certainly known to have buried treasure on an island – Gardiners Island, off Long Island in the state of New York. For all these reasons, the subject matter of pirates, islands, shipwrecks and treasure was appealing to readers, as Robert Louis Stevenson would have known very well from reading books such as Sir Walter Scott's *The Pirate* (1822) or tales such as Edgar Allan Poe's 'The Gold-Bug' (1843).

Robert wrote his pirate tale while mostly confined to bed because of poor health. His other best-known books – *Kidnapped* and *Strange Case of Dr Jekyll and Mr Hyde* – were also written while propped up on the pillows. The origin of the book lies in a rainy day spent with his stepson: to keep the boy entertained, they drew a map of an imaginary island together, after which Robert started to compose a story to bring the map to life. It wasn't long since Robert had returned from America with Fanny as his wife, after all his adventures, mishaps and near-death illnesses, and it was as though all these extreme ups and downs needed to be expressed in a wild rollercoaster of a story. He completed the first fifteen chapters in fifteen days, but then had to pause because of weakness and exhaustion. A short while later, while recuperating in London, he began work again. His father read the draft and was wildly enthusiastic about its page-turning appeal. He took a keen interest in the story's progress, and contributed to the plot during intense father-son discussions. The most memorable character in *Treasure Island* – the one-legged pirate Long John Silver – was possibly inspired by a friend, the poet W.E. Henley, though shorn of "all his finer qualities and higher graces of temperament, and to leave him with nothing but his strength, his courage, his quickness and his magnificent geniality".

Robert's original idea for the title of the book was *The Sea Cook,* because Long John Silver hides his piratical history under the guise of being a ship's cook. Only a month after beginning the story, the first chapters of *The Sea Cook* were published in a magazine called *Young Folks.* The whole book was issued in serial form in this way from October 1881 to January 1882, after which it was published in book form with the new title, *Treasure Island.* It was the author's first big success, both in terms of sales and critical reception, and established him as a celebrity among authors. By the end of the decade, *Treasure Island* was a much loved classic.

If *Treasure Island* has had a slightly smaller influence on popular culture than, say, *Strange Case of Dr Jekyll and Mr Hyde,* this is probably because the latter, as with Bram Stoker's *Dracula* and Mary Shelley's *Frankenstein,* creates a new kind of being which can be imagined in other environments and stories by subsequent storytellers – in fiction, film and other media. Nevertheless, the long-lasting appeal of *Treasure Island* is indisputable. Never out of print since it was first published, it has been translated into many languages, from Swedish to Swahili, and can boast scores of adaptations made for film, television and radio, including a silent movie in 1918 and the 2002 Walt Disney animation *Treasure Planet,* which reimagines the story in space with a cast of cyborgs and aliens.

## CHARACTERS

### Jim Hawkins

Jim, the teenage son of the innkeepers of the Admiral Benbow in Bristol, is the hero of the story and its main narrator. When an old seaman, Billy Bones, visits the inn and dies there, Jim finds a mysterious map in the old man's chest. This is the beginning of an adventure that will take him halfway across the world in search of treasure and reveal his best qualities – bravery, humanity and a spirit of adventure – as he strives to defeat Long John Silver's mutinous crew and to secure the hidden treasure for those who really deserve it.

### Mrs Hawkins

The whole adventure would never have happened unless Mrs Hawkins, Jim's mother, had insisted on opening Billy Bones's chest in order to look for money she was owed.

### Billy Bones

An old pirate on dry land at the end of his career, Billy Bones is laying low and hiding from other pirates because of the treasure map in his chest, which he wants to keep to himself. He drinks a lot and exhibits scary behaviour, but he is kind to young Jim too.

### Black Dog

An old shipmate of Billy Bones, the arrival of this pirate at the Admiral Benbow makes Billy Bones realize that his hiding place is no longer secure.

## Pew

Another pirate from Billy Bones's past, Pew comes sniffing around the Admiral Benbow trying to ambush Billy Bones and secure the map. A very violent and unpleasant man, Pew meets the end he deserves when he is later deserted by his "friends" and trampled by a horse.

## Dr Livesey

A local doctor and magistrate, Dr Livesey is a steady, rational, fearless man who is one of the treasure-seeking party. He is extremely fair-minded, and treats wounded pirates with as much care as his own wounded men. At times he is something of a father figure to Jim Hawkins.

## Squire Trelawney

The Squire, young Jim Hawkins and Dr Livesey make up the three main "good" characters who determine to find the treasure island shown on Billy Bones's map. He finances the endeavour and buys their ship, the *Hispaniola*. Fiercely patriotic and good-hearted, he is also quite gullible, and it is his foolishness which results in the treasure-hunting party hiring a bunch of murderous pirates as crew.

## Tom Redruth

Tom is one of three servants (the others being Richard Joyce and John Hunter) whom Squire Trelawney takes with him on the voyage to the island. A faithful, if grumpy fellow, his death at the hands of the pirates is the cause of great grief to the Squire.

## Captain Smollett

Skipper of the *Hispaniola*, Smollett has to deal with half his crew being inexperienced landlubbers, and the rest being cut-throat pirates waiting for the right moment to mutiny. No wonder he's in a bad mood. A rigid disciplinarian, his lack of flexibility in dealing with the pirates contrasts with Jim Hawkins's more imaginative actions.

### Mr Arrow

Captain Smollett's second-in-command, Mr Arrow, seems to be permanently drunk, and therefore not the best first mate a captain ever employed. It transpires that the secret pirate crew are supplying Mr Arrow with alcohol in order to neutralize him. Mr Arrow disappears – presumed to have fallen overboard while drunk, although there is also the possibility that he was pushed over by the pirates.

### Abraham Gray and Dick Johnson

These two hands on the *Hispaniola* suffer different fates, according to the choices they make. Dick Johnson doesn't resist the villainous piracy of Long John Silver, and so becomes corrupted by it. At the end of the novel he is marooned with the surviving pirates, fearful and feverish. Abraham Gray, on the other hand, despite being on his first voyage, has the strength of mind to throw in his lot with Captain Smollett rather than with Long John Silver, and wins a share of the recovered treasure.

### Long John Silver

The most vividly painted character in the story is Long John Silver – with one leg, a parrot and the capacity for both extreme violence and cunning charm. He has come to represent everyone's idea of what a pirate looks like and how he behaves. The secret leader of the pirate crew of the *Hispaniola*, he is taken on as the ship's cook. As adventurous, brave, and at times as appealing as Jim Hawkins, he is in many ways Jim's alter ego – a bad version of Jim – which perhaps explains why there is a grudging respect, and even a sense of affection between the two, despite their mortal enmity.

### Israel Hands

Coxswain of the *Hispaniola*, and the secret second-in-command of Long John Silver, Hands is both skilful and reckless. In one of the most tense episodes of the story, he and Jim, alone on the *Hispaniola*, reluctantly have to cooperate in order to beach the vessel, rather than let it drift away with them on it.

### Ben Gunn

Ben Gunn is one of the more complex characters in *Treasure Island*. A crew member of another great pirate, Captain Flint, he was deliberately abandoned on the island three years earlier. Somehow he has survived, but he is almost famous in the pirate world for being poor company, and Long John Silver's pirates have no time or respect for him. But what they don't know is that Gunn has found the treasure. He does a deal with Dr Livesey and friends – one thousand pounds and a berth back to England in exchange for revealing the treasure's location.

## FAMOUS PIRATES IN HISTORY

The golden age of piracy was from around 1660 to 1730. Pirates were a rampant peril in different places, such as around the Caribbean and eastern Pacific, where Spanish vessels were commonly targeted, and in the Indian Ocean towards the end of the period, when Muslim sailors and East India vessels were attacked in the Indian Ocean. Several of the best-known pirates have entered folklore, sometimes becoming almost unrecognizable in the process. What do we know of the real people behind the myths that have grown up around them?

## William Kidd (1645–1701)

Scotsman Captain Kidd should never have become a pirate. A respectable citizen of the new city of New York that was expanding on the west coast of North America, he started off in the privateering business – that is to say, he was employed to protect British fleets against pirates. Somehow, the gamekeeper turned poacher, and soon Kidd became an infamously effective pirate. Hiding treasure on uninhabited islands is a habit more common among fictional pirates than real ones, but in Kidd's case it really happened. He buried some of the plunder from one act of piracy on Gardiners Island – it was later recovered and used as evidence against him when he was caught. Captain Kidd was sent to England, put on trial and sentenced to death. His hanging was bungled, and he only died on the second attempt.

## Blackbeard (Edward Teach, c.1680–1718)

Of all the real-life pirates, surely the name Blackbeard is the most recognizable today. He was an Englishman, possibly from Bristol, and at his peak he was operating a small fleet of pirate ships. Despite his frightening reputation – partially derived from a fearsome appearance – he was less violent than many pirates, preferring to use the threat of force and the impression of ruthlessness rather than indiscriminate violence. By these means he was able to exploit not just ships, but places, blockading ports in America (which were then small towns) and ransoming the inhabitants. Justice caught up with him eventually when the Governor of Virginia sent out a party of sailors and soldiers to capture him. During a fierce battle in November 1718, Blackbeard was killed. After his death, his legacy was to become the incarnation of what a pirate is among generations of people fascinated by the pirate life.

*Anne Bonny (c.1700–c.1782)*

From the time of the Vikings a thousand years before to the Chinese in the first half of the 20th century, there had been female pirates attacking shipping lanes and plundering booty. Anne Bonny, born in Ireland as Ann Cormac, was the daughter of William Cormac, a married gentleman, and his female servant Mary Brennan. To escape his wife's angry relatives, Cormac moved his unconventional new family first to England and then to America. Cormac ended up making his fortune in business, but Anne never benefitted from it: a hot-headed girl, she married a small-time crook and pirate called James Bonny, and her father disowned her. Anne and James travelled to an island in the Bahamas, where many pirates went in order to lie low. It was there that she met another pirate, John Rackham, known as Calico Jack. Anne divorced her husband and married Jack, to make a formidable husband-and-wife pirate team. With another female pirate, Mary Read, they stole a ship called the *William* from Nassau harbour in the Bahamas, and spent some years plying their trade around Jamaica. Anne was a brave and feared fighter, and the *William* gathered a great deal of treasure. A ship under the control of the Governor of Jamaica eventually tracked the *William* down, and after a fight the pirates were captured. They were sentenced to be hanged – and Rackham was, but Anne was pregnant, so her execution was delayed. There is no record of the execution taking place later, and there are some indications to suggest that her father may have bought her freedom.

Did you read *Treasure Island* with the avid attention of a cut-throat pirate greedily poring over a long-lost treasure map? Try this multiple-choice quiz to find out. The answers are overleaf.

1. "*Fifteen men on the dead man's chest*," sings the old pirate Billy Bones as he approaches the Admiral Benbow inn in Chapter 1. "*Yo-ho-ho and a...*" Yo-ho-ho and a what?

    A) "Yo-ho-ho and a high crow's nest!"

    B) "Yo-ho-ho and a bottle of rum!"

    C) "Yo-ho-ho and the dead sleep best!"

    D) "Yo-ho-ho and a-here they come!"

2. In Chapter 6, Dr Livesey, Jim Hawkins and Squire Trelawney access the map of the island by opening up what?

    A) A rusty tobacco tin

    B) A roll of parchment

    C) An oilskin packet

    D) A packet of smoky-bacon crisps

3. The treasure on the island – 700,000 pounds – was originally accumulated by another pirate, and hidden there. What was the name of that pirate, and what was the name of his ship?

    A) Captain Flint of the *Walrus*

    B) Captain Dent of the *Seahorse*

    C) Captain Blunt of the *Mermaid*

    D) Captain Hunt of the *Kraken*

4. Because Long John Silver is the ship's cook, he is known by another name as well. What is it?

A) Gravy

B) Chowder

C) Pie

D) Barbecue

5. Where is Jim when he accidentally eavesdrops on Long John Silver and realizes that Silver is a pirate who intends to mutiny?

A) In an apple barrel

B) Up a mast

C) Under a hatch

D) Behind a sail

6. Of the twenty-six on board the *Hispaniola*, how many does Jim calculate are on the side of the true captain, Captain Smollett?

A) Six

B) Seven

C) Eight

D) Nine

7. Which food has Ben Gunn been dreaming of for three years?

A) A Subway twelve-inch

B) Trifle

C) Bread-and-butter pudding

D) Cheese

8. When Long John Silver and the remains of his crew are searching for the treasure, what unusual sign do they stumble across that points them in the right direction?

A) A dead shark pointing with its snout

B) Thirteen Bibles laid out in an arrow

C) A skeleton stretched out with its hands over its skull

D) An ancient cannon aimed east-south-east

# ANSWERS

1 — B
2 — C
3 — A
4 — D
5 — A
6 — B
7 — D
8 — C

## SCORES

**1 to 3 correct:** Maybe you'll be better at walking the plank... **4 to 6 correct:** Not quite a captain, but an excellent first mate... **7 to 8 correct:** Pieces of Eight! Pieces of Eight!

# Glossary

| | |
|---|---|
| **AB** | Able-bodied. |
| **abeam** | At a right angle to the ship's length. |
| **accoutrement** | A collection of clothes; also, an extra item. |
| **affy-davy** | See *davy*. |
| **after-part** | The rear part of a ship. |
| **ague** | Illness involving fever, usually malaria. |
| **aloft** | Above; upstairs. See also *alow*. |
| **alow** | Below. See also *aloft*. |
| **amphitheatre** | A seating area laid out in a semicircle. |
| **ankecher** | Handkerchief. |
| **aperture** | Opening. |
| **apoplexy** | Unconsciousness caused by a stroke. |
| **arrant** | Utter. |
| **assizes** | A court responsible for administering criminal law. |
| **astern** | At the rear end of a ship. See also *after-part*. |
| **athwart** | From one side to the other. |
| **bade fair** | Seemed likely. |
| **backstay** | A support that holds a mast in place. |
| **bandolier** | A shoulder belt with loops and pockets for gun cartridges. |
| **beam-ends** | Beams run across the width of a ship; if a ship lies on its beam-ends then it is lying on its side. |

| | |
|---|---|
| **berth** | Where a ship moors or drops anchor. |
| **blockhouse** | A one-storey building made of wood, used as a fort. |
| **blunt** | Money. |
| **boatswain** | The officer on a ship in charge of crew and equipment. |
| **booms** | The crossbars on a mast, to which sails are attached. |
| **bow oar** | One who pulls the oar nearest the *bows*. |
| **bows** | The front end of a ship. |
| **bowsprit** | The long pole that sticks out from the front of a ship. |
| **bumboat** | A small boat used to peddle provisions to ships that are anchored offshore. |
| **brace** | A pair. |
| **brand** | A piece of burning wood. |
| **breeches** | A type of trousers – short, fastened just below the knee. |
| **briers** | Thorny rose bushes. |
| **broadside** | The firing of cannons from one side of a ship. Also, the side of a boat or ship. |
| **broom** | Any one of a family of flowering, often evergreen bushes. |
| **buccaneer** | Pirate. |
| **bulkhead** | A wall inside a ship. |
| **bulwarks** | The walls formed by the edges of the ship's sides extending above the level of the deck. |
| **busts** | Statues of people from the head down to the chest. |
| **butt** | Object of ridicule. |
| **by the board** | Walked the plank. |
| **cache** | A hidden collection of items. |

| | |
|---|---|
| **calumnies** | False statements or accusations made about someone in order to ruin their reputation. |
| **candlelight** | Dusk. |
| **canikin** | A small can, often used to drink from. |
| **canting** | Tilting. |
| **capstan bars** | The large winch found on a ship, which was operated manually by pulling "bars". Normally used for lowering and raising the anchor. |
| **careen** | To turn a ship on its side to clean or repair it. |
| **catechism** | A summary of Christian teaching to be learnt by heart. |
| **cat's paw** | Nautical: a localized, slight breeze. |
| **caulker** | A waterproof sealant used for repairs. |
| **chains** | The planks that stretch across the middle of a ship; where one sits to row. |
| **chine** | Backbone. |
| **Christian** | Interchangeable with "person" – especially those who display kindness or fairness. |
| **chuck-farthing** | An old game – based on throwing coins into a hole. |
| **circumspectly** | Warily. |
| **clenching** | Affirming, making up for something. |
| **clove hitch** | A type of nautical knot – used as a metaphor for "mess". |
| **coltish** | Energetic, but awkwardly moving. |
| **companion** | A raised frame on a ship's deck with windows. |
| **conned** | Steered. |
| **connived** | Made plans to do something in secret. |
| **connoisseur** | An expert. |
| **consort** | A ship that sails in company with another; a companion. Also used as "search party". |
| **coracle** | A small, round boat made with wicker. |

GLOSSARY

| | |
|---|---|
| **cordage** | Collection of ropes; rigging. |
| **cove** | Bay. |
| **coxswain** | The person in charge of the steering and navigation of a ship. |
| **crosstrees** | Horizontal struts at the top of the mast. |
| **cutlass** | A short sword with a curved blade. |
| **cutwater** | The forward edge of a boat. |
| **davy** | Abbreviation of affidavit, a legally binding oath. |
| **deadlights** | A porthole shutter; used also to refer to eyes. |
| **desperadoes** | Reckless criminals. |
| **deuce** | The Devil. |
| **dingle** | A wooded valley. |
| **dirk** | A small dagger. |
| **dogwatch** | A short watch on a ship; either four until six or six until eight p.m. |
| **diot** | Small amount of money. |
| **doldrums** | A period of depression. |
| **doubloon** | A Spanish gold coin. |
| **downhaul** | The rope used for hauling down a sail. See also *halyard*. |
| **drub** | Defeat thoroughly. |
| **duff** | A boiled pudding |
| **durst** | Dared. |
| **dysentery** | An infection causing severe diarrhoea. |
| **easting** | Travelling east. |
| **ebb tide** | The tide going out to sea. |
| **enow** | Enough, for the moment. |
| **ensign** | Flag. |
| **ere** | Before; by the time. |
| **evil one** | The Devil. |
| **farthing** | Coin, worth a quarter of a penny. |

| | |
|---|---|
| **fathom** | Unit of length: equal to six feet or 1.8 metres. |
| **fawning** | Exaggerated flattery. |
| **fidges** | Fidgets. |
| **figureheads** | The carved statues on the front – or prow – of ships. |
| **first mate** | See *mate*. |
| **foc's'le hands** | Those lower-ranking sailors living in the *forecastle*. |
| **fourpenny** | Coin worth four pence. |
| **forecastle** | The front end of the space below deck on a ship; often where the crew's living quarters are. |
| **foresheets** | In a boat, just inside the bows. |
| **frigate** | A warship. |
| **fugitive** | Someone in hiding, usually to escape criminal charges. |
| **gabbling** | Fast, unintelligible speech. |
| **galley** | The kitchen in a ship. |
| **gallipot** | A small pot, used as a medicine container. |
| **gammon** | Defeat, deceive. |
| **garding** | Garden. |
| **garrison** | A group of soldiers stationed with defence in mind. |
| **gaskin** | Gasket: a cord used to tie up furled sails on a ship. |
| **genteel** | Exaggerated, false politeness. |
| **Georges** | Coins: a half-crown. |
| **gibbet** | Gallows. |
| **gigs** | Small, long, narrow boats (for rowing or sailing). |
| **girt** | Put on; secured to a belt. |
| **glim** | Candle. |

| | |
|---|---|
| **go bail** | Put up money and vouch for someone. |
| **grapple** | Fight. |
| **grog** | A spirit (often rum) mixed with water. |
| **guinea** | Money: just over £1, or 21 shillings. |
| **gully** | A large knife. |
| **gunwale** | The lip of the side of a boat. |
| **halyard** | The rope used for raising or lowering a sail or flag. |
| **hamlet** | A very small village. |
| **hand-barrow** | A frame with poles at each end, used by two people to carry large objects. |
| **handspike** | A wooden stick with an iron tip – used as a lever on a ship. |
| **hark back to** | Remember. |
| **hawse** | The part of the ship through which the mooring line passes. |
| **hawser** | The thick mooring line. |
| **hazed** | Annoyed. |
| **hazing** | Nautical term: receiving all of the least agreeable jobs. |
| **head** | Short for "headland" – a strip of land sticking out into the sea. |
| **headpiece** | A colloquial term for head or brain, suggesting great intelligence. |
| **helm** | The steering wheel of a ship. |
| **hilt** | The handle of a weapon – in this case, a cutlass. |
| **hoar frost** | A greyish-white covering of frost on the landscape. |
| **holus-bolus** | All at once. |
| **horseplay** | Rough games. |
| **hummock** | A small hill. |
| **imprecations** | Curses. |

| | |
|---|---|
| **in no wise** | Not at all. |
| **in stays** | Heading straight into the wind – sails flapping, without much power. |
| **irresolute** | Hesitant and uncertain. |
| **jine** | Join. |
| **jolly boat** | A small boat carried on a ship, normally suspended from the *stern*. |
| **keelhauling** | Being dragged through the sea under the ship as a form of punishment. |
| **keelson** | A line of floorboards on a ship which fixes the keel to the ship's floor. |
| **knolls** | Small hills. |
| **lancet** | A double-edged surgical knife. |
| **larboard** | *Port*. |
| **leer** | An unpleasant look. |
| **lee shore** | The shore lying downwind of a ship. |
| **leewards** | Downwind. |
| **lick** | A blow. |
| **link** | A torch. See also *brand*. |
| **livery** | A special servant's uniform. |
| **lock** | The mechanism in a gun that causes the powder to explode. |
| **long brass nine** | A type of gun. See also *swivel*. |
| **louis d'or** | A French gold coin. Also referred to as Louises. |
| **lubbers** | Someone who is unfamiliar with the sea – used to suggest that someone is clumsy. |
| **luff** | The edge of a sail. |
| **lugger** | A small sailing ship with two or three masts, each hung with a lugsail: an asymmetrical sail with four sides. |
| **lumber** | Furniture and oddments; suggests a mess of unwanted or useless items. |

| | |
|---|---|
| **made fast** | Tied up, moored. |
| **magistrate** | Person who judges criminal cases, such as those in the *assizes*. |
| **mail** | A vehicle used for delivering post. |
| **main hold** | The large space in the lower part of a ship. See also *forecastle*. |
| **mainstay** | The person or thing upon which someone or something else relies. |
| **man-o'-war** | An armed sailing ship. |
| **maroon** | Someone who is stranded. |
| **mate** | Second in command on a ship. |
| **merest trifle** | Very small amount. |
| **mind** | Remember. |
| **miscellany** | A mess or mixture of different things. |
| **mizzen** | The front, shorter mast of the ship. |
| **mizzen shrouds** | The rigging on the *mizzen*. |
| **moidores** | Portuguese coins. |
| **morass** | A boggy or marshy area. |
| **musket** | An old-fashioned gun – long barrelled, fired from the shoulder. |
| **nail** | Steal. |
| **nigh-hand** | Close by. |
| **noggin** | Small amount of liquid; normally about a quarter of a pint. |
| **oaths** | Swear words, curses. |
| **obsequious** | Subservient; exaggeratedly polite and attentive. |
| **painter** | A rope attached to a boat's bow, used for tying it up. |
| **paling** | A fence made from pointed posts. |
| **palisade** | A *paling* forming an enclosure or defence. |
| **pannikin** | A small metal cup. |
| **parlour** | A sitting room, often used for entertaining guests. |

| | |
|---|---|
| **peach** | Inform, tell on someone. |
| **pestiferous** | Filled with infection; diseased. |
| **piece of eight** | Coin: a Spanish dollar. |
| **pigtail tobacco** | Tobacco in a thin twist. |
| **pious** | Deeply religious. |
| **piping the eye** | Weeping. |
| **pitch** | Tar-like substance used to repair and protect ships. |
| **plate ships** | Treasure ships – normally Spanish. |
| **poll** | Scalp. |
| **port** | The left-hand side of a ship; as opposed to *starboard*. |
| **priming** | Preparing a gun for firing. |
| **promontory** | A high point of land jutting out into the sea. |
| **puncheon** | A cask of large volume. |
| **quadrant** | An instrument used in navigation, along with charts. |
| **quadrilateral** | A shape with four sides. |
| **quart** | A measurement of liquid, equal to two pints. |
| **quartermaster** | The person on a ship responsible for navigation; on a pirate ship, they were usually elected by the crew and second in command only to the captain. |
| **quid** | Chewing tobacco. |
| **reparation** | Amends. |
| **report** | A sudden, loud noise. |
| **rheumatics** | One of several conditions involving swollen, painful joints. |
| **sabre** | A type of sword, often heavy and with a curved blade. |
| **sallied** | Charged suddenly from a place under attack towards the enemy. |

| | |
|---|---|
| **salts** | Also known as smelling salts: used to revive someone who has fainted. |
| **score** | Dues, fees; what is owed. |
| **score** | Twenty. |
| **schooner** | A sailing ship; often large, with two or more masts. |
| **sculled** | Rowed – named after a scull, or oar. |
| **sea calf** | A seal; used to mean "idiot". |
| **shirking** | Lazy; avoiding work. |
| **shoal** | Shallow. |
| **six bells** | Three o'clock. |
| **skipper** | Captain. |
| **skulk** | Coward. |
| **slough** | Swamp. |
| **smit with** | From smitten, enamoured with. |
| **snipe** | A marsh bird. |
| **sojourn** | Stay; brief portion of time spent somewhere. |
| **soundings** | Measurements of water depth. |
| **spit** | A narrow point of land sticking out into the sea. |
| **squalling** | Crying; normally noisy and protracted. |
| **squalls** | Huge gusts of wind; storms. |
| **square** | Talk honestly, bluntly. Also used to mean someone is in agreement. |
| **starboard** | The right-hand side of a ship; as opposed to *port*. |
| **staunch** | Loyal; watertight. |
| **stern** | The very back of a ship. |
| **stirrup** | The metal hoop used to support the feet of a horse rider. |
| **stockade** | A fenced enclosure; a barrier formed of upright posts. |

| | |
|---|---|
| **stoving** | Breaking; knocking inwards. |
| **straits** | Narrow streams of water that connect two large areas of water. |
| **subaltern** | An army officer: one rank lower than captain. |
| **superintend** | Oversee. |
| **surf** | The shoreline, often denoting foaminess. |
| **swab** | Someone worthy of contempt. |
| **sward** | An area of short grass. |
| **swivel** | A type of gun. See also *long brass nine*. |
| **tack** | A change in direction. |
| **tallowy** | Greasy – from tallow: rendered animal fat. |
| **the horrors** | An attack of nervousness or anxiety. |
| **thwart** | A horizontal plank that serves as a seat in a rowing boat. |
| **ticklish** | A tricky problem requiring a delicate solution. |
| **tinderbox** | A box containing flint, tinder, steel, etc., for starting fires; the predecessor of matches. |
| **tract** | A large area of land. |
| **trim** | The act of rearranging cargo or people in a boat in order to adjust its tilt or balance. |
| **truculently** | Quick to argue or fight; used also to mean "snappily". |
| **trump** | An admirable person. |
| **wain** | Wagon. |
| **widders** | Widows. |
| **wrought** | Worked very hard towards an end result. |
| **yardarm** | The farthest reaches of the outside of a ship. |
| **yawed** | Twisted. |
| **yellow jack** | Another name for yellow fever – a virus affecting the liver and kidneys, causing jaundice, often fatal. |

# ALMA CLASSICS

ALMA CLASSICS aims to publish mainstream and lesser-known European classics in an innovative and striking way, while employing the highest editorial and production standards. By way of a unique approach the range offers much more, both visually and textually, than readers have come to expect from contemporary classics publishing.

～

1. James Hanley, *Boy*
2. D.H. Lawrence, *The First Women in Love*
3. Charlotte Brontë, *Jane Eyre*
4. Jane Austen, *Pride and Prejudice*
5. Emily Brontë, *Wuthering Heights*
6. Anton Chekhov, *Sakhalin Island*
7. Giuseppe Gioacchino Belli, *Sonnets*
8. Jack Kerouac, *Beat Generation*
9. Charles Dickens, *Great Expectations*
10. Jane Austen, *Emma*
11. Wilkie Collins, *The Moonstone*
12. D.H. Lawrence, *The Second Lady Chatterley's Lover*
13. Jonathan Swift, *The Benefit of Farting Explained*
14. Anonymous, *Dirty Limericks*
15. Henry Miller, *The World of Sex*
16. Jeremias Gotthelf, *The Black Spider*
17. Oscar Wilde, *The Picture Of Dorian Gray*
18. Erasmus, *Praise of Folly*
19. Henry Miller, *Quiet Days in Clichy*
20. Cecco Angiolieri, *Sonnets*
21. Fyodor Dostoevsky, *Humiliated and Insulted*
22. Jane Austen, *Sense and Sensibility*
23. Theodor Storm, *Immensee*
24. Ugo Foscolo, *Sepulchres*
25. Boileau, *Art of Poetry*

To order any of our titles and for up-to-date information about our current and forthcoming publications, please visit our website on:

# www.almaclassics.com

Debbie
JOHNSON

A Gift from the
Comfort
Food Café

HarperCollins*Publishers*

HarperCollins*Publishers* Ltd
1 London Bridge Street,
London SE1 9GF

www.harpercollins.co.uk

First published by HarperCollins*Publishers* 2018
2

A catalogue record for this book is available from the British Library

ISBN: 978-0-00-825885-6

This novel is entirely a work of fiction.
The names, characters and incidents portrayed in it are
the work of the author's imagination. Any resemblance to
actual persons, living or dead, events or localities is
entirely coincidental.

Set in Birka by Palimpsest Book Production Limited, Falkirk, Stirlingshire

Printed and bound in the UK by CPI Group (UK) Ltd, Croydon CR0 4YY

MIX
Paper from
responsible sources
FSC™ C007454

For Barbara Tomkinson (and Tinkerbell!)

# PART 1: ON YOUR MARKS . . .

# Chapter 1

My name is Katie Seddon. I am seven years old, and I am preparing to run away.

This is the first time, but it won't be the last.

It is Christmas Day, and I have gathered together all of the essentials, which include the following: a selection of gifts, including my mermaid Barbie, a colouring book and felt tip pens, a musical jewellery box with a wind-up dancing ballerina inside it, fluffy pink ear muffs, elf bed socks and a four-pack of custard creams wrapped in cellophane. The biscuits weren't under the tree that morning; I pinched them from the kitchen.

I look at my stash, and decide that I am ready for all that life can throw at me.

I pack my haul into my *Toy Story* backpack, and decide I will take a trip to infinity and beyond. Or at least to my grandma's house. She only lives two streets away, so it isn't exactly an intergalactic space quest.

I sit on my bed, and pause after I've zipped everything up. I wonder if my mum and dad will hear me as I sneak downstairs, get my raincoat, and leave – but a few seconds sitting with my head cocked to one side, listening to them scream at each other, reassures me that they won't.

I can only make out the odd word, and I've learned already not to try too hard. I won't hear anything good. It's a cacophony of shrieks and yells and thuds as they chase each other around the living room. The bangs of ashtrays being thrown and high-pitched swearing and the crash of plates are all perfectly normal to me. They're part of the soundtrack of my childhood; a reverse lullaby that keeps me awake and scared instead of sleepy and secure.

Looking back, with more complex thought processes than I possessed at seven, I know they are one of those couples who base their whole relationship on mutual contempt. On a good day, they tolerate each other. On a bad one, the only emotion in their eyes is hatred and bitterness. The overwhelming disappointment of what their lives have become.

I know now it's not uncommon – and that their conflicts were the glue that held them together. Maybe when they first met it was exciting. Maybe they thought the arguments were passionate. Maybe the first few serious rows were put down to fire and spice. Maybe they were different when they were young, and thought they were in love – but now, with my dad in a dead-end job and Mum stuck at home, it's not passion. It's fury.

At the age of seven, I don't understand any of this. I don't know what's going on in the big, nasty grown-up world – but I do know that I've had enough. That this is the worst Christmas ever. That they're both really, really mean when they fight. Dad is bigger and physically stronger, but Mum is like a wasp, constantly zooming in to sting him. It's horrible, and I'm leaving. Forever.

I tiptoe down the stairs and creep out of the house really quietly, although I needn't have bothered – they've reached critical mass by this stage and wouldn't pause if I did a conga through the living room wearing my flashing neon Rudolph deely-boppers. Which I am wearing, by the way – I've decided they will help me stay safe outside in the dark.

The walk to my grandma's is a bit scary. I've done it before, loads of times, but only with grown-ups. This time I am doing it alone, at night, and with nobody to hold my hand when I'm crossing the road. I'm a good girl, and do as I've been taught, waiting for the green man to come on at the traffic lights even though there are no cars at all. Mum sometimes goes when the red man is on, but she says that's all right for adults.

I knock on my grandma's door, and she opens it wearing her quilted dressing gown and tartan slippers. She lets me in without any questions at all. I realise now it's because she didn't have to ask – she knew exactly what was going on in my house, and exactly why I needed a refuge. A place to shelter from the storm of my parents' toxic relationship.

My nan was a very kind woman, and she always smelled of Parma Violets. To this day I still find it comforting whenever they turn up in a big bag of Swizzels. Halloween can be a bittersweet experience.

She settles me down with a bowl of custard-soaked jam roly-poly that she warms up in the microwave, and makes me a mug of instant hot chocolate. She even lets me sit in the big armchair that has the button that makes the footrest go up, tucked under a blanket. I hear her on the phone, but I'm so comfy and cosy and happy I'm not remotely interested in who she's talking to. The room is lit by the twinkles of her small plastic Christmas tree, and all is well with the world.

When she comes back into the room, she's all wrinkled smiles and loveliness, and we watch an episode of *ER* together. It's an exciting one, with a big fire and lots of drama. It may even have been that early brush with Nurse Carol Hathaway that planted the seeds of my later career.

By the time my mum drags herself away from her fight, Nan has put me to bed at her house. I'm in the spare room, which used to be Mum's when she was little and still has a giant cuddly lion in it that's big enough to sit on.

I lie scrunched up beneath the duvet, warm and full, and hear them talking down below. It's one of those little terraced houses with the staircase right off the living room, so the noise carries. Mum sounds tearful and her voice is wobbling and going up and down, like your voice does when you're trying to keep a cry in and can't breathe properly. Nan is telling her to leave me here for the night, and to stay herself as well. Telling her to consider staying for good – to finally leave him.

'There's never going to be a happy ending here, Sandra. You've both given it your best, but enough's enough, love,' she says, and I hear how sad she sounds. Sometimes I forget that my mum is my nan's little girl as well as my mum. Weird.

I wake up the next morning with my mum in bed with me, curled around me like a soft, protective spoon. She's already awake, watching me as I sleep, gently moving my blonde hair from my face. For a moment, all is well in the world.

Then I see that her eyes are all crusted together where she'd been crying, and her face is all puffed up, and she has finger-shaped bruises on the tops of her arms like small purple paw-marks. I burrow into her, and give her a cuddle – she looks like she needs one.

# Chapter 2

The second time I run away, with any serious intent, I am fourteen. I've been staying with my nan most weekends, to the point where it is my second home. Mum and Dad are still at it, the years giving them more frown lines but no extra restraint.

The fights don't get physical quite as often, but I still sometimes find the remnants of shattered crockery in the kitchen in the morning, or a mysteriously put-in window pane in the living room door, glass scattered on the floor in glistening zig-zags as I come downstairs for school.

I always creep down quietly, hoping they're still sleeping it off, praying for a peaceful bowl of cornflakes before I leave. I've learned to tread carefully in our house, in all kinds of ways.

The year I turn fourteen, though, things change. They change because my nan dies, and my escape hatch is gone. It's sudden and unexpected – a complication of diabetes. All those Parma Violets, I suppose. I am grieving and in pain and swamped with guilt – because as well as missing her, I am worried about myself as well. About how I'll cope without her, and her kind smiles, and our cosy nights in watching *ER* and *Casualty* and *Holby City*, talking about nothing but saying such a lot.

Mum and Dad had gone out for a meal together, a pre-Christmas 'date night'. As usually happens on those rare occasions, what started off well was ending with a row. Something to do with him drinking four pints of cider even though he was supposed to be the one driving, I don't know.

The verbal missiles start as soon as they walk in, and had obviously been fired first on the journey home from their *romantic* night out. I make a sharp exit, stage left, not really knowing where I'm going or what I'm going to do when I get there.

They don't even see me, and I stand outside the house on the driveway for a few moments, looking in at their drama unfolding. It's dark, and it's almost Christmas, and their row takes a festive turn when Dad gives Mum a mighty push as she screams at him. It's not a push with intent – more of a push to get an irritating insect out of his face.

She loses her balance and topples backwards, staggering for a few steps before she finally lands sprawling in the middle of the Christmas tree, taking it down with her.

I stay rooted to the spot for a few seconds, just to make sure she isn't, you know, dead or anything – but am strangely reassured to see her climb back up from the fake-pine branches, strewn in red and green tinsel. She's grabbed the nearest weapon to hand – the star off the top of the tree – and is brandishing it like a shiv in a jailhouse movie, threatening to poke his eye out.

*Okay*, I think. *God bless you merry gentlemen*, and away I go. It's very cold, and the streets are giddy with pitching snow and slow-moving cars inching through slush. I'm wearing a hoody and leggings, which isn't really enough. I haven't packed as well as I did last time, not even a spare pair of bed socks.

I wander the streets a little, wondering if I could hitch-hike to London without getting murdered or locked in someone's cellar, before my feet finally take me where I probably knew I was going all along.

I sit on the kerb outside my nan's old house, ice-cold snow immediately soaking through the seat of my leggings, and rest my chin in my hands as I stare across the street.

Someone else lives there now, of course. The house was sold within a couple of months of her dying, which will always, always piss me off. I'm a teenager now, so I swear a lot more than I did when I was seven. And this? Imposters in her home? That pisses me off. It should have been kept as some kind of museum. At least had a blue plaque outside it. Instead, it's like she was never even there.

I pull the cord of my hoody to make it tighter around my face, and look in through the front window. I see their brightly lit Christmas tree, and the cosy room, and occasionally even see a woman walking around, carrying a baby. I have no idea who they are, but I resent them. It might not be their fault that she died, but that doesn't make me feel any better. The people who live there are pissing me off as well.

I'm so sick of my parents' dramas. Sick of the tension, of not knowing when it's all going to kick off again. There was a temporary lull after Nan died, and both of them were on their best behaviour, but it didn't last.

Sometimes it comes after a flash point; sometimes it comes after days of simmering anger and snide comments and 'your dinner's in the dog' sniping. He'll go straight to the pub after work; she'll sit at home planning her revenge.

And I know now – because my mother has said it to me – that I am apparently the cause of their determined grip on marital misery.

'We didn't want you to come from a broken home,' she said – as though this was better. As though me bearing witness to a state of warfare throughout my childhood is beneficial, rather than filling me with dread.

I wade through a state of constant nervous energy every time I come home from school, standing in the hallway with my coat still on, weighing up the mood of the house, deciding whether I can risk venturing into the living room or if it would be better to run straight upstairs to my room, put on my headphones, and pretend none of it is happening.

So that's how I live. Hiding in my room with my music; hiding at friends' houses for way too many sleepovers, and running. Sometimes here, to my nan's. Sometimes to town. Sometimes just buying a day pass for the bus and riding around all day.

It's not an easy balance, and as soon as I am old enough, I go away to college to study nursing. I choose a college far enough away that I have to live in the halls, and think I have found paradise. Other teenagers are homesick – I'm just relieved. Relieved to have my own space, my own place, my own peace and quiet. Relieved to be alone.

# Chapter 3

By the time I am in my twenties, I'm sharing my own space and my own place and I don't have much peace and quiet any more. I'm definitely, 100 per cent not alone, either.

In fact, the third time I run away, I'm a grown woman, with a six-month-old baby, a job, a rented flat, and a boyfriend who never really wanted to be a dad.

That time, I run away for good. That time, I run away because of yet another screaming row – with Jason, my boyfriend.

It isn't pretty. These things never are. When we met, he was working as a hospital porter, and I was a nurse. At the time, I suppose I thought we fell in love – but now I see it for what it was. A lot of lust, some laughs, and a strange sense that this was what I was supposed to be doing. That women of my age should be looking to find 'the one' and building a relationship.

It was never, ever right between us, but when I got pregnant, we both pretended it was. Because everyone knows that having a newborn baby is really easy, and completely papers over the cracks in any relationship, don't they?

Of course, it didn't make anything better. It made everything worse. The flat was too small. We didn't have enough money. We were too young, and didn't have a clue what we were doing. Mainly, I think, we just didn't like each other very much.

While I was pregnant, we were able to pretend much better. We went to Ikea and laughed as we built cots from Swedish instructions and cooed over tiny little baby-grows. He said he'd give up drinking while I was pregnant, and even managed it for a couple of weeks.

After our son, Saul, arrived, the tensions started to build. I never slept. Jason was working extra shifts. When we did see each other, we were both filled with seething resentments – me because I was stuck at home, him because when he did get home, all I did was moan and nag.

The only good thing about any of it was the baby. He was perfect – caught between us, this chubby-faced, blond-haired angel who I always secretly thought we didn't deserve.

The night of the screaming row, I am especially tired. I've been on my own for so long, I've started talking to the kettle. It isn't answering yet, but in my delirious state of fatigue, it's only a matter of time.

Saul is teething and crying and irritable. Jason has been doing extra shifts to cover for other people's Christmas leave, and I am watching the big hand crawl around the clock in the kitchen, counting the minutes until I can hand Saul over and collapse onto my bed and cry silently into my pillow for a few moments, wondering what happened to my life.

We're out of nappies, and Jason is supposed to be getting some on the way home. Except he doesn't come home – not for another two hours. And when he does, he smells of lager and cigarettes and Calvin Klein's Obsession, which is a perfume I definitely don't wear. In fact the only perfume I wear these days is baby sick and desperation.

I could overlook all of that if he'd even remembered the nappies – but of course he hasn't. He has, though, remembered to pick up six cans of Fosters and a bad attitude.

I yell. He yells. We both say things we will regret, but also probably mean. It gets louder, and hotter, and angrier. We're both like subterranean geysers, all of our frustrations rising to the surface in one big, scalding explosion.

I pick up the nearest thing I can find – a dirty nappy – and lob it at Jason's head. He retaliates by slapping me so hard across the face I feel the red sting marks shine immediately.

We're both stunned into silence by this; me standing still, holding my stinging cheek, him staring at me, shaking his head, stammering apologies.

I'm so sorry, he says. I don't know what came over me, he says. It'll never happen again, he promises. He is full of remorse, full of regret, full of instant self-loathing. In a strange way, I almost feel sorry for him – our situation has revealed a side of himself he probably never knew existed.

I am hurt, and shaken, and weirdly relieved. It's like we've finally pushed ourselves over an abyss that we can't climb out of. I don't feel scared, oddly – I can tell he won't do it again. Not this time, anyway.

I'm trying to make words come out of my mouth when I notice Saul. Saul, my beautiful son, who has been sitting in his baby chair, in a dirty nappy and a Baby's First Christmas vest, watching all of this unfold.

His blue eyes are wide and wet, his pudgy fists held to his ears trying to block out the noise, so scared and confused he is screaming as well. He's probably been screaming for a while – but neither of us noticed, because we were too lost in our own drama.

I rush to the baby to comfort him, and know that I will be running away again sometime soon – not for my sake, but for Saul's. Maybe even for Jason's.

Now, when I look back using the magical power of hindsight, it feels like so many of the important moments in my life – like that one – involve running away. I could draw a time-map of when things started to go wrong, and add in a cartoon figure of myself zooming off in the opposite direction, vapour trails behind me.

The problem with all of these memories – all of these actions and reactions and inactions and overreactions – isn't really the running away. The problem is, I never had any clue what I was running towards, and usually found myself blown around by the breeze, like the fluff from one of those wispy dandelion heads, without any sense of direction and no control over my own movements.

Now, a few years have passed. Saul will be four on his next birthday, and life is very different. I'm less of a dandelion-head, and am trying very hard to take root.

It's different because the last time I ran away, I ran here – to a little place called Budbury, on the picture-postcard perfect coast of Dorset. I have a job. I have a tiny house. I have friends, who I've reluctantly allowed into my life. I have a community, in the Comfort Food Café that is the heart of the village. I have peace, and quiet, and most importantly, I have a gorgeously healthy little boy. Who definitely disrupts the quiet, but in a good way.

I have more than I could ever have imagined – and this time, I won't be running anywhere. This time, I am breaking all the cycles.

This time, I'm staying put – no matter how complicated it gets.

# Chapter 4

*This year, Christmas Eve night*

I've had enough. My head is pounding, and my eyes are sore, and every inch of my body from my scalp to my toes feels like it's clenched up in tension.

All I can hear is the screaming, rising in shrieks and peaks above the sound of festive music, a playlist of carols I have on my phone to try and drown it all out. The mix is horrendous: the sublime choruses of 'Hark the Herald Angels Sing' alternating with yells of abuse.

Saul is sleeping, but restlessly, in that way that children will – I can see his eyes moving around under his lids, and his little fists are clenched, and every now and then his legs jerk, like a dreaming dog. It's the night before Christmas – maybe he's thinking about Santa, flying over the rooftops in his sleigh. I hope so, anyway. I hope he's not about to wake up, and hear all the rowing, and the banging, and voices. I worked hard to protect him from this, but it's chased me down, rooted me out.

I'm in my own little house, but I don't feel safe here any more. I'm in my own little house, and there are too many voices. Too much conflict. I'm in my own little house, and I'm hiding upstairs, cowering beneath the bed sheets, paralysed by it all.

I'm in my own little house, and I have to get out. I have to get away. I have to run.

# PART 2: GET SET . . .

# Chapter 5

*Six weeks earlier*

It's the weekend. Saturday, in fact. But as anyone with young children knows, kids have absolutely zero respect for the sacred concept of 'the lie-in'.

Saul has always been high-energy. I mean, I don't have a lot to compare it to, but even the other little boys at the playgroups we've attended, and at his pre-school in the next village over, seem like they're on sedatives next to him.

He's a force of nature. A bundle of energy. A whirling dervish in *Paw Patrol* pyjamas – and he never stops talking. I know this is good – he has a crazy vocabulary for his age – but sometimes I remember the days when he couldn't speak or move oh so fondly. I am such a bad mother.

Right now, I'm lying in bed, in what my friend Lynnie calls the 'corpse pose'. Lynnie is in her sixties and has Alzheimer's – but no matter how much she declines, she always seems to remember her past life as a yoga instructor. Saul adores her, and she's even managed to get him into downward dog on a few occasions – sometimes for literally whole seconds.

It hasn't turned him into a zen master though – and he seems to think that 5.45 a.m. is the perfect time to come and climb into bed with me.

We live together in a teeny-tiny terraced house in the centre of Budbury village. There's only one road, which runs through the village like a ribbon, lined with a few shops and a pub, a community centre and a pet cemetery and a couple of dozen little houses. They're quite old, and face straight into the pavement, and were probably built for fishermen in ye olde days of yore.

Several of my friends – regulars at the Comfort Food Café, a few minutes' walk away on the clifftops – live on the same road. I used to feel a bit claustrophobic, living so close to people who were keen to be friends. I used to feel like the only way I could be independent and safe was to be alone. Sometimes, I still feel like that – but I try to beat it down with a big stick, because it's really not healthy, is it?

So, I know from my horribly early visit to the bathroom, in the grey pre-dawn November light, roughly what else they're all up to. Edie May, who is 92 and has almost as much energy as Saul, is still tucked up in bed, bless her.

Zoe and Cal, along with Cal's daughter Martha, also still seem to be a-slumber. Martha's 17, and from what I recall from that state of being, mornings are not to be touched at weekends. Lucky swines.

In fact, I can see lights on in only one other house – the one where Becca and Sam live. They have a baby girl – Little Edie – who has just turned one. She's utterly adorable and they both dote on her – but she's not one of life's sleepers.

Seeing them awake, and imagining Sam bleary-eyed and zombified as he tries to entertain Little Edie, makes me feel slightly better. There's no snooze button on a baby – he'll be up, and surrounded by plastic objects in primary colours, and elbow-deep in nappies. Ha ha.

Saul doesn't have a snooze button either – but he is easier to distract. This morning, by 6 a.m., I am not only in corpse pose – I am playing Beauty Parlour.

This is one of Saul's favourite games, and I have no idea where he picked it up. None of the women in Budbury are exactly dedicated followers of fashion.

Willow, one of Lynnie's daughters, has a pretty unique style that involves a lot of home-made clothes and a nose ring and bright pink hair. The teenagers – Martha and her pal Lizzie – definitely wear a lot of eyeliner. But there isn't a beauty parlour in the village – or possibly even in the twenty-first century. Even the words sound like something from the 1950s, and bring to mind those big space-alien dryers women sit beneath in old movies, before they go on a hot date with Cary Grant.

Anyway – I don't know where he got it from, but I'm glad he did. It's a game that can be played with me entirely immobile. The very best kind of game.

He's gathered my make-up bag and a collection of hair-brushes and slides and bobbles; even some hairspray and perfume. In all honesty, I rarely even use any of it, but like most women I've somehow managed to amass a gigantic pile of half-used cosmetics and hair products to clutter up the house for no good reason.

He's sitting cross-legged next to me, blond hair scrunched up on one side and perfectly flat on the other, working away with the foundation. I didn't know I even owned foundation, and I suspect it's some deep tan-coloured gunk I used after a sunny holiday in Majorca when I was twenty-one. He's blending it in with all the gentleness of Mike Tyson, but I don't care.

It's allowing me to stay in bed, so I just make the odd encouraging noise, and keep my eyes closed really tight when he starts on the eyeshadow. I ban him from mascara though, as I'd actually like to keep my vision.

'You're looking so beautiful, Mummy,' he says, when he pauses to inspect his work so far. 'But I think you need to highlight your cheekbones a bit more. I'll use some blusher.'

'Okay,' I mutter, half asleep. Where *is* he getting this stuff?

I hear the lids getting screwed off various pots, and know from his sharp inhalation of breath that he's probably just spilled something. In fact, the whole duvet cover will likely be covered in powders and lotions – but hey, that's what washing machines were made for, right?

He pokes at me with his fingers, rubbing in what I know

will be two great big clown-like spots on the side of my face, before sighing in satisfaction. Lipstick is next, after he's instructed me to make a 'kissy mouth' first. I bet I'm looking really sexy.

I glance through slitted eyes at the clock, and see that it is now 6.20 a.m. Wow. A massive lie-in.

'How's it going?' I ask, stifling a yawn.

'Really good. Really pretty. I think I might be finished. Shall we get up so we can watch cartoons before we go to the café for breakfast?'

Ugggh. Cartoons. I shrivel and die a little inside, and make a new suggestion: 'Hey – why don't you go and get my nail varnishes and you can do my fingers and toes?'

That fills in the next half an hour, and completely finishes off the duvet cover. I must admit he does a quite good job though, and am still admiring my brand-new multi-coloured fingers a little while later, when he is safely installed on the sofa watching shows on CBBC, shoving chunks of sliced-up banana into his mouth and laughing at the antics of a cartoon mouse who goes to school.

I put the duvet cover in the washer, and change it out for a new one – it's getting colder now anyway, and I'm already looking forward to snuggling up beneath the clean brushed cotton later. I live a wild and crazy life, what can I say?

I catch up on a bit of coursework for college – I'm trying to keep my nursing skills up to date, and since I met Lynnie,

I've become a lot more interested in community mental health – and organise some files. I do some ironing, in a vain attempt to get prepared for the week ahead, and I check my emails. Apart from being contacted by a Nigerian prince offering me an unbeatable investment opportunity, there's nothing.

My phone shows three missed calls from my mum, but I can't quite face that conversation just yet. It's never fun, getting Mum's weekly updates on what terrible crime Dad has committed recently. I love them both, but it's like being trapped between two angry pit bulls. Except with more spite and slobber.

I intermittently check in with Saul, making sure he's not eating the coffee table or swinging from the light fittings, and eventually take him upstairs to get ready for the day ahead. He's excited to go to the café, and I can't say that I blame him – it's become like a second home to us. A home that always has cake.

It's his favourite place in the whole world. I think it might just be mine too.

# Chapter 6

The Comfort Food Café is like no place else on earth. It's set on the top of a cliff on the gorgeous coastline, surrounded by the sea on one side and rolling green hills on the other.

You reach it by climbing up a long and winding path, and enter through a wrought-iron archway that spells out its name in an embroidery made of metal roses. Even the archway is pretty and welcoming.

The building itself is low and sprawling, and set in its own higgledy-piggledy garden. There are tables and benches that get packed in summer, as well as a barbecue area, a terrace, and as of this year, the adjoining Comfort Reads bookshop.

The bookshop is open by the time we get there, and Zoe – short, ginger, slim – waves at us through the window. She's sitting on her stool behind the till, a paperback propped up on her knees. Saul squeaks when he sees her, as the last time we were here she produced a Gruffalo mug for him.

Zoe moved here last year with her god-daughter Martha,

who is seventeen now, after her mother died. It's not been an easy ride for them, but they're settled now – along with Cal, Martha's biological dad, who she'd never even met before last Christmas as he lived in Australia. Yeah, I know – if Budbury had a Facebook page, it would need to set its relationship status to 'It's Complicated'.

I don't think anyone here is simple, or straightforward, or has had an especially traditional life. It's one of the reasons it's sucked me in, to be honest – these are people who lived through a lot, survived to tell the tale, and now seem to see it as their life's mission to make other people happy while feeding them carrot cake.

There's even some kind of weird vibe where they match people up with their favourite comfort foods – like me and jam roly-poly, which always reminds me of my nan. I must have mentioned it at some point, but I don't remember when – all I know is when I'm especially down or tired, that's what will be waiting for me there, even if it's not on the menu.

I still vividly remember the first time I came here. It was a couple of weeks after we'd made the move to Dorset – after leaving Jason, I lived with my parents for a while, but I soon realised that was a mistake. I knew I needed to get away properly, and started looking for a place with enough distance for a fresh start, but close enough to Bristol for me to get back and see my parents, and potentially for Saul to see his dad, if that's how things played out. It's not, but such is life.

Mum, amazingly, helped me find the money to move here – something to do with a 'nest egg' that my nan had left – but it took some sorting. Jason resisted initially, made some half-hearted attempts to persuade me to come back, but it felt hollow and fake – we were better off without each other, and we both knew it. Eventually he moved himself as well, all the way to Glasgow – fresh starts all round.

It was harder than I thought, though, leaving. Setting up on my own in a new place where I knew nobody, with a baby. I'd thought it was what I needed – but I didn't factor in how lonely I'd feel in those first few weeks. I had to stop myself from giving in, from calling my parents or Jason, from back-sliding.

Saul was almost eighteen months by that stage, and bloody hard work. I can say it now, because I'm his mum and it's in the past – but he was actually a bit of a demon child. Endless energy, constant battles, the terrible twos way before his birthday. I was exhausted, running on empty, and secretly convinced that my own child hated me. I had no idea how I was going to cope.

Then, one morning, I came here. To the café. Out of sheer desperation, really – the need to get out of the house and at least be in some proximity to the rest of the world. I was sitting there, Saul busily throwing bread soldiers at my head and mashing his egg up like it was his mortal enemy, feeling washed out and fatigued to the edge of insanity.

A woman I now know as Becca came up to me, and

brought me toast. Not Saul – me. Then another lady, who I'd thought was a customer but turned out to be the owner of the café, Cherie Moon, came and took Saul away. She's a big woman, Cherie, tall and robust, in her seventies with a weather-beaten face and wrinkles she wears with pride. She has a lot of long hair that she often has bundled up into a grey-streaked plait, and she has so much confidence that it practically oozes out of her.

Anyone else, I'd have worried about handing the baby over – more for their sake than his – but I just instinctively knew that Cherie could handle it. She'd walked him around the room, while I ate my toast and actually drank a hot beverage before it was lukewarm, and the sense of relief I felt was astonishing. In fact I had to disappear off to the toilets for a minute to compose myself – by which I mean sob relentlessly into wadded-up tissue paper.

These random acts of kindness – aimed at me, a complete stranger – were my introduction to the café. To the village. To the community that now, almost two years on, I am starting to dare to call my own.

It's taken a long time, because I am wary and stubborn and always cautious about random acts of kindness, but I understand it all better now. This place is like the island of misfit toys, and someone is always on hand with a sticking plaster and a spoonful of medicine for the soul.

These days, our lives are tied up with theirs in ways I could never have anticipated. The café gang help me out with childcare. I help them out with other things. We all look out for each other. It's like a big, tangled, misshapen ball of string, all directions leading to each other.

I'm still not the life and soul of any of the parties the café hosts or organises – I still dodge the big social events – but I'm getting there. Edging towards a security and comfort that I've never known since my nan died.

Saul thinks this place is home. He's little – he doesn't remember a life before it. He thinks Lynnie is his wacky granny, and Willow is a cartoon character because of her pink hair, and Cherie is the queen of the world.

He thinks Laura, who manages the café, is the cuddliest woman ever, and that Edie May is a magical tiny-faced elf who lives in a teapot.

He thinks all the men of Budbury – and there are several – are there purely to play football with him, or take him for walks on the beach, or help him hunt for fossils. He thinks the dogs of Budbury – Midgebo, Laura's black Lab, and Bella Swan, Willow's border terrier, and her boyfriend Tom's Rottie cross, Rick Grimes – are his own personal pooches.

I may have left behind my parents, and Jason, but what I gained was so much bigger – a whole village of the biggest-hearted people I've ever met.

He's tugging at my hand as we approach the doors, his little legs pumping as fast as they can, like a puppy straining on the lead, desperate to get inside.

Inside, where a world of fun awaits. Where the café starts

to get weird. Weird in a good way. There are lots of things you'd expect to find in a café – tables covered with red gingham cloths; a big fridge full of soft drinks; a chiller cabinet crammed with sandwich platters and salads and whopping great slices of cake; a serving counter and a till. So far, so normal.

Then there are the extras. The things that immediately let you know that you're not in Kansas any more, Toto. The multiple mobiles hanging from the ceiling, dangling home-made oddities like old vinyl singles and papier-mâché fish. Half a red kayak. The oars from a rowing boat. Fishing net tangled up with fairy lights. The shelves lined with random objects – an antique sewing machine; a giant fossil in a cabinet; rows of books and board games and puzzles.

It's like the anti-Ikea – as though the Old Curiosity Shop got together with a tea room and had a baby. Despite the clutter, though, it all still feels fresh and clean, and is washed over with the light flooding in through the windows on all sides.

On one side, you can see into the garden. On the other, it's the sea and the beach and the endless red-and-gold clifftops stretching off along the horizon. It's the kind of place you can lose hours, just watching the maritime world go by.

Saul bursts through the doors and strikes a dramatic pose, his little arms raised in the air, fists clenched, as though he's Superman about to take off.

'Everybody, I'm here!' he shouts, just in case they hadn't noticed. Laura is behind the counter, round and pretty and fighting a constant losing battle with her curly hair. She pauses in her work – slicing up lemon meringue cake – and her face breaks out into a huge smile.

'Thank goodness! I was wondering when you were going to turn up!' she says, wiping her hands down on her apron and walking out to see us. She crouches down in front of Saul and gives him a cuddle which he returns so enthusiastically she ends up sitting on her backside, his face buried in her hair.

I start to apologise, but she looks up at me and raises an eyebrow. That's a stern telling off from Laura, so I clamp my mouth shut.

Laura has two kids of her own – Nate and Lizzie, teenagers now – and understands children. She's told me approximately seven thousand times that I need to stop saying I'm sorry about Saul, when he's only doing what kids of that age do. She continues to stare at me, over the tufts of Saul's hair, but I can't figure out what I'm doing wrong this time, so I pretend not to notice.

I look around, and see Cherie sitting at a corner table, her feet in red and green striped socks, propped up on the chair next to her. Her husband Frank, who is an 82-year-old silver fox, is sitting opposite, drinking his thick tea and reading the paper. They both look up at me, and grin widely. They must be in an extra good mood this morning.

There is an actual paying customer here, still wrapped up in walking gear, perusing a guide book as he eats his toast. The café is on the Jurassic Coast and is often populated by people in padded anoraks and woolly hats, taking a break from their treks. He glances at the commotion, briefly widens his eyes when he nods good morning to me, and goes hastily back to his maps.

I glance around. There's nobody else here. Or at least I don't think there is, until he walks out of the gents.

He's tall by my standards – about six foot – but short by the standards of his own family, who are all giants. He's bulky, with brawn he earned travelling the world digging wells and building schools in the kind of places you see on the news during droughts. His chestnut hair is cropped brutally short, and he's wearing his usual uniform of care-worn denims and a long-sleeved jersey top.

He looks up, and our eyes meet across an un-crowded room. He has great eyes. Bright blue, on the Paul Newman spectrum. He smiles when he sees me, and I smile back, even though I feel the usual tug of anxiety I get whenever I'm around him. He's looking half-amused, as though he's remembering a joke someone told him on a bus some time, his gaze moving from me to Saul.

This is Van, and he's Lynnie's son, and Willow's brother. He came back from his life in Africa when Lynnie took a turn for the worse in the spring, and has been working for Frank as a labourer ever since. I wait, knowing that Saul will spot him as soon as he's emerged from Laura's hair.

Right on cue, I see my son look up and around, his eyes widening in excitement when he sees him walking towards us.

'Van! Van! Mummy, Van is here, look!' he squeals, leaving Laura lying on the floor, abandoned and forgotten, and me in a cloud of dust as he runs towards him. Van braces – this has happened many times before – catches him in his arms, scoops him up, and swings him around and around in a dizzying circle.

All I can hear is the ecstatic chuckling of my little boy as he whirls and flies through the air, shrieking for it to stop in a way that suggests he really doesn't want it to. Laura looks on and grins. Cherie and Frank look on and laugh. Even the random walker stifles a smile.

It's the kind of thing that makes everyone who sees it happy – an innocent expression of pure, unadulterated joy.

Everyone apart from me, I suspect. It doesn't make me happy. It makes me nervous. It makes me want to grab Saul back from him, and run away all over again. I vowed I wouldn't, no matter how complicated it all gets – but this is a whole new level of complicated.

Because in the same way that Saul seems to think that Cherie is the queen, and Edie is a magical elf, and Willow is a cartoon character, and all the dogs belong to him, he has views about Van as well. In his world, Van seems to have become the nearest thing he has to a real-life dad.

# Chapter 7

This, I am starting to think, could be a problem. Van is a nice man. Okay, he's a nice man who happens to be tremendously hot as well – and maybe that's the real problem. I like him, a lot.

In a fairytale world, that would be wonderful, wouldn't it? I'd complete my new move and my new life with a new relationship. We'd all live happily ever after, in a pink castle on a hill, surrounded by unicorns and rainbows. Everything wrapped up in a sparkly bow.

But this is the real world – my world. And in my world, all I've ever seen is relationships that start off good and go very, very bad. I'm determined not to let that happen to me again – or to Saul – and the best way to do that seems to be never to have a relationship at all.

That sounds very sensible when I say it in my head. I really, genuinely mean it. In my head. It doesn't seem to be my head that's the problem though – it's the rest of my body. Even here, now, in a café on a Saturday morning surrounded by other people, I feel that twitch when I look at him. The twitch that screams 'take me, take me', even when no words come out of my mouth beyond 'hi'. That's a blessing at least.

Van has done nothing to provoke this inner sluttiness, apart from exist, and I can't blame him for that. There are lots of good-looking men in Budbury, but they're all attached. There's Matt, the local vet and Laura's boyfriend. There's Sam, Becca's partner, who looks like a surfer and has the cutest Irish accent. There's Tom, Willow's fella, who has a superhero geek thing going on. There's Cal, Martha's dad and Zoe's man, an Aussie who manages Frank's farm and is pretty much the dictionary definition of 'rugged'.

But none of them have ever given me the twitch. Maybe because they're taken, and I just don't do that kind of thing. Maybe because I simply never felt that kind of chemistry with them even before I knew who they were and exactly how taken they are. It's weird, isn't it, the way you fancy some people and not others?

Weird, and in this case, inconvenient. I'm way too busy to even be wasting time thinking about such things, never mind doing them. I'm a single mum, I have my college course, and I work part-time in the village pharmacy, which is run by Auburn, Van and Willow's sister. Not an hour of my day is unaccounted for, ever. No, I definitely don't have time for a man in my life.

Even if I did, Van's never given any overt hint that he's even interested. He's probably not. In fact he definitely isn't. I'm nothing special – I'm perfectly average in every way.

I'm petite – I get that from my mum – and I'm almost-blonde. Which, if you look at it from the other direction, means I'm almost mousy. I'm not the kind of woman men look at and have sexy thoughts about.

'You look stunning today,' says Van, just as I'm thinking about how plain I am. He's stopped spinning Saul, and now has him on his shoulders, where he's using the extra height to fiddle with a mobile made of sea shells.

'Yes, you really do,' chimes in Laura, now busily getting my coffee ready. 'It's good to see somebody making an effort around here.'

I'm quite confused by this stage, especially as Frank and Cherie are visibly shaking with compressed laughter as they look at me over their newspaper pages.

'Erm . . . okay? Thank you,' I say, touching my hair self-consciously, noticing that it feels a bit stiff. Probably the salty sea air.

Saul realises what's being said, and grins at me before saying: 'I did that. I made her so pretty. I did Mummy's make-up in my beauty parlour this morning. She was being a lazy bones and staying in bed.'

I feel a horrifying blush sweep over my cheeks as the realisation sinks in. Luckily, my face is probably already so red that nobody will even notice.

My hands fly up to hide myself, and everybody bursts out laughing at my reaction. Even the walker, who I've never met in my life.

Oh God. I did it, didn't I? I played beauty parlour all morning just to get an extra few minutes in bed, and then was so busy and tired I didn't even look in a mirror before I left the house. Saul is perfectly dressed, perfectly groomed, with his teeth brushed and his hair neat and tidy. Me? I probably look like an escaped circus clown.

It does, at least, explain all the strange stares when I walked in. Maybe they thought I'd deliberately done it – me, a woman who rarely even wears make-up at all, and sees not being noticed as a tick in the win column.

Laura comes over and pats me on the shoulder in consolation. She's trying to look sympathetic, but the tears of amusement rolling down her cheeks don't match her tone.

'We've all been there, love,' she says, casting her eyes over my new look. 'I once went to Tesco with my hair sprayed into a mohawk, when Lizzie was going through a creative stage. Completely forgot until I was in the checkout paying for my sweet potatoes and toilet roll. What time did he get you up?'

'Umm . . . before six,' I reply quietly. I feel embarrassed and awkward and want the floor to open up, like in one of those films about earthquakes, and swallow me whole. I want to say more – to see how funny this is and shrug it off. Play it like Auburn would, and do a spontaneous mock-fashion catwalk around the room, showing off my new look.

But I'm not Auburn. I don't have her energy or confidence

or 'I'm-all-out-of-shits-to-give' attitude. I'm me. I'm almost mousy, and my default setting is to stay as quiet as possible so the predators don't notice me.

I try on a small smile for size, as Van looks at me in concern. Maybe he can see the slight trembling in my hands, or the ever-so-annoying sheen in my eyes. He nods at me once, sharply, and says: 'Come on, Saul – we're going on an adventure in the garden. Buried treasure. Let's give your mum a chance to look less beautiful and have a coffee, and see what we can find. What do you say, pirate lad?'

Saul grabs hold of his ears as though they're handles, and shrieks: 'Aye aye, Captain!' as they walk towards the doors. I watch them go, feeling both relieved and worried.

I don't have time to ponder the worried part, because Laura takes me by the arm and leads me away to the ladies. She's produced a packet of baby wipes – she's one of those mumsy women who always have a fresh pack of hankies about her person – and perches on the fake zebra-skin stool that's in there while I start to clean myself up. She looks a bit tired herself, now I come to notice.

The mirror in front of me reveals that my stylish look is even worse than I'd anticipated. I have purple eyes, the colour swirling all around the socket and across my eyebrows, and my skin is the deep tan of a terracotta warrior – up to my chin, where it suddenly goes milky white again. Two giant, circular blobs of bright red adorn my cheeks like apples, and the remnants of scarlet lipstick are lining my mouth. My hair is sprayed into a kind of cone on my head, like a strange hat – he must have covered it in lacquer, and massaged it upwards like the Eiffel Tower.

I stare at my reflection for a couple of seconds, then start to attack the whole mess with the vigour of a woman vowing never to let such a thing happen again.

'I remember those days,' says Laura, watching me and smiling. 'The early mornings. The constant demands for attention. I know it doesn't feel like it now, but you'll miss it when it's gone.'

'Really?' I say, unable to keep the disbelief from my voice as my fingertips get caught in my beehive.

'Oh yes,' she replies, nodding. 'Definitely. These days, budging Lizzie and Nate from their bedrooms is a challenge. Getting their attention is even harder. They still need me – but mainly for money and food and lifts to their friends' houses. I'm not the centre of their worlds any more, and even though that means I get more sleep, I do miss them being little. Of course, it was different for me – I had David around, then.'

Laura married her childhood sweetheart when they were barely out of school, and had her kids young. From what I can gather, theirs was a perfect life – until David tragically died after an accident at home.

A couple of years after that, she packed the children up and moved here for the summer. A summer that turned into forever, after Nate and Lizzie settled so well, and she met Matt.

She's another one of the Budbury survivors who has fitted into the routine of life here in this far-off corner of the world.

'Well, it's not too late, is it?' I ask, as I wipe my eyes within an inch of their lives. 'You could have another baby, if that's what you and Matt wanted.'

She snorts out a quick laugh, and slaps her own thighs.

'I don't think so!' she answers, looking part amused, part wistful. 'I'm knocking forty, you know. I think those days are behind me. Matt . . . well, he'd be a great dad. But I think he's happy with being a kind-of step-dad . . . I don't know. We've never even discussed it, to be honest. Anyway, I'm exhausted enough dealing with the kids and Midgebo.'

She gazes off at something I can't see, and I wonder if I've said the wrong thing. If I've touched a sore spot without even trying. She snaps out of it and smiles at me again, as though to reassure me.

'Anyway. You know what this place is like,' she says. 'We share our problems and we share our joys – and that means we all get to enjoy having Saul in our lives. We're glad you're here.'

I feel a sudden wash of gratitude towards her – for the baby wipes, for the conversation, for the reassurance. For the way she makes me feel so welcome.

'Thank you,' I reply, as I tackle the blusher spots. 'It's . . . well, it's taken me a while to settle in, but now I have, I'm glad I'm here as well. I'm not . . . not the sort of person who opens up too easily.'

She nods, and I can practically see her making an effort not to dive right in with a load of questions. The crowd here doesn't know much about my background, or why I left Bristol. They don't know about the way I grew up, or about Saul's dad, other than he lives in Scotland now. I have my privacy settings on high, and always have had.

Even as a kid, I was guarded. There are only so many times you can bring friends home from school just to have them walk into a parental war zone before you decide not to bother any more. It was embarrassing, at an age when you're mortally embarrassed about having a spot, never mind your mates seeing your mum whack your dad around the head with a frying pan.

'I know,' she says, when I don't add anything. 'And that's fine. We're all different, aren't we? I hope you know, though, that we're always here for you if ever you need a listening ear. Or some cake.'

'Or some baby wipes.'

'Yes! I always have baby wipes . . . even if I don't have the baby. Anyway, come on out and have a coffee and some toast. Or do you want some jam roly-poly? I know you like that.'

'Isn't it a bit early for jam roly-poly?' I ask, smiling.

She feigns shocked horror and says: 'Hush your mouth, child – it's never too early for jam roly-poly! I didn't get a figure like this by watching the clock, you know!'

She gestures down at her own body, which to be fair is

a little on the round side. She's not fat, not by any means. Just . . . comfortable. And curvy. And perfect.

'Thank you. Toast would be great,' I reply, as we emerge back into the café. There's another couple of customers now, a fresh-faced teenager and what looks like his granddad, and I feel momentarily bad that I took Laura away from her work. She glances at my face, and seems to know that immediately.

'Don't worry,' she says, patting my hand. 'Cherie's sorted them, look. About time she got off her lazy backside anyway.'

She says the last part extra-loud, and Cherie laughs from behind the counter, waving a spatula at her threateningly.

'Watch your cheek, lady,' she answers, grinning. 'You're never too old for a good spanking!'

Frank looks up from his newspaper, blue eyes twinkling, and adds: 'You're right there, love!'

This is something of a conversation stopper, and Laura and I exchange wide-eyed glances as we both try very hard not to imagine Frank getting his 82-year-old bottom smacked. Crikey. Grey panthers rule – and they've definitely got a better love life than me.

Laura does a mock shiver and settles me down at one of the tables. She knows I won't want company, and doesn't push it. The ladies here, in particular, tend to gather at the café for mammoth sessions of gossip and world-righting. I often see them, clustered around a couple of tables shoved together – Cherie and Laura and Becca and Zoe, Edie and Willow and Auburn. They always look so comfortable with each other; sitting there guzzling endless rounds of freshly baked scones and hot chocolates.

Sometimes, I want to join them. I want to take that simple step of walking in, sitting down and chatting with the tribe. But I never have, so far – in fact I've sometimes turned away from the café once I've seen them there, not quite ready to break my solitude.

Maybe one day I'll take the daring step of joining them for one of their sessions.

Not quite yet, though, I decide, looking on as the new customers stare around the room in wonder. They'll always remember this place – the weird café on the cliff they found when they were out walking. They'll probably tell their friends about it, go home and try to describe it. I see the teenager whip out his phone and start taking photos – because, of course, teenagers don't settle for just describing something when they can post it on social media instead.

Cherie comes over with a mocha – my favourite – and a plate heaped with granary toast. The butter is laid on so thick it's melting and oozing over bread that I know Laura will have baked herself. I have died and gone to heaven.

'There you go, love,' says Cherie, laying one gentle hand on my shoulder. 'Fill your boots, as they say. That little dynamo of yours will be back in soon, so enjoy the peace. Oh, by the way, did Laura tell you there was a phone call for you?'

I already have a mouthful of toast when she asks this, and all I can do is shake my head, butter dripping down my chin, looking up at her inquiringly.

'Laura!' she bellows, so loud that small mountain ranges in Nepal probably shake and quiver. 'When did you take that message for Katie?'

Laura stops what she's doing – slicing tomatoes for the day's salads – and stares up, looking horrified.

'Oh no!' she says, biting her lip. 'I'm so sorry – I completely forgot about it; I don't know where my head is today! Katie, your mum called – she said can you call her back, please? She also said, "Don't worry, nobody's dead." Which is nice.'

# Chapter 8

Van walks back into the café at that stage, Saul trailing behind him, cheeks rosy from the autumnal chill and his hair ruffled.

'Mummy!' he shouts, dashing over full of excitement. 'We found treasure!'

He grabs hold of my knee with one muddy hand, and in the other brandishes his booty – a one pound coin. I'm guessing that Van managed to distract him while he buried it in the garden, then helped him re-discover it. He winks at me over Saul's head, and I blink rapidly in response.

'It's a Spanish doon!' Saul says, spinning it around on the table top. He looks so thrilled, it momentarily distracts me from Van, my mother, and wondering what the hell is going on back at home.

'A Spanish doon? Wow!' I say, widening my eyes in suitable awe. 'That's amazing!'

'Shop?' he asks, hopefully, his tone slightly wheedling. He might think it's a Spanish doubloon – or doon, I should say – but clearly still expects to be able to exchange it for a carton of juice and a chocolate bar.

'Later, sweetie,' I respond. 'I'll take you to the shop later. Right now it's time for me to take you to see Lynnie and Willow while I go to work. How does that sound? You can show them your Spanish doon.'

He ponders this, and I see him weigh up the pros and cons with his little boy brain. On the one hand, no shop. But on the other – fun times! Luckily, he lands on the side of Lynnie and Willow, which is exactly where I want him. Life is much easier if you don't have to argue with a toddler. I mean, I usually win the arguments – I am technically the grown-up – but it's tiring.

'Lynnie will love my doon,' he pronounces, pulling up the hood of his coat in the way he does when he wants me to know he's ready to go somewhere. It's like his signal – *I'm ready for action, Mummy!*

I nod, and cram as much toast in my mouth as I can without choking. I swill it down with my mocha, feeling disrespectful – it deserved better than that. Life with a small child often leads to indigestion, I've discovered.

I glance at Cherie apologetically, feeling bad for my lack of appreciation, but she just nods and gives me a 'don't-worry-about-it' wave as I put my coat on. I'm wondering already how I'll manage to call my mum, and plan to try and fit it in on the walk to Lynnie's cottage. I have a few hours to do at the pharmacy, while he's on his weirdly formed playdate.

'I'm heading back,' says Van, now wrapped up in a navy fleece jacket and wearing a beanie hat that makes him look a bit like he should be in some mountainous ski resort in the Alps. 'I'll walk with you, if that's okay?'

I see Laura watching us, pretending not to, and know that she'll be thinking what a nice couple we make. Laura is a great believer in happy endings, despite all her own trials and tribulations. I catch her eye and raise one eyebrow, and she at least has the grace to blush and start bustling around with a cheese grater.

'Okay,' I say simply, as Van waits for a reply. I mean, I could hardly say no, could I? Even if I wanted to.

We say our farewells and start the short walk to the cottage. It's a beautiful day, cold but sunny, with that fresh, crisp light you sometimes get in autumn. Dazzling blue skies hover over the sea, the colour so bold and solid it looks like you could reach out and touch it.

The coastal pathways are slightly muddy from the melted morning frost, and the sound of birdsong is melodically present in the background, along with the gentle hiss and hum of calm waves lapping the sand.

We leave the cliffs behind us, and emerge onto footpaths that criss-cross Frank's farm. Tucked between glorious green hills, the fields are literally covered in seagulls and other birds, hovering and flapping over the ground like a living carpet made of fluttering wings.

'Why all the birdies?' Saul asks, tugging at Van's sleeve

and looking up at him inquiringly. He correctly assumes that I wouldn't have a clue.

'Ah,' replies Van, pointing across at them. 'That's because it's after harvest, and we've been getting the fields ready for their new seeds. We spread muck on it – cow poo! – and then we plough it and all the soil gets squished and turned over. When we do that, lots of worms come out to play, and the birds come along for an extra big dinner time. It's like the Comfort Food Café for seagulls, but instead of cake, they eat long, wriggly worms!'

Saul immediately giggles at the mention of cow poo, obviously. I know from my dealings with men that this will be the case even when he's thirty. He watches the birds and makes wriggling gestures with his fingers, making them into worms and laughing.

He's trotting along, feet squelching, one hand in mine and one in Van's, occasionally asking us to 'give him a swing'. We usually oblige, and his squeals of delight as he flies up into the air are joyous to hear. Anyone looking on would assume we were a young couple out for a stroll with our son, and the thought chokes me a little.

Maybe it's that, or maybe it's an underlying worry about my mum, but I'm quiet as we walk. Smiling, so I don't look like a complete misery-guts, but not exactly chatty either.

'Are you all right?' asks Van, giving me a sideways glance. 'You seem a bit . . . off, today.'

I snap myself out of my fugue state and reply as breezily as I can: 'Yes, I'm fine. Sorry. Just a bit tired, you know?'

'I can imagine. Maybe you need a night off. Maybe . . . we could go for a pint. Together. Like grown-ups do, or so I'm told. I don't know many of those.'

'Oh . . . well, I don't think I could. I wouldn't have a babysitter.'

He sighs, and when I look up at him, his blue eyes are crinkled at the corners. He looks partly amused, partly exasperated. Wholly gorgeous.

'Katie, you have a whole village full of babysitters. Saul could stay over at the cottage. Becca and Sam would have him for a few hours. Edie would sit in with him. Cherie and Frank would love to have him. Laura would probably see it as a treat and bake a whole oven full of cupcakes for him. There are several teenagers who would be desperate to earn a tenner for the privilege of sitting on your sofa using their phones. Babysitting isn't a problem.'

'Right,' I say, trudging on, half wishing that Saul would fall face first into a cowpat or something so I could use the excuse to end this particular conversation. He remains annoyingly upright, singing a song to himself about a worm that lives at the bottom of his garden. I recognise it immediately, and find myself singing along: 'And his name is Wiggly-Woo . . .'

Saul giggles again, and carries on singing. Van is quiet, but not in an annoyed way – coming from his family, I'm guessing he's used to eccentric women who randomly burst into song. I know Willow does it all the time, often serenading us with her highly individual versions of Disney classics.

'Right,' I say again, brushing my hair away from my face and feeling annoyed with myself. I don't know quite why, but I feel silly, for a whole variety of reasons.

'Well then,' I continue, trying to stride ahead but not managing it, as Van is so much taller than me. 'Maybe I will come out for a drink some time. Maybe I won't. I suppose what I'm saying is that I'll do it when and if I want to. Is that all right?'

He grins, and then laughs. I'm not sure I expected him to laugh, but it's better than him being offended.

'I love that thing you do,' he answers, looking on as Saul trudges off to investigate a pile of Wiggly-Woos.

'What thing?'

'That thing where you say stuff in a quiet voice that makes you sound apologetic and shy, but when you actually look at what the stuff you said was, it's the opposite of apologetic and shy. You sound all weedy, but you're actually kind of channelling a Chaka Khan "I'm Every Woman" vibe.'

I glance at him from beneath my fringe, and can't help but smile. He's totally right, of course. The new me is striving to be a strong and independent woman – but my attitude hasn't quite caught up with it. I'm like a mouse trying to roar.

'I'm a work in progress,' I reply, smiling at him. 'And by the way, I think your mother is on her way to meet us . . .'

He looks up and squints into the sunlight to make her out. Lynnie is cutting a path in our direction, wearing her pyjamas, a faux fur stole, and a pair of ancient Hunter wellies. Now, Lynnie does have Alzheimer's, but in all honesty, dressing like that probably isn't part of her symptoms – the whole family has what you might call a relaxed approach to social conventions.

The rolled-up yoga mat under her arm, though? That's usually a sign that she's decided to set off somewhere to give a class. At a guess, the café.

Sure enough, Willow isn't far behind her, eating up the distance with her stupidly long legs to catch her up, pink hair streaming in the breeze. Bella Swan, her Border terrier, is next in line.

We all meet up in the middle, Willow puffing slightly, Lynnie looking confused at all the fuss. It's hard to know how she'll react in situations like this – sometimes a gentle reminder of the here and now sets her back on track. Other times, she understandably lashes out at the fact that a group of strange people are trying to kidnap her.

Luckily, Saul is usually the salve in all of these scenarios. He runs straight up to her, and wraps his arms around her legs, making delighted sounds muffled by his scarf.

'Well, hello!' says Lynnie, squatting down to get on eye level with him. 'Where are you off to, little man?'

'Your cottage, silly billy!' he replies joyously, reaching out to stroke the faux fur around her shoulders. 'Mummy's going to work at the chemist shop and I'm coming to look after you.'

I meet Willow's gaze, and see the frown lines and anxiety on her face. She tries to hide it, and often manages, but it's all there – the worry and the fatigue. She's one of life's optimists, Willow, always seeing the best in the world and the people she meets – but having a sunny disposition doesn't always count when your mum has dementia.

We all wait to see what Lynnie's reaction is going to be, and there is almost a communal sigh of relief when she stands up straight and offers her hand to Saul.

'Come on then,' she says, heading back to the house, him ambling at her side. 'If you're going to look after me, we'd better make some toast to keep our strength up.'

She nods at me and Van politely as she goes, as though we are strangers deserving of a pleasantry as she passes. It's more than Willow gets.

'I'm the bad guy today,' she says sadly, as we follow on. 'She didn't want to take her tablets, or eat her breakfast, or get dressed. Then she waited until I was in the bathroom and made a break for it. Crazy like a fox, that one.'

Van nods and stays silent. I know he struggles more than his sisters with his mother's condition. Maybe it's because he's not been back as long; maybe it's a gender thing – he's the kind of guy who's used to being able to fix things. Build things. Make things work properly. Now he's facing something that isn't fixable, and I know it eats away at him.

'If it's too much to have Saul around, I can take him with me,' I say, touching Willow's arm as we walk.

'No, honestly, it's fine,' Willow replies, pasting a smile onto her drawn face. 'It's actually easier when he's here. It's like having a kid around somehow overrides the other impulses; some instinct kicks in and she just enjoys being with him and playing with him. Besides, can you imagine Saul in a pharmacy?'

I grin as I picture this, and bite back a giggle.

'I know. It'd be dangerous, wouldn't it? He'd be snorting athlete's foot powder and painting his face with antibacterial cream . . .'

'Not to mention swigging the Gaviscon, getting high on caffeine pills, and possibly treating the antibiotics like Skittles.'

We all pause as we let these images sink in.

'You're right,' I say, finally. 'He's banned from the pharmacy for life. Anyway . . . if you're sure?'

'Of course I'm sure,' she says, gently but firmly. 'I'd speak out if I needed to, don't worry. No, off you go – might as well make a break for it while he's distracted. I'll see you this afternoon, all right? He'll be fine. I'll be fine. We'll all be fine. Tom's coming round anyway, so he can ride Rick Grimes around the garden like he's that dog-dragon in *The Neverending Story*.'

Rick Grimes is part Rottweiler, part golden retriever, part mystery. He can be unpredictable with other dogs, but adores children. As we don't have any pets of our own, it's a good set-up – Saul gets all the fun, and I get none of the responsibility.

I nod and say goodbye to her and Van, and head off towards the village. I seem to spend my life traipsing across various fields and footpaths, juggling time and childcare and favours. Life might be easier if I had a car – but as I can't drive, maybe not. Perhaps, I think, as I leave them behind and follow a different path, I should invest in one of those motorbikes that has a sidecar I can put Saul into. He'd love that.

I'm still smiling about that particular image when I arrive at the pharmacy. It's in the centre of the village, and is imaginatively called The Budbury Chemist. It's quite quaint and old-fashioned looking on the outside, with mullioned windows and a wooden sign that hangs like the ones you find outside old pubs. On it is a painted version of an old apothecary symbol, a pestle and mortar, with a border made of green ivy. The place used to be owned by a lady called Ivy Wellkettle, who left to live with her daughter last year, and the sign has stayed as a reminder of her.

I push the door open and hear the familiar jingle-jangle of the bell as I make my way inside. The warmth of the room envelops me, and makes me realise how cold it's been getting recently. This will be my third winter here in

Budbury, and last year's was a humdinger. At least Saul is walking much more now, so I won't be wrestling his pushchair through the snow as often.

I look around at the well-stocked shelves and the pristine counter and the various posters about flu jabs and controlling asthma and giving up smoking, and spot Auburn sitting on the sprawling sofa at the back of the main room, next to Edie May.

You don't often get sofas in chemists' shops, but this is Budbury. Everyone likes a place to sit wherever they go – otherwise, they might have to stay upright while chatting. This sofa was a gift from Cherie, and it shows – it's in the shape of a giant pair of bright red lips. Like an enormous lipstick-on-tissue kiss that's been stuffed and covered in velvet and given little legs. Personally, I find it quite scary, and always feel like I'm about to be eaten by a cartoon alien whenever I sit on it.

Auburn is, as her name suggests, a red-head. All of Lynnie's children were named after characteristics they had when they were born – Van had a wonky ear (it looks fine now); Willow was long and lean, and their other brother, who lives in Aberdeen, is called Angel because he was so cherubic. He's the black sheep of the family – he changed his name to Andrew.

Today, Auburn's hair is pulled back into a glossy ponytail, cascading down the side of her white-coated shoulder. She looks professional and competent, and every inch the pharmacist, until you notice the bulge in her chest pocket. That'd be her Zippo and pack of cigarettes, which she regularly sneaks out into the courtyard at the back to puff away on. She's always saying she's going to give up, and even put one of the especially graphic anti-smoking posters in a back window so she can look at it as she wheezes. The photos of black lungs don't seem to have deterred her.

Next to Auburn is Edie, the village's 92-year-old elder stateswoman. She's tiny, with a face made entirely of wrinkles and creases, and twinkling blue eyes that belie her true age. Her white hair is recently permed, and forms a pouffy helmet around her head.

The other quirk about Edie is the fact she apparently believes her long-dead fiancé is still alive. He was killed during the Second World War, but there was never any body. Over the years, I'm told, she settled into a delusion that he was still around – and always takes home extra food for him from the café.

It's the way Budbury works that everybody simply accepts this, and doesn't allow it to get in the way of the fact that Edie, despite her age, is still one of the most active and popular people in the village. Nobody asks too many questions, nobody thinks she's any weirder than anybody else, and nobody even blinks when she mentions him.

The two of them – Edie and Auburn, not Edie and her ghost fiancé – are currently sharing a catalogue of some kind, pointing at pictures and giggling.

They look up as I walk towards them, and Edie pipes up: 'Katie! Just the girl! We were just considering a new range of novelty condoms and over-the-counter sex aids . . . what do you think? Is Budbury ready for that?'

I find myself blushing, and try to shake it away.

'I don't know . . . do you think there'd be much demand?' I ask, trying and failing to not look at the glossy photos of soft-focus boudoirs.

'Who knows?' replies Auburn, closing the catalogue, standing up and stretching. 'I think there are hidden depths of perversion in this town. It's all sweet and sugar-coated on the surface, but there's got to be some heavy-duty swinging and dominatrix action going on behind the lace curtains . . .'

My mind flickers back to Frank's comment about spanking, and I blush even more.

Auburn, being Auburn, carries on regardless: 'And you know what? That catalogue came in the same post for a brochure about Harry Potter merchandise we might want for Christmas! Imagine if they'd mixed up the two, and we'd got a Harry Potter-themed sex selection? That would be fun . . . Voldemort's Length, for *your* Chamber of Secrets!'

I shudder, and try not to show it.

'Well,' I say, hiding my discomfort as well as I can, 'you could always open an X-rated store in the back room, couldn't you? Adults only. Ann Summers kind of vibe. Laura would probably make you some cakes in the shape of penises.'

Edie bursts out laughing and claps her tiny hands together in delight.

'Oh yes! Buttercream willy cake! How funny – they'd flock here from as far away as Devon! We'd all become famous for our willy cake! Can you imagine?'

Sadly, I can – and it prompts me to offer a round of hot beverages instead of working further on our masterplan of filth. One minute it's a joke; the next I'll be selling fluffy handcuffs to the postman's wife.

'Been busy?' I ask, as Auburn follows me behind the dispensing area. This is pristine and clean, with a big fridge and well-organised shelves and various containers and pieces of equipment; reference books with exciting names like *Stockley's Drug Interactions*, a computer and printer for the labels, and a big locked cupboard that contains the heavy-duty controlled pharmaceuticals. The 'Party Cupboard', as Auburn very irreverently calls it.

It leads into a tiny kitchen area, which is slightly less pristine, and beyond that a stock room. We stop in the kitchen, and Auburn leans back against the counter-tops, pulling her cigarettes from her pocket in preparation for a trip outside.

'A bit, this morning. Some repeat prescriptions for that lady who has a lot of problems with her arthritis, lives a few miles off? Plus some blue pill action for a bloke who actually lives much further towards Dorchester, but is obviously too embarrassed to get his fix locally. Few people came in for cough and cold stuff. Sold some of those handwarmers you put in the microwave. But not exactly a tsunami of custom, no. How are things with you? Did you drop Saul off today?'

I nod and bustle around getting the cups ready. She sounds slightly edgy as she asks, and I know that's not because of Saul – it's because she's worried about her mum.

'Yep, everything is fine,' I reply, smiling at her. Okay, that's stretching the truth a bit – but it won't do her any good to know Lynnie was having one of her wandering star moments. Auburn in particular gets stressed out about those, as the first time she looked after her mum overnight, she made a run for it and ended up in hospital with a broken ankle. Not her fault – but like most women, she lives to blame herself for everything that ever goes wrong in the entire universe.

'Good . . . well, while it's quiet, I'm going to nip out for a breath of unfresh air. Oh! By the way – I completely forgot. You got a phone call earlier – from your mum. Said there was no answer on your landline, and she'd been trying you on your mobile, and could you please call her back? If you're not too busy. But don't worry, nobody's died.'

# Chapter 9

Before I make the tea, I get out my phone and check it. Missed calls from Mum, yes, but annoyingly no messages that might shed some light on what's going on. And as for the landline, that'll be because I unplugged it and forgot – Saul called 999 a few days ago to tell the police that two seagulls were having a fight outside the house. They saw the funny side, but in that stern *warnings about wasting emergency services' time* kind of voice.

I quickly look into the shop, to make sure there's not a giant queue of customers waiting to buy hand sanitiser and Strepsils, and call my mum's number. It goes straight to voicemail, and I leave a quick message saying I'm sorry I haven't called back, I'm glad nobody's dead, and she can get me on my mobile later.

I give it a few moments' thought, then try my dad as well. Also voicemail. The landline just rings out and out, and I can picture it, chiming away in the hall at home, on the little table that has a seat attached to it – an antique relic of a bygone era when people had to sit at home and talk to each other.

It's weird that neither of them is answering. It's Saturday, so Dad might be out at the pub with his mates. Mum's usually at home, though, watching the clock and getting annoyed with him.

I chew my lip a bit, and decide there's nothing else I can do for the time being. And, as I've been told, nobody's dead.

I distract myself by making the tea, and walk back through to give Edie a mug. She's chortling away at the sex aid catalogue, and peers at me over her glasses.

'Oh my! The things these people come up with!' she says, wrapping her papery-skinned fingers around the mug. 'Where do they get their ideas from?'

'I really don't know,' I reply, smiling at her infectious amusement. 'It's probably best not to think about it too deeply.'

She nods sagely, and stands up to her spectacular height of five foot nothing. She's dressed in her usual beige cardigan and matching tights, with sensible shoes and a fluorescent orange Vans backpack draped from her slender shoulders. It's like Edie's uniform. She downs her tea in one – decades of experience.

'You're probably right, dear . . . say goodbye to Smokey McChuff Face for me, will you? Thanks for this lovely tea, but I must make a move. Busy day today – I'm judging in a sausage-making contest in the big city! I wonder what the sex catalogue people would make of that, eh?'

I grimace, and wave her off. The 'big city' actually means

the next village over, Applechurch, which is a regular metropolis compared to Budbury. They have three pubs, and a school, and their very own GP surgery. Dizzying stuff.

I try my mum again and get no reply. To try and stop myself from worrying, I do some stocktaking, and by the time Auburn comes back in with her own mug of coffee and a plate of café-made cookies, I've discovered that we need more cold sore cream. Heaven forbid the lips of Budbury should go untreated. I make a note on my little pad, and take one of the chocolate chip sin-balls that Auburn offers. I have no idea why everyone in Budbury isn't obese – must be all the walking we do to offset the sugar.

I tell her goodbye from Edie, and carry on stalking the shelves, counting up boxes of Kleenex and wondering why chemist shops always seem to sell those lollipops that are made in the shape of whistles.

Auburn follows behind me like a shadow. She's hovering so close at one point that when I back up to get a wider look at our frankly stunning range of scented candles, I crash right into her.

'Sorry!' she yelps, jumping out of the way, the word muffled by her mouthful of cookie crumbs.

'Can I help you with something, Auburn?' I ask, smiling at her to take any potential sting out of my words. Full of confidence and brazen flash on the surface, she's actually pretty easily offended – like she's waiting for the world to notice she's not all that.

'No . . . I'm just bored, I suppose. I've got all the prescription requests done for Monday; I've checked my stocks in the dispensary, and I've eaten seven thousand chocolate chip cookies. So now I have a massive sugar rush and nowhere to go. I talked to Van while I was outside, by the way, just to see how things were going.'

'Right – everything okay?' I ask, perching myself on the stool behind the counter. Just in case we get a mad flood of customers – and also to stop Auburn from invading my personal space. I'm very protective of my personal space.

'Yep. Mum's teaching Saul how to knit. He says he's going to make you a scarf for Christmas. And Van says he asked you out for a drink and you said no.'

'I didn't say no. I said maybe I would, maybe I wouldn't. Was he upset? I didn't mean to upset him. I just . . . didn't want to agree to something I wasn't sure about.'

She grins, full wattage, and seems delighted with it all. Van is her big brother, but not by much, and there's a definite sibling rivalry that age and maturity hasn't managed to erase.

I'm an only child, and being involved with big families is always a magical mystery tour for me – no matter how old they get, there always seems to be part of them that stays feral, and wants to hold the other one down on the floor while they dribble spit on their faces.

'No, he's not upset. In fact I think you've accidentally mastered the art of treat 'em mean and keep 'em keen without even trying. Most people would just lie to get out of something.'

'I don't think I have the imagination to lie,' I reply, quietly. 'And I spent too much of my life tiptoeing around other people's feelings to feel comfortable with it. Not so long ago, I'd have just said yes to please him.'

'But not now?' she asks, one eyebrow arched up in question.

'No. Not now. Anyway, what lie would you have told?'

She narrows her eyes slightly, as though she's letting me know that she knows that I'm changing the conversation, steering it away from any personal revelations. I nod, to show that I know that she knows, and that I'm not about to start spilling my guts like I'm on *The Jeremy Kyle Show*. Budbury, for all its many charms, is not a great respecter of privacy. So, we both know what we know – and leave it at that.

'Well,' she replies, staring off into space as she thinks about it, 'there are a variety of lies that would suit that scenario. If you'd met him in a club, you could give him a fake phone number. And a fake name. I used to pretend I was a nurse called Lorraine when I met men for the first time. This is different, though . . . you'd have to go for either something halfway believable, or a complete whopper.'

'Examples, please. I live to learn at the knees of Lorraine.'

'Okay – well, halfway believable. Tell him you're a lesbian.'

'What?? Do I look like I might be a lesbian?'

She bursts out laughing, and I have to join in.

'Not that there's anything wrong with that,' I add. 'And it has its appeal – I could be the only gay in the village.'

'That we *know* of,' replies Auburn, nodding like she's stumbled across the world's greatest conspiracy theory. 'Statistically, there must be some. I should probably organise an official survey. And lesbians, I believe, can look like absolutely anybody – so that's a daft comment. Admittedly, you have a child – but you could say that was a one-off, and you've since had a personal epiphany of a Sapphic persuasion.'

'I could, if I knew what that meant. All right. That's one – how about the complete whopper?'

'Those are more fun,' she says, unwrapping a whistle-shaped lollipop and pausing to blow through it. 'You could say you're a nun on sabbatical. Or that you have a terrible sexually transmitted disease that's made your lady parts fall off. Or that your dog ate your foot. Or wait until the night you were supposed to go out, and say a giant pterodactyl shat on your head.'

'Or,' I reply, taking the lollipop out of her hand and throwing it into the bin – the last thing she needs is more sugar – 'I could just be honest. I'm really not at a point in my life where I want to be dating. Not that it was a date. Not that he implied that. Not that I'm being up myself, and assuming he's interested in me that way. Because I'm sure he's not – he's a very attractive man, and there's no way he'd fancy me. And even if he did, I'm not saying that I fancy him. Even though he is very attractive. And . . .'

I run out of steam at that point, which is a good thing, as Auburn is already practically wetting herself laughing at me.

'Aye aye, Captain Careful,' she says, giving me a mock salute. 'Message received, over and out – you're not interested. Even if he was interested. Which is all very interesting. And as he's my big bro, and I still think of him in terms of sweaty socks and acne, I can understand you saying no. But if not him, then what about someone else? I mean, you've been here for ages, and presumably single for ages, and . . . well, don't you need a shag by now?'

She looks genuinely bewildered by the concept of someone being celibate for this long. Auburn, for all her bluster, is actually almost as guarded as me when it comes to her emotions – she covers them up under layers of sarcasm and nonsense.

She's the same with her personal history – I know she lived away from home for over a decade, travelling and working, in South America and Asia and Europe. There must have been significant others, but she's never talked about them. Now, she seems to have a selection of blokes she refers to as her 'he-man harem', who she occasionally pays visits to. Presumably not to discuss the meaning of life.

I shrug and try to look nonchalant.

'I'm the mother of a very active small child. That changes everything. For a start, I'm too tired to even think about sex, never mind actually do it. And . . . well, maybe I'm just not built like you, Auburn. You can separate sex and feelings. That's never been my strong point, and life is already complicated enough without throwing that into the mix. For now, I'm content with things the way they are.'

She ponders that, and nods.

'You're right. Separating emotions from pretty much everything else is one of my strong suits. And I get what you're saying – but Saul won't be around as a human shield forever, will he?'

I'm not keen on that phrase, but let it pass. She doesn't mean any harm by it, I know.

'Nope. And maybe when he's left home, I'll turn into a nymphomaniac to make up for lost time. At the moment . . . well, I'm too busy washing pterodactyl poo from my hair, aren't I?'

'That's the spirit!' she says, patting my hand. 'By George, I think she's got it!'

She gazes outside, at the quiet main street that flows through Budbury, which is sleepy even on a Saturday. I know she's thinking about her mum, and what's going on at home. She usually stays until just after lunchtime, to be available for pharmacist duties, and it's now almost twelve. Crikey, I think – I've managed to go to the in-bed Beauty

Parlour, show off my new image at the café, say no to a not-really-a-date with a hot man, drop off Saul, and look at sex aids with a nonagenarian already this morning.

'Why don't you go home?' I suggest, following her gaze. 'I think we've had our rush. If anyone comes in with a prescription, I can tell them to collect it on Monday. Or if it's urgent, I'll call you and you can come back. I can lock up at three and meet you back at the cottage.'

She bites her lip, and I can see her weighing it up in her mind.

'If that's okay with you, I think I might,' she replies. 'Van said Willow had headed off to the café to help out – Laura wasn't feeling too good, apparently – so that might not be a bad idea.'

She sees the concerned look sprout on my face – I can't help it – and quickly adds: 'They're fine, honest! Mum and Saul are knitting, and Van's watching football on the telly. Everything's good. But . . . if it's all right with you, I might head off, yeah. Need to walk off those cookies, apart from anything else!'

'Yep. Walk away from the whistle pops, and make a move. I'll see you later.'

She nods, and bustles about getting her white coat off and her leather jacket on, and eventually leaves – giving me a wink as she grabs one more whistle pop 'for the road'.

I sigh a little as she goes, unfairly looking forward to an hour or so on my own. Barring customers, of course.

I never get time on my own, and when I do, it's precious. Not that I don't love Saul, or enjoy the pleasant, predictable bustle of my life, but every now and then, being in a room alone, without anybody needing me to do anything for them, is balm for an aching soul. I spent a lot of time alone growing up, and sometimes I miss it.

I won't be lazy – I'll do some cleaning, or unpack a new delivery of supplies, or order some cold sore cream online – but I'll be alone while I do it. Blissful.

Unfortunately, the universe has other ideas, and literally two minutes after the bell dinged to mark Auburn's exit, it dings again. I look up from my perch, and see Laura walk in. Her eyes have a slightly deranged look to them, and her pretty face is drawn and pale and . . . scared?

# Chapter 10

Laura glances around furtively, checking for interlopers, before heading in my direction. She's bundled up in a thick, hot pink puffa jacket, hands wrapped in black gloves that have skeleton bones painted on the fingers. I suspect she stole those from Lizzie, and I also suspect that they might glow in the dark. It's started raining outside, and her hair is bursting out from her hood in frizzy strands. She tugs the hood down, revealing a severe case of hat head.

'Hi!' she says, her voice shrill and way too perky. 'Is there anyone else here?'

'No,' I reply, coming out to her side of the counter. 'Auburn just left.'

'I know . . . I was hiding around the corner and saw her go.'

'Okay,' I say, calmly. Of course, I'm wondering why she was hiding, and why she sounds so weird, but I don't push. I've worked in healthcare the whole of my adult life, and sometimes people just need a little space. If they want to talk, they'll expand to fill the silence.

'Would you like a cup of tea?' I ask instead, in that ultra-British way that actually means 'I'm worried about you and don't know what else to do.'

She stares at me for a minute, slowly peeling off her skeleton gloves, and shakes her head.

'No, thank you. I'm just . . . well, I just thought I'd pop in and see how things are going?'

She doesn't even sound convinced by this herself, and I see her automatically reach out and pick up a cookie from the plate. She takes a bite and pulls a face.

'Not as good as they could have been,' she says, frowning. 'I made these at home to take to the café, and Midgebo ran into the cottage being chased by a cat. Poor thing was terrified.'

'The cat?' I ask, not unreasonably, as Midgebo is a very large, very lively black Labrador.

'Oh no – Midgebo! The cat was a monster! Seriously, the biggest ginger tom I've ever seen. It chased him around the kitchen, trapped him in a corner, then as soon as his job was done, gave me a look, like "yeah, puny human, your kingdom is mine", and strutted back out again. I've never seen him before, but I suppose people must have cats . . . I mean, a lot of us have dogs, don't we? And Becca has those goldfish. But perhaps other people have cats . . .'

She's wittering now, and doesn't seem able to stop. I recognise the wittering for what it is: self-distraction.

'Laura, are you all right? Auburn said you'd left the café

because you didn't feel well. Is there anything I can do for you?'

I'm thinking it might be bowels. The great British public seems, as a race, constitutionally unable to say the word 'bowel' in public without at least attempting to whisper it.

She bites her lips viciously, and I'm horrified to see tears springing up in her eyes. Laura is one of the most cheerful people I know, and seeing her crying simply does not compute. I know she's had her share of hardships and tragedy, but since I've known her, she's been such a happy soul. Kind of like Mary Poppins in café cook form, always upbeat and positive, and carrying a big bag full of everything you could ever need in life.

'Yes. No. Maybe . . . is the chemist like a doctor? Or a priest? Or Vegas?' she asks, in a tumble of words, all falling over each other.

'You mean, are there rules about confidentiality?'

She nods, her curls bobbing up and down with the motion, and the tears finally spilling down her cheeks.

'Well, *I* have rules about confidentiality, and they're probably stricter than any laws, so don't worry. Now, come on, what's the matter? Don't be upset. It can't be that bad – and don't be embarrassed, whatever it is. I'm a medical professional, you know, even though I didn't look like one when I walked into the café this morning!'

I intend that last line as something of a joke, and she looks pathetically grateful for it, swiping her hands across her face to remove the tears as though she's angry with herself.

'Yes,' she says firmly. 'You are. And thank you. It's kind of related to what we were talking about then, anyway. I've been really tired recently, and was just putting it down to getting older and being busy and the fact that I eat way too much cake and not enough quinoa or whatever. But then me and you had that conversation, about how exhausting it is to have a baby around, but how quickly it goes, and how it completely and utterly changes your life, and how it's both the best and the worst time you ever have?'

We'd barely touched on any of that, but clearly, in her head, we had, so I just nod encouragingly.

'Well, after that, I was in the kitchen, making a toffee caramel sauce for the puddings, and I suddenly hated toffee caramel pudding. I mean, look at me, Katie – I'm not the sort of woman who hates toffee caramel pudding!'

The last few words come out in a kind of desperate wail, and I suddenly start to get an inkling of what might be bothering her.

'Ah . . . so you're wondering why you hate toffee caramel pudding? And why you're tired?'

'Yes, and . . . well, having looked at the calendar on my phone, I suppose I'm also wondering why I'm ten days late with my period as well . . . I mean, it probably means nothing. I'm probably going through early menopause. And

I'm probably going to love the pudding again tomorrow. But . . .'

'You thought maybe you should check? Just to put your mind at rest?'

She nods, looking forlorn and deflated now she's finally admitted what's bothering her, and I walk over to our high shelf full of slightly adult items – by which I mean condoms and pregnancy tests and other things that would make a teenaged boy blush. I grab one of the packages, then turn the sign hanging on the door to 'closed'. I hope we don't get a sudden rush – but even if we do, Auburn would understand.

'Come on,' I say, leading her through to the back rooms. 'Are you ready to go? Or do you need that tea?'

'No, I'm bursting,' she says, managing a smile. 'I drank a whole bottle of water on my way here, just in case. If you hadn't been in, or you'd been busy with a customer, I'd have probably just weed myself quietly in the corner and hoped nobody noticed.'

We approach the loo – a common or garden loo, with a small wooden sign showing a gnome urinating on the door – and I feel her slowing up. Like a dog who recognises the entrance to the vet's, and tries to drag its heels as you take him in.

'No point waiting,' I say, firmly but, I hope, kindly. 'If you're not pregnant, then you can start eating some quinoa and maybe take some vitamin D, which I can find for you here. If you are pregnant, then ignoring it won't make the problem go away. And it's not even necessarily a problem – just an adjustment.'

She snorts out a quick laugh, and finally takes off her puffa jacket.

'It would be less of an adjustment, and more of a "holy fuck what am I going to do next?" kind of thing, really. I don't even know what I want it to be . . . negative would be easier, and, you know, I do like my life as it is. But positive would be . . . well, it would be a baby, wouldn't it? A new life. A bloody miracle . . .'

Laura rarely swears – at least out loud – and it's a sign of what a tizzy she's built herself up into. She hands me her jacket, gives me a brave smile, and says: 'Right! I'm going in . . . if I'm not back in ten minutes, call the fire brigade!'

I nod, and tell her I'll be waiting back in the shop. I mean, nobody can pee properly while they know someone's outside listening, can they?

I feel jittery and nervous on her behalf, and calm myself down by checking up on our stocks of pre-natal vitamins and nappies. You know, just in case? By the time I've decided we're fine for both, and dusted the already dust-free shelves they're sitting on, Laura emerges from the back.

Her skin is still pale, and her lips are quivering, and she's crying again. I don't know whether it's from relief at not being pregnant, shock at being pregnant, or a combination of all of the above. I fight the urge to run across the room and shake her shoulders, screaming 'what was it???', and instead just smile. Whatever the news, she doesn't need some hysterical shop assistant getting in on the action.

'Well?' I ask, then hastily add: 'If you want to tell me, that is. It's completely fine if you don't, I respect your privacy.'

She holds out her hands, inviting me to take them.

'Don't worry, I did wash first . . .' she says, grinning, as our fingers interlink. 'And it was positive, Katie. I might need to do another seven, just to be sure, but . . . well, I think I might be just a little bit pregnant!'

'And how do you feel about that?' I ask, keeping my tone even – she's smiling, but I still can't 100 per cent figure out what's going on in her head. Probably she can't either.

'Well, I feel terrified. And shocked. And worried. Concerned about how Matt will react, and how Lizzie and Nate will react, and how I'll manage at my age. How I'll fit in work, and how that might affect Cherie. And I'm cursing that night away we had for Matt's birthday, and all the cheap prosecco we drank that might have made us a bit careless, and that Princess Leia outfit Becca bought me for a laugh that made us definitely a bit careless . . .

'And I'm even a little tiny bit sad about David, my husband who died? Which is extra stupid – but this seems such a big deal, and I really want to talk to him about it. And . . . well, there are a lot of problems. The house is too small. I have a job that involves toffee caramel puddings. I have teenagers. I have a crazy dog. I'm overweight and middle-aged and . . . oh lord, Katie, mainly, I'm just absolutely delighted! The minute that second line appeared on the pee stick, I was just filled with joy . . . I can't believe it, still, but I'm over the moon. Thank you! Thank you so much!'

She pulls me into her arms, and we do a crazy, unbalanced jig all over the room, bumping into shelves, knocking over cardboard display stands, and generally wobbling and whooping and waving our hands around. Anyone passing by outside who happens to glance in will wonder if we've been getting high on our own supply after breaking into the Party Cupboard.

Eventually, we come to a standstill, both wearing matching grins on our faces – her hysterical level of happiness is completely infectious.

'What will you do now?' I ask. 'Apart from seven more tests. And maybe you should make an appointment with the GP. And . . . well, I'd suggest having a drink to calm yourself down, but that's not really appropriate, is it?'

Her expression momentarily clouds over – understandable, as I've just pointed out she'll be teetotal for the next few months – but soon bounces back into happy mode. Then confused mode. Then frowning mode.

'I need to tell Matt, obviously. I think he'll be okay about it, but . . . gosh, this is a really big thing, isn't it? I think I might need an hour to myself.'

'Go to my place. There's a spare key in the soil of the hanging basket. Excuse the mess, but make yourself at home – have a cuppa. Have a think. Take your time. I'll be here for a bit, then I'm off to Willow's to collect Saul, so there's no rush.'

She bites her lip, looks through the window at the rain, and nods.

'Thank you. That's a good plan. Nobody will look for me there . . . I'll just sit for a minute, and try and get my head a tiny bit straighter before I go and see Matt. Oh my . . . how do you think he'll react?'

That's a tricky one. The truth is that even though I've technically known Matt for a long time, I don't actually *know* him. Matt is the local vet, and he definitely seems to communicate better with animals than people. Like myself, he's a private kind of person. Always polite, always the type of guy you know you could count on in a crisis, but also always slightly guarded. Like he doesn't quite trust you if you only have two legs and no tail.

'I couldn't possibly say, Laura. You know him better than anyone. Trust your instincts. And try not to worry – I'm sure it'll all be fine.'

'Yes, you're right . . . I'm sure it'll all be . . . shit!'

'What?' I ask, as she tries to hide behind me – a foolish decision, as she's at least two inches taller, significantly more round, and has huge hair. 'You think it'll be shit?'

'No! I meant – oh, hi, Matt! How are you?'

He walks into the room, accompanied by the sound of the doorbell tinkling, having clearly decided to ignore the closed sign. It's starting to feel a tiny bit like a French farce in here now, with all the comings and goings.

Matt – tall, brawny, looks a bit like I imagine a blacksmith would look if I'd ever met one – nods politely at me. That takes approximately one nanosecond, before he turns all his attention to Laura. His face visibly softens as their eyes meet, and for a second I see a glimpse of what Laura's Matt is like. Not the public Matt – but hers.

They share a smile, one of those smiles that makes you feel like you might just be invisible, and he reaches out to touch her amusingly large hair.

'Cherie texted me,' he says, simply. 'Said you'd gone home sick? And that you felt repulsed at the idea of caramel toffee pudding?'

Laura laughs out loud, and replies: 'Yes, well. I'm amazed she didn't call 999 at that stage. I'm all right . . . I'm . . . erm . . .'

I feel so awkward, so much of a spare part, that I begin to edge backwards out of the room. This is private. It's personal. It's special. It's nothing at all to do with me. I try and think up a quick and believable excuse for leaving the two of them alone that doesn't involve a pterodactyl with the runs, but soon realise I don't need to.

I am still invisible, and they don't even see me as I skulk off to the back of the building, through the dispensary, and into the relative sanctuary of the stock room and the tiny kitchen.

I close the door behind me, leaving them alone, which technically I'm not supposed to do in case they raid our drug supply – but I'm convinced they have other things on their minds than selling asthma inhalers on the Budbury black market.

I stand still and listen – relieved when all I can hear is the low-key hum of their voices and not any actual words. I look around, and see that I am surrounded by unopened boxes, shelving stacked with trays of plastic bottles and random objects like a pricing gun and shampoo samples and an as-yet-unassembled Christmas tree, lurking in one corner like a festive ambush.

I lean back against the counter, absentmindedly wiping up some spilled tea with the dishcloth, not even noticing for a few moments that I'm actually crying as I wipe.

It's not sad crying – nothing sad has happened – it's just . . . girl crying. You know the kind – when you're just feeling overemotional and a bit off balance and you don't really understand why.

I let myself have a small weep – nobody can see, it'll be my little secret – and then swill my face with cold water so I don't look too blotchy.

I'm being daft, I know – I have nothing to cry about. Sometimes, though, you just don't need a reason, do you?

I distract myself for a few moments by washing and

drying the mugs and spoons that are in the sink, and then tiptoe to the door to see how things are getting on. I can still hear voices, and some laughter, and then a silence. I'm kind of hoping they don't get into some huge debate, or a mammoth life-planning session, and forget I'm here.

Just as that thought crosses my mind, I hear Laura shouting: 'Katie! Katie, where have you gone?'

I emerge back onto the shop floor, and am immediately wrapped up in a big Laura hug. I glance from beneath her hair at Matt, who looks stunned, dazed, and utterly soppy.

'He was pleased, then?' I whisper.

'Ecstatic. Honestly, if I'd known he'd be that happy, maybe I'd have done it on purpose . . .'

She smiles as she walks back over to Matt, who places a protective arm across her shoulders, and nods at me. This time, it's a nod with a lot of warmth.

'Thank you,' he says simply. 'For looking after her.'

'Not a problem,' I reply. 'Any time at all. And obviously, I won't mention this to anyone, until . . . well, until you make it official.'

After a few more moments of faffing, and Laura insisting on paying me for the pregnancy test she used and the spare she takes home 'just in case', they finally leave.

I flip the shop sign back to 'open', and watch them amble down the main street together, laughing and giggling, wrapped in each other's arms. They're a funny sight – her in the hot pink puffa, Matt in his far more sensible navy blue Berghaus – and completely lost in each other and in their own secret world. They don't even seem to notice the rain, as neither of them has bothered pulling up their hoods.

I settle back behind the counter, looking on as they pass the pub and head for Matt's surgery. I'm smiling, but I still feel a bit unsettled. A bit melancholy. A bit . . . just not quite right.

I can't put my finger on what the exact emotion is, until I realise that I can no longer see Matt and Laura and their little bubble of intimacy and happiness. They've disappeared off from view, and now I'm just staring at my own reflection in one of the pharmacy's tiny window panes. Rain is streaking down the glass, creating a weird optical illusion where it looks like my face has been chopped in two.

I look away from the double me, and let out a breath I didn't know I'd been holding. I'm one woman. Alone, on a stool. Still breathing. Still holding on.

I'm so happy for them. And I'm so sad for me. Because all of a sudden, it hits me like a cartoon anvil dropping from the sky – I'm very, very lonely.

# Chapter 11

Luckily, I don't have too much time to ponder that realisation and feel even more sorry for myself, as we have a veritable rush in the Budbury Chemist.

A small group of walkers comes in, one of them looking for blister plasters, one looking for Imodium, and one looking for sore eye drops. They seem remarkably cheerful considering their shopping list, and set off again in a flurry of chatter and clattering boots and those weird walking poles that are probably helpful on hills, but out of place on pavements.

After that, Scrumpy Joe Jones, who runs the local cider cave, arrives to pick up a prescription Auburn's made up for his wife Joanne, who has 'one of her headaches'. He rolls his eyes at me as he says this, as though I completely understand what hell that implies for him.

As Joe leaves, I get a visit from the Teenagers, who roam Budbury in a relatively benign pack – less likely to vandalise the bus-stop than to walk your dog for you.

There's Martha, Zoe's kind-of-daughter, who is seventeen,

and Lizzie, Laura's daughter, who is in the year below at college.

The girls look very different – Lizzie blonde, Martha dyed black; one on the short side and one getting that tall, willowy look that young girls take for granted. They both, though, feature heavy black eyeliner use, Dr. Martens boots, and various shades of black, purple and green clothes. They look like they could form a band, and be the star attraction at Wednesday Addams' birthday party.

With them is Josh, Lizzie's boyfriend, and the son of the just-gone Scrumpy Joe. Like his dad, he's tall and skinny and dark, with big brown eyes and an ever-present beanie hat. Nate, Laura's son, is a couple of years younger than them but has learned to fight for his place in the pack.

Like my Saul, I suppose, he's been without a dad since David died – but the menfolk of Budbury stepped in and he now never goes short of a footballing friend or someone to act macho with.

Last week, Laura caught him having a wee in the grid outside their cottage, and his response to her outrage was to tell her that Cal 'says it's manly'. I think it's fair to say both Nate and Cal were feeling a bit less manly by the time Laura had finished with them, and there will be no repeat performances.

Tailing along is a new face – Ollie, Martha's relatively new boyfriend. He's eighteen, and looks an unlikely boyfriend candidate for a Goth princess, with his surfer-dude blond hair and the kind of clothes and build I associate with adverts for Abercrombie & Fitch. For some reason, even though he's called Ollie, he's always known as Bill. I daren't ask why, in case they tell me.

They all mooch around for a while, sniffing the candles and briefly perusing the abandoned sex aids catalogue until I manage to wrestle it from Martha's amused grip. Eventually they all buy a whistle pop each and disappear off down the street, trying to perform the theme tune from *In The Night Garden* entirely with sugar whistles. I watch them go, a flurry of pushing and shoving and giggling, and think how weird it will be when Saul is that age. And how my life will look by the time he really starts his.

He's already at nursery, with his little friends and minia-ture social life that consists of parties at soft play centres, and he'll actually be starting in reception at primary school next September. It's so weird with babies and little kids – every day of amusing them seems to last forever, but in the blink of an eye a whole year has gone. It must still seem like yesterday to Laura that her two were tiny, and now they're part of the Budbury Massive.

At the moment I'm measuring Saul's progress in small things – like when he'll be able to reach the light switch, or write his own name with the 'S' facing the right way – but before long, it'll be much bigger things. Like his first day at little school, then big school, then maybe Uni or work. One day he's stretching on his tippy toes to try and put the lights on, next he's walking down the aisle and becoming a father.

As all parents probably know – and I've just this second realised – that way madness lies. It's not worth thinking about, apart from as a reminder to perhaps tend to my own life a tiny bit more.

Once you have kids you lean towards not noticing your own birthdays, or time passing – you're so focused on theirs. This is natural, and right, and good – but it doesn't mean I should forget about myself entirely.

All of these thoughts are hurting my brain a bit, and by the time I lock up the shop and finish for the day, I'm trying really hard to think less and do more. I've had a message from Auburn saying that Lynnie has gone for a nap, and Saul is helping her make jam tarts, and there's no rush to get back for him.

Usually, I'd still rush – reluctant to believe that everything was actually fine, that Saul was behaving, that I didn't need to go and relieve them as soon as humanly possible. That relying on people was a necessary evil to be reduced to the absolute minimum.

But I've been here for a while now. These people are my friends. I've just helped one of them find out that she's having a baby. I help Auburn and Willow with Lynnie when I can. I sometimes clean Edie's windows for her, after I saw her climbing on a stepladder as I went past one day, cloth in her 92-year-old hand. I helped Cherie talk sense into her hubby when Frank sprained his ankle and was insisting on carrying on working on the farm. I babysit for Little Edie so Sam and Becca can have the occasional night out.

I do things for them, because I want to – because I like them and because I enjoy helping. Being part of their world. But so far I've been so selective with how much a part of their world I allow myself to be; always backing off when things have felt too intense.

Like Edie's ninety-second birthday party earlier in the year – it had a *Strictly Come Dancing* theme, as it's Edie's favourite show. Cherie organised ballroom lessons for us at the café, and I attended all of them. I love dancing. But when it came to the big night, and everyone else was dressing up and heading to the party, I cried off. Made an excuse and stayed at home. It felt too big, too overwhelming, too public.

I think I have to start making more of an effort to change that. To believe that I am welcome, that these people like me, and that every favour doesn't make me a burden or leave me with a debt they'll demand to be repaid.

So, instead of doing my normal mad dash over to the cottage to act apologetically about ever having gone to work at all, I head to the café. I check my phone as I go, and see a text from my mum: 'Sorry not answering, love. Bit busy. Don't worry about me. See you soon.'

I tap out a quick reply, asking her if she's sure she's all right, and try not to worry too much. I remind myself that my mother is not exactly averse to creating a little drama around herself, and that maybe it's just because I haven't paid her enough attention recently.

And I haven't, really, I know that – I've been busy and haven't spoken to her as much as I should. I haven't been back to visit in a couple of months either. I feel bad about that, now. I mean, she can be a bit of a nightmare, but can't we all, in our own way? She's still my mum, and I still love her. I'm sure she's always done her best.

I try not to hold onto anger about the way I grew up, because it does me no good at all. Wishing it had been different won't make it different. Fantasising about a childhood where my family was happy doesn't create an alternative reality. It all happened, it all had an effect, and none of it can be changed – all I can change is the way I build my own life, not the way my parents built theirs.

I shake my head as I climb the path up the side of the hill that leads to the café, and put my phone away. Thoughts for another time. Or not. Mum says not to worry – so I need to try not to worry.

After I make my way under the wrought-iron archway and into the garden, I pause for a moment and look out at the bay. It's still drizzling, and the sky is fifty shades of grey, but the sun is trying desperately to break through the clouds. It's a strange and beautiful effect: dark clouds, dark sky, with one or two dazzling fingers of gold poking through to cast yellow streams down onto the waves, where they shimmer and shine as the water rolls inland.

There are dog walkers down there on the beach, and a couple of mums with toddlers wrapped up so well they look like fat eggs you could roll down a hill, and someone who appears to be fossil-hunting. Out of season, quiet, but still stunningly beautiful. In summer, it's completely different – the café is bustling, the beach is full, the sounds are a blend of squealing kids and the ice cream van's tune and the chatter and buzz of holiday fun.

I reluctantly turn away from the view and walk towards the café. It's after three now, and as I'd suspected, the only people left there are the regulars. I pause and look through the windows. The light outside is dim and grey, so the contrast is stark: the café is vivid and warm and bright, its fairy lights shining, the glass panes slightly steamed up.

I can see a few tables pulled together to form one big, haphazardly assembled mega-table, and the ladies arranged around it. Cherie has her head thrown back in laughter; Becca has Little Edie on her lap; Zoe has a paperback in her hands, and Willow is doing some kind of mime to entertain them.

They look perfectly relaxed. Perfectly comfortable. Perfectly terrifying.

I take a deep breath, and push open the door. They all turn and look at me, and I see Cherie's eyes widen in surprise. I get that feeling, the one I'm way too familiar with: the feeling that I've walked into a room where I'm not welcome. Where I'm interrupting something.

'Come on in then!' bellows Cherie, waving at me. 'And don't let the weather come with you!'

I nod and shut the door – I hadn't even noticed I'd been holding it open, as though clinging to the option of running away, back down the hill.

By the time I've crossed the room, Willow has pulled an extra chair over for me, and headed to the kitchen to get me a coffee from the ancient machine. I hear it hiss and spit as I sit down, smiling politely, wondering what on earth I'm going to talk about now I'm here.

'We were just discussing the relative feminist merits of Disney princesses,' says Zoe, her ginger curls pulled up into a cascade of fire on top of her head.

'Oh . . . well. Maybe Mulan?'

'She definitely kicks ass,' replies Becca, bouncing Edie up and down on one knee. The baby responds with a series of gurgles that implies it's the most fun she's had in her entire life. 'As does Pocahontas.'

'Yes, that's true,' says Zoe, 'but for me it's got to be Merida from *Brave*. Because she's a warrior, she doesn't want to be forced to be married and, most importantly of all, she's a ginger. And as we all know, gingers rock.'

Willow places the coffee – a lovely mocha – in front of me, and pushes a big slice of chocolate fudge cake in my direction.

'Eat that,' she says, firmly. 'And then agree with me that it's *Frozen*. The film, not the cake.'

Cherie starts to hum 'Do You Want to Build a Snowman?', and within seconds, everyone has joined in. The debate is paused for a few seconds, until we run out of lyrics – apart from Willow, that is, who knows all the words to pretty much every big Disney song ever.

'I think,' Becca says, once the discordant chanting has stopped, 'that I'd also cast a vote for Moana. I know it's recent, and some of you old fuddy-duddies won't have seen it yet, but it's very cool. No princes. No magical kisses. Just a feisty chick and her friend the demi-god, saving the world one song at a time. Plus, The Rock. You're welcome.'

She sings the last two words in the tune of the song from the movie, but only me and Willow get that part – Zoe and Cherie just look confused.

Becca takes in their lack of understanding, and shakes her head.

'Clearly, we need a movie night. Maybe we can do it here. Get rid of the blokes for the evening, and ideally the kids too, and have a Disney film marathon. Wouldn't want kids at that, would we? Or . . . maybe not here, just realised there's no telly. Duh.'

'We could do it upstairs, in the flat,' replies Cherie, pointing above her head. 'Bit of a squeeze, but that would add to the ambiance. You supply the movie, I'll supply the

Baileys. We'll let Laura do the cake, as soon as she's feeling better.'

Everyone nods in agreement, even me. Laura, of course, may not be feeling 'better' for a while, but it's definitely not my place to point that one out.

I'm interested in seeing Cherie's flat. I've never been upstairs, to her near-legendary bolthole. She lived there for years, after the death of her first husband, until she finally moved in with Frank at his farmhouse.

Since then, it's been used as a kind of emergency pit-stop for the Budbury ladies' brigade. Becca lived in it until she and Sam properly got together, and Zoe used it as an escape hatch when she first moved here.

I've never been up there, but I've heard the stories – Cherie was a bit of a rock-chick in her day, hanging around with a hippy crowd and going to festivals before glamping was invented, and she's still partial to the occasional herbal cigarette and cranking up the volume on her record collection. The flat, I'm told, is a perfect reflection of all of that.

'So,' says Cherie, giving me a gentle kick beneath the table, 'what brings you to our door, lady? Not that we're anything but delighted to see you. We were beginning to think that you didn't like us.'

She's smiling, so I know she's not really serious.

'What makes you think I like you now?' I ask, licking oozing fudge off my spoon. 'I'm here for the cake.'

'Cheeky! You're very welcome, anyway, my love. Much as

we adore our menfolk, we do need our little get-togethers. Stops us getting lonely.'

It's interesting that she uses that word. Lonely. I mean, I can't imagine any of these women feeling lonely – not now, anyway. But when I think about it, I can see that they all have been. That they all know how lonely feels.

Looking at them now, they all have solid, robust relationships, full lives, and this circle of friendship – but it wasn't always that way. They've all been through the grinder, and somehow all emerged whole. They've pulled each other out of holes, like a human chain of emotional support – and I'm starting to think that maybe I need a bit of a tug in the right direction myself.

'That's why I came,' I say quietly, as I glance at them all. 'I was feeling a bit lonely. Took me a while to notice, because I'm basically really happy with my life. Like our Disney heroines, it's not a needing-a-man thing . . . maybe it's a single mum thing. Or a still-feeling-new-in-town thing. Or just a me thing. I don't know – but I thought I'd come along and see what you all get up to when the café's closed.'

There is a slight pause after I speak; not long, but long enough to make me wonder if I've somehow misjudged this terribly. If I'm not eligible to join their club after all. If I should just crawl under the table and pretend I don't exist.

'Well, mainly we eat cake,' says Cherie, reaching out to squeeze my hand. 'And drink coffee. Occasionally, when we're feeling really wild, we crack open a bottle of Amaretto and have a little toot . . .'

'And sometimes we dance,' adds Willow, grinning at me. 'Or even sing. We do both of those things really badly, but we don't let that stop us.'

'Willow speaks only for herself,' chimes in Becca, lowering a now-sleeping baby into her pushchair, 'I have the voice of an angel and moves that would make Beyoncé weep. When we're not dancing, singing, or eating cake, by the way, we're talking about Daniel Craig.'

Zoe pipes up: 'And sometimes, looking at pictures of Daniel Craig, on the iPad. But that's only if Big Edie's here – she's a total pervert. I mainly sit here half-listening, half-reading a book, until I spot a chance to say something snarky or sarcastic. If I'm not here, Auburn takes over on the sarcasm front; we're a bit like a tag-team. Laura's job is to ask us questions about our love lives, talk way too much about *Bake Off*, and supply the cake. It's like a badly oiled machine – we all have our roles to play.'

I look from one to the other as they take turns talking, wondering what I could possibly contribute. Whistle pops?

'Mainly, my love,' says Cherie, obviously realising I may be struggling here, 'we make sure that none of us get lonely. We've all been there, and know how it feels. It's hard, sometimes, to reach out to other people – especially when you're trying to be all Little Miss Independent. But reaching out for help isn't a bad thing – it's a good thing. Come here whenever you like, and listen to us witter on. You'll soon get the hang of it. It's a bit like a club . . . a cake club.'

'Are there any rules?' I ask, looking around at their intent faces. 'Will you abduct me at midnight and put a sack over my head and I'll wake up in Frank's turnip field?'

'Not unless you want us to,' she replies, shaking her head slowly. 'Although, now I seem to have named it Cake Club . . . we probably should have some rules. And the first rule of Cake Club is: you don't talk about Cake Club.'

'Unless you want to, obvs,' adds Willow, 'then it's totally fine.'

'Yeah. Then it's fine,' says Cherie, somehow keeping her face straight.

I nod, and feel stupidly grateful for their humour, and the way they've made me feel welcome without making too big a deal of it. The way I do feel, quite suddenly, a bit less alone in the world.

'Well,' I say, eventually, eating some more cake. 'I do like Daniel Craig.'

# Chapter 12

The next major development in my life comes two days later, and is covered in fur.

Matt knocks on my door in the morning, just after I've got back from taking Saul to nursery. He's shuffling, looking sheepish, and not quite making full eye contact, as is his tendency when dealing with humans.

'Hi,' I say, trying not to look annoyed. I think this is possibly the first time anybody has ever knocked on my front door, and it feels strangely intrusive. 'Is everything okay? Is Laura all right?'

I gesture for him to come into the hallway, as yet again it's pelting with rain. November is turning out to be nothing but rain.

His face creases into a huge smile as he steps inside, even the mention of Laura's name transforming him into something completely different.

'Yeah, she's great – sorry, didn't mean to worry you. I was . . . well, I was wondering if you could help me out with something. Laura was all for turning up with him in tow, but . . . I wanted to ask first. It's a big responsibility. And you might be allergic.'

I am completely befuddled by this whole exchange, and it obviously shows on my face. Matt shakes his head, and apologises again.

'Let me start over,' he says, grinning at his own ineptitude. 'Did Laura mention the rogue cat at all – the one that's been hanging around the Rockery?'

The Rockery is the holiday cottage complex where both Laura and Matt live, in separate houses – although for how long, who knows? Zoe and Martha lived there for a while too, before they moved into the house next to the pharmacy with Cal. It's owned by Cherie, who seems to have a habit of turning her holiday lets into permanent homes for the Budbury strays – now including a cat, from the sounds of it.

'She did, briefly – she said he'd had a showdown with Midegbo and won. Sounds like quite a cat.'

'He is – pretty much the biggest I've ever seen. A ginger tom, probably about three or four, but looks like he's been in the wars. He was starting to make a bit of a nuisance of himself at the Rockery, finding his way into the cottages, chasing the dogs, probably worrying the sheep, planning world domination . . . usual cat stuff. The kids all tried to catch him, but he was too clever for them.'

'Cats usually are,' I reply, smiling at the image of the teenagers chasing a ginger phantom all over the gardens.

'Yes. They are. Anyway, I did manage to catch him . . .'

'Being a professional animal whisperer and all?'

'Being someone with a lot of experience of cornering unwilling felines. I brought him into the surgery, and gave him a good look over. He's a bit of a softy once you get close up – loves a fuss and a treat.

'Anyhow – he's not microchipped. No collar or ID of any kind. From the state of him, he's not been living in a home for a while, and he's been out and about getting feisty with the locals. The tip of one ear is gone, and he has a line of fur missing where it's not grown back over some scar tissue on his face. I've called around all the local shelters and the police station and checked the pet registry, and nobody's reported him as lost. I think he's been stray for a while, and sadly nobody's looking for him. I'm keeping him in for a day or two, giving him a course of vaccinations, and . . . well, performing the necessary operation to prevent a ginger tom epidemic.'

'Ouch . . . that'll make you popular!'

'It's only a small op – I'll keep him with me for a few days, make sure he's not a stitch-remover. But as I'm sure you've guessed, I'm here about what happens to him next . . . I need to find him a good home, and Laura suggested you, because Saul loves animals.'

I pause, and ponder this idea. It's not terrible – but it's not brilliant either.

'Well, Saul also loves dinosaurs, but we're not adopting one of those,' I point out.

'They're extinct.'

'I realise that – but . . . well, what do you think? What's your professional opinion? I'm out a lot, and I'm busy. I'm sure Saul would love it – he loves Midgebo and Bella and Rick, and pretty much every other animal he comes across – but Saul is three. He's not in a position to make mature decisions.'

Matt nods and looks thoughtful. This is easily the longest conversation we've ever had, and I'm finding it easier than I thought to be blunt. Matt is a straightforward man, which makes life so much simpler.

'It's better to think it through,' he agrees. 'I see too many cases of people taking on pets they're not equipped to deal with, and it ending badly. But I would say this – cats are a lot less high-maintenance than dogs, on the whole. This one in particular seems pretty independent, very robust physically, and has a nice nature. Even when the kids were chasing him around, and Midgebo was barking at him, he never once scratched or lashed out, which is usually a sign of a good, stable personality. Maybe you could come and meet him, and bring Saul?'

'If I bring Saul, it's a done deal – I won't be able to resist the pleading! If it's okay with you, why don't I pop in now, while Saul's out? I must admit, I do kind of like cats . . .'

He gives me a small and understanding smile – like I've just made a life-changing admission – and waits while I grab a coat and an umbrella. I feel like I have the umbrella permanently glued to my side these days. It should be made part of my arm, like a cyborg limb. Robo-Brolly.

Together, in what I have to describe as a companionable silence, we make our way down the slight hill to his surgery, which is closed until the afternoon. Neither of us seems to feel the need to fill the time with small talk, which is refreshing – and leaves me free to save all my spare oxygen to use in the outrageous coo-ing sounds I make the minute I lay eyes on the cat.

He's in a big kennel in the back of the building, next to a sorry-looking Dalmatian who I'm told is recovering from knee surgery. Opposite, there's a far more feisty French bulldog, who is turning round and round in circles, so happy to see Matt he's almost climbing the walls. Matt makes a few comforting noises, lets the bulldog lick his finger through the cage door, and gives me a few minutes to make the acquaintance of the ginger tom.

He is ginger – but with gorgeous stripes of so many different shades that he almost looks multi-coloured. He's absolutely enormous – especially for a stray – but a lot of that looks to be made up of a very thick, very fluffy coat. His tail is fanned, a bit like a golden retriever's, and he has bright green eyes set in a very wide face. His feet are all white, like he's wearing little boots, and I can see the ear with the tip missing and the scar Matt mentioned.

He gazes at me that way that cats can – the way that

says they can see into your soul, that they know all your secrets, and that they'd quite like a can of tuna now, please.

Matt has opened the cage door, and after a few moments of getting to know each other, he finally trots to the edge, and gracefully leaps to the floor. Once there, he winds in and out of my legs, purring and snuffling, rubbing his fur against my jeans and basically totally flirting with me. I lean down and stroke his head, and he leans into my hand, giving me a quick lick with a sandpaper tongue.

Matt's right. He is a big softy. Also, I suspect, a big softy who knows a thing or two about human manipulation, and is putting on a good show of adorableness.

'So,' says Matt, after a few minutes of this dance, 'what do you think? Take some time if you like. It's a big decision, I don't want to rush you . . .'

'I'll take him,' I say quickly, tearing myself away from my new friend and standing straight. Because suddenly, I can't imagine our little home without this cat in it. He is clearly some kind of cat Jedi, and has totally mind-controlled me.

Matt lets out a quiet laugh at my undoubtedly soppy expression, and leans down to scoop the cat into his arms. Said cat looks at me pleadingly as he is reinstalled in his prison, and lets out a few plaintive meows to let me know he expected better of me as I stand by and allow him to be jailed again.

'It's okay, sweetie, I'll be back . . .' I murmur, poking my finger through the door to touch his fur. He gives me one sad look before curling up in a giant fluffy ball, as if to say 'yeah, right . . . I've heard that one before.' I suspect he's a cat who's had a lot of humans disappoint him in his time. Or – just possibly – I'm reading too much into it.

'Okay,' says Matt, walking me back into the reception area. 'Good decision. I think he'll settle just fine, and I'm always around if you need me. What are you going to call him? Not that it makes much difference with cats.'

'I don't know,' I say, putting my coat back on, and smiling. Smiling because I'm genuinely happy – almost excited in fact – at the prospect of getting a cat. I really should get out more.

'I'll leave that up to Saul,' I decide, looking around at the posters about worming tablets and neutering programmes and the importance of vaccinations.

I stay for a few more minutes, chatting to Matt about Laura and the impending life-changing arrival, and find out that she's started back at work, that she's feeling so excited it seems to be helping override the less pleasant physical symptoms, and that they have an ultrasound booked in a few weeks' time. After that, assuming all goes well, they'll start telling people their news. Until then, it's their little secret.

Or, I suppose, mine too. Mine and the cat's – because he undoubtedly read my mind and knows all about it by now.

# Chapter 13

I leave the surgery and stand beneath the porch roof for a few moments, sheltering from the rain while I decide what to do next.

I have another couple of hours before I have to go and get Saul, and am fighting the urge to rush out and buy luxury cat beds and a box full of toy mice. Cats, I know, rarely care for such things – they're far happier on the luxury bed that they find in your bedroom, and Budbury is definitely full of real mice that will be a lot more fun.

Instead, I decide to go to the café. Of course. It seems to exert some kind of magnetic force on everyone who lives in the village, and there's little point resisting. Besides, I'm already halfway there, and I can get warm and dry, and eat home-baked bread slathered in fresh dairy butter. What's not to like? Especially as the only bread left in my own house is half a packet of wholemeal pittas that are destined for the bin.

Anyway, I'm overdue a visit. I've not made it there for a few days, after my initiation into the Budbury Cake Club, and feel like I need to make the effort. Like if I leave it too long, it'll be harder to join in again – like when you don't use your earrings for ages and the holes are a bit healed over and you end up having to semi-pierce the skin. Or maybe that's just me. I could, of course, start my Christmas shopping instead, but I don't quite have the energy to tackle that one – plus I have to wait for payday at the end of the month. I already know what Saul wants – I trick him into writing a very early letter to Santa so I can be prepared – and none of it is going to be difficult to get. I've already half decided that I'll probably combine the shopping with a trip back to Bristol anyway, as I really do need to see my parents.

Dad has stayed radio silent for the last couple of days, but that's not actually unusual. He's not a fan of mobile phones, and thinks social media is the work of the devil. He may of course be right on that one.

Mum has sent a few more texts, which are a strange combination of attempts at reassurance blended with a subtle sense of mystery – like 'I'm fine, love, or at least I will be . . .'; or 'Don't worry about me – what doesn't kill you makes you stronger!' Like that.

She is a drama queen, and I tell myself not to overreact. I always reply, tell her to call when she can, and make the appropriate concerned noises. But after a few days of this kind of exchange, I'm starting to think there's nothing actually wrong at all. That she's just short of attention and needing a moment in the spotlight.

My nan always used to call her Judy Garland, because

of her tendencies towards melodrama and tears. Looking back, her combative relationship with my dad was definitely not helped by this personality trait. Maybe the fact that he always engaged with the script was part of the attraction.

It also made it hard to distinguish between her real moods and needs and the ones that she was playing out like a B-list movie star, placing herself centre stage in a kitchen-sink drama.

She was, admittedly, in an awful situation – the constant fights, the physical tussles, the ongoing battle for supremacy with a man who was supposed to be her partner, but only was if you added the word 'sparring' in front.

With them, it was never as simple or horrendous as her being a victim. They drove each other on to increasingly nasty levels of conflict. So sometimes when she was sitting in a tearful heap at the kitchen table, looking around at the smashed plates and overturned chairs, it was genuine. She'd sob and weep and her shoulders would shake with the pain of it all; at the grief and disappointment over what her life had become.

But other times, there'd be a strange sense of glee in her upset. The teenaged me would pat her hand and try and console her, and she'd look up at me, and through the tears I'd see it – I'd see that she was feeling like she'd won. That she was triumphant. It was all very odd and confusing, and definitely taught me not to accept everything she says at face value.

As I trudge my way yet again up the hill to the café, I

make a small plan in my mind. I will continue to exchange these texts with my mum; I will continue to try and contact my dad, and I will definitely make a weekend trip back to Bristol to combine seeing my parents and hitting the mega toy stores at the outlet village. Simples.

I don't pause and admire the view down to the bay this time – it's raining too much to see anything other than dirty grey clouds and dirty grey sea. I just plod my way across the garden, which is starting to resemble some kind of marshland nature reserve, and push open the doors to the café.

The warmth wraps around me like a blanket fresh from the radiator, and the aromas of cinnamon and ginger tell me Laura is not only back, she's already experimenting with her Christmas menu. This is a tradition of hers – and a very fine one. We all get to be guinea pigs in the great Christmas bake-off preparation, and I for one am a very willing participant.

Nose twitching, I glance around the room as I shake off my umbrella and stash it in the big holder Cherie has placed near the door. It's made of wrought iron and is in the form of a giant sunflower, which seems cheery even when it's full of soggy brollies.

I see Laura behind the counter, apron on and covered in floury fingerprints, putting together some bacon butties and garnishing an omelette. I see Cherie, standing next to her, waiting to take the orders out to customers. I see the customers – a table full of middle-aged women laughing so hard that I assume someone has just told the world's best joke. They're soaked to the skin, and have obviously been walking the coastal paths.

I see Zoe, leaving the counter holding a mug of coffee and a plate bearing some kind of muffin, heading in my direction as she exits with her takeaway.

'Christmas muffins,' she says, giving me a wink. 'In November! God, I love this place . . .'

I nod in agreement as she bustles past, doing a mad dash over to the bookshop. Her hair is still massive and frizzy from the mad dash over here, and I anticipate it being the size of a Renault Clio by the end of the day.

I see Edie, in her usual perch on a high stool next to the counter, probably playing online Boggle on her iPad. She has an astonishing knowledge of arcane and random words that make her cackle in delight every time she finds them, especially if they sound rude. I thought she might pass out from laughing when she once found 'fellatio' on the grid.

I see Cal, Zoe's boyfriend, watching her as she leaves. His blond hair is damp from the rain, and he's wearing an actual denim cowboy shirt that makes him look like he's about to engage in a spot of rodeo riding. He's sitting at a table for two, chatting to someone with her back to me.

I hang up my coat and make brief eye contact with Laura. She gives me a quick thumbs-up to show that all is well, and then pulls a weird face and nods over towards the tables. She looks a bit like she's swallowed a wasp, and

I have no idea what she's trying to tell me. Cherie notices me from the other side of the room, where she's deposited the breakfast orders with the table full of amused ladies, and makes a similar gesture. Her eyes are wide, and she seems to be nodding in Cal's direction.

I nod and smile, and don't question their behaviour too much. I know I don't have Beauty Parlour hair and make-up today, so I'm not too worried. Besides, sometimes the Budbury Cake Club ladies are just plain weird.

There are plenty of empty tables, and I'd usually choose one as far away from the rest of the crowd as usual – that's just been my vibe since I got here. But now, embracing my brave new world, I decide to aim higher, and head for the table next to Cal's. Apart from anything else, he looks like a cowboy – one of life's simpler pleasures.

I nod to him as I walk over, and his eyes crinkle up in amusement. I resist the urge to double-check my hair, but do glance briefly down at my shirt, in case I've missed a couple of buttons or something. Nope. All present and correct.

It's only when I go to pull a chair back at the table beside him that I realise what's going on. When I realise who he's chatting to.

'Better pull that chair over here, love,' he says in his Aussie drawl. 'I've got an old friend of yours here with me . . .'

I stare at him. I stare at her. And finally, I say: 'Mum! What are you doing here?'

# Chapter 14

'What, can't a mother decide to spontaneously visit her only daughter now and then?' she says, sounding half amused and half annoyed. I recognise the tone – it's her Disappointed Joan Collins voice.

She glances up at Cal, sees him watching our interaction, and lets out a ridiculous little laugh. It's the kind of ridiculous little laugh teenaged girls let out when they're busily flicking their hair at a boy they fancy. Mum has short hair, so she can't do that, praise the Lord.

The hair in question, I notice, has been recently touched up, taking her from almost-blonde to definitely blonde. She's wearing more make-up than usual as well, but it doesn't quite detract from the fact that her eyes look tired, and the lines around her mouth more pronounced. She's wearing her favourite jumper, the one with sequinned love hearts on it, which she always calls her 'cheer-me-up-top'.

There's a black coffee in front of her, along with an untouched Christmas muffin that is oozing some kind of spicy syrup filling. She's been 'watching her figure' for as long as I've been alive, my mum – although I have no idea why, as she's still got the build she had as a 20-year-old, and is, like myself, on the petite side. She even joined Slimming World once, where she made herself highly unpopular by claiming to be struggling with her weight in a room full of women who really were.

She's smiling at me, and at Cal, and anyone who didn't know her might think she was perfectly happy and perfectly relaxed. It's probably only me who spots the warning signs of tension: the strain in her face, the gentle tapping of her fingers on the table top, the slightly higher than normal pitch to her voice.

These are all signs I grew up learning to recognise, and signs that immediately put me into placatory mood in an attempt to offset any escalation.

'Of course you can!' I say, blinking my eyes rapidly to shake off my surprise and, if I'm entirely honest, any visible signs of the fact that I'm not 100 per cent thrilled to see her. I'm starting to think that I'm not a very nice person.

'It's lovely to see you,' I semi-lie, 'but why did you come here, and not to mine?'

'I did try yours first, but there was no answer. I thought perhaps you were still in bed so I didn't keep knocking.'

I try not to laugh at that one – as if I'd still be in bed, with Saul in the house! I also feel a bit like she's sneakily trying to make me sound lazy in front of Cal. She probably isn't, I'm just being paranoid. And defensive. And basically acting like a kid. Funny how you slip into your old roles around people you've known the whole of your life.

'Oh, well – no. You must have called while I was taking Saul to nursery. Probably just missed you. Anyway, I'm glad you're here.'

Cal looks from one of us to the other, his face set in a pleasant smile, his shirt sleeves rolled up around arms that are thick with muscle from a lifetime of manual labour. It would be easy to underestimate Cal, but he's a lot more perceptive than he looks. He's fitted into this world a lot more easily than I have, even though he grew up on the opposite side of it.

He stands up and stretches. There's a brief moment where I notice pretty much every woman in the room stop what they're doing and watch him, including the table full of middle-aged walkers, Laura from behind the counter, and even, dear God, my own mother.

'Ladies,' he says, placing his battered cowboy hat on his head and tipping it towards us, 'it's been a pleasure, but I have to get to work. Sandy, enjoy your stay, and I do hope we get to see more of you.'

She giggles in response – actually giggles – and reaches out to pat his hand.

'Oh, so do I, Cal, so do I,' she says, with a flutter of mascara-clad eyelashes, waving at him as he leaves.

'Mum,' I say, something of my horror creeping into my voice, 'why did he call you Sandy? And were you . . . flirting with him?'

She shoots me a sideways look and shrugs.

'Well, sweetie, of course I was flirting with him – have you got eyes? I'm fifty-three – not dead. He said he was going to shorten my name to Sandy, because Australians always shorten names, and because I reminded him of a young Olivia Newton-John when she was in *Grease* . . . anyway, I'm sure he's used to being flirted with. No harm done.'

I nod, and have to concede that she has a point. He is used to it, and frankly seems to enjoy it. He's a man who likes women, and women always seem to know that.

'Fair enough. But if a man called Frank comes in – he's tall and dresses like a farmer, because he is one, and has silver hair – then don't flirt with him, okay?'

'Why not?'

'Because he's Cherie's husband, and she'll squash you like a bug.'

Mum lets out a confident snort, and replies: 'Hah! I'd like to see her try!'

I glance over at Cherie, who is back behind the counter with Laura, helping her get ready for lunch. She's tall, powerful, and a completely dominant presence, both physically and socially. I decide I'd quite like to see her try as well.

Mum and I sit in silence for a moment, looking at each other. As the silence stretches into something more awkward, I can see she's putting on a show here; that her bravado is definitely covering something up. Something she doesn't feel in control of.

She's had her nails done, and decorated with little love-heart gems, and she's wearing dangly earrings also in the shape of love hearts. Combined with the sequinned jumper, that's a whole lot of love hearts going on. She's put a lot of effort into her appearance, but despite it all, she still has the look of a woman brought low. Of someone fighting off the sadness inside.

'You'd better eat that muffin,' I say, pushing the plate towards her. Now that I notice it, it looks as though she's lost a bit of weight as well, which she can't really afford to lose. 'They shoot people in here for not eating muffins, you know.'

She uses her knife to slice it in half, giving one side to me. She plays with it a bit, crumbling it up into pieces and moving it around the plate in the syrup that's spilled out, but never actually eats any.

'Sorry, love,' she says, after a few seconds of muffin-bothering. 'I don't have much of an appetite. I stopped at the services on the M5 and had a big cooked breakfast. Wasn't sure if you'd have anything in.'

She's lying about that, and we both know it. She didn't eat breakfast. I'd be surprised if she's been eating much at all. The wave of sympathy I feel is slightly tempered by the fact that she added in that barb about my housekeeping skills, but the sympathy wins out.

'Mum, I'm glad you came. I really am,' I say, holding her hand just to stop her incessant tapping on the table. 'But why are you here? What's going on? The mystery phone calls, the texts, the fact that I've not been able to get hold of you for days? Is everything all right?'

'Well, nobody's died . . .' she says quietly.

'So I believe. But clearly something else is wrong. You've come all the way here, so you might as well talk to me. I can't help if I don't know what's wrong, can I?'

She bites her lip and stares off in the opposite direction. I see her clock Frank as he walks through the door, and that at least makes her smile.

'That's him, is it? Cherie's hubby? Quite the gent, isn't he? Like a sexy granddad . . .'

'Mum!' I say, slightly louder than I probably should have. I'm getting exasperated now. She's only been here for half an hour and my nerves are already fraying.

She pulls a face at me, and replies: 'All right, all right . . . don't get your knickers in a twist. It's your dad.'

'What about Dad? Is he all right? I thought you said nobody was dying?'

'He's not dying, Katie. He's . . . well, he's very much living. Living with Fiona Whittaker from the next street over, in fact.'

'Fiona Whittaker?' I say, incredulous. 'Fiona Whittaker, the woman who used to drive the ice cream van?'

'Yes, her. She still does drive the ice cream van.'

'Fiona Whittaker . . . the one who looked like she ate all the ice cream in her ice cream van?'

My mum simply nods, and starts opening sugar sachets for no good reason other than to give herself something to do with her hands.

'The very same Fiona Whittaker, yes.'

I am momentarily so stunned by this that I simply can't speak. There is so much wrong with what she's just told me that I can't quite take it in.

No disrespect to Fiona Whittaker, but she's not your stereotypical image of a femme fatale home wrecker. She must be a good twenty stone, and looks a little bit like Jeff Goldblum. I mean, that works for Jeff Goldblum, but it's not so good on a chick. She did, though, always have a jolly smile and an infectious laugh, and seemed to genuinely enjoy her job dispensing ice cream to the children on the estate.

Still, you couldn't get much further away from my mother's physical type than Fiona Whittaker if you actually sat down and designed one for effect. And I'd stood with my dad buying ice cream from her on probably hundreds of occasions, and never picked up on any simmering sexual tension. Then again, I probably wouldn't when I was six.

So him running away with Fiona Whittaker is, by itself, kind of weird. But weirder than who he's run away with is the fact that he's done it at all.

For all of their fighting and all of their mutual contempt,

I'd always worked on the assumption that they'd be together forever, my mum and dad. Right up until the point where one of them gave the other a heart attack, or killed each other in a spatula duel gone bad.

I'd genuinely wanted them to split up when I was younger. I yearned for a scenario where I could visit them both in separate houses, and not be caught in the middle of it all; not be used as a pawn or an emotional human shield. Where we could do normal things together without the risk of someone getting shoved into a Christmas tree, or having a bowl of cereal emptied over their head at breakfast.

A world where I could come home from school and not lurk in the garden first, checking that nobody had thrown the other one's clothes out of the window. I once found my dad's Y-fronts hanging off a potted conifer, and never quite recovered.

And yet, they never did split up. They stuck together through what felt like sheer bloody-mindedness, clinging to a marriage that was so long dead it was practically a zombie. They seemed to despise each other, but cling to their stand-off. Maybe, I'd always thought, deep down they love each other – they just do the world's best job of hiding it. And whenever I heard that phrase about there being a thin line between love and hate, I'd think of them – and how they lived their whole lives skipping over that particular line.

Once I'd left home in my teens, it was easier to deal with.

Easier to accept them for what they were, and not to spend any more time wishing I could find out I was adopted and that my real parents were out there looking for me. And over time, I stopped being angry – I knew they loved me, and that they did their very best.

Trips home were still sometimes tense, although I'd laid down some pretty strict ground rules once Saul was on the scene. No fighting while he was there – ever. They mainly managed to stick to that, and limit themselves to barbed comments that he didn't understand. So the tension was all on my end, not his – he didn't have a clue; I on the other hand was constantly waiting for the ding-ding of the bell that signified the start of round 9007 in their battle royale.

But one thing I never expected was this. That one of them would finally call time on it all, and leave. That one of them would make a break for freedom and happiness, and presumably, in my dad's case, free 99s with strawberry sauce whenever he fancied.

'So,' my mum prompts, making me realise that I've been sitting in silence doing an impression of one of Becca's goldfish. 'Don't you have anything to say?'

'Um . . . gosh. I don't really know what to say, Mum. I'm completely shocked. What's the situation now, then? When did all of this happen?'

She starts chopping up the muffin with the knife, reducing it to a sugary rubble, scraping the blade on the china and generally looking a little tiny bit psychotic.

'I found out last week, but obviously it'd been going on a while. I knew there was something wrong – or I'd suspected anyway, for a few months. He was all . . . I don't know . . . quiet. *Content*. He started working later shifts, and then going to bed early, and not complaining about anything, and . . . well. He just wasn't himself.'

'You mean he stopped fighting with you?'

She nods sadly, and I see a faint gleam of tears in her eyes. I think, from her body language, that they're real. Only in her screwed-up world would a husband who seemed content, and stopped fighting, signify disaster. And yet it did – and I completely understand why. It must have totally confused her; she'd have felt like the rug of life had been tugged from beneath her feet.

'Have you spoken to him since you found out? Have you sat down and properly talked?'

'Well, he did come around on Monday night. To collect his things. I told him he'd find them in the garden, and that was that. He wasn't even bothered, Katie – just walked back outside and started picking everything up off the lawn!'

I grimace inside, but try to keep my face calm and non-judgemental. That was a typical Mum move – and one that would usually have incited my father into a fit of purple-faced anger. The fact that he didn't even rise to that kind of bait must have been terrible for her – all her expectations dashed. All of mine, too, to be honest.

If he'd stopped caring enough to fight with her, then he'd stopped caring. That would be the simple equation in her brain, and it was one I probably agreed with. I was sad for her, confused for me, and, I suspected, actually pretty impressed by my dad. If he'd done that when I was younger, it might have saved us all a lot of trouble.

'All right, Mum. I'm so sorry. But you're here now, and we can spend some time together, and it'll get better – it really will. I know it might not feel like it now, but it will. You'll stay for a bit, will you?'

'If that's okay, yes. I left my bags in the car. I just couldn't stand it at home any more . . . it was just so quiet all the time. And I kept finding things of his lying around the house, like his shaving stuff in the bathroom and his old copies of *Auto Trader* in the downstairs loo and those tins of Irish stew he likes in the kitchen cupboard . . . and . . . well. I had to get away for a bit, love. The only thing I was grateful for was the weather – so she wasn't driving around in the bloody ice cream van, looking all smug and loved up . . .'

I shudder slightly at the image of a female Jeff Goldblum getting loved up with my dad, and instead start calculating some logistics. Saul can sleep in with me for a few days, and Mum can have his room. She'll have to sleep in a small single bed decorated with *Paw Patrol* stickers, but them's the breaks.

'I get it, Mum. I do. And don't worry. The only way is up.'

'Like Yazz used to say.'

'Exactly. Now, come on – let me introduce you to a few people . . . and remember. No flirting with Frank.'

'I'll try,' she replies, managing a smile. 'But Sandy can't make any promises . . .'

# Chapter 15

After that, my life goes from busy but straightforward to something resembling a complicated American sitcom. Without evil twins or fake deaths – at least so far.

Mum takes root in Saul's room, which he finds hilarious. On the first night, he tucks her in, surrounded by approximately 7,000 cuddly toys, telling her all their names and back-stories in a solemn way that suggests he might test her on them in the morning.

She's tired, and clearly struggling with what has happened in her life, and being put to bed by a toddler beneath a *Paw Patrol* duvet cover must have only added to the sense of the surreal for her. It doesn't get much less surreal, but luckily I have a busy spell with work and college, and she seems happy enough keeping herself amused.

Then, two days after that, The Cat arrives in all his ginger glory. Matt brings him round, fully recovered from his 'small op', but I suspect still harbouring some resentment. He definitely gives Matt an untrusting glare that wasn't there before as he strolls out of the cat carrier, and inspects his new home like the Queen inspecting her guards on parade.

He prowls around the room a while, looking supremely confident and 99 per cent disdainful, while Saul sits on his hands almost bursting with excitement.

I've had some Big Talks with Saul about pet etiquette, and how to handle the cat, and how important it is to let him settle in and get used to things before we smother him with affection. Also, about how pulling tails and tweaking ears isn't a good thing under any circumstances. He's playing along so far, but is literally vibrating with anticipation as the cat carries out his initial patrol.

I half expect him to just take off upstairs, find somewhere quiet and ignore us – but he surprises me by padding over to Saul and curling up on his lap. The look on Saul's face is priceless, and actually makes me cry. There's just something so pure and joyous about seeing a young child react to the presence of a pet – the simplest and most honest of reactions.

Saul looks up at me, as if asking a question, and I nod and tell him it's probably okay to go ahead and touch now, as the cat seems to have made up his mind about us. Or Saul at least.

Tentatively at first, he runs his tiny hands along the cat's back, and when he hears a purr, plunges his fingers into his thick fur. Within minutes, they're best friends, and everyone in the room seems to sigh a communal breath of relief.

One hand on the cat's head, Saul looks up at us with what is officially the world's biggest grin, and announces: 'We're going to call her Tinkerbell!'

I look at Matt. Matt looks at me. We both shrug – what does it really matter? It's not like the cat will ever respond to its name, unless he thinks there's something in it for him. And if Saul has, for some reason, decided the cat is female . . . well, that's not going to do any harm anyway.

The cat looks up at us, snuggled and comfy, and pauses in his leisurely paw-licking to give us a smug cat stare. He's borderline ugly, this fella, with his scar tissue and bald patches and missing ear tip and sheer brute size. If not ugly, then definitely not pretty.

'Tinkerbell,' I say, reaching out to stroke Saul's blond head. 'That's perfect, love.'

After this initial outburst of affection, Tinkerbell becomes slightly more reticent – finding hiding places all over the house, and making his base camp in the dirty washing basket. Saul just thinks it's a splendid game of hide and seek, and even counts to ten (give or take a six) to give the cat time to find a new spot, so that's not a problem.

My mum, after being open and honest that first night, also becomes a bit more reticent – although thankfully she doesn't start hiding in the dirty washing basket.

We have two evenings in, where I cook and she damns with faint praise, and we both shuffle around the small living room trying to be neutral. I'm struggling with her sudden arrival, if I'm honest – I've not spent this much time with an adult human being since I moved to Budbury, and I've definitely become set in my ways.

I'm also confused by what's happening with my parents – and the fact that I'm so bothered confuses me even more. I'm a grown-up. They had a terrible marriage. Why should I be concerned at all that it appears to have come to an end?

I don't really have an answer for that, other than change is hard. Even when it's change that we know, deep down, is a good kind of change, a change that was necessary, it's a tricky fish to land.

So when she's being especially annoying – dusting the TV stand when I only did it the day before; insisting on watching *Gardeners' World* and making saucy comments about the size of Monty Don's pitchfork; rearranging my kitchen cupboards so they 'make a bit more sense' – I remind myself of that.

I remind myself that no matter how confusing this is for me, for her it's a million times worse. Yes, their relationship was beyond dysfunctional – but it was theirs. It was all she'd known for most of her adult life, and suddenly, it was gone. She'd been rejected for a woman she would most definitely not have seen as a love rival, which also had to sting.

She's still not eating much, and still wearing too much make-up, and seems to have developed a taste for skinny jeans – all, I suspect, in an attempt to somehow boost her self-confidence. She's still flirting with everyone from the postman to Scrumpy Joe, which is quite amusing to watch. Scrumpy Joe just looks confused by it, and asks if she likes cider.

Surfer Sam responds like Cal, with a generosity of spirit that brings a smile to her face. Matt simply stares over her shoulder, as though trying to figure out how to escape. Tom, Willow's boyfriend, engages her in a conversation about Jean Grey from the *X-Men* comics, which is a joy to behold – that'll teach her to say he looks a bit like a much younger Hugh Jackman.

She does, however, leave Frank well alone – she might be in crisis, but she's clearly had the good sense to get the size of Cherie and decide to live another day. Not that Cherie would actually squash her like a bug – not physically. Truth be told, Farmer Frank enjoys a good flirt, and she never seems to mind, but my mum doesn't know that.

By the third night, we're both getting a bit stir-crazy. Tinkerbell is housebound for the first fortnight on the advice of Matt, so he gets used to the idea of this being his home before he's allowed out into the wilds, and he's not especially liking being cooped up with us. I think me and Mum feel exactly the same, as I come down from the stairs after putting Saul to bed.

'So,' she says, stretching out on the sofa that used to be my spot, 'I was thinking we might give Netflix a miss tonight. We've done *Jessica Jones* and watched the best bits of *Friends*, and I did enjoy that one about the president with Kiefer Sutherland in it. But I'm all tellied out, I think.'

I settle down into the armchair and nod in agreement. She's right – we have watched a lot of TV. She hasn't seemed open to much conversation about any issues more weighty than whether Ross and Rachel were really on a break when he slept with the girl from the copy shop, despite my attempts to gently prod her into it.

It's like she's built some kind of wall of unreality around it all, and that's probably easy to do here – where she's away from the house she shared with my dad, away from the risk of bumping into him in the street with Fiona Whittaker, away from the grim everyday-ness of her current circumstances.

I understand that, and in all honesty I've been happy enough to just binge-watch TV with her. We love each other but we've never been especially close, and this enforced proximity is obviously taking its toll on us both.

'Okay,' I say eventually, jolting slightly as Tinkerbell makes a sudden appearance, leaping up onto the back of the chair and splaying himself along it. I can feel his breath on the side of my face, and wonder briefly if he's planning to eat my eyeballs. 'So what do you want to do? Early night?'

I could probably go for an early night, I think. I mean, I usually can – because I will definitely be getting an early morning, and not much rest in between. I love the very bones of my little boy, but he is not an easy bed companion – he tends to sleep horizontally across the mattress, his legs splayed across my tummy, curled up in a comma shape so his face is always millimetres away from mine.

Sometimes it's cute, and I do tend to lie awake staring at his beautiful features, listening to his little sounds, simply adoring this wonderful creature. But other times . . . well, I'm pretty exhausted, let's leave it at that.

Mum looks at me and smirks. It's an annoying smirk – one that says, 'My God, what kind of a woman are you?'

'Katie, it's just gone half seven. That's no kind of bedtime for a woman in her prime!'

'Right. Yes. You have a point. So . . . what, then?'

'Well, I was thinking I might go out,' she replies, stretching a bit like the cat. My first thought is: *brilliant – if she goes out, I can have the sofa. And the remote controls. And a whole bloody night on my own.*

My second thought is: *hang on a minute . . . aren't I a woman in my prime, like she says? And isn't she the grandma here? And shouldn't she maybe be babysitting so I can go out?*

As soon as I think it, I see that it's a silly thought. A ridiculous thought. I mean, where would I go? What would I do? The café is closed. My friends all have busy lives too. I've not had a night out without Saul since . . . well, ever, actually.

'Is that all right with you?' she asks, arching her eyebrows. 'It's not like you seem to have much of a social life, beyond your cake club and work. Seems a shame for us both to be stuck in. Anyway, you have Tinkerbell for company.'

The cat nuzzles the back of my neck on cue, and I realise that she's kind of right. I am a complete saddo, now I come to think of it. Not even thirty, and already one of those ladies who spends every night with a cat. If I'm lucky, by the time Saul's left home and I reach my own mother's age, I might have fifteen of them and wear a dressing gown twenty-four hours a day and never leave the house at all.

The weird thing is, if Mum wasn't here, I'd actually be quite happy with that prospect – a quiet night in with Tinkerbell, I mean, not my ultimate fate as a reclusive cat lady. But something about the way she says it, something about her expression (I think the best word for it might be 'pitying'), rattles me. Puts my back up. Sends me into a rare mood where I actually think, *no – that's not right.*

I'm used to taking the back seat, and I'm fine with that. I've never enjoyed the spotlight, never been at the heart of a dizzying social whirl. I'm usually happier alone than with other people. All of that is true, but it doesn't mean I want my own mother patronising me because of it.

'Actually, Mum,' I say, firmly, 'I wouldn't mind going out myself. I never get the chance to normally, because of Saul.'

'Oh!' she says, her eyes widening in surprise. 'Why's that? Can't you get babysitters in this part of the world? I'd have thought all your wonderful friends would have been pleased to help!'

There's a definite edge of cattiness to her voice as she says this – and it's a cattiness I've heard many times before. One designed to provoke and push and start a row. She wants me to leap in and defend my friends, and give her the chance to criticise them, and for all of this to end with a big argument where she can slam some doors and storm out.

It usually used to work with my dad – he was just as bad as her, and always up for having his buttons pressed. But I'm not my dad and she's not my wife, and this is not her life. This is mine, and Saul's, and I'm not going down that road, ever.

So instead, I take a deep, calming breath, listen to the sound of Tinkerbell's purring for some extra zen, and reply: 'You're probably right, Mum. They would have, if I'd ever asked. I just haven't for some reason. That's my fault, not theirs. But it's different with you, isn't it? You're Saul's grandma and he loves you, and I'd feel comfortable leaving him with you. But maybe we can do that another time – maybe tonight, you can go out, and perhaps at the weekend I can take a turn. How does that sound?'

She bites her lip, leaving her teeth stained with bright pink lipstick – she wears lipstick all the time these days – and considers what I've just said. My tone seems to have taken the wind out of her sails, which is exactly what I'd hoped for.

'Well, when you put it like that, I see what you mean. It's not my fault you moved away, but I've not done much on the grandma duty front. I do love our little man, and I'd be happy to look after him for you. Anyway, I can go out any time. I was only planning to go to the pub over the road anyway, see if I could make some new friends . . . I don't mind staying in if you have something you'd like to do, love.'

Suddenly, of course, I feel guilty. My poor mum, trying to rebuild her life and her self-confidence, was only wanting to make some new friends. And I chose that exact moment to start being selfish about it all. I'm on the verge of opening my mouth to apologise and insist that she goes out instead, when she starts speaking again.

'While you're out, I could give the bathroom a good deep clean. I swear I saw some mould growing around the shower curtain this morning . . .'

Let me make this clear: there is no mould growing around my shower curtain. There is no mould anywhere in my house. My house is very clean, even if it sometimes gets messed up by having a small child around. This is a mould-free zone, thank you very much.

I look across at her and see that she's staring around the living room – the very clean living room – with a critical eye. I follow her gaze and see that yes, there is a pile of toys left out in the corner. That Saul's little art table has a higgledy-piggledy heap of colouring books on top of it.

That there may, in fact, be one brightly coloured sock poking out from beneath a sofa cushion. But no mould, anywhere, definitely. I keep a clean house.

I realise, as my nostrils flare in annoyance, that for the good of our relationship, it is suddenly very important that at least one of us gets out of the house tonight.

I stand up, dust myself down and make my mind up.

'Right. That's great then. I'll go out, and you can look for mould, and we'll both be fine.'

'Yes. It's a plan. But where will you go – you know, in case of emergencies? And who will you be with? Everyone here seems coupled up already.'

'Well, I'm not looking for a place on *Love Island*, Mum – just a quiet night out. I'm sure I can find someone to play with, don't you worry.'

Her eyebrows are raised again, and it's starting to really wind me up. I wonder if maybe I could sneak into her room late at night and shave them off without her waking up.

'Okay, sweetie, that's fine. Even if you just go out for a little walk on your own, maybe that'll help calm you down.'

As anyone who has ever had an argument knows, being told you need to 'calm down' is a sure-fire way to strip you of any calm you did, in fact, have left. Again, though, I don't rise to it. I smile sweetly and walk into the kitchen, where I spend a good five minutes crushing up recycling into small cardboard squishes. When you're a single parent, you soon find healthy ways to release your frustration.

After that, I'm left with a problem – I've now won a battle with my mother, and put myself in a situation where I have to actually go out. Minutes ago I was pondering an early night, and now I have to somehow dredge a social life up from absolutely nothing.

I grab my phone, and consider who I can call. Even if it's just to go around to theirs and sit with them for an hour. It's still lashing it down outside, so I can't even resort to plan B and go and hang out at the bus stop with a bottle of cider like a teenager.

I try Laura first – a quick text asking if she's up for a visit. She replies with the not unsurprising news that she's already in bed, followed by a long line of smiley faces. Then I call Becca, but there's no answer. I'm on the verge of trying Zoe, but then I remember that her and Cal and Martha are away in Oxford for the night, visiting the college Martha's applied to.

Next up is Auburn, who answers on the first ring.

'Madam Zelda's House of Bondage – whom may I say is calling, and what is your safe word?' she says, before erupting into laughter.

'Erm . . . hi, Madam Zelda. It's Katie.'

'I know that. I can see it on my phone. I was just having a bit of fun. How's tricks?'

'Well, I seem to have got myself into a bit of a predicament, and need to find a buddy for the night. Do you fancy a pint?'

'Hmmm,' she says, dragging it out into a thousand syllables, 'ordinarily I'd love to, but I was just out in the garden having a fag, and this passing pterodactyl did an enormous shit in my hair . . .'

I snort out loud at that one, and she continues: 'Seriously, I did actually just wash my hair. Not because of a pterodactyl or anything, obvs. I was planning on having an early night in with Mum. But *Van's* around. He's doing nothing more interesting than waxing his balls and painting his toenails tonight . . .'

She says the last sentence with such obvious glee that I can tell he's within earshot. I'm tempted to hang up on her, admit defeat, and let Mum go out while I carry on with a surreptitious mould-check in the bathroom.

I hear a scuffle at the end of the phone, and the sound of Auburn yelping and shouting something about someone being officially the world's biggest bastard. In a way that suggests she really, really means it.

Seconds later, Van comes on the line.

'Hi. Auburn's indisposed at the moment. She was wearing one of those towel turbans on her head, like all you ladies do and men are incapable of making, and someone accidentally set it on fire with a nice lavender-scented candle.'

I'm not sure if he's serious or not. I mean, it sounds like

a crazy thing to do – but my only-child mindset under-stands that in theory, siblings actually do things like that just for fun. The sound of a running tap in the background suggests that possibly Auburn is now dunking her towel in the kitchen sink.

'So,' I say, feeling a little unsettled by it all. 'What colour are you painting your nails?'

Obviously, I avoid referring to his balls. It wouldn't be polite.

'I'm thinking a nice shade of coral . . . but I'll happily sacrifice my mani-pedi if you're finally at a loose end. Assuming I read Auburn's end of the conversation correctly. I'd ask her, but she's busy right now. You know. Putting out the fire and all.'

'Well, it's not that urgent. I was just . . . wondering what people were up to. You don't need to change your plans,' I reply noncommittally. I'm not sure I'm ready for a night out with Van, now or ever. It all feels a bit too delicious. A bit too exciting. A bit too scary.

'In fact I think I might stay in after all,' I add, as much to myself as him.

'Oh. Right. Sorry, I must have got the wrong end of the stick,' he says, sounding disappointed. 'I'll pass you back to Auburn.'

At that moment, my mum bustles into the kitchen, with a whispered 'don't mind me!', and starts poking around in the cupboard under the sink, once she's figured out the child lock. She emerges with a bottle of spray-on Mr Muscle, a wire scrubber and several cloths, waving them in the air triumphantly as she leaves the room.

I watch her skinny-jeaned backside go. If I stay in, there might be blood. I should have told Van yes. I should have agreed to go out with him.

'He is such a wanker,' says Auburn, once she's back on the phone. 'I could have died. I'd have become a cautionary tale on the internet: this young woman died from drying her hair . . . anyway, you okay?'

'Yeah. I'm okay.'

'Really? You sound about as okay as Meghan Markle is ugly.'

'I'm sorry,' I reply, smiling at the way she pulls these crazy images from thin air. 'I'm out of practice at sounding enthusiastic. To be honest my mum's driving me nuts, and I told her I was going out and she agreed to babysit, and now . . .'

'Now you feel like a big fat loser with nobody to play with?'

'Exactly. Don't worry about it. I'll see you at work.'

'Oh no, missus,' she says firmly. 'You have opened the lid to Pandora's Box. Be at the pub in an hour, okay?'

I nod, realise she can't see me, and agree. It's done. I'm going out!

# Chapter 16

It actually feels weird, going out. On my own. At night. Luckily, I'm only actually on my own for about forty-five seconds, which is as long as it takes for me to cross the road from my house and reach the Horse and Rider on the opposite side. It's about three doors down from the Budbury Chemist, which is a slightly longer commute of about a whole minute.

Having set out my stall as a busy woman-about-village for my mother's benefit, I found myself having to go the whole hog. Clean jeans, a fresh top, a touch of grown-up make-up rather than Beauty Parlour style, and even an attempt at doing something with my hair. Admittedly not much – just a slightly off-centre French plait. I always find my arms aching way too much to do them well.

I give myself a spritz of perfume, and pull on my trainers. Okay, so it's not a hike and I could have gone for heels – but it's only my local pub. And it's only Auburn.

It's only Auburn, and it could have been Van, and a tiny part of me regrets my choice. Still, it was the right choice. The sensible choice.

I tell myself this repeatedly as I get ready, tiptoeing around upstairs so I don't wake up Saul. The cat follows me silently, looking at me with what I can only describe as scepticism.

'Don't look at me like that,' I whisper, as he perches on the toilet seat and watches me put my slap on. 'I'm not ready for anything like that, okay?'

In response, he twists one leg up and elegantly licks his own bottom. Well, that told me.

Now, after bidding farewell to my mum and telling her where I'll be in case of emergencies, I'm out. Standing in the doorway of the pub, wondering if it's not too late to change my mind. The bus stop with a plastic bottle of cider is looking more attractive by the second.

I make my way inside, and am amazed at how different it is at night. I've brought Saul here in the day once or twice, just to fill in time. He likes it well enough, but there's only so long a little boy stays amused by a glass of orange juice and a bag of Quavers.

It tends to be quiet in the day, a few locals, a few walkers, the aroma of pub grub wafting around the place, the tinkling sound of the fruit machine. That sound always makes me smile, and remember holidays to Somerset as a kid, where my nan had pots full of coins to use in what she called the 'one-armed bandits'.

Tonight, though, it's bustling – a veritable cacophony of chatter and laughter and cheers from the corner, where some kind of highly competitive game of darts seems to be going on.

I glance around and nod to the few people I know, giving a wave to the landlord as I walk past the wooden-topped bar. It's a good, old-fashioned boozer, with two main rooms and various tucked-away alcoves and corners, and every chair and stool seems to be occupied.

I search the crowds, looking for Auburn's distinctive hair, and failing to find it. I mill around a bit, checking in the corners and cubbies, wondering if I'm early or if I've gone to the wrong pub. That, though, would be difficult, as there's only one in the village – the other one roughly classed as local is a drive away.

I'm on the verge of giving up and creeping back home in shame when I spot a familiar face over in the back room.

Familiar, but not what I expected. It's not Auburn, for sure. It's Van.

My heart does something skippy and thuddy that under normal circumstances would have me heading straight to A&E, and I stand still, staring at him. He hasn't seen me yet, so I could still make a run for it. I silently curse Auburn and chew my lip, and manage to be both excited and terrified at the same time.

It's Van – not Count Dracula. It's Van, who is my friend, and why can't we have a friendly night out as friends, discussing things that friends do?

Because I fancy the arse off him, that's why. And I think

he feels the same about me. And there's alcohol in this pub. And . . . no, this is a terrible idea.

I'm on the verge of turning around and leaving when he spots me, and waves. He's grinning at me, and looks so happy that I can imagine him as a little boy. Damn. I can't just snub him like that. I have to stay, even if it's just for one Diet Coke.

It still takes me a moment to force myself forward, though, climbing over discarded bags and umbrellas and random legs until I reach him.

He's managed to hook a small table by the fireplace, which is one of those that begs to be described as roaring, logs blazing and crackling in a massive stone hearth so big you could roast a suckling pig in it. He already has a pint in front of him, which looks like a member of the real ale family, and probably has one of those borderline rude names like the Bishopric or Old Bessie's Buttock.

Unlike me, he hasn't been able to do much with his hair – it's cut so short – but he is wearing a navy blue T-shirt that stretches over his shoulders and brawny upper arms in such a snug way that I can almost imagine him without it.

This, obviously, is not the kind of thought I want to be having as I walk over to the table, especially as this is not a date. This is just two friends, out for a friendly chat about friend things. As friends. It's not my fault that one of us looks like he does. Probably not his either, but . . . well, he could've worn a baggier top.

I giggle to myself as I think this, as it is a ridiculous thought to have had. This confuses him as it coincides with me arriving at the table.

'What?' he asks, looking down at himself self-consciously. 'Did I accidentally wear my pyjamas or something?'

'No, no . . . just me. Being weird. No pyjamas involved. Do you wear pyjamas? You don't strike me as a pyjama kind of man.'

'You're right. I'm not. I'm usually a buck-naked kind of man. But I don't half feel the cold, living here, after years travelling around much warmer places. Winter in Budbury is not a prospect I'm relishing. Last night I used a sleeping bag and two duvets, and I was still a wuss about it. You look nice, by the way – I like that hair thing. Makes you look like a ballerina. What would you like to drink?'

This is a good question, especially right after his distracting buck-naked comment. It's also skipping right past the other, more glaring question that needs to be asked.

'What are you doing here, Van?' I ask, trying not to sound upset. That would be rude.

'I'm meeting you for a drink . . .' He frowns, looking as confused as I feel, then continues: 'Didn't you know I was coming?'

'Umm . . . no. I'd arranged to meet Auburn.'

'She said she had a migraine, because I'd set her on fire. She said she couldn't come, but didn't want to let you down at the last minute, and she said she'd told you and it was fine.'

He takes in my bewildered expression, and the way I'm hovering by the chair but not actually sitting on it, and I see a moment of hurt flicker across his face before he wrestles it into something more neutral.

'I take it from your reaction that she didn't?' he says. I nod, and he smiles at me.

'Well, don't worry,' he adds, standing up. 'It's not a big deal. Either stay for a quick one, spend the night with me getting hilariously drunk, or we'll call it a night right now and go home. I don't mind. It's your choice.'

Every single one of those options sounds both acceptable and wrong. There is no right thing to do – so I go for the middle ground.

'I'll stay for a quick one. Or maybe two. That'd be nice.'

'Are you sure?' he asks. 'Because the way you say "nice" makes it sound a bit more like "I'd rather be stung by a thousand angry bees."'

'Sorry. I was just surprised to see you. I'm staying, honestly.'

'All righty then . . . well, as I'm up, what do you want to drink? Arsenic? Invisibility powder? Man repellent?'

'Hmmm . . . just a Bacardi and Coke please,' I reply, grinning. I used to drink that when I was much younger, and it seems as good a time as any to revive the tradition. He raises one eyebrow in what might be surprise, and goes off to fetch it. I quickly grab my phone out of my bag, and see a text has just landed from Auburn. Well, not so much a text as a screen full of devil emoticons and laughing faces.

I tap out a reply that informs her in simple language that I am planning to kill her the next day.

'So,' says Van, when he returns with my glass – complete with little umbrella, very fancy – 'how are things going? With your mum? I'm guessing not brilliant if it's actually driven you out.'

'That's a harsh assessment,' I reply, taking my first sip and trying not to sigh out loud. 'But an accurate one.'

'I can imagine. I know how weird it is being back with your family after years away, believe me.'

For him, of course, it must be even weirder – he's been abroad for so long, and now finds himself not only back in Dorset, but sharing a house with his sisters, and a mother with Alzheimer's. So, yeah, I believe him when he says he understands.

'Well,' I reply, staring into the fire, 'it's a work in progress, I suppose. I mean, it's not easy – she's not easy. But she needs to be here for a while, and that's okay. Half the time I want to hug her, and half the time I want to kill her. But that's kind of normal for families, isn't it?'

'I think so. It's easy to love your family – but not always easy to like them. Have you spoken to your dad yet? And how do you feel, about the whole them-splitting-up thing? Are you sad? I know you're not a kid or anything, but it's still got to hurt.'

I let out a laugh at that one. I can't help myself.

'No, it doesn't hurt. It's confusing, and strange, and part

of me doesn't even believe it yet – mainly because I've not spoken to him beyond a couple of texts. He's not good at texting, or apparently using phones at all. Mainly, to be honest, I just wish they'd done it years ago.'

Van looks understandably flummoxed by this, so I explain: 'They've been making each other miserable as long as I've known them. Seriously, I grew up in a war zone, Van. They fought constantly. It was one long line of rows and screaming matches and actual physical fights.'

'What?' he says, looking distraught. 'He hit her?'

'Yes, but it wasn't that simple. She hit him too. She's small but scrappy, my mum. It wasn't one of those mean-dad scenarios – they were both mean. I've seen her literally hanging off his back trying to gouge his eyes during one of their spats. He was more of a shover and a grabber. Basically, neither of them ever came out of it unscathed.'

'And neither did you, from the sound of it. That must have been terrible. My childhood was hardly conventional – you know, born in a hippy commune, Dad died young, moved here and got raised by Lynnie during the Yoga and Incense years. But it was never, ever like that. Mum was all for peace and self-expression – she never even raised her voice. The only violence in our house was between us lot when she wasn't looking.'

'Still the same now, isn't it?' I reply, smiling. 'Did you really set Auburn's towel on fire?'

'Just a little tiny bit. It was all under control, honest.

And you're avoiding the subject. Is that why you came here, to get away from them?'

I chew my lip for a moment, and then decide to break the habits of a lifetime and actually talk openly about all of this stuff. *Maybe*, I think, *it'll help. I've joined the Cake Club. I'm in the pub. Maybe things are changing, and I need to push them along a little instead of being a passive witness to my own life.*

I don't think I'd have had this conversation with Auburn – we are both highly skilled at talking about nothing of consequence for hours on end – but with Van, it feels more natural. More organic. Maybe that's what scares me.

'Not just them,' I say. 'I needed to get away from Saul's dad as well . . . from everything, to be honest. Me and Jason – well, we were heading down the same path as my parents.'

I see him stiffen slightly as I say this, and his hand clenches into a fist on the table top.

'Don't get all macho on me,' I say, trying to keep my tone light. 'I never let it escalate. It was about me and what I needed as much as him – we were never going to work as a couple. But that's the past, and this isn't one of those situations where some big tough man can come to the rescue and sort my life out, okay? I sorted my own life out, and, I think he's sorted his out too. He lives in Scotland, with the woman who's now his wife, and that suits us all fine.'

'What about Saul? Doesn't he see him?'

'He did, a bit, when he still lived in Bristol. And he stays in touch, sends cards and presents, that kind of thing. He was talking about making a trip down to see him a while ago, but it hasn't materialised . . . I suppose I'm kind of hoping it won't, which is very selfish of me. He's still Saul's dad, at the end of the day, and sometimes I do worry about him growing up without one. I'm not very good at football, you know.'

Van gives me a little grin as he replies: 'I bet you are. And there's more to being a dad than playing football anyway. I grew up with Lynnie as the sole parent, and I turned out . . . well, maybe I'm not the best example, I'm just a professional backpacker and basic New Age slacker. But I did learn how to play football, and Saul will too. He has all of us for that as well – it's not like you're on your own with him.'

He's just vocalised, in a nutshell, the very thing that I struggle with. All of these baby steps – going to the café more, my job, socialising – are taking me somewhere I have mixed feelings about going. Most of me wants to be more rooted, more involved, to give Saul the stability and sense of community that this place offers us both.

But part of me is still anxious and concerned – what if it all goes wrong? What if things break? What if I need to leave? What will that do to Saul, and to me? And more importantly, why am I such a nutter that I always assume the worst? I seem to live my life waiting for the other shoe to drop – in fact, waiting for an enormous great boot to not only drop, but land firmly on my head and squish me into the ground. It's about as much fun as it sounds.

I'm trying to override it, to be brave and sensible and

optimistic, but unfortunately, I don't seem able to completely change my world view. It's my default setting. I don't suppose there's any point analysing it – I just have to try and manage it, and not let the fear of things going wrong get in the way of things going right.

Just now, for example, I am sitting in a pub, finishing off a delicious Bacardi and Coke, getting a supportive pep talk from a man who makes my girl-brain tingle. Why can't I simply relax and enjoy it? Maybe I just need to drink the rest of the bottle of Bacardi and go with the flow.

'You're freaking out inside, aren't you?' he asks, grinning. 'You're feeling overdosed with community spirit, and too involved, and wishing you could run away to your nan's house?'

'How do you know about my nan?' I ask, genuinely surprised.

'You told me about her. You told me you used to run away there when you were fed up at home – although you didn't explain why. You told me she was kind and sweet and fed you cake and custard and always smelled of Parma Violets. You tell me a lot of things without even noticing, Katie. I'm like your stealth confidante.'

All I can do to that is make a small hmmph sound, and decide that ever so possibly he's right. When I'm with Van, I do open up more than when I'm with other people – he just seems to have this easy knack of peeling back the layers of self-protection. It's probably why I've avoided being alone in a pub with him for so long.

'Do you want another?' says Van, pointing at my empty glass. I think he's picked up on the fact that this has all got a bit too serious for me, and is giving me time to process it all.

'It's my turn to go,' I reply, preparing to move.

'No. Let me. I have to get rid of my big tough man urges somehow, you know. At least allow me to be a caveman when it comes to your booze requirements.'

He doesn't give me much choice, as he's already walking away, chatting to people from the village as he goes. I lean back, and feel the warmth of the fire on my face, and the warmth of the alcohol in my system, and I have to say – it does feel pretty good. Like I said, baby steps.

By the time he comes back, I've snapped myself out of whatever morose and overly analytical mood I was heading for, and restart the conversation on a different tack. One that isn't about me. I'm bored of me.

'So,' I say, nodding in thanks for both the drink and the bag of dry roasted peanuts he offers, 'tell me about travelling. Tell me about Tanzania.'

He immediately smiles, but also looks a little wistful. A little sad – like he's happy to be here, but he's also missing his old life.

'Well, that's a big topic. I left home when I was nineteen, and apart from a few visits back for birthdays and such, kept moving until this spring, when I came home again. I'm thirty-three now, so that's a lot of years spent with a backpack on my shoulders. Mainly, I spent my time getting

149

dirty, getting drunk, getting high. They were the early years – when I was hanging around with posh kids called Tristram who were on their gap years. It was a lot of fun, but it does start to wear you down after a while – you start to yearn for more in life, like a clean toilet.

'So then I stayed in Tibet for a bit. That was . . . amazing. It taught me a lot, about myself and others and the whole big world. Made me realise I needed to find a different path, not to go all Dalai Lama on you or anything. And that's when I started working for charities.'

'In Africa?' I ask, genuinely fascinated. The furthest I've ever travelled is for holidays in the Canary Islands, where you eat and drink yourself to death in an attempt to break even on your all-inclusive deal. And since Saul was born, I've never left the UK – or even the southern half of it. Very lame indeed.

'Thailand initially, then Tanzania. I've been there for the last few years, setting up a school. It's . . . well, it's a beautiful place. But complex, like most beautiful things.'

'Do you miss it?'

He blinks hard, like he's trying to clear his mind, and replies: 'Only every day. I think I left a part of myself there, to be honest. I miss the air, and the space, and the landscapes, and the people. Mainly the people. The kids. The kids were so great . . . it's hard to get used to things the way they are here, you know? Over there, even though life is harder in so many ways, they're also so much happier when things go right. They don't take anything for granted; there's a kind of joyfulness over small triumphs. But I'm okay here, honest. I love my family, even when I'm setting their towels on fire, and my mum . . . well, she needs us, doesn't she?'

'I think your sisters need you too. I can only imagine how hard it is to settle back down to normal life.'

'Ha!' he snorts, laughing. 'Normal is a relative term in our house, between the Alzheimer's and the dogs and the fact that we're all basically crazy anyway . . . but it's all right. I'm enjoying lots of it. This, for instance. I'm enjoying this. It's nice to be out with someone I'm not related to and don't work for.'

I smile at him and nod. This Bacardi is possibly making me a bit more flirtatious than usual. Or maybe it's the dry roasted peanuts acting as a little-known aphrodisiac. Either way, I feel it – I feel the tug of attraction between us; that's always been there, ever since I first met him.

'I can imagine,' I say. 'In fact I think that's the only reason you've been asking me out. You're swimming in a very small dating pool.'

'Outrageous! You do know there are places outside Budbury within swimming distance, don't you? I could have a harem in Applechurch for all you know. Or a cougar in Dorchester. There's even ways to meet people on this wondrous new invention called the internet . . .'

'Have you ever tried that?' I ask. 'I've heard tell there's a whole world of singletons out there.'

'I did sign up to Tinder, yes. But I came off it again straight away when my first match was Auburn. I mean, I know we're in the countryside, but I draw the line at my sister . . . she's really not my type.'

'What is your type then? What was your last girlfriend like?'

'She was called Annika, and she was Swedish. She worked for the same charity as me, and had that whole blonde-one-from-Abba thing going on.'

'Ah. Did she take a chance on you?'

'She did,' he replies, grimacing slightly. 'And it's not one that paid off, because I upped sticks and moved back here, didn't I?'

'Oh – was she upset? Are you kind of still together?'

I know this thought shouldn't bother me – we're just two friends, out for a friendly chat about friend things, as friends – but I have to admit that it does anyway. Feelings don't always do what they're told, I've found over the years. I feel low-level anxiety thrum through me at the thought of Van being with someone else, even if she is on the other side of the world.

'No,' he says hastily, shaking his head. 'It's a transient world. People who work in it sometimes make long-lasting connections, but much of the time we're on the move. No, we're definitely not still together, in any sense. Don't worry.'

I'm about to launch into a response about how I'm not worried, I have no reason to be worried, and that I'm worried that he thinks I would be worried – but luckily we're saved all of that by the arrival of Willow and Tom. Who looks worried.

Willow is wearing her pink hair tied up into a scrappy ponytail, and a dress that seems to be made of Miss Haversham's wedding gown, coupled with her usual Dr. Marten boots – extra-long ones that almost come up to her knees. Willow is really, really tall, and really, really slim. Tom is even taller, and must have spent a lot of time since his move to Dorset ducking to avoid banging his head on all the random low-flying beams.

He's wearing a T-shirt that tells the world The Truth Is Out There, and seems stressed. A bit like Matt, Tom isn't one of life's chatters. He's geeky and warm and always a tiny bit awkward, and is currently clinging on to his phone for dear life.

'Mind if we join you?' asks Willow, as Tom troops off to the bar to get us all more booze. We scuttle around making room for their stools, and I end up squashed next to Van in a way that isn't entirely unpleasant.

'What's wrong with Science Boy?' Van asks, nodding off in Tom's direction. 'He looks like he's just found out the Force isn't real.'

'Hush your mouth, big brother,' she replies, reaching out to swat him across the head. 'Of course the Force is real. And he's . . . well, he needed a drink. Rough night at genius camp. He has a house full of mega-brainiac boffins at Briarwood, all trying to build time machines or next-generation handheld microwaves or whatever – but one of them at least hasn't figured out how to use a toaster. Set one of the kitchens on fire.'

She takes in our shocked expressions, and adds: 'Only a bit. Nothing that couldn't be solved by me and a fire extinguisher. But I think he's worried about it all – some of them are young, some of them are borderline other-worldly, and some of them are partying a bit too hard. So he's playing house dad and not enjoying it.'

Briarwood is a big old Victorian mini-mansion just outside the village, on top of a huge hill. It used to be a children's home – where Tom was raised after his parents died, and where Lynnie used to work, and where he and Willow first met when she was only eight. Tom seems to have made a bundle of cash from inventing some kind of doo-hickey nobody really understands, and bought the old house when it came on the market earlier this year.

He's turned it into a kind of hot-house for budding beautiful minds, people who had brilliant ideas but needed the time and space and investment to bring them to life.

They mainly keep to themselves, but every now and then you'll see a stray wandering around the village or coming into the café – always easy to spot by one or all of the following signs: trendy glasses, awful glasses, bowl-cut hair, long hair, sci-fi reference tops, flannel shirts, odd socks, pens behind their ears, ear buds in the shape of skulls, membership cards to the Stephen Hawking Fan Club, the ability to speak Elvish and/or any of the languages of Middle Earth.

Tom himself fits right in, apart from the fact that he's also very, very good-looking – if mainly unaware of it, or at the very least unconcerned with it. He's also back at the table with a tray of drinks, and yet more snacks.

He sits down, raises his glass in a 'cheers' that we all join in with, and gives us an uncharacteristically outgoing grin.

'I've solved the problem,' he announces happily.

'While you were at the bar?' asks Van.

'Of course while he was at the bar – my man is a born solver of problems!' says Willow, leaning in to give him a quick smacker on the lips. 'Go on then – hit us with it.'

'I'm going to employ someone,' he answers, gazing off at the fire, the cogs of his super-tuned brain almost visible as he fleshes out his plan. 'I'm going to create a new job – I don't have a title for it yet, but for the time being, I'll stick with Star-Lord. Because he or she will be the Guardian of the Briarwood Galaxy.'

Van frowns a little – I guess living in Tanzania has dulled his knowledge of pop culture references beyond Abba songs – but doesn't ask.

'And what will Star-Lord do?' Willow asks. 'Apart from some cool dancing.'

'Star-Lord will live at Briarwood, and basically be in charge of the geek squad. He'll bring order from chaos, and make sure they occasionally sleep, and check the oven isn't left on after late-night pizza, and be the keeper of the keys to the

Red Bull cupboard. He'll be part-father, part-boss, part-benign-dictator. I don't suppose you'd be interested, Van?'

Van looks shocked by the very idea, and quickly replies: 'Me? God, no! Thanks for asking, but that would drive me nuts. Little kids I can handle – adult ones, not. I'm happy to carry on doing the maintenance and gardening for you, big man, but I'm not your Star-Lord.'

'Okay,' says Tom, looking temporarily disappointed. 'No worries. I'll find him, even if I have to scour the entire galaxy . . .'

'Or,' I suggest quietly, 'you could go to a recruitment agency?'

'Or that, yes,' Tom says, grinning. 'Anyway. How are you two?'

I finish up my latest Bacardi, and decide that that's enough. I'm starting to get tempted to rest my hand on Van's jean-clad thigh, and that wouldn't be a good idea. Who knows what kind of lovely trouble it could cause?

'I'm a bit drunk,' I reply, and stand up. 'So it's time for me to leave. Saul will be jumping on my head at six a.m., and it won't feel better with a hangover.'

I gather my belongings, and Van insists on walking me home – all the way across the street. We manage that without any incidents at all other than a close encounter with a crisp bag that flies at my head in the breeze, and end up standing awkwardly outside my house.

I feel a bit like a teenager who's been out with a boy for

the first time, a feeling that isn't dissipated by the fact that not only is Tinkerbell lying in my windowsill, staring out at us with his all-seeing cat eyes, but noticing a twitch of the curtains as my mother takes a quick peek as well.

'So,' he says, grinning at me, blue eyes somehow managing to pick up on the moonlight and look ever-so-slightly wolfish, 'that was nice. We should do it again some time.'

'Yes,' I reply, fumbling for my keys in my handbag and trying not to gaze up at him in a way that might invite A Goodnight Kiss. He's moved in closer, and he looks so good, and smells even better, and it would be a matter of millimetres for my body to meet his. Holding my keys is the only thing stopping me from reaching out and resting my hand on his chest, just to see what it feels like.

'It was,' I say. 'And we should. And now I've got to go . . .'

I get the key into the door with shaking hands, and slam the door open so hard it bangs the back of the hallway wall.

I dash inside like a woman being pursued by a pack of hyenas, and bang the door shut again.

'You big chicken!' I hear him shout outside, before he starts laughing. I peer at him through the frosted glass at the top of the door, watching his hazy image walk back over the road to the pub.

I take a deep breath and try to calm myself down. I have nothing to be ashamed of – now I just need to convince Tinkerbell that's true.

I lean against the door and breathe hard, and try not to imagine what would happen if I opened the door again. Called him back. Took this to a level that wasn't just friends being friendly.

I'm too much of a big chicken, like he said. Too frightened. Or, being kinder to myself, just not ready. Kissing someone is just no good if you're not ready to lose control, to surrender yourself to it – and I know I'm not.

I stand and listen for a few seconds, making sure there's no noise from above, and tiptoe up the stairs. I go to the loo, and notice the flush on my cheeks that wasn't just caused by the cold, and close myself into my bedroom.

I slump down on the duvet, and wonder if he's back in the pub now. If he's thinking about me. If he even wanted to kiss me at all.

My phone beeps, and I lazily pull it out and look at the screen.

It's a photo, from Van. A picture of the Cowardly Lion from *The Wizard of Oz*.

I smile, and read the message: 'One day, Katie – one day xxx'

I close my eyes and kick off my trainers, and drift off into a sleep full of dreams that make me blush.

# Chapter 17

It's the first Saturday in December, and I am sitting in a Costa Coffee in Bristol, waiting for my dad. This used to be my favourite coffee place, with all the little pastries and biscuits and things, but I think I've been spoiled by the Comfort Food Café now. Or maybe I'm just a bit freaked out by being back here, and knowing I'm about to have an awkward conversation.

I'm stirring my mocha while I wait, feeling slightly nervous about seeing him. Mum has continued to take root at my house, and we have continued to try and find a balance that makes it manageable for both of us. I'm not sure if we're succeeding, but so far, there's been no need to involve the local constabulary or call an ambulance, which is possibly as good as we can expect.

She has, to be fair, started to make herself very useful – the fact that she has a car and a lot of spare time has definitely made my life simpler when it comes to logistics at least. Having someone to give me a lift to college, or drop Saul off at nursery, has been a rare luxury. It's only now I realise how insanely hectic our lives were – a carefully orchestrated performance pulling together times, places, and various bus timetables.

If the last weeks of November were nothing but rain, then December is so far nothing but pain. The incessant lashing has stopped, but the temperatures are starting to plummet and the wind is wild and unforgiving. Back in Budbury, especially, you feel it whipping up from the bay, slapping your cheeks and making your eyes water as you walk down the street.

Van, who is still doing work for Frank at the farm and also gardening for Tom, is now bundled up in sweaters and shirts and body warmers and gloves, his tanned skin out of place in a small village in England, making him look like some kind of exotic refugee.

We've seen each other a few times, always in the company of others, always as friends – but every now and then I'll catch him looking at me, and he'll smile, and the corners of his blue eyes will crinkle up in amusement, and I'll have to fight off a swoon.

In other news, Tom has a shortlist of potential Star-Lords who he's planning to interview, and Auburn has asked if she can come along. Just for fun and to see if any of them look like Chris Pratt.

Tinkerbell is now allowed out, and has become one of those cats who owns multiple people – I'll be crossing the road from the chemist, and see him draped along Edie's window ledge, or sitting on Becca's doorstep. It seems to fulfil his need to roam, and he always comes home at night to see his best buddy Saul.

Martha has been to her interview at Oxford, and both Zoe and Cal are understandably pipping with pride – now they have to wait and see if she made it through the selection process. Josh, Scrumpy Joe's son, is hopefully off to East Anglia to study chemistry, which will be quite a change for both him and for Lizzie.

Lizzie herself seems thrilled with two developments in her teenaged life. One is that she's started a 'small business' doing pet portraits. She's always taking snaps, Lizzie, and like most teens seems to feel like life hasn't been lived unless you've shared it on social media. But she does have more of an interest in photography than most, and got a new camera for her birthday. Midegbo, Bella Swan, Rick Grimes and Tinkerbell have all been her test portraits, and now she's promoting herself via Matt's veterinary surgery.

She's also delighted about Laura's news – which has now been made public. I think Cherie had already figured it out, because it takes quite a lot to get one over on Cherie, and she'd already told her sister Becca, but everyone else was shocked. Not, maybe, as shocked as Matt and Laura – when their ultrasound revealed that she's expecting twins.

Apparently this is more common in 'geriatric pregnancies'. She was about as thrilled as you'd imagine at the use of that particular term, and is currently walking around in a state of shock as she tries to get used to the idea of not only one baby, but two.

You'll see her in the café, staring into space as she beats a bowl of buttercream or blends up smoothies, and it's obvious her head is elsewhere. Cherie's made an executive decision that she shouldn't be allowed near knives or the chopping board any time soon, telling her she won't be able to change all those nappies if she lops her fingers off.

So, in the way of life in Budbury, not a lot has happened – but a lot has happened. It's the way things work there, marching to the beat of a gentler rhythm than the rest of the world.

Now I'm here, back in the big city, that feels especially noticeable. There are so many cars and vans and buses and bikes. So many people and voices, and so much noise. Everybody seems to be in a hurry all the time, and have that streetwise always-aware look on their faces as they dash from one crowded shop to another – like they're not being funny, but keeping a close hand on their bags.

I'm probably overthinking it. I usually do. But life in my small, sleepy corner of the world is a lot slower than it is here – and while it was exciting for the first hour of getting swept along by the tide of humanity, blissfully anonymous, I'm now feeling a bit worn down.

I have a heap of bags at my feet at my corner table, mainly for Saul's Christmas stash, and my hands have finally warmed up after being wrapped around my mug for a good five minutes. The place is packed with fellow survivors of the Great Christmas Shopping Disaster of 2018, all of us with the same weary look. Keeping a chair for my dad is getting harder by the minute, and I'm relieved when I finally see him poke his head around the door and scan the room for me.

He comes over when I wave to get his attention, looking a little bit sheepish but none the worse for the emotional wear of what's happened.

He's only about five ten, my dad – but compared to me and my mum he always seems like a giant. He has dark hair that's thinning on top, and a moustache he's insisted on keeping since the Eighties, and has the tiniest touch of a beer belly. In short, he's a normal-looking middle-aged bloke, wearing a leather jacket that looks like he stole it from *The Sweeney*.

We share a hug when he makes his way through the crowds and randomly discarded shopping bags, and he gets us both another coffee before finally sitting down at the table. I'm guessing, from the look on his face, that he's been feeling a bit nervous as well.

'So,' he says, poking my bags with his toe, 'been shopping for the nipper, have you?'

'Yep. I'm all shopped out. It's like a war zone out there.'

'I know, love – season of goodwill hasn't quite kicked in yet. Still the season of sharp elbows and queue anger. How is he, Saul? And how are you? And how is . . .'

He trails off, staring into his coffee for answers.

'Mum?' I supply helpfully. He nods, and tries to smile.

'She's not so bad, Dad,' I reply. 'Seems to be quite enjoying herself in the village. No idea how long she's staying, but I'm assuming for a bit longer as she asked me to call in at the house and pick up some more stuff for her. I was hoping you could give me a lift there later?'

He nods, looking miserable at the prospect, and stays silent.

I give him a few moments, then have to prod: 'Well, go on then. Tell me your side of the story. Did you really run off with the woman from the ice cream van?'

He stalls for a while longer by helping a woman lift a pushchair over some abandoned coats, then finally sits back down, looks me in the eye, and says: 'Well, it's not quite that simple, Katie.'

'I'm sure it's not – but as I'm the one picking up the pieces with Mum, I think I at least deserve to know, don't you? And anyway – I've been worried about you as well.'

'No need to worry about me, and as for your mum . . . she'll be okay, once she gets her head around it all. And . . . well, no, I haven't run off with the ice cream woman, all right? I am staying at hers, but we're not a couple.'

'What do you mean, you're not a couple? Mum seems to think you're love's old dream . . .'

'Less of the old, cheeky. I told your mum I was moving in with Fiona, and she jumped to that conclusion.'

'Much as Mum's doing my head in a bit at the moment, I can't blame her for that – it seems like a logical conclusion when your husband leaves you to live with another woman!'

He nods, as though conceding that I might have won that point on a technicality.

'Yes, well. It was the wrong conclusion. Fiona – well, Fiona likes ladies, love, you see? And I'm not a lady, am I?'

A trick of unfortunate timing means that as he says this, I have just taken a mouthful of coffee. Coffee that is immediately spat out in one of those full-force snort-laugh-sprays that results in your whole face getting spritzed. After that, I choke for a second or two, while Dad passes me a napkin to dab my chin with.

'She likes ladies?' I repeat.

'Yes. Is that so shocking in this day and age? I thought you young people were all up with that LGBTTQQ stuff . . .'

'Hang on – what's the QQ bit?'

'Queer and questioning. There's also intersex, asexual, allies and pansexual, if you're interested . . .'

'Since when did you become an expert?'

'Since I became housemates with an L,' he replies smugly.

I screw the damp tissue up into a ball and throw it into the saucer.

'Anyway. That's by the by,' I say. 'And of course I'm not shocked that lesbians exist. But I am shocked that you're currently living with one, and maybe even more shocked by the fact that Mum thinks you're loved up with the lesbian in question – and you're letting her think that. Do you have any idea how much make-up she's wearing at the moment? Or how much she's flirting with any man she meets? How much weight she's lost? All to try and make herself feel better because she thinks you've rejected her for Fiona Whittaker!'

He's quiet again by the time I finish, all traces of smugness gone. He reaches out and pats my hand in an attempt to comfort me. I'd been so busy being annoyed by my mum, I hadn't quite realised how worried about her I was.

'I'm sorry, love – no, I had no idea. Though I should have guessed; it's not like I don't know how much of a drama queen she is. I just . . . it seemed easier to let her think that. Fiona's not ashamed of herself for being what she is, and quite right too – but she also doesn't shout it from the rooftops. People can still be old-fashioned, can't they? She's kind of a public figure as well . . . but you're right. Maybe what I mean is it's just easier for me. The truth's a bit more complicated, I suppose.'

I gesture for him to go on, although part of me is convinced that he's about to tell me he's actually gay. That he's been living a lie for the whole of his life, and couldn't do it any longer. And, you know, that would be fine – eventually. Once I got used to it. I'm just hoping he's not one of the T's though – he'd make a terrible woman.

'Okay,' he says, looking at his coffee wistfully. 'Wish I

had some brandy in this . . . anyway. I got to know Fiona better over the summer. I've always known her, like you, for the ice cream van. Then one day, when I was getting a Magnum, we started talking about Lee Child books. You know, because it's a gun? And then we talked a bit more, about other books – she's a big fan of James Patterson, like myself. And eventually, she asked me if I fancied joining her book club.'

This conversation is most definitely not going the way I expected it to. I don't quite know if it's going worse, or going better, but it's definitely heading off in a surprising direction. I find myself thinking, oddly, that the image of my dad sitting in a room discussing Jane Austen is potentially weirder than everything else.

'Right,' I reply, nodding. 'You always did like James Patterson. So, you joined the book club . . .'

'I did. And met some really interesting people, as you can imagine. Broadened my horizons a bit. Then one thing led to another . . . the occasional night at the theatre. A comedy club. Meals out. Even the ballet. All very friendly but nothing more, love, honest. For all my flaws I've never been unfaithful to your mother . . . I think I've become a bit of an A, to be honest.'

There are all kinds of answers to that, but I bite my lip. Being flippant won't help anyone.

'That's why she thought you were having an affair – the nights out, time away from home? She actually said she knew there was something wrong because you stopped fighting with her.'

He looks so sad when I say this that I almost feel sorry for him.

'That's the problem, isn't it?' he says gently. 'For so many years, that's been all we've had. I've done things I'm ashamed of. I've let myself get sucked in, every single time. I don't know, love, I'm no expert on relationships – but I think to make a marriage work, you have to be the very best you can be. And all me and your mum ever did was turn each other into the worst possible versions of ourselves. Spending time away from it, with different people . . . well, it just opened my eyes a bit, I suppose.'

'I can understand that, Dad – I really can. But why now? And why didn't you at least try and talk to her about it?'

'Have you met your mother?' he jokes, absentmindedly ripping open sugar sachets. It reminds me of my mum, that first day in Budbury, trying to find something to do with her hands.

We're both silent for a while, and then he says: 'But you're right. I should have done. I got home from work one day, and we had a huge row. This won't come as any surprise to you, but it was a real humdinger – all over the fact that I said the potatoes were a bit salty. Serves me right, on the one hand – she'd cooked my tea, and I was sitting there moaning about it.

'But then the usual happened, and before I knew it, we're

standing up screaming, and she threw the salt mill at my head, and I threw the pepper mill at hers, and . . . God, I was just so tired of it. We'd been there so many times. She'd carry on sniping, and eventually I'd snap and give her a shove, and she'd threaten me with the electric carving knife, and . . . I just couldn't face it any more. It all got worse after you left, Katie.'

I'd like to pretend I'm confused by this, but I know exactly what he means – I was their buffer zone. Without me or Saul around to at least temper them, it must have been a free-for-all.

'Without you there, we only had each other,' he continues. 'And it wasn't enough. So I walked out and went to Fiona's, and she offered me her spare room, and that was that. It's not been easy. Sometimes I miss your mum, love – we've been married a long time, and it wasn't all bad. But I knew that I couldn't go back, not the way things were. I'm sorry – sorry for being such a coward and landing you with her, and sorry for the fact that you must have felt horrible when you were a kid. Trapped in the middle of it all. And I'm glad you got away.'

'Got away from you?'

'Yes, I suppose – although I hope you won't always feel like that. I hope now things are different, eventually you won't feel like you need to escape from us.'

'I can hardly escape from Mum right now,' I reply, pointing my spoon at him accusingly. 'She's living in my house.'

'I know. But again, that won't be forever, will it? It'll get better. And I'm glad you got away from Jason as well. I didn't mind Jason, I really didn't – and you've never told us why you left him. I'm not soft, though, and I can imagine – I think you were following in our footsteps. When your mum said she wanted you to use what was left of the nest egg your nan had left, so you could make your move, I was pleased. I was proud of you for being so strong. I still am, Katie.'

I let out a big breath, and kind of slump back into my seat. I'm exhausted by all of this, I really am.

'Okay, Dad. This is all big stuff. I'm glad you're happier, I really am – but you've got to talk to her, all right? You can't just ignore it. You need to see her and sort things out, and act like a grown-up. Stop letting me deal with it all, because that's what's happening right now, isn't it?'

He nods, and finishes his coffee.

'All right, love. Again, you're right – and I will. Just give me a bit more time, will you? Don't tell her for the time being. Just let me sort my head out for a bit longer, and then I promise, I'll talk to her. Now, after all that . . . shall we nip to the pub for a quick one before I drive you round to the house? Don't know about you, but my nerves are shot.'

# Chapter 18

The next time I go to the café, a few days after seeing my dad, it's turned into a Christmas wonderland.

I'm not a stranger to the café at this time of year, so it's not a total surprise. It's slightly different each Christmas, though, with new decorations added, and old ones revived. The bookshelves are lined with neon green plastic holly wreaths bearing berries in a colour not found in nature; all of the dangling mobiles have been adorned with glittering lametta, and there's a whole display featuring a small electric train whirring through a snowy landscape like *The Polar Express*.

Outside in the garden a giant inflatable Father Christmas is wibbling and wobbling around, almost as tall as the building, tethered to the ground by ropes like a tent. I remember them having a snowman version in previous years, but Midgebo decided it was a chewy toy and managed to puncture claw- and teeth-shaped holes all over it.

It all reminds me that I need to get our house sorted – find a tree, unpack the decorations from the attic, maybe buy some of that fake snow you can spray on windows. Saul would love that. This year, though, we'll have to cat-proof it all.

Today is cold but bright, and I've called in to fill in some time after pre-school. I've done a shift at the pharmacy, picked up Saul, and walked straight from the bus stop to the café. The alternative was going home, which wasn't that appealing as Mum is on one of her missions.

She's decided to change the curtains in every single room in the house, and I've left her to it. I don't really want my curtains changed, but I don't seem to have much choice. She's also taking the opportunity to give all the windows 'a proper clean' – as opposed to the improper clean I must have been giving them.

She'd waved at us as we walked past, cheery as heck, still wearing her pink lipstick and a pair of dangly earrings that would look right at home on *RuPaul's Drag Race*. She's super-glammed up to change the curtains, presumably in case Fabio happens to wander down the street and she needs to look her best.

I'd waved back and walked by, noticing Tinkerbell in Edie's window on the way and making a mental note to pick up some soup for her from the café – she's been under the weather with a cold recently.

I've had some cinnamon-dusted coffee and a slice of Green Velvet cake – Laura has decided that it shouldn't be limited to Red alone and is making them in a variety of

Christmassy colours. Now I'm sitting at a table, waiting for Cherie to finally say what's on her mind.

She's sitting opposite me, a slight frown on her face. Her hair is in a fat black-and-silver plait dangling over her shoulder, and she looks a bit tired. She's sent Laura home early, and the fact that Laura didn't object tells you how exhausted she must be feeling.

Willow is scurrying around doing some clearing up, assisted by Saul with his very own bin bag, and Frank is fixing the coffee machine, which is temperamental at best. The clanging and hissing provides a melodic backdrop to the conversation I feel is coming.

Cherie is uncharacteristically quiet, and seems to be turning something over in her brain before she speaks. She's looked thoughtful and pensive ever since we sat down together.

'I was thinking,' she says, between spoons of her Green Velvet Cake, 'about your mum. And you. And the twins.'

This is slightly out of left field, as we don't know any twins – so I am assuming she is referring to the as-yet-unborn ones currently exhausting our poor head chef and café manager.

'Okay,' I reply, closing my eyes as I eat my own cake – something about green cake just makes me feel weird, and I don't want my eyes to tell my taste buds not to enjoy it. 'What were you thinking?'

'You've not said much, Katie, as is your way,' she pauses

for effect, as though giving me the chance to disagree. I remain true to type, and simply raise my eyebrows in acknowledgement.

'But I get the impression that it's a bit crowded in your house at the moment. Saul says you and him are having sleepovers every night, which I can't imagine is as much fun for you as it sounds for him.'

'You're right there,' I reply, rubbing my side. 'He boots me in the ribs constantly.'

'Ouch. Anyway . . . I also think I need to get a bit of help in here. Laura's doing her best, but she's wiped out – and it's not like it's going to get much easier. So I was thinking about asking your mum if she wanted to come and work with us for a bit. And as part of the deal, if she wanted to, she could also use my flat upstairs?'

I pause with the spoon halfway to my mouth, and hope the disloyal wave of euphoria I feel at that concept doesn't show on my face. She's my mum. I love her. But God, I would so love to get rid of her for a bit . . .

'What would you need her to do? She's okay at cooking, but she's no Laura.'

'Well, we still have Laura to be Laura – she just needs to be a bit less of a Laura. I was thinking she could still do the baking and the creating, but cut down on everything else. I can easily come in and do more, we have Willow, who's a bit more flexible these days, and your mum could give us a hand with the rest. So it'd be taking orders, serving, and preparing the easier stuff – the toasties and paninis and coffees. Plus cleaning up afterwards.'

'She does love cleaning . . .' I reply, putting my spoon down and giving it some proper thought. To me, it sounds ideal – but my judgement may be clouded by the prospect of her moving out, if I'm brutally honest.

'I'm talking to you about it first because I wanted to check you were okay with the idea,' Cherie continues. 'I know you like to play your cards close to your chest, but this isn't the time to suffer in silence; if you think it's a bad idea, or if you think I'm an interfering old busybody – which I am, by the way – or if you want her to stay with you and Saul, then just tell me. You don't get to be this old and this ugly without learning how to deal with being told no every now and then.'

This, I've learned, is fairly typical of the way Cherie operates. Yes, she is an old busybody. Yes, she does meddle. But she always meddles in a respectful way, if that makes sense.

'Personally I think it's a great idea, Cherie,' I reply after a few more moments of thought. 'It *is* crowded at ours, and it would be nice to get my bed back. But as well as that, I think it might be good for my mum. It might make her feel more involved. Give her a bit of purpose. Make her feel a bit more . . . needed?'

'Well, that's something we all like, isn't it? Whether we realise it or not. Feeling useless is an absolute curse in life. So, tell her to pop in, and I can talk to her about it. Unveil my latest masterplan . . .'

She lets out a fake evil-villainess laugh as she says this. Or at least I think it's fake – if she is an evil villainess, she seems to have very benign motives.

With the masterplan in place, I finish my cake, and ask Cherie if she can carton up some soup for Edie.

'How is she? I must call in and see her,' she says, as she ladles delicious-smelling pea and ham into two takeaway cups and prepares two slices of cake. One for her, one for her fiancé, of course.

'She was on a *Stranger Things* marathon when I saw her yesterday,' I reply, beckoning Saul over to begin the process of re-coating him. 'She was sniffly, chesty, and seemed a lot more tired than usual, but I'll keep an eye on her. Tinkerbell was keeping her company when I walked by this morning; she usually lets him back out about now so he can come home for his tea.'

'In that case, I'll pack him one of these leftover salmon fillets as well . . .' says Cherie. The pets of Budbury are as pampered as the rest of us.

Once I've managed to get Saul's hands encased in the mittens he has threaded through his coat on a string, we walk back down the hill and into the village. It's still very, very cold, but the sun is shining and that makes it somehow feel better.

We entertain ourselves with one of our favourite games – making animal noises and guessing what they are – and by the time we reach Edie's, I'm letting Saul think he's completely bamboozled me with his silent mouth-gaping impression of a fish.

'Is it a parrot?' I ask, looking confused.

'No! Silly! Parrots go squawk, or say pretty boy! Try again . . .'

He continues his silent cheek-puffing, and I suggest: 'Is it a rhinoceros?'

'No again! Rhinocerosseses . . . rhinoseroos . . .'

'Shall we just say rhinos for short?'

'Rhinos go . . . oh, I don't know what noise they make! But mine was one of Becca's goldfish. I win. Mummy, what noise *does* a rhino make?'

I've trapped myself with that one, because I frankly have no idea, not ever having been up close and personal with one.

'I'm not sure, sweetie. Maybe we'll ask Matt?'

Saul thinks about this, and decides it's a sensible course of action.

'Yes. Matt knows how to talk to all the animals. We'll ask him. Will Matt's new babies be people or puppies?'

'They'll be babies, sweetheart,' I reply, laughing at the look of disappointment on his little face. He continues his chatter as we approach Edie's house, and becomes excited when he spots Tinkerbell through the window.

I, on the other hand, become slightly concerned when I spot Tinkerbell through the window. We have a bit of a routine going, along this street. Tinkerbell eats his breakfast at ours, then we let him out for a wander, and he heads to Edie's or

Becca's. They've agreed never to feed him, so he always comes home – and they always kick him out at about three.

It's past that now, and Tinkerbell is still there. He spots us, and is pacing back and forth on the window ledge, tail up, mouth moving in a way that tells me he's making a bit of noise.

'Wouldn't it be funny, Mummy,' says Saul, pressing his face up against the glass and creating a cloud of steam, 'if Tinkerbell could play that game? If she could pretend to be a sheep and baa, or a cow and moo?'

'It would, love, it would . . . maybe she'd know what noise a rhino makes as well . . . Saul, I'm going to drop you off with your nan for a bit, okay, while I give Edie her soup?'

He's perfectly happy with this, thankfully, and I bustle us both further up the road to our house. A house that now has purple and gold curtains in every single window. Yikes.

'What do you think?' Mum shouts, as she hears us come into the hallway. 'Gorgeous, aren't they? Best windows in the street! Move over Laurence Llewelyn-Bowen!'

She looks so proud of herself as she emerges from the living room that I have to agree, even if the new curtains make the house look a bit like the set of an especially gaudy pantomime. Princess Jasmine would love these.

'Beautiful, Mum – thanks so much, you've done a great job. Look, can you keep an eye on Saul for a minute? I just want to check on Edie.'

She can tell from the tone of my voice that I'm worried, so she just nods and hustles Saul away.

'Course I can. Off you go. Saul, do you want to make some cookies with me? I know your mum always buys them from the shop, but they taste so much nicer when you make your own . . .'

I roll my eyes at that one – she has this supreme talent for making digs without even knowing she's doing it – and concentrate on the task at hand.

First, I try the obvious, and call Edie – thanks to her army of nieces, nephews, and the great and great-great versions of both, she's never short of new technology, and actually has a better phone than me. Sadly, there's no reply.

Then I nip out again and try Becca's – she's really close to Edie, and I suspect she has a spare key to the place. Unfortunately there's no answer to my knock on the door there either, so I make my way over to the pharmacy. Auburn's in there, perched on the stool behind the cash desk, looking at her phone and twiddling with her hair.

'Been busy?' I ask, smiling.

'Rushed off my feet. You okay? You look a bit hassled. Nice new curtains, by the way – did your mum buy them at a bankrupt brothel sale?'

'Ha ha, very funny. Look, I'm a bit worried about Edie. I can't see her, and she still has the cat, and she's not answering her phone, and she's not been well, and . . .'

'She's ninety-two?'

'Yes, that. I tried Becca's to get a key but she's not in. What do you think I should do?'

She jumps down from the stool, and replies as she hits buttons on her phone: 'She's probably fine. Knowing Edie, she's out running some committee about allotments or planning her Christmas social life or at one of her niece's houses . . . but I'll get Van over. He has a *very* impressive toolbox, you know.'

She raises her eyebrows at me as she speaks, somehow making a reference to a container for screwdrivers and nails sound filthy. It's a skill.

I listen to her end of the conversation, which is short, to the point, and serious enough to remind me that Auburn is, at the end of the day, a healthcare professional. It's easy to forget when she's puffing away on her ciggies, or making double entendres about me and her brother.

We sit and wait for about fifteen minutes, while Van explains what's going on to Frank and Cal and drives over from Frank's farm. Lynnie's at her day centre, giving the Longville siblings a day to themselves.

We try and make small talk until he gets there, but I'm feeling more nervous by the minute. I don't know why – I have no real evidence that anything is wrong – but for some reason my instincts are all telling me that something is.

'Right,' Van says, once he's parked his truck and jingle-jangled the bell on his way in. 'Let's do a bit of breaking and entering, shall we?'

Frank follows behind him, looking concerned – which is not a look I associate with Frank at all. He's only ten years younger than Edie himself, but apart from the usual aches and pains of getting older, seems stupidly fit. Must be his active lifestyle, although he swears it's down to a pact his mother made in a fairy dell on the night he was born.

Auburn closes up the pharmacy, and we make our way to Edie's in a small pack. We're going to look seriously stupid if she answers the door to us after all this.

We start with a knock, and Frank leans down to shout through the letterbox. Tinkerbell is the only one to respond, running to the hallway and meowing frantically at him through the gap. I call Edie again, just in case, and as we all strain our ears we just about make out the sound of her ring-tone – the *Strictly* theme tune. The phone is in there – which means Edie might be as well.

'Nothing else for it,' says Frank, frowning. 'We need to get in there. She'll forgive us.'

Just to be sure, he shouts through the letterbox again: 'Edie! It's Frank! We're coming in, so make yourself decent!'

Van nudges his way to the front of the small crowd, and inspects the door.

'That's a solid lock on there. Might be easier to go around the back and break a window – and cheaper to fix afterwards.'

We all follow him down the narrow alleyway that intersects the houses after each small terraced block. Edie's is at the end, so he doesn't have to scale everyone else's back wall as well.

He nimbly climbs up onto the top of the wall, pulling himself up with no trouble, and perches on top.

'No point you all following me this way,' he says, eyes crinkled in amusement as we all gaze up at him. 'Much as I'm sure you've all got amazing parkour skills, be easier if you went back to the front door, and I'll come and let you in!'

It seems obvious now he's said it, and I'm glad I'm not the only one who dumbly followed. Frank, Auburn and myself make 'duh' noises and traipse back to the road, feeling a bit stupid. Within seconds we hear the sound of glass being smashed, and soon after Van comes and opens the front door.

Tinkerbell shoots out like a ginger bullet, pausing only to twine himself in and out of my legs for a bit before heading off home. I remember just at that moment that I left all the food from the café in the hallway, and suspect I'll get back to find that he's rooted through the lot of it tracking down the smell of salmon. Such is life.

Frank is first through the door, and I wait until Auburn's in there before I follow. Now we're doing this – going in to find out if she's okay – I'm gripped with fear and reluctance.

My mind's playing tricks on me, associating the sights and smells of Edie's neat little home with my nan's. The embroidered covers on the arms of the chairs; the porcelain figurines; the distinctive smell of mothballs and an old-fashioned perfume that I vaguely remember being called something equally old-fashioned like White Shoulders. It does look and feel familiar – apart from the life-sized cardboard cut-out of Anton du Beke in one corner and the giant flat-screen TV.

Anton and telly aside, it's the home of an old lady – and Edie really is very, very old.

We soon see that she's not in the living room, and Van, who broke a small window panel in the kitchen to let himself through that way, knows she's not in there, so we head upstairs. It's set out like my own house, two bedrooms and a small bathroom, and it's in one of the bedrooms that we find Edie.

She's tucked up in bed, a paperback copy of *The Handmaid's Tale* on the pillow next to her, a glass of water and her little wire-rimmed specs on the cabinet beside the bed. In the corner of the room I see a box full of old black-and-white photos and letters, which I know must be from Briarwood – Tom found them there, all relating to the building's past and its role during the war, and Edie, a former librarian, is archiving them for him.

Edie herself, though, doesn't look like she'll be archiving anything in her current state. She's still, and pale, and looks covered in sweat. Her breathing is coming in fast but laboured chugs, accompanied by a nasty-sounding wheeze.

'Edie!' Frank says, as he dashes over to her side. 'Edie, are you all right?'

I move over to him, kneeling at Edie's side, checking her pulse while he tries to rouse her. It's too fast, and I notice that her fingernails look a bit blue in the sunlight that's dappling through the window. I touch her forehead, and look up at Auburn, who's hovering a little in the doorway. I suppose nurses are more used to this kind of thing – her patients are usually at least capable of getting to a shop.

'She's got a fever. Pulse is up. Don't think she's getting enough oxygen,' I tell her.

'Pneumonia?' she suggest in response. I nod – that's exactly what I think it is. Pneumonia is a lot more common than people think, and isn't usually anything to worry about – but with a woman of Edie's age, no matter how sprightly she seems, there's a lot to worry about.

Auburn bites her lip, and immediately uses her phone to call an ambulance. She also uses all the right terminology to get them here as quickly as possible.

Edie is rambling slightly, her eyes half open, talking but not making any sense. I make out the words 'my fiancé', and 'new dress', and 'legs like Betty Grable', none of which relate to her present circumstances in any way. Edie is lost in her illness, and my eyes sting with very unprofessional tears.

I feel Van's hand on my shoulder, and lean back against his legs for comfort.

'She's a tough one, Edie,' he says gently. 'Don't worry – she'll be okay.'

I nod, and screw my eyelids shut to get rid of the tears, and hope that he's right.

# Chapter 19

The scene in the waiting room at the hospital is, I know from experience, a doctor's worst nightmare. The place is packed with the distraught members of Edie's fan club – friends and relatives, all of them upset, all of them desperate to know how she is.

Her clan of nieces and nephews and their children and grandchildren range in age from teenagers through to her sister's daughter, who is in her seventies, and added into that is me, Van, Cherie, Tom, Frank and Becca, who came as soon as she heard. Becca's a tough cookie, but her eyes are sore and red from crying, and she looks like she wants to punch somebody.

Auburn's gone home to help Willow with Lynnie, who's come home from the day centre in a bit of a state, and that's added to the vaguely apocalyptic sense of doom.

As soon as I see the harassed-looking young doctor walk through into the crowds, I notice the fleeting look of horror that crosses her face at seeing us all in various stages of pacing and worrying and sipping scalding hot coffee from the vending machine.

She looks up, confused, trying to figure out who Edie's next of kin might be amid the mass of humanity. As it turns out, it's her niece, Mary, who strides forward accompanied by Cherie. The rest of us assemble in a kind of loose circle around them.

'Miss May has been admitted to intensive care,' the doctor explains, doing a great job as she makes eye contact, uses her patient's name and never once needs to look at notes.

'She's currently on strong antibiotics and fluids. We're giving her extra oxygen, and at the moment, that's helping. We think she might have pleurisy as well, which isn't uncommon at her age, but so far she's still breathing on her own.'

This, I know, is very good news – I couldn't imagine Edie getting off a ventilator again if they put her on one. Cherie glances at me, and I realise I probably sighed out loud. She gestures me forward to stand next to her, probably thinking it won't do any harm to get a translator in.

'Will she be all right?' asks Mary, in the no-nonsense voice of a woman who has seen her share of hospitalisations.

The doctor tries to maintain a neutral face, but doesn't quite manage it. Her blonde ponytail is wilting, and a pen has leaked ink in the pocket of her white coat.

'Well, we can't really say at the moment. We're doing

everything that we can to help her recover, and to keep her comfortable. But given her age . . .'

It's the second time she's mentioned Edie's age, which is completely understandable as she is in fact ancient. In hospital terms, that's a major factor – but in Budbury terms, it's a complete red herring.

I see Cherie stand up very straight, which must be unnerving for the doc – who maybe scrapes five foot in her flats. She looks fierce, and I suck in a breath – I really hope she's not about to kick off. The doctor is only doing her job, and speaking a truth that medically is extremely relevant. Everyone here might like to imagine that Edie is going to live forever, but science says otherwise.

Cherie squints slightly at the doctor's name tag, and then says: 'Doctor . . . Sullivan? We all know how old Edie is. And none of us are idiots, we know that's a factor. But I'd ask you to remember something, when you're treating her – her age doesn't matter to us. To us, she's just Edie, and we love her. She's treasured, she's precious, and our lives wouldn't be the same without her. We don't expect you to perform miracles, but please – don't write her off.

'That woman has lived through so much, for so long, I really wouldn't give in to the idea that because she's old she won't fight. She will. And I'd like you to help her – when you look at Edie, please don't just see a geriatric patient. See your own mother. See your own grandmother. See Mother Theresa if it helps – but please, see her as someone who deserves every possible chance at surviving. I know you can't promise us she'll make it – but can you at least promise us that?'

The doctor blinks rapidly a few times – she looks tired, as all hospital doctors seem to – and nods.

'Yes. I can. I can promise you that. Now, she's not really conscious at the moment, and I'd suggest the best thing you can all do is go home, get some rest, and come back tomorrow. If anything changes, I'll make sure we let you know.'

'I'm staying,' pipes up Becca, making her way to the front. 'If that's all right with you, Mary? I'll stay.'

Mary smiles and nods, and pats Becca's hand.

Dr Sullivan looks like she thinks this is a bad idea, but wisely decides not to object.

Becca goes off to one side making phone calls, presumably to explain the situation to Sam and maybe Laura, and everyone else starts to make moving-away noises. It's a strange sight, like the air being sucked out of a room – Edie's family trooping off in twos and threes and fours, all promising to stay in touch and giving Becca smiles and hugs on the way out.

Cherie and Frank stay a few minutes longer before leaving in Cherie's car, and Tom follows not long after.

Eventually only Becca, Van and I are left, in a waiting room that now feels empty and hollow, even though there are still people in it. People dealing with their own dramas and traumas who are, entirely probably, relieved to see the back of the Edie May club.

I glance up at the clock on the wall, and am actually shocked to see that it's almost ten p.m. Everything takes so long in hospitals – or at least it feels like that when you're waiting. When you're on the sharp end, the hours fly by in a frenzy of activity. I definitely prefer the sharp end – or at least the end that doesn't involve a person who you're very fond of lying in a bed fighting for her life.

Becca comes off the phone and joins us. She looks jittery, and I know she's had too much coffee. She shouldn't be here – but I think Dr Sullivan recognised a losing battle when she saw one.

'Everything okay?' I ask, reaching out to touch her shaking hand. 'Is there anything we can do for you?'

She shakes her head, and bites her lip hard enough to draw blood. I can practically hear the 'pull yourself together, woman' speech she's giving herself.

'No, it's fine. I've spoken to Sam. He'll be okay. Maybe tomorrow you could pop in and make sure he hasn't set the house on fire, or let Little Edie eat Pot Noodles?'

'Of course. And what about you – do you need anything? Clean clothes, a book, some food, anything at all?'

'Nah, I'm good. I don't mind being grubby. And Laura will undoubtedly send Matt over with enough cake to feed the whole hospital before long. You know how she gets.'

I do know. And she's probably right. Laura will have the

oven on as we speak, to show her concern in the way that comes naturally to her.

'Was everything the doc said right, Katie? I mean, from a hospital perspective?'

She looks so desperate as she asks this, like she's hoping for me to promise her something I can't in all good faith promise. Like she wants the doctors to be wrong, and for Edie to be twenty-one, and for all to be well in the world.

'From what I heard, they're doing everything they should be doing, Becca. Following all the best protocols. And yes, Edie is old – but they don't know Edie like we know Edie. The odds might be against her, but you see small miracles every day in hospitals, and if anyone can come back from this, it's Edie.'

She nods, and gives me a very quick hug – she's not one of life's huggers; it's like Laura got all of the tactile genes between the two sisters – before backing off again.

'Okay. Well, I'll let you know if they tell me anything,' she says briskly. 'So you two bugger off, all right? I'm just going to grab another coffee . . .'

'Are you sure that's a good idea?' says Van, smiling gently. 'You look kind of wired already.'

Becca snorts out loud in response, and gives a quick laugh.

'Wired? This isn't wired. This isn't even slightly strung out. You know, before I moved here, I don't think I'd had a proper night's sleep for years . . . I was a complete insomniac, one of those people who lie awake looking at the time all night and then finally doze off an hour before dawn? It's Edie who changed that. In a lot of ways, it's Edie who changed everything. Without her, I probably wouldn't have had the guts to stay – and then I wouldn't have had Sam, and Little Edie, and everything . . .'

There's not a lot that we can say to this. She's clearly devastated at even the idea of losing her friend, and for her sake as much as Edie's, I hope those antibiotics are currently coursing through her and kicking some nasty bacterial ass.

'All right, Becca,' says Van quietly. 'We'll be off then – you know where we are if you need anything. And you stay there – I'll go and get you another coffee. Black, right?'

She nods gratefully, and I ask: 'Okay. Do you have baby wipes?'

Baby wipes, as most mums discover, are incredibly useful items.

'Duh!' she replies, grinning. 'Of course I have baby wipes! Plus a packet of organic rice cakes, and an almost-full pack of jumbo crayons in case I get bored . . . the full mama kit and caboodle!'

She taps the side of her bag as she says this, and it makes me laugh. You can probably tell the age of a family's child by the contents of the parent's bag. Mine, for example, does contain a small envelope of wipes, but also two Hot Wheels cars, one of those multi-coloured pencils that comes apart and stacks up again, and a pack containing a strawberry-flavoured Yoyo.

After Van returns with the coffee, we finally leave. It's dark outside, so cold our breath puffs out clouds of steam as we walk across the car park, our way zig-zagged by headlights of new arrivals and the flashing orange of ambulances. I feel a slight crunch beneath my feet, and suspect we're in for the season's first proper frost tonight.

'I got her decaf,' Van says, as he unlocks the truck and we get in.

'Probably a good idea . . .' I reply, nestling back into the seat and rubbing my hands together as Van puts the hot-air blowers on full. He messes with the radio, and we end up with a show playing Motown classics. 'Tracks of My Tears' and 'Tears of a Clown' and a variety of broken hearts doing a variety of things to a toe-tapping beat.

We drive back to Budbury in relative silence, apart from the music, both processing the day's events. We're tired, and worried, and we both skipped dinner. I know Saul is okay with my mum, because I've spoken to her, but it still feels strange having been away from him for so long. Relinquishing control is a lot harder than I expected.

Van, I know, is also unsettled by the fact that Lynnie has been upset. She's asleep now, Willow's told him, but it had been a rough night. Life, just right now, feels like a lot to handle.

He makes his way through largely empty roads, skimming

the coast before driving through the central street that ribbons through Budbury, pulling up in the parking spots on the opposite side to my house.

We both sit for a while, without speaking, waiting for Lionel Richie and Diana Ross to finish singing about their 'Endless Love'. The truck is cosy and warm, and the music is beautiful, and part of me wants to delay reality for a few moments longer. To stay in this cosy bubble for just a little while.

'Tough day,' says Van, once the song draws to a close. He turns the radio off, just in case another impossible-to-leave track starts playing. 'Will you be okay?'

I'm not used to people wondering if I'll be okay, and it takes a second to adjust.

'Yeah,' I reply quietly. 'I'll be okay. I was upset, though. It all reminded me of—'

'Your nan?' he supplies, smiling gently. I look at him in surprise, and reply: 'Yes – my nan. Why are you so clever?'

'I'm not clever,' he answers, reaching out to squeeze my hand comfortingly, 'about anything but you.'

I stare through the windscreen and say: 'You're the only person I told about my nan. And about Jason. And what it was really like growing up. I tell you things I don't tell anyone else. I don't know why that is.'

He twines his fingers into mine and replies: 'You'll figure it out one day, I'm sure. And it's the same for me. I never told anyone else how much I miss being in Tanzania, you know.'

'Oh. Right. What about the fact that you were in a relationship with the blonde one from Abba? Did you tell anyone that?'

'No. That's top secret. The paparazzi will be all over me if that one gets out . . .'

His grin lights up the car, and it's a bit of light relief we both need. A bit of light relief I'm not quite ready to say goodbye to.

'Do you want to come in for a coffee?' I ask, tentatively. 'Or a glass of milk. Or a bottle of whiskey. Might even have a chocolate Yazoo in the fridge if you're lucky. Saul and Mum have gone to bed.'

He stares ahead for a moment, gazing at the dark street and the starlit sky that leads down to the shoreline, then replies: 'Yeah. Thanks. That would be really nice – I'm feeling a bit wired myself, to be honest. If I went home now I'd probably have to sit out in the garden and do some deep breathing while contemplating the meaning of life.'

I have to smile at that – Van might look like a rough, tough kind of guy, but nobody could grow up in Lynnie's house without having mastered some advanced breathing techniques.

'That doesn't sound like fun,' I reply, as we climb out the truck, quietly close the doors – we'll wake up half of Budbury if we slam them – and tiptoe into my house.

Van's never actually been in here before, I realise, as I watch him take it all in. In fact, only Matt has been in here before and even then, he only made it as far as the hallway. I've been so protective of mine and Saul's territory, keeping it safe and cosy and just for us.

That seems to be unravelling these days, and I'm both exhilarated and terrified by it. I've always told myself that if things don't work out, we could just leave – pack our bags and move on. But now I'm not so sure that still applies. We'd be leaving behind an awful lot – friendships and support and free cake and the kind of community that most people dream of. Saul will be starting school in September, and that will be yet another nail in the coffin of my escape plan – perhaps it's time I start letting go of that, and come up with a staying-put plan.

'Nice curtains,' says Van, as we walk through to the living room.

'Auburn's already made the brothel joke,' I say quietly, gesturing for him to sit down on the big, squishy couch that dominates the room. The sofa was my one extravagance when I moved in here. I reckoned if I was going to be spending lots of nights in on my own, I should at least have a place to lounge around.

'I wasn't going to make a brothel joke,' he replies, looking scandalised. 'I was going to make a Sultan's harem joke. And apart from the curtains, your house is really lovely, Katie.'

I'm getting us both a glass of wine while he says this – wine has been appearing in the fridge a lot more often since my mother moved in – and hand it to him as I sit down on the armchair. Just the one – there wasn't enough room for more, and I never anticipated a time when I'd be hosting glamorous soirees.

'Thank you. Although it's just a normal house.'

'Yeah, that's what's nice about it,' he answers, looking around. 'Not an incense stick in sight! No, seriously, it just feels . . . cosy. You can tell a kid lives here, and if I was that kid, it's the kind of home I'd feel safe in. That's all I meant.'

'Thank you again. That's what I aim for. I can barely remember life before Saul came along . . .'

'I can imagine. I can't imagine you without him. Or Budbury without him – he's everyone's favourite little man, and a complete credit to you. You're a great mum.'

I feel my face break out into a smile – what mother doesn't feel proud of comments like that? I spend way too much time worrying about doing things wrong; it's nice to bathe in a moment of reflected glory.

We're quiet for a few moments, sipping our wine, and I am quite surprised to realise that almost against my will I am relaxing. It feels natural, sitting here, chatting and not chatting, with Van. Just . . . being. I do a quick mental calculation to figure out when I last felt like that, and come to the conclusion that it was sometime round about never.

Me and Jason were never suited, and we plunged head-long into parenthood way too fast. I don't regret Saul for a moment – he was the most blessed of mistakes – but his dad and I shared little other than a sense that we should give it a try, and a tendency to get very drunk and have loud sex. Loud, but not that good, if I'm honest. Apart from Jason, and a few other failed experiments while I was at college, I've never actually slept with anyone who made me feel like we're all led to believe we should feel.

You know, when you grow up watching romantic movies and reading saucy books and thinking that the slightest touch of a man's lips will leave your knees trembling? Nobody really tells you about the reality – that your knees might be trembling, but it's usually because of an excess of WKD in the college bar. That sex can be awkward and embarrassing and many men wouldn't know a clitoris if it walked up and introduced itself.

I find myself shocked at even thinking the word, never mind ever saying it, and cast a quick glance at Van, hoping he can't read my mind. He's sprawled on the sofa, stroking Tinkerbell, who has magically appeared on his lap. For a rough, tough street cat, Tinkerbell likes a bit of TLC.

I have the feeling it would be different with him. The sex thing, that is. I like to think it would, anyway. And as I plan to never actually do it, I am at least preserving the fantasy that this would finally be the man to rock my world in the bedroom.

'I know what you're thinking . . .' he says, grinning. I blush immediately, and reply: 'I really don't think you do.'

'You're thinking how much nicer it would be if you came

and sat next to me. How we both probably need a hug tonight. How we could even have a little snooze once we've finished this wine . . .'

I laugh out loud as he talks. He has his eyebrows raised in an outrageously suggestive way, telling me that he's joking. Probably.

'Right,' I say, putting my wine down and vowing not to drink another glass. 'That would work out well. We'd pass out, and my mum and Saul would find us collapsed in a heap of drool and cat fur in the morning. No, thank you. Drink up, Van – your own bed is calling.'

He grimaces, and I understand why. The cottage he shares with his family has three bedrooms. When he was a kid, he shared one with his brother Angel, and the others were taken by Lynnie and Auburn and Willow.

After the older siblings left, and Willow struggled to care for her mum alone, she understandably claimed a bedroom all to herself – and is, again understandably, staying put. Which leaves Van with the options of either sharing a room with Auburn, or sleeping on the couch. It's not ideal for a grown man – a man who is already missing the wide open spaces of the country he left to be here.

Van nods, and is stretching his arms up into the air as he prepares to leave. I can't help but notice his T-shirt untucking from his jeans, because I'm clearly the world's biggest lech.

He's about to stand up and make a move, which

Tinkerbell senses. He leaps from Van's lap and disappears off into the windowsill, where he'll lie above the heat of the radiator like a feline draught excluder.

Before Van gets a chance to stand upright, Saul barrels through the door, slamming it behind him dramatically. He's dressed in his stripy PJs that make him look like a junior pirate, and his blond hair is tufted all over his head. He's unbearably cute, standing in the doorway, rubbing his eyes with tiny little fists as he takes in the scene before him.

He spots Van, and his little face breaks out into an unquestioning smile as he runs straight to him. Van manages to catch him as he stumbles, scooping him up into his arms as though he weighs nothing, and nestles him into his lap. Saul snuggles in, his head on his chest, his small arms thrown around his neck.

'Van! Did you come and visit me?' he says, sounding thrilled at the whole idea.

'Of course,' replies Van, smiling. 'What else would I be doing? I was a bit of a silly, though, and didn't realise how late it was, so I was having a chat to your mum instead.'

Saul nods, accepting this as completely obvious, and yawns.

'It's okay,' he murmurs. 'I'm wide awake now – do you want to play Twister?'

I have to laugh at that one. Saul is basically still half asleep, and Van is exhausted, but I can still imagine both of them at least giving it a try – moving their hands and feet very slowly to the coloured spots and trying not to fall over.

I'm about to pick Saul up and carry him back to bed when my mum follows him into the room. She also pauses in the doorway, and is wearing vivid purple pyjamas that match the curtains in a way that instantly makes me feel a bit nauseous.

Her short hair has been backcombed into a Frankenstein version of a beehive, and her face is covered in multi-coloured make-up. I mean, she usually wears plenty of slap these days, but this is next-level stuff – a kind of space alien Seventies disco look.

'Have you been playing Beauty Parlour with Saul, by any chance?' I ask, biting my lips so I don't start giggling.

She looks momentarily confused, then her hands fly to her face as she realises.

'Yes! Where does he get that stuff?'

'I have no idea . . . but it's taught me the importance of at least glancing in the mirror in the morning before I leave the house. Was everything all right?'

'Yes,' she says, her eyes glued to Van and Saul. They both seem to be snoring – probably getting some rest in before their game of Twister. I can almost see the cogs turning in her brain, and wonder how long it'll take before she has me married off to a man I barely know.

To my surprise, she stays quiet on that subject, and quietly asks: 'How's Edie?'

I check that Saul's not earwigging – he has an amazing ability to hear things he shouldn't – and reply equally quietly: 'She's in the best place. We'll just have to wait and see.'

She nods and yawns, and asks: 'Do you want me to take Saul back up? So you and Van can . . . carry on with whatever it was you were doing?'

I roll my eyes a bit – funny how we all turn back into teenagers again in the company of our mothers – and say: 'We were just having a chat, and he was about to head off home. You get yourself back to bed, I'll sort Saul out.'

She nods reluctantly, her gaze returning to the sleepy pair in the sofa, and replies: 'Okay, love. You can fill me in in the morning.'

I know she'll be reading more into this whole situation, but I'm going to have to disappoint her – because there really isn't anything to fill her in on. Maybe I'll make something up just to keep her happy while we eat our cornflakes tomorrow.

I hear her pad up the stairs, and stand looking at Van and Saul. As soon as I close the door behind my mum, Van opens one eye.

'Is it safe?' he asks, grinning at me over Saul's head.

'It is, you big faker – I can't believe you were pretending to be asleep! Are you scared of my mum?'

'Of course I'm scared of your mum,' he whispers. 'It's the lipstick.'

He gestures down at Saul, who is definitely not faking it, and adds: 'What shall we do with this little fella? Do you want me to carry him back up? To be honest, I'm really comfy – I could probably just pass out for real . . .'

I can hear the fatigue in his voice, and remind myself that he's probably been working since six this morning – farm work starts early. Then he helped us rescue Edie, dealt with the crisis at home on the phone, and was stuck with the rest of us at the hospital before going out of his way to drive me home.

'Stay there,' I say, disappearing off upstairs to the airing cupboard.

I tiptoe, so I don't disturb my mum, but might as well not have bothered. She was clearly waiting to pounce, and emerges from Saul's room with her inquisitive beehived head tilted to one side. I put my finger to my lips to tell her to be quiet, and she nods.

'Just thought you could do with a freshen up . . .' she whispers, before padding out onto the landing and liberally spritzing me with some Calvin Klein Obsession – her signature perfume for as long as I can remember.

I cough and splutter as it hits my face, and fight very hard not to punch her in hers.

'For goodness' sake, Mum!' I say, trying hard to keep my voice quiet despite my annoyance. 'I'm not heading down there to seduce the man – I'm just getting a blanket! It's not been the sexiest of days, you know?'

She takes a step back, using her hands to waft the perfume around me.

'Well you never know,' she says, giving me a wink from mascara-encrusted eyelashes. 'Never hurts to be prepared . . .'

I ignore her, grab what I need, and walk back downstairs. Saul and Van are out for the count – although both their nostrils twitch in their sleep as I enter the room, bathed in a toxic cloud of Calvin's finest.

I lay a blanket over them both, tucking it in at the sides, pausing to look at them. Saul is completely encased in Van's arms, his tiny body curled into a contented comma, his fingers splayed on his chest. Van has one leg on the sofa, one leg off. I consider hoisting the second one up, but he looks perfectly comfortable. He's loosened the laces of his work boots, and I tug them off as gently as I can, grinning at the fact that he's wearing socks with Homer Simpson's face on them.

He sleeps through my assault on his feet, and I forgive him the fact that they're a bit on the ripe side considering the day he's had. I collapse down into the armchair, and tug a fleece over myself as well. Tinkerbell decides he wants in on the action, and curls into a fluffy ball by Van's feet.

Everyone is settled. Everyone is warm. Everyone is happy, despite the horrors of the day.

I look at the snoozing threesome on the sofa, and can't quite figure out how I feel about it. I'm exhausted, and I've had a glass of wine, and my brain is a mish-mash of Edie and Saul and Van and my mother. There's a lot going on in there, and I don't have the emotional resources to pick my way through the tangled threads.

I've been worried about how close Saul is to Van. Frankly, I've been worried about how close I am to Van. But right now – here in my cosy home, surrounded by the people most important to me – I simply feel content.

And that, I think, is possibly the most worrying thing of all.

# Chapter 20

I'm woken up the next morning by Saul banging sauce-pans at the side of my head. Any parent out there will understand this: it's perfectly normal. I startle into consciousness with a rush of adrenaline, my body preparing me for battle or buggering off.

Saul is still in his PJs, and is slamming a frying pan against the milk pan, singing an extremely annoying song he's learned at pre-school that seems to be a constant repetition of words involving 'wake up' and 'shake up'. Luckily this morning, at least, it doesn't include make up.

'Get up, sleepy-head!' he shouts, clattering his pans and jumping up and down on bare feet. 'Time for my breakfast!'

I practise opening my eyes one at a time, eventually building up to the full set. I glance at my watch and see that it's 6.30 a.m. Oh joy.

The sofa is empty, the blankets neatly folded up and left in a squishy square on the corner. Tinkerbell is mewing by my side, having clearly been woken, and shaken, and now looking forward to some food. I can hear footsteps upstairs, and the sound of the toilet flushing.

I stand up, stretch myself out, and force myself out of my stupor for long enough to give Saul a morning cuddle.

'Where's Van?' I ask, yawning.

'He's gone up for a wee-wee,' says Saul, putting his hand over his mouth and giggling. Bodily functions – is there anything more amusing to a 3-year-old boy?

'Okay. Right. Well, what do you want for breakfast?' I say, hoping he says cereal. I don't feel up to anything more complicated. Even that might be a challenge.

Saul ponders this important question, looking serious for a second, then bangs his pans together as though creating a drum roll.

'Pancakes!' he announces gleefully. 'With blueberries! And squirty cream! Just like Laura makes them!'

I frown at this. I'm not sure I have blueberries. Or eggs. In fact I think I only have the squirty cream.

'How about something even better than that . . .?' I say, as I walk through into the kitchen. He looks as though he's going to argue, but his face lights up when I get the cream canister out of the fridge and wave it in his face. I squirt a cream beard on his chin, and he dissolves into a fit of laughter as he tries to manoeuvre his tongue low enough to lick it off.

Tinkerbell jumps up onto the table to try and help him, and I shoo him away. I know as soon as my back is turned

Saul will let him, but it's my parental duty to at least try and stop the human-feline bacteria exchange.

I pop some bread into the toaster, and sip a glass of water, leaning back against the sink. I'm already thinking about Edie – if I'm honest, wondering if she's even made it through the night. It's by no means guaranteed that she has, and I can't imagine how Budbury will look without her. I feel tears sting the back of my eyes, and shake it off – no use worrying about that until I know for sure.

The toast pops up, slightly burned as usual, and I put it on one of Saul's dinosaur-patterned plastic plates. He watches closely, fascinated by what I'm planning, as I cut it into triangles. I then take the cream, and squirt it all over the slices, so thick it wobbles.

'Squirty cream on toast! Mummy! That's brilliant! I can't wait to tell Auntie Babs about this . . .'

I give him a mock curtsy, and hand him the plate. I smile, but inside I'm grimacing. Auntie Babs is one of the ladies who runs his pre-school, and she's a bit of a dragon. A retired head teacher who will probably report me to social services for serving my child such a nutritionally reprehensible breakfast.

I'm wondering how I can avoid seeing her for the next few days when Van walks into the room. He's clearly had a quick shower, and his closely cropped hair is still damp and shining. He's wearing yesterday's T-shirt, his plaid flannel jacket thrown over one shoulder. He looks like a lumberjack, and way too big for my small kitchen.

'Squirty cream on toast?' he says, peering at Saul's plate as he trundles off towards the sofa to watch TV.

'Yep. I thought it was about time I gave someone else a shot at winning the Mother of the Year Award.'

'Can I have some?' he asks, grinning at me and looking for all the world like an overgrown kid himself. 'Such delights were only dreamt of when I was growing up . . . Lynnie was way ahead of the curve on the whole holistic diet thing. It was a multi-grain and lentil kind of house.'

I nod, and do the honours on the next slice. He crunches into it, his face blissfully happy, a huge cream moustache left above his lips.

He suddenly leans in and kisses me on the cheek before I have time to dodge him, holding me by my shoulders so I can't escape.

'Right – I'll be off!' he says, darting out of the kitchen in case I retaliate. 'Just wanted to leave you with a little reminder of the first night we spent together . . .'

I hear him say goodbye to Saul, and the sound of the front door closing behind him, closely followed by the clunking of his truck doors and its engine revving up.

I'm still standing there, wiping squirty cream off my face, when my mother walks into the room. She has a full face on – a fresh one, not the one Saul did in his Beauty Parlour, which was possibly slightly less garish. She's still in her pyjamas, and the pink lipstick set against the purple fabric is not something easily beheld on an empty stomach. Or probably any stomach. I pop some more bread in the toaster for us both and hope I don't get a migraine.

She raises her perfectly plucked eyebrows at me, takes in my face – by now bright red as well as creamy – and says: 'I thought we had company?'

'He's gone to work,' I reply, pouring us both some orange juice and sitting down at the little dining table. I clean up my cheeks with a wad of kitchen roll and hope she doesn't ask what happened.

'These countryside types don't half start early . . .' she says, sitting herself down. She stares at the toast – devoid of cream – and pushes it around her plate a bit before taking a tiny, mouse-like nibble. I am reminded again that despite the newly found obsession with make-up, my mum is still in a painful place.

'Any news? About Edie?' she asks, for which I give her credit. I know what she really wants to ask about is Van, but she reins herself in and makes an effort to be polite first.

'Not so far,' I reply, having checked my phone and not seen anything. No news, I tell myself, is definitely good news in this particular case.

'So . . . what's going on with you and Van then? He's quite rugged. Reminds me of a young Clint Eastwood when he was in those Spaghetti Westerns, but, you know, bigger. And without the poncho.'

It's taken her over a minute to get there, which is longer than I expected.

'Nothing's going on, Mum,' I reply patiently. 'He's just a friend, that's all.'

'He's great with Saul, isn't he?'

'Yes, he is.'

'And he seems to really like you . . .'

'Well, yes. I like him too.'

She ponders the whole thing for a few more moments, still barely touching her toast, before saying: 'Mind you, they say Alzheimer's runs in the family, don't they? Might be for the best to keep him at arm's length.'

I'm initially left speechless by this. Not only has she thought as far along the line as me and Van having a future together, possibly even procreating – she's decided it's potentially a bad idea because of the tragic circumstances Lynnie and her children have found themselves in.

I shake my head and take a deep breath. She really is quite a piece of work, my mother.

'All kinds of things run in families,' I reply. 'And that's irrelevant. I'm not looking for a man, Mum. I don't need one.'

She nods and chews on her lip, and looks thoughtful. I wonder what kind of fresh hell I'm about to be subjected to, before she says: 'Not need, no. Maybe not. But perhaps you might . . . want one, at some point?'

I say a silent prayer that she's not about to start talking

about my libido, at least partly because I have no defence on that front – much as I try and play it cool, Van definitely sets off a few earthquakes whenever I'm near. Even if he's just kissed me with squirty cream.

'Maybe I will,' I answer. 'And I promise you'll be the first to know. But at the moment, I've got my hands full with work and college and mainly Saul. I want things to just . . . settle down for us.'

She lets out an unladylike snort and replies: 'Settle down? Crikey, Katie, if your life gets any more settled you'll be comatose! I know you've got Saul to think about, but you're still a young woman. You need to think about living a little. Think about your future. You don't want to end up like me, a dried-up old crone, useful to no one, thrown into the gutter like yesterday's chip wrapper . . .'

She delivers this speech with such fervent pathos that I'd feel sorry for her if it wasn't also a bit funny.

'Mum, you're not dried up, or a crone! You're in the prime of your life. And Dad . . . well, maybe it's more complicated than it seems. I'm sure it's not just that he threw you in the gutter.'

Of course, I have the advantage of knowing more about it than she does. I've promised my dad I won't say anything just yet – but his time is running out. I decide to text him later to express exactly that. It's not fair on Mum, and it's definitely not fair on me, being caught between them. Again.

'Well, that's what it feels like! All those years together,

and now this . . . dumped for the ice cream lady! It's . . . well, it's crap, to use a vulgar word. Just crap. And I'm lonely, if I'm honest. And sad. And . . . I don't want you to end up the same way. I want you to find someone, Katie – someone nice, who'll treat you and Saul well, and build a good life with you.'

She doesn't add 'someone like Van', but I wonder if she's thinking it – or if she's discarded him as a potential suitor and provider of further grandchildren due to his suspect gene pool.

'I understand that, Mum,' I say, reaching out to cover her hand with mine. She's so thin her bones feel like a sparrow's beneath her skin.

'And I know you want the best for me . . . but I'm not convinced that getting married and spending the rest of your life with someone is the answer. I mean, I can't deny that I find Van . . . not disgusting. And it might start out well. But how long would it last? How long before we started to annoy each other, or get bored, or start being cruel and snippy? How long before all the excitement magically disappears, and we start fighting about whose turn it is to put the bins out? How long before Saul gets stuck in the middle of it, and ends up losing Van all together? What if it ended up getting so messy, we had to leave Budbury, just as we've started to fit in? It's a small place, you know – we wouldn't be able to avoid each other, it'd be terrible! And then we'd have to start all over again . . .'

Once I start, I find I can't stop. The words pour out, vocalising the exact thing that worries me about the whole situation. Mum squeezes my hand and stares at the table top. I see a tear sneak its way from one of her eyes, and feel terrible.

Before I can apologise, she speaks: 'Well, I'm really sad you feel like that, love. It's not always like that, you know? You and Jason weren't right for each other . . . but that doesn't mean it always has to end badly. Look at your friends here in the village, and how happy they seem to be with each other.'

'I know, and I'm happy for them,' I say. 'Every single one of them. But I'm still not sure that's part of my future.'

She draws in a deep breath, and looks up at me from her spidery lashes.

'I know you're not, Katie. And I know you probably didn't have the best role models, did you? Me and your dad were hardly examples of marital bliss when you were growing up. We did our best, but I'm not stupid – I know our best wasn't good enough.'

We're both silent for a moment, and it strikes me as strange that the only time either of my parents have acknowledged my less-than-idyllic childhood is now, when their marriage is in tatters. It's taken a complete breakdown in their relationship for them to see it as it really was, rather than the way they probably had to tell themselves it was in order to survive.

I always thought I'd relish this moment – feel some sense of victory or vindication. But now it's happened, I just feel sad. The way she's talking isn't the way you want to hear your mother talking – she's broken, defeated, lost. The fact that all of this is unfolding to the background sounds of Saul chortling away at a mega-loud TV show about a family called the Thundermans, who are all secretly superheroes, makes it even more weird.

Meanwhile, back in the real world – literally feet away in the kitchen – none of us are superheroes. None of us are villains. We're all . . . just doing our best, like Mum said.

'I had an interesting conversation with Cherie . . . erm, yesterday, I suppose. God, it feels like a longer time ago than that. But it was yesterday.'

'Oh? What about?' asks Mum, apparently welcoming the opportunity to change the subject, swiftly wiping her purple pyjama arm across her leaky eyes.

'About you, actually,' I say, raising my eyebrows at her. She perks up immediately, sitting straighter and suddenly looking much more lively. She might be an ego-maniac – but she's my ego-maniac.

'Me? Why? What was she saying? Was it about my lipstick? She was admiring it the other day and I did offer to give her a few make-up tips . . . I don't mean to be rude, but I think she needs them.'

I grimace inside but manage to keep my face neutral. The thought of Cherie in a full face of slap simply does not compute. She's a woman who would never dream of hiding a wrinkle or dying her hair – she's happy with who she is and doesn't give a damn if the rest of the world disagrees.

'No,' I reply slowly, 'but that was very kind of you. She was actually saying that she could use some help at the moment. That they're struggling for staff, what with Laura being in a delicate condition and all that. She was actually wondering if you'd like to work there . . . and even live there?'

I add the last part cautiously, not wanting for a minute for my mum to feel like I'm trying to get rid of her. I am, of course – but it's a secret, much like the Thundermans' super-powers. She's in far too fragile a state to be able to cope with another perceived rejection, so if she quails even slightly, I want her to know that she's still welcome here.

'She has a flat,' I explain, 'in the attic of the café. It's really nice, she used to live in it before she married Frank. So if you wanted to, you could use it for a while. But only if you wanted to. You're a huge help here, and I'd miss you, obviously, so don't feel any pressure. I love having you here, and you're welcome to stay as long as you like.'

I'm treading carefully, not to mention outright lying, all to spare her feelings. I really needn't have bothered.

'Oh God, yes! I'd love to!' she shrieks, jumping to her feet as though she plans on running right upstairs and packing her suitcase this exact moment. She realises that might have sounded a little overeager, and sits down again.

'I mean . . . only if it's all right with you, Katie? I'll stay if you want me to, you know I will. Family comes first.'

I'm laughing inside as we look at each other across the tiny kitchen table. Laughing at the games we all play in an attempt to be decent – the lies we tell in an attempt not to be hurtful.

It's completely obvious to me now that my mother has been struggling with our enforced proximity as much as I have – she couldn't have been keener on moving out if I'd offered up Cal and Sam stark naked and covered in icing sugar to help her with her luggage. She's been hiding it as much as I have – and now we're both sitting here pretending that we want to do whatever the other one wants. If we're not careful she'll let me talk her into staying, and we'll both lose.

'That's okay, Mum,' I reply, without a trace of laughter in my voice – we both need to keep up the pretence of enjoying each other's company a little while longer so we can escape with our mother-daughter dignity intact.

'I think it'd be really good for you,' I add, watching as she actually starts eating her toast. 'And Cherie needs the help. Maybe you're not as dried up and useless as you thought, eh?'

'Maybe not!' she says, her eyes sparkling.

It's the happiest I've seen her in years.

# Chapter 21

A couple of hours later, Mum sets off to take Saul to pre-school, still full of verve after my news about her new life and new temporary home, and I make the long commute across the road to the pharmacy. There's a light sheen of frost on the windowsills, and the air is bitingly cold again. Tinkerbell didn't follow me out onto the street but stayed glued to the radiator, and I can't say that I blame him.

The shop door is open, but nobody seems to be at home. I walk through, and predictably I find Auburn out back, having a cigarette. Less predictably, she's jogging on the spot as she smokes, the cigarette waving around between puffs in her fingerless-gloved hands.

'Why are you doing that?' I ask immediately.

'Smoking? Because I have an addictive personality, an oral fixation and no will power. Have you met me?'

'Yes, and I get all of that. But why are you jogging on the spot?'

'Oh!' she says, her ponytail bouncing. 'It's my new fitness

plan. You're supposed to do, like, 10,000 steps a day or something stupid, aren't you? And even with walking to and from here from the cottage, I don't do anything like that. So I thought I'd maximise my time by doing a quick thousand or so every time I'm on a ciggie break. Cool, right?'

It is, of course, one of the most counter-intuitive things I've ever heard – but possibly it's better than having the smoke without the jogging. I nod, still feeling bemused at the psychedelic wonderland that is Auburn's mind.

'I'm going to patent it,' she says, sounding slightly out of breath now. 'I'll call it the Fag Break Fitness Plan. I'll start a blog, and I'll probably get a book deal, maybe even an exercise DVD . . .'

'Excellent idea,' I reply. 'Not long now until you're on one of those health promotion posters we have in display in the shop. You and your Marlboro Gold.'

She grins, and smokes, and then starts to jog more slowly.

'It's important to always cool down after vigorous exercise . . .' she announces, eventually reducing her speed until she looks like a man on the moon in gravity boots, taking super-slow steps.

I'm about to leave her to it when she speaks again: 'Talking of which – did you get any vigorous exercise last night, Katie?'

I frown and shake my head. I have no idea what she's talking about until she adds: 'Because I couldn't help noticing that my big brother didn't make it home at all . . .'

'You have a dirty mind,' I reply, turning my back on her to go and make some tea. I'm blushing, and don't want her to see my weakness.

'Maybe,' she says, following me back in, puffing and wheezing slightly, 'but my lungs are clear as mountain air! Did he stay over, though? At yours?'

'He did,' I answer, busying myself with less troublesome things like a kettle and tea bags. 'But in case you were wondering—'

'I was.'

'He slept on the sofa. Nothing happened, and even if it did, I wouldn't tell you.'

'Spoilsport,' she says, sounding like a sulky child. She leans back against the sink, and I notice that she looks tired too. There are dark circles beneath her eyes, and the nails showing through her fingerless gloves are chewed so far down the skin looks raw.

'Everything all right at home, with your mum?' I ask, putting the pieces together.

'They've been better,' she replies, shrugging and looking sad. 'We've made an appointment to go and see her consultant. She was really wound up yesterday, one of those "I don't know who you are, why are you holding me captive?" scenarios.

'When Willow suggested she read her book – the one that reminds her who she is and who we are and where she is – she threw it at her head so hard the spine cut her

219

eyelid. After that, Mum went and barricaded herself in her room with the bookcase and a Buddha bust. She's done this before, and we know it's possible to move it all eventually – but if you do it while she's still upset, it just makes her even more scared and agitated.

'So Willow let her cool down, and Tom came over, and they waited until it was quiet and managed to get in. In the meantime Lynnie had conked out, and went to sleep for about twenty hours – except it didn't look restful, you know? More like she was in a coma, which she'd wake up from every hour or so to have a good shout and thrash around in bed like she was fighting someone.'

I hand Auburn her tea – plenty of sugar – and say: 'That's awful, for all of you. I'm so sorry. What do the team at the day centre think?'

'They think maybe it's a sign she's going to decline. Or maybe it's a sign she has some other illness she can't tell us about. Or maybe it's a sign that her meds need upping. Or maybe it's a sign her meds are having side effects. Or maybe a sign she's in pain, but we don't know where. Basically it's a sign that nobody has a fucking clue.'

It's not uncommon for Auburn to swear – she's that kind of girl – but it's usually in fun, or for comedic effect. This time it's a reflection of her frustration and anxiety.

'I'm so sorry, Auburn. You've done the right thing making the appointment. She's really fit, your mum, physically – but there might be something else going on. She might have another urinary tract infection, like she did earlier in the year. They can test her easily for that. Or she might have a bump or a strain or any number of things. Is she up to date with her routine scans and checks?'

'Hmmm . . . I don't know. I'll check,' replies Auburn, already fingering her cigarette packet in a way that implies she might soon be going for another jog.

'You might ask if she can have her bowels looked at as well. It's a common problem, and anything going wrong down there can make even the most healthy of people get wound up and cranky. Have you noticed any changes in her toilet habits?'

Auburn sighs, and I can't say that I blame her.

'No, but I've not been paying close attention. I will now . . . that'll be fun.'

'Well, it's worth asking the doctor about. Anything like that could be what's causing the problem.'

'Or,' she says, staring at me while she chews her lip viciously, 'it could be that she's entering the end stages. I should know this – in fact I probably do but I've deliberately forgotten it – but what is life expectancy with Alzheimer's?'

I do know the answer to this, but it's not one she's going to like.

'It varies massively,' I say, cautiously. 'All kinds of factors come into play – her physical health and wellbeing, the level of support she has at home, her treatment plan. All of which I'd say are excellent.'

'Yes, but . . .?'

'For someone diagnosed like your mum was, in her early sixties, it averages between seven and ten years. But it can be much longer.'

Auburn nods abruptly, her nostrils flared and her lips pinched tightly together. I can only imagine what she's going through, how complex and devastating all of this is for them, and say a little prayer of thanks for the fact that my mother, no matter how annoying, is still my mother. Hopefully she'll be annoying me for a long time to come.

I'm wondering if Auburn's going to ask me more questions, and decide that all I can do is answer them honestly, when both our phones make beeping noises to tell us a message has landed. We exchange a glance, knowing it's likely to be about Edie, and both reach to check.

Sure enough, there's a text on mine from Becca – obviously sent in a round robin to everyone waiting to hear the morning's news. I hold my breath slightly as I start reading it, telling myself that if it was bad – if there was no more Edie – then Becca wouldn't be telling us by text. She just wouldn't.

Luckily, I'm right on that – and the news is good.

'Ahoy sailors!' it says, bizarrely. 'Better news on the Good Ship Edie. She's awake and talking and drinking her tot of rum. Waiting to see the Captain on her rounds. Jolly Roger that, over and out, Able Seawoman Becca.'

I smile – because it really is good news – and then frown. Because it's also confusing.

'Why did she go all nautical-but-nice on us?' asks Auburn, also frowning.

'I have no idea!'

'And do you reckon they really give you rum for breakfast in hospital?'

'Not in my experience, or it'd be a lot more popular. But it's good news anyway – really good. Becca's probably just knackered. Have you seen Sam this morning? I said I'd check in on them for her.'

'Yep, I saw him when I was opening up – he was taking little Edie into work for the day. Said it's never too young for your first ammonite.'

Sam works as a ranger, and gives guided walks along the Jurassic Coast, pointing out the fossils that get washed up on the shore or are embedded in the cliffs. Looks like Little Edie's getting her first lesson in fossil hunting.

'Anyway . . . didn't get a chance to say it yesterday,' says Auburn, putting her phone down on the counter. 'But well done. You were a bit of a hero.'

'What do you mean? What did I do?' I ask, genuinely bewildered.

'You saved Edie's life. Didn't want to actually say that out loud until we knew how she was doing – but you did, Katie.'

'Don't be daft,' I scoff, embarrassed. 'All I did was notice the cat in her windowsill and call for help. It hardly makes me Natasha Romanoff, does it?'

'Well, I'm sure you'd make a great Black Widow, but heroes come in different forms, don't they? You could just as easily have not noticed the cat. Or not wondered why the cat was still there. Or decided it didn't matter. Or told yourself you were imagining things, and ignored your instincts and gone home. You're a nurse – you know how bad she was. You know it was touch and go. If we hadn't found her when we did, she might not have made it through the night. So don't argue – you saved her life.'

I don't agree, but I also don't argue. There's no point with Auburn. I just smile, and walk back through into the shop with my tea.

I settle in on the scary lipstick sofa for a minute, and text my dad, telling him he needs to get his arse into gear and sort stuff out with Mum. She's happy right now, because of the obviously exciting idea of moving out of my house, but it's still not fair.

I don't expect any kind of reaction from him, because he's usually so bad with his mobile, but I actually get a reply straight away. A reply that makes me want to scream, but I don't suppose you can have everything in life.

He's going away for a bit, he says. On a mindfulness retreat in Tenerife. With Fiona and some of her friends. But, he assures me, he'll be down before Christmas to talk to Mum.

I sit still for a moment, drinking my tea, and trying to be more mindful myself. Maybe it's a good thing, I decide. I have my blood pressure to consider.

*Maybe it's for the best*, I think. Maybe he'll come back with some answers. And long term, who knows? He was definitely a changed man when I saw him – and that can't be a bad thing. Mum's a changed woman as well, but that's different, and a lot less positive – hers is change she's had forced on her rather than chosen. No wonder she's a mess.

I shake my head, and leaf through the sex aids catalogue almost without realising what I'm doing. As soon as I get to a brightly coloured page full of pastel-shaded vibrators, I throw it away, wondering if I now need hand sanitiser.

It's all so strange, this family stuff. Here, in Budbury, I've made friends better than I've ever known. I've become part of an extended family that I chose for myself, rather than the one I was born with. But family is still family – still part of my history and my genetic make-up and my future. I wonder about Saul, and what he'll make of it all when he's older. Right now, he accepts that his dad lives in Scotland and he lives here and that's all fine.

But Saul is only very small, and knows no different. This is the only way he's ever known it to be. Maybe that will change once he's old enough to ask questions. When he's at school, and has his own friends, who all might have perfect little Mum-and-Dad set-ups. He's bound to be curious – to want to know why his dad isn't around; why we split up, why he's not in his life more. It's only natural, and I know that day will come – and I'm surely dreading it.

I idly mess around on my phone, feeling low-level stressed about pretty much everything. About Edie, about my parents, about Lynnie, about Van, about Saul. I find myself on Facebook, which I rarely use as I never have any pictures of nice meals to post.

I flick through my newsfeed, laughing at the fact that Lizzy's page is now full of photos of Tinkerbell and the dogs, and press like on them all. I see that Laura's shared a picture of her Green Velvet Cake and like too.

I see that my mum has updated her profile pic – the first time she's posted since she set up her account four years ago. It's a selfie with trout pout, taken against the backdrop of my purple curtains, and looks frightening. Still, I like that as well, as Facebook hasn't as yet introduced a button for 'that scares the shit out of me'.

Barely thinking about what I'm doing, I type in Jason's name and search. I scroll through the results, and find that there are an improbably large number of people with the same name as him online. Eventually, after investigating a few, I find him.

Feeling guilty and sneaky and really hoping he can't tell I've been looking, I open his page. I'm met with a photo of him and his wife, Jo, at their wedding. It looks nice, one of those candid shots with confetti fluttering across their laughing faces. She's about my age, Jo, but couldn't look more different – she's brunette, almost as tall as him, with one of those Amazonian figures that makes her look like Wonder Woman.

I know she's a teacher, and that they've been together for the last two years, getting married this summer.

I roll the page down, looking at their various joint posts, at the numerous pictures – Jason and Jo on honeymoon; Jason and Jo at a barbecue; Jason and Jo on a mini-break to Paris; Jason and Jo eating spaghetti.

They look happy. They look good together. I feel strange about it – not out of any sense of jealousy, but out of a weird sensation that I'm intruding on a life that has nothing at all to do with me. Except it does – because for better or worse, this is Saul's dad.

Jason and I communicate mainly by email, which is easier because we both get to think carefully about what we're saying. He always remembers Saul's birthday, and Christmas, and even sends Easter eggs and boxes full of creepy chocolate treats at Halloween.

He's mentioned coming to see him a few times, but it's never happened. I don't know whether that's down to distance, or something deeper – whether Jason doesn't push for it to happen because he doesn't want to see me. I don't suppose my lukewarm response has helped – I've never said no, but I've never shown any enthusiasm either.

That, a tiny little voice whispers into my ear, probably

isn't fair. Maybe if I'd been more open, more encouraging, he'd have made the effort. The way Jason and I ended was horrible – but I don't for one minute see him as a threat to me, or to Saul. Not a physical one, anyway.

With the hindsight of a couple of years away from him, and with my parents as examples, I can see quite clearly how easy it was for us to descend into the arguments and bitterness. It wasn't by any means inevitable that it should end the way it did – not all men who fight with their wives slap them. But I also don't think it was typical of Jason, or indicative of the way he is now. I genuinely believe it was a one-off – one he was as horrified by as I was. Although maybe that's what all women think, who knows?

I do know, though, that in some ways it gave me an excuse to finally end a relationship we both knew wasn't working. And then I ran away, and I've kept him at arm's length ever since. He's probably still ashamed, and hasn't pushed as hard as he could have to stay in Saul's life – and perhaps I need to have a think about it all. I don't like thinking about it, obviously – things go much more smoothly when I don't think at all.

But with everything that's been happening – my parents, Edie, even Van – the time has come. I don't want the complications. I don't want the mess. I don't want my orderly little life to be disrupted by all this tangled emotional stuff. But this isn't about what I want; it's about Saul's future.

On the spur of the moment, I hit the button that sends

a friend request. I immediately feel a little tremor of panic run through me as I do it, and jump up to do something else. Anything else. I don't know why it feels weird – it's not like we never communicate. We do. But somehow a 'friend request', and this little foray into his personal life, feels too intimate – like I'm inviting him to be more to me than he currently is.

I need to find work to distract myself, and decide to rearrange our display of Rimmel make-up – the lipsticks are all in the wrong places, so it's pretty urgent. I'm still stubbing plastic tubes into plastic holes when Auburn trots through from the back room. She's taken her coat off but is still wearing her fingerless gloves after goodness knows how many cigarettes while she pulled herself together.

'I feel great!' she says breezily, completely transformed from the maudlin state she was in a few minutes ago. 'I think I might run the London marathon next year!'

'Will you smoke while you do it?' I ask, wondering if anybody has ever done that – and whether they'd get on TV cameras if they did.

'Only a few – you know those little places they have set up on the course, where they give you bottles of water and whistle pops?'

'I've never seen them handing out whistle pops, but I know what you mean.'

'Well, maybe I'd just stay there for a minute, and have a

quick puff. I don't think I'd actually smoke while I was running – it wouldn't be ladylike . . . anyway, there's time to plan for all of that later. I've got some prescriptions getting sent in from the surgery in Applechurch – let me know when they land, will you? And by the way – there's a big dinner at the café tonight. By royal decree of Cherie – says she wants everyone to get together to have a feast to celebrate Edie being on the mend.'

The nurse part of me is worried by that – because while the Good Ship Edie might be doing better today, it's by no means guaranteed that it's plain sailing from this point on. She's fighting pneumonia, she's 92, and she's in hospital – where there will be other people, with other infections, potentially sharing their germs with her. She's still very, very poorly.

It seems churlish to mention this right now, though, so I keep my thoughts to myself. Dinner at the café will be lovely. Saul will be the centre of attention; there'll be dogs for him to play with, and the food will be a heck of a lot better than the chicken kievs I have in the freezer. Plus my mum can talk to Cherie about her glamorous new life as a member of Team Comfort Food.

Van will probably be there too. Which is fine, I tell myself – that will also be lovely, and I won't be drinking. It's all under control.

'Okay. Great,' I reply, finishing with the lipsticks and moving over to the dispensing area to turn the computer on. We get prescriptions sent electronically from local GPs, and get them ready either for patients to collect, or for us to sometimes deliver. Auburn does most of that part due to my childlike inability to drive a car.

I'm checking through our files, keeping myself busy, when I hear an alert from my phone. I get it out of my pocket, and check to see what it is.

It's a notification from Facebook. Jason has accepted my friend request, and Facebook wonders if I'd like to send him a message or wave to him.

What I'd actually like to do is rewind the last hour, and not contact him at all. But I somehow suspect that's beyond Facebook's power.

# Chapter 22

I'm grateful to be in work for the rest of the morning, and equally grateful to have to go to college in the afternoon. I've passed three of the four modules I'm studying already, and only have one more to go. Having Mum around has, at least, taken off a lot of the pressure around childcare.

Before, it was a workable but ad hoc arrangement with my various friends – and with Laura now very much in the family way, and Lynnie taking a downward swing, I'm glad I don't have to impose.

I'm also glad I've had something to occupy my mind, as Jason and I have been exchanging messages all day. There's something about the whole messaging thing that makes it feel more personal than an email – like we're talking to each other in real time.

He's now seen the few photos I have of Saul on my account, and seems interested in all of them – and in our life here. I suppose that's kind of what I wanted, but it also feels vaguely unsettling. Like I've opened a can of worms that's now going to crawl all over me; that I'll still be shaking off my skin even when they're gone.

It also seems that Jason was on the verge of contacting me anyway – partly to ask what Saul might want for Christmas, and partly to share some news.

His wife, Jo, is pregnant. Again, this weirds me out – not because I still have feelings for Jason, but because it means that Saul will be getting a little brother or sister in about six months' time. Logically, I knew that my life would always be connected to Jason's through our son – but this news makes it all the more real. More complicated. A whole lot more difficult to ever run away from. I feel strangely trapped by it all, and can't quite understand why.

The absolute last thing I feel like doing is going to the café for a big group dinner. I love my pals, I really do, and I've taken big strides in getting more involved with village life. But I now realise that when I feel conflicted, or worried, my instinct is still to hide away from the world and sort it out myself. To shut all the potential stress factors down and retreat to my bunker.

It's a pattern I'm now familiar with, but only really identified when I briefly attended a support group for single mums. We had a group counselling session where we were all asked to mark important turning points in our 'journeys'.

I left the support group after two weeks – to be honest, I'm not very communal, and I also felt like a bit of a fraud. I definitely hadn't suffered enough in comparison to some of the other women there, and was worried I might start making things up just to fit in.

But I do always remember that session. I remember sitting in a circle on a hard plastic chair, Saul in the crèche off to one side, probably trying to eat Duplo, my eyes closed and hands wrapped around a plastic cup of hot coffee. I think that was half the attraction, the hot coffee.

I sat there, eyes closed, and I saw that pattern. Saw it, and took it home with me to examine later. That night, when my precious baby boy/demon spawn was finally asleep, I sat sprawled across the sofa, watching repeats of *Through The Keyhole* and remembering things I'd thought dead and buried. Reliving moments so painful I'd hidden them deep under seventeen layers of denial.

I'm feeling the same now, and the sensation of being under attack reminds me of when I was a kid, and things were getting heated downstairs in the Land of the Lunatics. The way I'd lock my bedroom door and listen to music, or walk the streets for hours on end just to escape from the insanity and the noise and the anger.

I kind of want to do that now – or at least to not have to be in company I'm not fit to be in. I know how this will go: I feel pressurised, so I'll retreat. It'll be like the time earlier in the year when Edie was having her ninety-second birthday at Briarwood. I'd been to all the dancing lessons, I'd helped plan the event, but when it came down to it, I couldn't face it – there were too many people, and too much attention.

I'd wussed out and stayed at home with Saul instead.

On the bus ride home today, I'd briefly toyed with the idea of coming up with some excuse to wuss out again, but the text messages from pretty much everyone I know reminding me to be there by 7.30 were making it patently clear that that wasn't an option.

So, my brain a simmering pot of stress stew, I find myself walking to the café on my own, through village streets that feel deserted – probably because everyone is at the café.

Mum has headed over early with Saul, keen to talk to Cherie about her job and the flat, and I'd had time to get ready on my own. It should have felt like a luxury – but it actually felt like torture. My make-up was applied half-heartedly, and I wasn't even sure what my hair was supposed to be doing.

In an empty house, I had too much time to think, too much time to worry, too much time to wonder about how my life would look if Saul wasn't in it. If, for example, he was spending time away in Scotland – with his dad and his new baby brother or sister.

The whole thing feels like a case of 'be careful what you wish for' to me. Hours ago, a lifetime ago, this morning in the pharmacy, I'd been thinking that it would be a good idea for Saul to get to know his dad better. To not grow up feeling unwanted or rejected in any way. To not only rely on me for love and nurturing and approval.

Now it looks as though that might be happening, I'm

frankly terrified. I know that doesn't say anything good about me, but it's how I feel. I can't change the situation – it is what it is – all I can do is try to adapt. To stay calm, and get through it. If life crises have taught me anything, it's that with time, things won't always feel as bad as they do in the heat of the moment.

I tell myself this over and over again as I walk, far too slowly, towards the café. It's dark, and chillingly cold, and snow has been forecast overnight. I'm wrapped up warm but, without a balaclava, still have icy cheeks that feel as though Jack Frost has rubbed his bony fingers all over my skin.

By the time I get to the café, lit up with its fairy lights, I've decided that I'll only stay for an hour. I can fake it for an hour – then I'll come up with some reason, like Saul being tired or Tinkerbell needing a foot massage, so I can make my excuses and leave.

I trudge my way reluctantly up the path and into the garden, where the giant inflatable Father Christmas is wobbling around, half in shadow from the illumination spilling from the steamed-up café windows.

I take a deep breath, tell myself I can hide in a corner and leave as soon as possible, and push open the door.

I'm immediately struck by two things. One is the heat – the place is warm and crowded and suddenly makes all my coats and scarves and gloves feel unnecessary. The other is the noise.

As soon as I step through the door, the whole place erupts into a chorus of 'For She's a Jolly Good Fellow', loud and discordant and threaded through with the one or two voices that are actually hitting the right notes.

I freeze, rooted to the spot, and actually look behind me – checking to see who it is they're singing to.

As there's nobody else there, and there's also a huge banner strung up along the serving counter that says 'Well done Katie!', I come to the inescapable conclusion that they're actually singing to me.

I don't know how I must look to the assembled masses standing in front of me, but I'm guessing that it might involve the words 'deer' and 'headlights'.

Saul dashes forward and hugs my legs. He's getting bigger now, taking after his dad in height rather than me, and I kneel down to hug him back. And, you know, to hide the look of sheer horror on my face.

These people, these wonderful people, have thrown me a party to congratulate me for doing something that wasn't even a big deal. And in return, all I feel is a driving need to run screaming back down the hill, through the village, and into my own little house. Except my own little house doesn't even feel that safe any more – it has weird curtains, and my mum's stuff all over it, and people have started to *visit* me. I've had Matt in the doorway and Van on the sofa and in my shower, and it all feels too big – too invasive.

I school my face into something that hopefully doesn't

reflect this – because I know I'm being crazy – and stand up straight.

Everyone is there – apart from Edie, of course. Everyone is looking at me, and grinning, and cheering. There's a trestle table set up and groaning with food and drink, and the whole place is draped with little fairy lights in the shape of Christmas presents.

If I was here in the background, celebrating somebody else's heroism, I'd be thinking how pretty and lovely it all is. Instead, I'm still wondering how quickly I can escape.

Becca steps forward and envelops me in a huge hug.

'Thank you,' she whispers into my ear. 'The doctors are all amazed at her. They keep bringing students in to meet her – I think they're considering writing some kind of paper on the Edie May miracle! Nobody thought she was going to survive, but she is. I know she is. But she wouldn't have done if it wasn't for you.'

'And Tinkerbell,' I add, overwhelmed.

'Yeah. Tinkerbell too. Cherie has a whole plate of salmon for him as well.'

I nod, and smile a stupid smile, and keep the stupid smile on my face as everyone troops over to thank me and hug me and pat me on the back. Laura's there, looking tired but happy; Zoe and Cal; Sam and Little Edie; Willow and Tom and Auburn and Van and Lynnie.

Lynnie's looking confused but not distressed, which is

a blessing, and Van gives me an extra tight squeeze when he reaches me.

'You can do it,' he murmurs into my ear. 'Just keep on smiling!'

That does at least make me laugh – he's obviously seen right through my less-than-brave face. I just hope all the others haven't.

Finally, after a large round of thanks from Edie's family, Cherie is by my side. She's wearing a kaftan – an actual kaftan – decorated with tiny pom-poms, like something she picked up from a little boutique in an Aztec village.

'We made you these,' she says, 'me and Saul. Just for you.'

First, she shows me a big cardboard love heart, decorated in pink glitter, with the words 'Our hero!' written on them in neon-coloured marker pen. The heart is attached to some stripey blue and white fabric used as a necklace. I think it might possibly have been a tea-towel in a previous life. She drapes it around my neck like a medal, and flips my hair out at the back.

Next she produces a kind of cape, obviously made from an old tablecloth, also decorated in glitter. It shimmers under the fairy lights as she wafts it around, shining specks of glitter flying off and into a sparkling cloud around our heads.

There's a makeshift clasp at the corners made out of glued-on press-studs, and she fastens it around my neck.

'There,' she says, smiling at her handiwork, 'your very own superhero cape. Give us a twirl!'

I blink rapidly and do as she says – it's the path of least resistance, and I'm hoping that once I've endured this last suffocating act of kindness, I can fade into the background.

Everyone cheers and claps as I twirl, and then, thankfully, attention starts to move away from me. Cherie calls out for music, and I see Matt, who always seems to end up manning sound systems at parties, switch it on. I think it's his way of hiding – the anonymity of being the guy in charge of the buttons.

Bizarrely, the first song on is Beyoncé's 'Single Ladies', and everyone immediately starts busting out some dance moves and laughing. I feel the beat, and wish I could join in – I love dancing, and I'm good at it, but right now I just can't. I wish I was the kind of person who could just twirl their superhero cape and throw herself into the party, but I'm not. I'm too much of a coward.

I see that Saul is doing that thing that kids like doing, where he's got his feet on Cal's feet, and Cal is dancing him around the room. I see Laura sit down with a sigh of relief, and Matt bring over a glass of water and a paper plate laden with food. I see the teenagers, dancing in their own little circle, mock-twerking and pulling faces as they look at the old people gyrating. I see Willow and Tom cutting it up, and Auburn to one side, sitting with Lynnie. I see my mum, and she catches my eye across the room, giving me a huge grin and making a 'thumbs up' sign.

Everyone is happy. Everyone is relieved. Everyone is grateful that Edie has lived to fight another day.

I, on the other hand, am shrivelling up inside, and hating myself for it. I slink away to the ladies, smiling and chatting to people as I move through the room, feeling more and more brittle with every conversation.

I finally make it, leaning back against the door once I've locked it, breathing a sigh of relief. I just need a moment, I tell myself. A moment to regroup. To calm down. To shake off the feeling that I'm some kind of imposter – that I shouldn't be here, amongst all these people, on the receiving end of their love and support and thanks. That if they really knew me, they wouldn't like me at all.

Even as these thoughts flitter through my mind, I realise how silly they sound. Why shouldn't they like me? What have I ever done that's so bad? I shoplifted a mascara once, when I was fourteen. Technically, that's about the worst of my sins.

But this runs deeper than that, I know. It started young, feeling like I was a spare part in my parents' drama. It developed into my teenaged years, where I always felt I had to keep people at arm's length, that I needed distance from people who might hurt me.

Now, I'm here, with a child and with friends and with a life. And yet I still feel like I don't quite belong. Like I can't quite connect with them in a genuine way. I'm still playing a part – and it's not the one of a superhero.

I splash my face with cold water, and swish my hair around to get rid of some of the glitter, and stare at myself in the mirror.

'Don't freak out – just don't,' I tell myself out loud. It's been a big couple of days. Edie being ill. Everything that's going on with Dad. Van sneaking further and further into our lives. And, with ultimate bad timing, facing up to the fact that I need to sort myself out when it comes to Jason.

It feels like things are changing – and I don't want them to. I've only just steadied myself with the basics of this community, my place in the world. And now I feel like I'm being fast-tracked on to an advanced level I'm not quite prepared for. Like if I'd gone into work as a nurse and someone expected me to perform brain surgery.

I'm taking some deep breaths – the kind Lynnie has taught me to do when I'm feeling stressed – and turn the taps off.

I'm preparing to leave when there's a knock on the door. I assume I've been a toilet hog for too long, and someone – probably Laura – is desperate for a pee.

'Coming!' I shout, aiming to sound perky and bright and happy. In other words, the exact opposite of what I actually feel.

I open the door, fake smile plastered onto my face along

with the stray glitter, and see Van standing outside, leaning against the wall. He looks at me and grins.

'Nice look,' he says, pointing at the glitter. 'I'm here to rescue you.'

'What do you mean, rescue me? What makes you think I need rescuing from anything?' I reply, my voice rising about seven million octaves by the end of the sentence.

'The look on your face when you walked through the door. The fake smile you're currently using. The fact that your voice sounds like Minnie Mouse on helium. And the fact that I know you, Katie, and know that this isn't your idea of a good time. Come on – let's sneak through the kitchens and out the back door. Saul's fine, and if we're quick nobody will notice we're gone. I promise I'll have you back by midnight so you don't turn into a pumpkin.'

I look beyond him, to the packed café, where The Mavericks are helping everyone just dance the night away. Saul is now on Cal's shoulders, tangling up some of the dangling lametta in his fingers, and my mum is doing her usual Eighties party dance with Frank. The idea of plunging back into it all makes my stomach clench into knots.

I look back at Van, who has somehow figured all of this out, and nod.

'Okay,' I say quietly. 'I'll let you rescue me.'

# Chapter 23

We make our way through the kitchens, for some reason tiptoeing as we do – I don't know why, it's not like anyone would be able to hear our footsteps over the music.

Van pauses at a cupboard near the back, where Cherie keeps a stock of plaid fleece blankets for customers to use when they're sitting outside in winter, and grabs a couple before we leave.

We head off down the path, and I find myself smiling at the thought of anyone noticing us – two dark figures, doing a runner like a pair of fugitives. My superhero cape is fluttering behind me in the breeze, and I kind of wish I was also wearing tights and red pants just to make it even more ridiculous.

Once we're down by the bay, I feel a physical sense of relief wash over me. It's as though gaining even this amount of distance from the party has allowed my adrenaline levels to calm down to something approaching normal.

We walk out onto the beach, which is completely

deserted. I can still hear the beat of the music from the café, and when I look up I can see its bright lights and the dancing figures inside, but it's all small enough to feel less intimidating.

*Van was right*, I think, sucking in some cold night air – *I did need rescuing. And maybe, once the shock and surprise of the ambush party has worn off, I'll be able to simply go back in and enjoy myself, like a normal human being.*

I just walk, grateful for the chilly air against my overheated skin, while Van amuses himself in the way of overgrown boys everywhere – by throwing sticks and stones into the sea. As we get further along the coast, the sound of the music fades, and all I can hear is the gentle hiss and fizz of waves lapping up onto the sand, and the occasional splash when he lobs one of his beachcomber finds into the water.

Eventually, after about ten minutes or so, I decide to stop. I can't just keep walking until I hit Devon – I've left my son in the café, apart from anything else. I sit down on one of the big, water-smoothed boulders that line the bay by the cliffs, and Van joins me.

He places one of the fleece blankets over our knees, and one over our shoulders.

'We could have had one each,' I say, smiling.

'I know. But that would have foiled my masterplan to get you to snuggle up to me. Anyway, it's not too disgusting, is it?'

I feel my thigh crushed up against his, and his arm

around my shoulder, and realise that I feel small and warm and safe.

'Not completely, no,' I admit, staring out at the sea and the shimmering stripes of the moonlight, rippling across the undulating waves.

'So, what's up, then? Apart from the party, that is. I can tell there's something else going on. Is it your mum?'

I shake my head, and wonder how he can possibly see so much in me. It's like he has some kind of spyglass set up in my brain.

'No, she's fine. In fact she's more than fine – Cherie's offered to let her stay in the flat for a while, so she'll be moving out.'

'I hope she takes her curtains with her.'

'Me too. But that's all good . . . it's other stuff.'

'Oh,' he says, seriously. 'Other stuff. Well, that can be a bastard. Would you like to be more specific, or should I start guessing?'

I laugh, and gently poke him in the ribs. After that my hand somehow finds its way to his thigh, where it decides to stay. He covers my fingers with his, and links them into mine.

'I was in touch with Saul's dad today,' I explain. I clearly need to talk to somebody about this, and Van is the person who knows more about it than any of my new friends. That I've been here for two years and not shared any personal information with anyone else probably tells me all I need to know about my privacy issues.

'Okay. Is that uncommon?' he asks.

'Hard to say. We've always stayed in touch, but it's been by email – maybe three times a year. All very civil. Very distant. Very grown up – like we were both trying to make up for the lack of civility we were displaying by the time we split up. This time, though, we were messaging each other on Facebook, which I know makes me sound like a teenaged girl—'

'Teenaged girls wouldn't use Facebook,' he says, grinning. 'They think it's for old people. They think it's something from the past, like thimbles, and soap dishes, and flip-phones.'

'Thank you, Mr Down-With-The-Kids. Anyway, being an old person, I do use Facebook. Occasionally a soap dish, but never a thimble. So, we were chatting. Jason and me. And he wants to see Saul, and his wife is pregnant, and Saul is going to have a baby brother or sister, and—'

'It all feels like a bit too much right now?'

'Exactly! He's even talking about meeting up when he's back in Bristol for Christmas. And I know it's not a bad thing – I know he's Saul's dad, and I don't want to be the kind of mother that keeps them apart, and ends up giving Saul all kinds of daddy issues. But even though I know that, I still feel worried.'

'Do you trust him?' he asks, frowning. 'After . . . what happened with you two?'

I know what he's alluding to, and I reply: 'Yes. I think

so. He wasn't ever that keen on being a dad, to be honest. He was too young, and we were incredibly ill-matched. But when he was with Saul, he was never anything but kind.

'After we split up, before I moved here and he moved to Glasgow, we saw each other – and there weren't ever any problems. No rows. No raised voices. Nothing . . . else. Just two people who had gone quite a long way down the path of destroying their self respect. I don't think it's a coincidence that we both ended up relocating – it's like we both needed a fresh start. That was right for us both, then – but now I suppose I also need to think about what's right for Saul.'

He nods and ponders this silently, his fingers tracing swirling patterns on the palm of my hand.

'And I suppose,' he says eventually, 'that this has all assumed monstrous proportions in your mind? In your imagination, it's gone from something small, like meeting up for a coffee, to something huge? Like Saul going there for holidays, and his dad deciding he wants to keep him, and your whole life falling to pieces?'

I let out a short, sharp laugh. He's battered the nail on the head.

'Of course. I am female. That seems to be one of our specialist subjects, doesn't it – blowing things out of proportion?'

'I couldn't possibly comment. I live with three women and I'm not falling into that trap, thank you very much. What I would say is that perhaps you need to break it down; take it one step at a time. Deal with each development as it comes, rather than try and control it all and freak yourself out with the what-might-be scenarios. That's one thing I've learned through Lynnie being in the state she is.

'Maybe you could try to concentrate on the what is happening, rather than the what-could-happen – and at the moment, the thing that's actually happening could be really positive. He's not talking about abducting Saul and running away to Marrakesh – he's talking about meeting up in your home town. And if his wife is having a baby, maybe you'd like to meet her as well? If – and I mean "if" – Saul ends up spending any time with them, it would be good to meet her. It could put your mind at rest.'

I think about what he's said, and know that he's right. So right there's no way I can argue with it – except, I do.

'That's all true,' I say sadly. 'But somehow it's not helping. I know what I should do – but at the moment, I don't seem able. It's like it's all set off some kind of chain reaction inside me, and I'm on the verge of exploding. And yes – I need to meet his wife. And I want Saul to like her, and her to like Saul. Eventually, if it goes that far. But if I'm being honest, even that freaks me out . . . because what if she's so fantastic, Saul prefers her to me?'

*There*, I think. *I've said it.* It makes me feel like poo, but at least I've made myself acknowledge it – the deep, dark fear that's stubbornly lurking inside me.

I don't know quite how I expected Van to react to that admission, but I have to say, it wasn't with laughter.

Laughter is what I get, though – big, full, whole-hearted laughter. The arm around my shoulder squeezes me in tight, and he rests his chin on top of my head, his body shaking with amusement. I'm taken aback by this, and also considering punching him in a place no man likes to be punched.

'Oh, Katie, I'm sorry,' he says, once he's regained control of himself, 'but that is so stupid the only sensible response is to laugh! I can actually understand why you feel like that – it's always been you and Saul against the world and this feels threatening. But to even think for a minute that the little man would prefer someone else to his mum? A mum who loves him and laughs with him and makes him feel like the centre of the whole world? Well, that's a step too far.

'I know you don't have a lot of confidence, and I know life has taught you not to believe in yourself as much as other people do. As much as I do. But you have to listen to me when I say this: you are a great mother. Saul adores you. Nothing will ever break that bond – Saul's world getting bigger just means he'll have more people to love him, not less love to give. Is there any way you can try and believe that?'

I nod, and tell myself he's right. That I'm being foolish. I'm not sure I'm convinced, but I need to take my anxiety down a notch or ten before some vital part of my brain snaps in two.

'I'll do my best,' I say. 'And thank you. For the cheer-leading.'

'It's one of my specialist subjects,' he replies. 'I'll dress up for you next time, if you like.'

'With pompoms and everything?'

'If that's what floats your boat. Look, if you want me to, I'll come with you. When you go to Bristol. If you need the moral support or, you know, a lift.'

'I'm not sure that would help,' I answer honestly. 'It's only going to make an already awkward situation even worse, me bringing my . . . friend along. And I'm not convinced you won't go all macho on me.'

'I promise I wouldn't. I might look like a caveman, but I don't always act like one. Anyway. No pressure – just keep it in mind. You're not alone in this. Not if you don't want to be. Now, do you think you might be ready to go back to the café? They might have noticed they're missing their guest of honour by now.'

I make a sound that is a suitable expression of my lack of enthusiasm for being the guest of honour – the noise a whoopee cushion makes when you sit on it – and he laughs again.

'I get it,' he says, 'I really do. This place can be so claus-trophobic sometimes. Everybody is always in your face – in the nicest possible way. I struggle with it too. At least it's by the sea. Sometimes, when I'm feeling a bit hemmed in, or the cottage feels like a battery chicken cage, I come and sit out here and tell myself it's all okay – I'm perched at the edge of the world.'

'It must feel so small,' I reply, gazing around us. 'The village. Compared to what you're used to.'

'Well the village itself feels like a major metropolis to be honest – there's a fish and chip shop for starters. Running water. Usable roads. All the big city attractions. But yeah – the landscape is very different. The culture? Not so much. People get in your face in Africa too, once you're part of the community. But you're only ever minutes away from the most beautiful wide open spaces; the best sunsets and sunrises, the animals . . . it's a special place. Maybe I'll take you there one day.'

I stand up and stretch out my limbs. Now we've been still for a while, the cold is catching up with me, and even my eyelashes feel frosty.

'Maybe you will,' I reply, smiling at him. 'Wouldn't that be something?'

'It would,' he answers, standing up to join me. 'We'll do it, I promise. When Saul's all grown up, and I'm not sleeping on a sofa, and life is simpler. If life ever does actually get simpler. But for now . . . I'll settle for this . . .'

He's standing so close to me I can feel the warmth of his body, and the touch of his breath. He places his hands on my shoulder, and leans forward to kiss me.

It's tentative at first, as though he's giving me the chance to slap him away. I probably should, I know.

But when I don't, his arms close around me, pulling me closer, his hands sliding up to tangle into my hair, the intensity of the kiss building.

I can't deny that I've fantasised about this moment. I've imagined the touch of his lips on mine; the feel of his fingers on my skin. Of my hands, splayed across the width of his chest. I've thought about it many times – and I can honestly say that everything I'd hoped it would be is nothing at all compared to the reality.

From the minute we make contact, I'm swept away. Every thought, every anxiety, every worry – swept away. Every doubt, every question, every self-recrimination – swept away. Every pain from the past, or fear for the future – swept away. All that's left is the present: me, and Van, and the sound of the waves and the bright stars in the dark sky around us.

I don't know how long we stand there, tangled up in each other, tangled up in the moment. It could have been a minute. It could have been a lifetime.

All I know is that when we finally pull apart, our bodies still touching, our eyes locked, every part of me is tingling and alive.

'Wow,' says Van, giving me a crooked smile, his fingers still stroking my hair, his breathing coming fast and hard. 'You really do have superpowers.'

# Chapter 24

Laura takes forever to get out of the car, me and Saul waiting by her side as she constantly finds reasons not to leave it. She checks for her glasses in the glove box (where she just put them); she carefully places the CD we've been listening to back in its sleeve, and she puts the handbrake on and off repeatedly. Once she's out, she uses a bottle of water to clean an already clean windshield.

Eventually, when that's done, she locks the doors approximately sixteen times, checking each one individually, before slowly walking with us out of the car park. When we reach the entrance to the building, she pauses, and eyes it slowly and warily – as though it's a rabid dog about to bite her.

'Are you okay?' I ask, laying a gentle hand on her arm. Frankly, she looks like she might be about to pass out. Her skin is drawn and pale, and her pretty face is furrowed into a deep frown.

'Yes. I'll be fine. I just . . . don't like hospitals,' she replies, shaking her curls and very clearly trying to snap out of her fugue state.

'Not many people do,' I say, keeping a tight grip on Saul's hand. He's jogging up and down, pipping to get inside and visit Edie.

'I'll be okay. I just need a minute. It's because of David, you see . . . he died after a head injury, and we had to turn the machines off, and it was all very, very grim. So sometimes, in a hospital, I have a bit of a funny turn. If I do, don't worry – it's not related to me being pregnant or anything.'

I nod my head, and keep my hand on her arm. Between her and Saul, I'm fully occupied now.

'I understand,' I say quietly, 'take your time. If you want to stay in the car, that's not a problem – I'll tell Edie you weren't feeling well.'

I'm not a stranger to hospitals, and they hold no fear for me – luckily they're places I see as work, not vivid reminders of hellish personal trauma. But I've been around them long enough to appreciate the fact that for most people, they don't signify a long shift and beans on toast in the canteen – they signify something much more upsetting. Especially in a case like Laura's.

Saul picks up on some tense adult thing going on around him, and gazes up at Laura's face. He inserts himself between the two of us, and takes one of our hands in each of his.

'It's okay,' he says to Laura. 'I'll look after you.'

She stares down at him, her distress causing a bit of a time lag between him speaking and her processing the words, then breaks out into a big smile.

She ruffles his hair, and beams at him as she replies: 'Thank you, sweetie. I feel much better now. Shall we go and see Edie?'

She puts one brave foot in front of the other, and together we make our way inside. Through the familiar corridors, through the familiar smells, through the familiar worried faces and harassed-looking medical staff. She blanches slightly when we pass a room with a bleeping monitor, but shakes it off and carries on.

Eventually, we reach Edie's ward. It's evening visiting, and busy, crowded with family and friends all searching for extra chairs and looking for a spare surface to lay down their chocolates and flowers and cards. I can hear that weird low-level buzz from the strip lighting humming behind the bustle and chatter, and resist the urge to start looking at charts.

We find Edie in a corner spot by the windows, propped up on pillows, her silver head bowed over her iPad. I pause for a moment myself, and say a little prayer of thanks to whoever might be listening. I don't think anybody quite realises how miraculous this is – for a woman of her age to recover from pneumonia. If I'd been pushed at the time, having seen the state of her lying in her bed at home, I'd have bet against it.

Saul breaks free as soon as he spots her, dashing straight over to her bed, and clambering right up to sit next to her. He throws his small arms around her shoulders, and gives her a kiss.

I follow on quickly, worried that she might still have an IV in, or be in some discomfort that an agile three-and-a-half-year-old chunky monkey might exacerbate.

I needn't have been concerned. Edie is hugging him back, and is blessedly free of a drip. There's still a cannula in the back of one hand, and the skin around it is purple and bruised, but other than that she looks good. Frail, as is to be expected, but good.

I gently pull Saul down from the bed, and lean forward to give Edie a kiss on the cheek. Her wrinkled skin feels like parchment, but her grip is firm as she takes hold of my hand.

'Thank you,' she whispers. 'For finding me. I'll be home in no time, and it's all down to you.'

I smile and tell her it was nothing, and settle myself in the chair next to the bed, Saul on my lap. Laura hovers at the end of the bed, apparently not quite ready to commit to actually being seated.

'How are you, my dear?' asks Edie, peering at her over her tiny specs. 'How's the precious cargo?'

Laura's hand instinctively goes to her tummy, and she manages a smile.

'All doing brilliantly, thanks, Edie. You look great. I'm so sorry I haven't been in before, but . . .'

She trails off, and Edie waves her papery hands, dismissing the comment.

'Don't be foolish,' she replies firmly. 'I wasn't fit company for the first few days anyway. Afraid I put poor Becca through the mill, acting as though it was still wartime, all kinds of nonsense! It's wonderful to see you all . . . especially you, Saul. There's a new episode online, you know.'

Saul perks up at this, stops fidgeting, and stares at her intently.

'Can we watch it? Can we? Please?'

Edie nods, and fiddles with the screen of her iPad while Laura and I exchange confused looks. Within seconds, she's found what she was apparently looking for, and hands it to Saul. I peer over his shoulder to try and see what it is that they're both so excited about.

It's something on YouTube – something that comes with some terribly cheesy music, some vivid coloured graphics, and lots of animated cartoon make-up and hair products who have tiny hands and feet and faces. They all do a little dance around one of those lightbulb framed mirrors you see in film versions of a star's dressing room, and then the lipstick speaks: 'Kick off your heels, kittens! Sit back, and prepare to be pampered . . . it's time for your session at the Beauty Parlour!'

Saul is completely enraptured as a lady with a pink beehive, wearing a Fifties style pencil skirt and a pink polka-dot blouse, starts to explain that in this episode, we'll be able to discover 'everything you ever wanted to know about the bouffant and the bob'. I can't say that I ever wanted to know very much about either, but Saul is fascinated by the flashed up pictures of Jackie Kennedy and Grace Kelly and other

Fifties stars, along with the voiceover that promises that within the next fifteen minutes, you'll learn all the secrets to recreating your own Hollywood look.

It does, of course, explain a lot – including my frequent makeovers. It also, thankfully, looks like it's going to keep Saul thoroughly entertained. I'm guessing he's been a regular viewer with Edie, all those times he's been sitting with her in the café.

'Mummy,' he says, without even taking his eyes from the screen, 'these are really nice looks. Maybe I can do one before Van comes to have tea with us . . .'

Laura's eyes widen, and she makes a 'oooh' noise as she grins at me. Edie follows up with a speculative 'Oh my!' I try not to take the bait, but can't help a very small smile.

It's been four days since Van and I kissed on the beach. Four very busy days – the usual stuff, like work and college and Saul, but also sorting Mum out in her new temporary abode, helping Sam with Little Edie while Becca's been doing shifts at the hospital, and spending a few hours with Lynnie when all three of the siblings were otherwise occupied.

Busy is good. Busy distracts me from worrying about things, like our impending trip to Bristol to meet Jason and Jo. It distracts me from the fact that my dad is AWOL, getting all mindful in the Canary Islands. It distracts me from the fact that my mum is now at the café, which makes it no longer a place of refuge. It distracts me from the fact that Christmas is almost here, and I don't feel quite ready for it.

It also distracts me from my main distraction – which is reliving that one kiss, over and over again. That wouldn't be a problem if not for the fact that even thinking about it makes me go all wobbly and weird, like I suddenly start seeing the world through a soft focus lens. I try and keep a lid on it as I go about my daily business, but I usually find my mind drifting in his direction as I lie in bed at night. Which, you know, leads to some interesting dreams.

If you'd asked me how I'd feel before it happened, I'd have expected the kiss to have made things more complicated. To be concerned about it, and what it might mean, and how it might affect our future.

In reality, something quite strange has happened – all I actually feel about it is happy. And excited. And curious as to how it would feel to do it again. To kiss him, and touch him, and lose myself in him. Basically, I think I've probably turned into a sex maniac, and that's somehow managed to override the worries about what could go wrong. And all it took was one kiss. Who'd have thought it? Not me.

'It's nothing to raise your eyebrows at, ladies,' I say, hoping none of my newfound lustiness shows in my face. 'Just a friend, coming round for some dinner.'

'He's bringing us a Christmas tree,' pipes up Saul, eyes still glued to the screen, a slight lisp on the 'r' of his words that makes him sound super-cute.

He's sounding less babyish every day now, apart from the brilliant way he gets words mixed up – the radiators are the 'radios', yellow is sometimes still 'lellow', hedgehogs are 'spikely', a combo of spiky and prickly. The rolled 'r' only comes when he's distracted or sleepy, like now. I can't believe he'll be going to school next year, my not-so-tiny baby boy.

'Oh! How lovely!' gushes Laura in response to Saul's comment, finally bringing herself to perch on the end of Edie's bed. 'Matt brought me a tree the first Christmas we were together . . . it was so macho I almost melted into a puddle! Lizzie said I was betraying the spirit of Emmeline Pankhurst by being such a pushover!'

'We're not together,' I reply hastily, hoping that Saul isn't listening any more.

Edie and Laura share knowing looks, and Edie adds: 'You just tell yourself whatever makes you happy, dear. But I'm betting the Budbury magic has worked its charm again. Give it time – you might be in the same state as Laura in a few years!'

Saul, obviously, *is* listening. He looks at me, and then looks at Laura, frowning in confusion.

'You mean she might have curly hair?' he asks innocently.

'That's exactly what I mean, young man,' replies Edie seriously. 'Now, ladies . . . fill me in on all the gossip! I don't want to lose touch with the real world, like some of the old dears in here . . .'

As Edie herself is 92, I'm slightly flummoxed by what her idea of an 'old dear' is, but Laura and I oblige. We stay for another half hour, telling her all about the party, and updating her on Tinkerbell's bird-hunting missions, telling her about my mum being added to the café staff, and describing the new range of Christmas-themed puddings that Laura's put on the menu.

Edie sounds excited about that, and declares that 'my fiancé' will love it too. I know she's asked Becca to keep an eye on her fiancé while she's been gone, and Becca, bless her, has actually gone and stood in Edie's empty house. She said it was quite spooky, and she was half expecting the ghost of the long-gone Bert to wander in from the kitchen.

By the time we leave, Saul is yawning, and so is Edie. He gives her another full-body hug, and we make our way out of the hospital.

'Phew,' says Laura, once we're safely back in her car and Saul's installed in his car seat. 'I actually feel like I can breathe again. She looks great, doesn't she? I'm glad we came – but I'm relieved to be out of there. I'm dreading the whole birth thing, you know? I was trying to persuade them to let me have the babies at home, but apparently that's a no-go, because it's twins and because I'm so . . . *geriatric!*'

She hisses the last word with about as much enthusiasm as any woman would, as she starts the car engine and navigates us out of the car park.

'Well, obviously you're not geriatric in the real world, Laura. It's just one of those terms medical people sometimes use without thinking it through. And twins can be more complicated, so I have to agree that maybe you'd be better off in hospital . . . anyway. Maybe it'll change the way you feel about them.'

'What?' she scoffs. 'Hours of agony followed by an emergency C-section? I can't imagine that's going to be a barrel of laughs!'

'No. Probably not – but there's no guarantee it'll happen like that. It'll probably all go smoothly. And after it, however it happens, you'll be a new mum. You'll have two beautiful, healthy babies, and Matt will be a dad, and Lizzie and Nate will have little brothers or sisters, and it'll be the start of a wonderful new adventure. I bet that's worth a trip to hospital, isn't it?'

She keeps her eyes on the road, but I see a slow smile creep over her face as she thinks about it.

'You know what, Katie? That's completely true. It will be worth it. And maybe I'll replace my last hideous hospital experience with something so much nicer . . . new life, rather than losing someone I love.'

'Exactly. It's so exciting.'

'Exciting, and a tiny bit terrifying . . . it always is, starting something new. Especially when you have kids to factor in. I can imagine that's how you must be feeling, about . . . Van!'

She whispers the last word, presumably for Saul's benefit – but she needn't have bothered; he's completely conked out behind us, head lolling on one side, chubby fists splayed at his sides. Like someone's taken out the batteries.

'We're just friends,' I insist, though I suspect the twitch in the side of my mouth might give me away.

'You'd make a terrible poker player,' she says, laughing. 'But if you don't want to talk about it, that's fine. Do you? Want to talk about it?'

She sounds so young and so curious and so hopeful that I'm almost tempted to crack. It would be a relief in some ways, to get it out in the open – to gossip about it like a pair of teenagers, discussing the cute boy in the year above who always winks at us outside the PE hall.

'No,' I say, firmly – because I'm not a teenager any more, and I don't even know what's happening with Van myself – never mind enough to discuss with anyone else.

She makes a disappointed 'hmmph' sound, and we make the rest of the journey without touching on the subject again – for which I am truly grateful.

By the time we reach the village, the roads are quiet, the night's frost already adding a diamanté sheen to the pavements. I see fairy lights glittering in Becca's window, and the outline of a tree in Cal and Zoe's house, and have to admit that it's beginning to feel a lot like Christmas.

Even more so when we spot Van, standing at the back of his truck, wrapped up in a body-warmer and a dark beanie hat, his gloved hands waving at us as we approach. Laura pulls up in her Picasso, but doesn't get out – can't say that I blame her.

She waves at Van, gives a beep of the horn, and then

drives off in the direction of the Rockery. I wonder briefly how they're going to sort their living arrangements when the twins arrive – at the moment Laura and her kids are in a three-bedroomed cottage called Hyacinth; Matt is in the biggest of the buildings, Black Rose. Maybe they'll merge. Maybe they'll keep it like it is. Maybe it's none of my business.

I gather a sleepy Saul in my arms and cross the road, standing in front of Van and eyeing the contents of the back of the truck.

Saul briefly wakes up, grins at Van, and passes out again. He's slobbering on my neck. One of those lovely motherhood moments.

'Your truck is taking up half the pavement,' I say, smiling to show I'm joking. 'That's very inconvenient for people with pushchairs, you know.'

'I can only apologise,' he replies, reaching out to swirl his fingers gently across Saul's tufty hair. 'But as the street is completely deserted I think we'll get away with it. I'll move it after I've unloaded; I didn't fancy carrying this beast any further than I need to. Not that I'm not strong enough or anything, before you go doubting my manliness.'

I raise my eyebrows – that's one thing I definitely don't doubt – and stagger to the front door. This boy of mine is getting very heavy now. I manage to get the key into the door and kick it open, a complex manoeuvre that mothers soon get used to – juggling a child in one arm, doing something completely different with the other. I can make tea, load laundry, and put pizza in the oven, all with one hand.

Tinkerbell rushes to greet us in a flurry of ginger fluff, then suddenly seems to remember he's a cat, and starts to play it cool instead. He winds around my ankles a few times, then heads off into the street to investigate his kingdom.

I carry Saul into the living room and lay him in the corner of the sofa. I hand him a cushion, and he hugs it to him, like I knew he would.

He's awake, but still half asleep, if you know what I mean. On any other night I'd take him straight up to bed, but I know the chances of him sleeping through Van being here, and the Christmas tree arriving, are non-existent.

Besides, I wouldn't want to deprive him of the chance to start the decorations. He's far more aware of Christmas this year, and is at the age where he totally believes in all the magic – I know that won't last forever, so I need to treasure it.

As ever, my brain does a complex analysis of when Saul last had a wee, and if he might need to go to the toilet – he's at the stage where he's definitely out of nappies, but still occasionally has an accident if he leaves it too late to ask, or is so engrossed in doing something exciting that he forgets. This can include, but is not limited to, watching cartoons, playing with his Crocodile Dentist game, eating

Mr Freeze ice pops, applying my make-up, or reading *The Gruffalo*.

I remind myself he went just before we left the hospital, so all is good. I get him a beaker of watery juice from the kitchen, and he sits sucking on it, curled up in a ball with his cushion, still recovering from the trials and tribulations of being three.

I sit myself down on the armchair, and prepare to be entertained. I hear the clank of the truck gate being lowered, and some huffing and puffing as Van hoists the tree down. The huffing and puffing develops into a full-on swear as he attempts to get it up the front step and into the house. There's a sudden pause, as he realises what he's done, then he shouts: 'Sorry for the language!'

'Do you need any help?' I shout back, kicking off my trainers and tucking my legs up beneath myself on the chair. I'm guessing he'll say no.

'Nope, I'm fine . . .' he yells. 'Or at least I will be, once I get this . . . *flipping* thing through the door!'

Eventually, he makes it, and emerges into the living room with the tree trunk over his shoulder, and the green pine-needle laden branches drooping all around him. His face peers out, like he's in a jungle filming a wildlife video, and he grins in victory.

'Where do you want it?' he asks, trying to hide the fact that he's slightly out of breath.

'In the corner . . . or maybe by the window . . . oh, I

267

really can't make my mind up. Can we try it in a few places and see which looks best?'

He stares at me from behind the foliage, eyes narrowed, until I crack: 'Just kidding. Over in the corner. Thank you.'

He nods, and carries the tree to the spot I point at. He's already attached a kind of wooden disc at the bottom for it to stand up on, and he fluffs the branches out once it's stable.

'What do you think?' he asks, standing back, wiping sweat from his forehead.

'It's not as big as I thought it would be . . .' I say, actually delighted at that – I'd expected him to bring the biggest he could find, which would have been a mistake, as our house is only small.

'I bet you say that to all the boys,' he replies, laughing. 'Have you no respect for the fragile male ego?'

'Well, perhaps I should rephrase that. What I meant was, it's not too big, and not too small, and not too bushy, and not too sparse. It's perfect. It's the kind of tree Goldilocks would have chosen – exactly right. Thank you. It's really kind of you.'

He nods, once, and looks pleased, before noticing Saul curled up on the sofa, back asleep. I gently take the juice beaker from his hands and put it down on the table. He murmurs but doesn't open his eyes.

'What shall we do about the little man?' he asks quietly. 'Let him be, or wake him up with a party popper?'

'Let him be for twenty minutes. We'll wake him up to do the decorating in a bit. He'll be cranky if he needs a nap, and it'll give me time to start dinner, and you to . . . I don't know. Whatever it is that fragile male egos need to do.'

'In my case, move my truck so I don't inconvenience any passing pushchairs. But before I do that, just nip into the hallway for a minute, I've got something for you.'

I tear my gaze away from admiring the tree, and tiptoe out of the living room door behind him. I'm still pondering how much tinsel we're going to need when he takes hold of my waist, pushes me back against the wall, and kisses me. I use one foot to kick the door closed in case Saul wakes up, then wrap my arms around his neck and kiss him back.

It's another absolute powerhouse of a kiss, and definitely proves the first one on the beach wasn't a fluke. I let my hands explore the bulk of his shoulders, the firm outline of his arms, drifting down to his side and slipping my fingers beneath his T-shirt. He's pressed up hard against me, and the touch of his skin beneath my hands is completely intoxicating.

His lips move to the side of my neck, kissing their way down to my collarbone, and I groan as I feel his hands pull my hips even closer to his. I'm on the verge of losing what little self-control I have by this point, and am wondering how it would feel to wrap my legs around his waist and get even closer.

When Van puts his hands on the wall either side of my face and pushes away a few inches, my first thought is, *please bring back the nice thing*. The second is, *pretty please bring back the nice thing*. But my third, to be fair, is, *my son is sleeping in the next room and could walk through at any minute*.

Van takes in my disappointed expression, the flush I can feel creeping over my cheeks, and smiles. He leans his forehead forward so it touches mine, and says: 'I didn't want to stop either. I promise. Don't look so crestfallen. But . . .'

'Yeah. I know. But. I'm pretty sure we could tell Saul we were playing a game, but he'd just tell everyone else all about it next time we're in the café. This is tricky, isn't it? Not that I really know what this is.'

He nuzzles my neck for a few seconds before replying: 'Me neither. But I like it. I like you. And I don't want to rush it – it took me months to even persuade you to come to the pub. I know it's complicated. I know you'll want to take things slowly, and that's fine with me.'

I drape my arms around his waist, and close the small gap he's opened up between our bodies. I can feel that he's still very, very interested in the physical aspects of this, and it makes me grin. It's been a long time since I had that kind of effect on a man, and I can't deny it feels good. Especially as I feel exactly the same.

I duck from beneath his arms and sit on the stairs, patting them to invite him to join me. He tugs his rumpled

T-shirt into shape and sits by my side, one arm thrown across my shoulders.

'Thing is,' I say, laying my hand on his thigh and telling it to behave itself, 'that at least part of this is very simple. The sex part. As in, I want to have sex. With you.'

He jolts very slightly, and I realise I've shocked him. To be honest, I've shocked myself as well.

'Look,' I say quietly – this is not the kind of conversation I want Saul overhearing – 'I know there are all sorts of complications. Both of us are at this weird stage of our lives where everything seems to revolve around other people. For me, it's Saul mainly, but also my parents right now. For you, obviously, Lynnie's needs come first.'

'Go on,' he says, nudging me. 'I'm intrigued.'

'Well, despite all of that, I still can't stop thinking about you. Specifically, about kissing you. And touching you. And being . . . with you.'

I glance up at his face, and see that he's grimacing slightly – which isn't the reaction I'd anticipated.

'Sorry,' he says, when he notices me looking. 'It's just that I'm a bloke. A bloke who's just kissed a hot woman. And now you're saying things like this, and it's making me . . . uncomfortable again, if you get my drift.'

I do indeed get his drift. I can pretty much see his drift as well, which is both amusing and gratifying.

'So,' he continues. 'You're saying you want this to . . . progress?'

'Yes. I do. But even as I say it, I'm a bit worried about it. Because it might get messy. It might get complicated. We might screw everything up, and neither of us has time for drama. I have to be totally honest with you, Van – I'm not looking for a big heavy relationship. I don't have the time or the energy or the courage. That's why it took me so long to go to the pub with you – maybe I always had a sneaky suspicion that we'd end up like this.'

'With me in agony on your bottom step?'

'Not precisely, no . . . sorry about that. But I knew I found you attractive, and I was worried about where it might lead.'

'And now you're not? Worried?'

I sigh and bite my lip, struggling to find the right words to express how I feel – mainly because I don't even know.

'I am about some aspects of it. But I'm also . . . ready. More than ready. For the physical side of it, anyway. I know it's complicated. Everything is – and I'm sick to death of complicated. But the way I feel when you kiss me? That's the only time things feel simple.'

'So,' he replies, a smile in his voice, 'the obvious solution is that I should just kiss you twenty-four hours a day?'

'That's a nice idea,' I say. Because it is. 'But I don't think it's practical. Might cause a few issues at work.'

He nods, and I see him turning all of this over in his mind. I'm hoping he has some answers for me, but I'm not sure any of this makes sense to me any more.

'I'm just trying to decide,' he eventually says, 'whether I feel insulted at being used as your sex toy, worried about breaking your heart, or excited about the prospect of seeing you naked. I've got to say, option number three keeps intruding on the other two – but the other two do matter.

'As I've said, I like you. I'm not getting down on one knee and proposing or anything, but I like you enough to think this might be more than sex. More than just physical. I enjoy your company, and feel relaxed when I'm with you, and see you as a friend. A friend I fancy. I'm not quite sure how all of that fits in with your version of things?'

'Me neither,' I reply, shaking my head and laughing. 'And I must warn you, I usually overthink things – so it's entirely possible that I'm saying one thing now, and then I'll feel differently later. It's a rollercoaster. You're so lucky to have me in your life to confuse you.'

He tugs me up against him, and kisses the top of my head.

'I am lucky,' he says. 'And horny. And yeah, now very confused. I was all set for a slow burn here, just to feel things out and see how we worked through it. Now you've gone and messed up the masterplan.'

'My specialist subject,' I say, leaning my head against his chest. 'Anyway – I don't suppose it's something we need to decide right now. As my son is asleep in the next room, this is about as sexy as it's going to get tonight. And I don't know when that will change – I share my house with a curious toddler who already thinks you're God's gift to the planet and follows you everywhere, and you share a cottage with your elderly mother and your sisters. We're not exactly rocking it on the *sexy night in* front, are we?'

'I suppose not – not yet at least. Though I had a chat with Tom about that the other day. He found me on the floor in a sleeping bag. Auburn was being a nightmare – she was all hyper because she's helping Tom out with these interviews to find his Star Lord. I couldn't face another night in a single bed in a room with her, and my legs are wrecked from being crammed on a too-short sofa, so I ended up on the floor. As you say, not sexy. So Tom offered to lend me his camper van.'

'His camper van? Doesn't he live at Briarwood? Aren't there enough rooms there for him?'

'He does have rooms at Briarwood, and a flat in London and, knowing Tom, a bolt-hole on the moon as well – but he also has this really nice, retro VW van he used when he first moved here. It's parked up in the woods near Briarwood.'

'Oh. So would you move there?' I ask, frowning. It's very possible the excitement of the last few minutes has blown a brain circuit.

'No. It's on wheels, see? It's mobile. He'll drive it to the cottage and we can park it up on the drive, so I'm still around, but everyone gets a bit more privacy.'

'I'm not convinced that's much better. I'd feel a bit . . .

weird, right outside your cottage. What if your mum heard us?'

'How loud are you planning on getting?'

'I don't know . . . you tell me!'

We grin at each other, and it feels good. Natural. Easy. I haven't flirted for many years, and I'm enjoying it.

'Well, we'll have to wait and see,' he replies. 'But again, I refer you to the fact that it's on wheels. The world's our lobster.'

I nod, and roll that around in my mind. Okay, so it's hardly a mini-break to Paris – but the idea of spending a night with Van in a camper, somewhere secluded and quiet and beautiful, isn't exactly repellent. And with my mum here at the moment, I could probably even make it happen, if she agreed to have Saul for a sleepover.

Crikey. I'm starting to think this might even happen. And I'm even starting to think I might go for it.

I hear muffled movement from the other room, the sound of small feet padding around, and then the ever-so-gentle screech of 'MUMMY!!! Come and look at our tree! It's giant-gantic!'

It might happen, for sure. *But not*, I think, standing to my feet and walking back into the living room, *tonight*.

# Chapter 25

I'm not especially keen on reptiles, but at least it's warm in here. Outside, it's bitterly cold, and snow is forecast for later today.

I've dragged out the snakes and geckos and giant tortoises for as long as I can, and Saul's attention is waning. He wants to see something more exciting, like the gorillas or the lions or the little hippos. Or his dad – one of the lesser known exhibits at Bristol Zoo.

Frankly, I'm nervous, and would probably rather walk into the lion enclosure than stroll across to the café, where we're due to meet Jason and Jo. I've played it as casually as possible with Saul, trying to strike the balance between this being a real treat, and it not being too big a deal. He knows his dad lives in Scotland, which he talks about as though it's an incredibly exotic place, and he knows his dad loves him and always sends him presents and cards.

He's spoken to him on the phone as well, on his last birthday, but he hasn't actually seen him since a time he was too small to even remember.

Saul actually seems very cool about it all, accepting it without too many questions and with an open-hearted sense of anticipation that reassures me I'm doing the right thing. The right thing for him, anyway.

Because while Saul might be okay with today's meeting, I'm basically pooing my pants. It's all very, very strange.

We came to Bristol last night, and stayed in my parents' house. That in itself was weird and a bit melancholy. Mum is down in Budbury, and Dad is due home from Tenerife very soon, and the home I grew up in felt oddly quiet and empty without them.

Saul enjoyed it, laughing at the photos of me on the wall in frames: me with pigtails and missing front teeth; me in my ballet outfit after a dance performance; me on the beach on a family holiday to Cornwall. No child ever easily imagines their own parents as young, do they? Even when we're adults, and technically know they were, once, tiny little humans – it still seems unlikely.

Saul thinks the photos are hilarious. I on the other hand feel sad when I look at them. Sad because I'm always on my own – no brothers and sisters, no playmates, not even any happy, smiling family group shots.

For me, they're a reminder of lonely times. A reminder of the chaos around me that the lens never quite caught. The night of that dance recital, Mum locked Dad out of the house because he'd turned up with the smell of beer on his breath.

After the triumph of the show itself – I must have been about eight, I suppose – I recall the rest of the night being fraught with drama, Dad banging on the door and Mum screaming at him from the bedroom window. That might have been the night one of the neighbours actually called the police, I don't know – they all fade into one big row with the passing of time.

And the family holiday in Cornwall was one of the worst weeks of my life – all three of us crammed into a two-bedroomed caravan on a park near Bude. They'd drink too much in the leisure club where we'd watch the entertainment staff sing hits of the Seventies, and a giant bear mascot prowled around scaring the kids. After the drink, there'd be the fighting – and the walls of a caravan are even thinner than the walls of a house.

I'm not sure it was a good idea, going back there. But again, Saul seemed happy with the arrangement, and that's what matters. He got to sleep in my old bedroom, and I showed him pictures of my nan and told him all about her, and I took him to the little play park nearby where I'd gone as a child myself.

And now we're here. In the zoo. Approximately five minutes away from meeting my ex and his new wife and soon-to-be mother of Saul's baby brother or sister. I tell myself it's a good thing. That it's important for Saul to feel good about his relationship with them. That maybe having a sibling will make his childhood a lot less lonely than mine, because it seems unlikely I'll ever be providing him with one.

I can't even find it in myself to commit to a relationship, never mind have a baby. I do wonder sometimes if something inside me is simply broken, and I'll never be able to fix it. Having Van in my life should feel wonderful – and when I'm with him, it usually does.

But when I'm away from him, like now, it all feels different. It feels frightening and anxiety-inducing and probably not worth the risk. I turn into a big fat coward, basically. Poor Van. He deserves better. Like the blonde one from Abba, or at the very least a woman who doesn't blow hot and cold like a faulty car heater.

I glance at my watch, and tell Saul it's time to go.

'Will my daddy be there now?' he asks, scurrying along so fast he's taking two steps to every one of mine as we leave the reptile house and emerge into an arctic blast of wind that makes my eyes water.

I quickly bend down to fasten up Saul's coat and tug his bobble hat back down over his ears, and nod.

'He will,' I reply, trying to put some much-needed enthusiasm into my voice. 'Isn't that exciting?'

'It is,' he replies, gripping my hand with his mittened fingers. 'He's come all the way from a different country. Do they have lions in Scotland? And will Daddy be able to make a lion noise? And will the lady called Jo speak in a different language because she's from Scotland?'

I answer all his rapid-fire questions as well as I can – only in zoos, definitely, and no – as we make the short walk to the café. We pause in the entrance, and I take off his hat and unbutton his coat again. It's an exciting life, looking after a small person. A rollercoaster of indoor-outdoor clothing logistics.

I scan the room, filled with shivering refugees from the icy weather, looking for them. Maybe, just a tiny bit, hoping they haven't turned up.

Of course, they have – I spot Jason easily, even after all this time. He's very tall, even sitting down. The woman with him is almost the same height, and it occurs to me that their child is going to inherit some mighty genetics.

Jason waves hesitantly, and I suspect he's just as nervous as I am. Maybe he was secretly hoping we wouldn't turn up as well.

'Is that him? Is that my daddy?' Saul asks, when I wave back. I nod and smile, and feel a creaking sensation inside me, like a rotten floorboard being stepped on.

We walk over to their table, and as we approach, Jason never takes his eyes off Saul. Saul, who is keen to run towards them, and possibly the muffins they have on a plate. I let go of his hand, and he dashes the last few feet, the mittens on strings streaking behind him.

He stops right in front of Jason, who crouches down to be on the same level as him, and smiles at him. He plays it just right – not grabbing hold of him and freaking him out, not showing his own tension, just talking to him in a soft voice, saying how lovely it is to see him and asking what animals he wants to see and wondering if he prefers chocolate or blueberry muffins.

He hasn't changed that much, in the last few years. He looks a little leaner, maybe, and his hair is a bit longer. Jo, sitting beside him, glances up at me and smiles, giving me her own little wave. I linger a few steps away, not really sure of how to behave. There aren't really any rule books for this kind of situation, and I'm sure we're all scared of getting it wrong.

Luckily, we have a talkative toddler with us – possibly the world's best ice-breaker.

'I like blueberry,' Saul says, perching himself on the seat next to Jason and chattering away as though all of this is completely normal. 'Laura makes blueberry cake for me at the café.'

'Does she? I bet it's yummy,' replies Jason, looking on as Saul tears off his coat and grabs hold of a muffin. He's going to perform his usual trick of reducing one cake to a billion small pieces, I know – but I don't suppose it matters.

'It is. The yummiest. You should come and taste it.'

'Maybe I will,' says Jason, glancing at me over Saul's head. I finally make the move to sit down, and he nods at me. 'Saul, this lady here is Jo.'

'Hi, Saul!' she says brightly. I know she's a primary school teacher, and it shows in her voice – the kind of voice that kids automatically respond to; that you can imagine leading an assembly or singing the times tables. 'It's really nice to meet you. Blueberry's my favourite too.'

Saul squints at her slightly, while he chews his first mouthful. His fingers are working on the rest.

'You sound funny,' he eventually says. 'Mummy said you wouldn't speak different.'

'I said she wouldn't speak a different language, Saul,' I add, explaining. 'Not that she wouldn't sound different. People who come from different parts of the world have different accents. Like Laura is from Manchester and she sounds different to your nan, who's from Bristol.'

He chews this over as thoroughly as his muffin and decides it makes sense.

'Did you have to come on an aeroplane?' he asks, perking up again. He's obsessed with going on an aeroplane at the moment, and decided after watching a film called *Monsters vs Aliens* that he wants to be an astronaut when he grows up, so he can make friends with little green men.

'Not this time, no,' replies Jo, automatically sweeping some of the crumbs from the table in a way that suggests she's done it many times before. 'We came in the car, but it took us two days.'

'Did you sleep in the car?' Saul asks, frowning.

'No, we stayed overnight in a hotel on the way. A nice one with a swimming pool that had pancakes for breakfast.'

'I like pancakes,' he concedes. 'Laura makes those too. Mummy does as well, but Laura's are nicer.'

I raise my eyebrows and let out a small laugh. I can't argue that point, and it's good that he's honest, after all.

Saul stops destroying his muffin, and looks at the map of the zoo that they have spread out on part of the table. Jason uses his finger to point out where we are, and where the reptile house is, and where some of the other animals are.

'Do you know a lot of animal noises, Daddy?' he asks earnestly. It's the first time he's addressed him like that, and I see a quick and sudden sheen of tears in Jason's eyes. I bite my lip, because I feel a bit like crying too. I know my reasons for agreeing to this were sound, but I'm simply not a big enough human being to not feel threatened by it. I need to toughen up.

'Yes. It's one of my best things,' answers Jason seriously. 'What do you want to hear?'

The two of them spend the next few minutes challenging each other to recognise various roars, squeaks and howls. I go to get myself a coffee to give them a bit of space, and to give myself a breather. I kind of wish there was a brandy in it.

By the time I come back, Saul is on his feet, doing that mad little bouncing-on-the-spot thing he does when he's excited about something.

'Mummy, can I go and see the gorillas with Daddy? We

both want to see if they answer us when we make our gorilla noises! Please please please!'

Jason's eyes meet mine across the table, and I'm so nervous I slosh my coffee into the saucer. The gorillas are literally only minutes away. He's not asking for custody, he's asking for ten minutes. It's normal, it's natural, and it's nothing to get choked up about. I gulp in air, and manage to nod.

'Of course you can,' I say, aiming for relaxed. 'Just make sure you put your coat and hat back on. Say hello to the gorillas for me.'

Jason mouths the words 'thank you' at me, and the two disappear off in a flurry of scarves and excitement. I see Saul slip his hand into Jason's, and feel a mix of relief and desperation. He'll be back before I know it, but he still takes a tiny piece of me with him.

'He's gorgeous,' says Jo, as I sit down opposite her. Her accent doesn't sound Glaswegian to my admittedly untrained ear. It's soft, and lilting and gentle.

'He is, isn't he?' I reply, smiling as best as I can.

'He'll be starting school next year, will he?'

'Yes. The local primary. He can already read some words and write his name, as long as you have a liberal stance on which way round the letter "S" should face.'

'Well he'll be off to a flying start then. I teach P1, which is like reception in England, and I can tell he won't have any problems at all – I bet he'll be more than ready.'

I grimace as I sip scalding hot coffee, and reply: 'I hope so. I'm not sure how ready I am, though.'

'That's always the way,' she replies, using a napkin to clear up the coffee I've now spilled. 'The kids come through the gate full of excitement, and the mums are weeping in the playground.'

I nod, unable to think of a single thing to say. It's like my brain has gone completely blank, and my tongue has superglued itself to the roof of my mouth.

'This must be weird for you,' she says eventually.

'Um . . . yes. But I think it's probably weird for everybody, apart from Saul, apparently.'

'That'll be down to you, raising a happy and confident little person. Look . . . it doesn't have to be weird. I can only imagine how you must be feeling, us turning up, a baby on the way, suddenly part of Saul's life. All I can say is that we're genuine – both of us – about wanting to get to know Saul better. You're his mum, and obviously a good one – but one day before too long, he'll have a brother, and it would be great for them to know each other.'

I stare at her, my eyes flickering to her stomach against my will. She's wearing a thick jumper, so I can't tell if she's showing or not yet. I remember those days – the combination of excitement and terror. Or maybe, in her case, there is no terror – she's older than I was, and obviously happy in her marriage, and she teaches kids for a living. Maybe she doesn't just look like Wonder Woman. Maybe she is Wonder Woman.

'Yes, it would,' is all I can manage. 'It's a boy?'

Her hand goes to her tummy, and she grins.

'At least that's what they think, yes. So thank you – for this. For seeing us. It means the world to Jason, and to me. He told me, you know . . . what happened between you. All of it.'

For some reason, I cringe as she says this. I don't know why. I have nothing to be ashamed of, and it's only natural that he has. Proof that they have a much better functioning relationship than Jason and I ever did. But I still feel somehow exposed – like this woman knowing so much about one of the darkest times in my life makes me somehow vulnerable.

'Oh. Okay,' I murmur, still apparently in shut-down mode.

'And you should know, it changed him. He probably won't tell you all of this, because he's a man. But it changed him. He's not touched a drop of alcohol since that day, and he went to counselling. Still does, every now and then. He hated what he'd done, and that's probably why he left Bristol. But . . . well, I'm sure you know that.'

I nod, and avoid her eyes. She has vivid blue eyes that I suspect can see right into my soul.

'I know. We . . . brought out the worst in each other. It's why I moved as well. But you two . . . you seem to bring out the best in each other.'

She beams at me, and passes me another napkin. I'm

really not managing very well with this whole advance level coffee-drinking business at all.

'We do, I hope. I just wanted you to know that I understand. And that we won't be putting any pressure on you, or on Saul – we just want to know him. To be part of his life in any way that works for all of us.'

I know she means well. I know she means every word she says. I even know she's right.

But that still doesn't take away the fear. The fear that bit by bit, I'm falling to pieces. That all the control I've worked so hard for is crumbling. That everything is about to change, and I don't want it to. That I want to take Saul, and possibly Tinkerbell, and run as far away as we all can.

That, I realise, is ridiculous. It's an outdated impulse, a knee-jerk response to a perceived threat. Something I need to manage or analyse or possibly just ignore until it goes away.

I nod firmly, and force myself to look up from the napkin-strewn table and meet her eyes.

'Okay,' I say simply. One word. A lifetime of meaning.

# Chapter 26

I get three calls from Van during the journey home, and I ignore all of them. Then he texts me, asking if I want a lift from the train station in Applechurch. Then I turn my phone off, and slam it into my bag. I can't face anyone right now – I need some space to process all of this.

The rest of our visit with Jason and Jo passed well enough. Nobody cried, even me. Saul was happy to see them, but happy to say goodbye as well. Jason bought him a giant stuffed toy gorilla from the gift shop, and it takes up its own seat on the train. Saul drifts in and out of sleep all the way home, tired out from all the excitement and walking. He cuddles up on my lap on the bus for the last part of the journey, and is perfectly content to collapse in a heap on the sofa when we finally get home.

He's watching *The Jungle Book*, the old cartoon version. The gorilla next to him, Tinkerbell curled in a ball by the toy's side. The three musketeers.

Once he's settled, I wander into the kitchen and make myself a cup of tea. It takes a lot longer than it should, due to my impaired mental state. First I put the kettle on to boil without any water in it. Then I put the water in, but forget to switch it on. Then I put both coffee granules and a tea bag in the same mug. Then I add a lovely dollop of mayonnaise to the tea instead of milk. I'm really not feeling like myself.

It's not that late – just after 8 p.m. – but it's pitch black outside. The snow is coming down in gentle flurries, and I'm grateful for the warmth and cosiness of our little house. The Christmas tree lights are switched on, a blaze of yellow sparkles, and the sound of the movie fills the house. I'm here. Saul's here. We're safe. The bear necessities of life.

I lean back against the kitchen counter, and sip the tea I've finally managed to make. I look through to the other room, at Saul with his juice, and the gorilla and the cat, and realise how exhausted I am. Not just by the journey, but by everything.

My parents. Jason and Jo. Van. The trip down memory lane in Bristol. The complications of everybody else's lives – Lynnie, and Edie, and Laura. Love them as I do, they all add extra layers of mess to my life – a life that used to be much tidier.

It used to be me and Saul. Saul and me. It was straight-forward and simple and all very, very manageable. Yes, sometimes I was lonely – but, to use a comparison that would probably fit if I could drive, I was like the only car on a secluded country lane, going at my own pace, never worrying that someone might crash into me if I braked too suddenly.

Now I feel like I'm driving on a crowded multi-lane motorway at rush hour. Everybody seems to want to be part of my life. Everyone seems to want something from me.

Even as I think that, I know it sounds awful. I've gained far more than I've lost, and usually I like the hustle and bustle of my life here. But right now, when I'm physically and mentally wiped out, it all feels like too much. Too many people. Too many complications. Too many demands. I just need to shut it all down for a while. Get Saul settled in bed, and follow right behind him. Get some sleep. Clear my mind. I'm sure everything will feel different in the morning.

I finish my tea and rinse the cup out in the sink, deciding that there's no time like the present. So what if I go to bed at 8 p.m.? There's no one around to judge.

I walk through into the living room, and scratch Tinkerbell behind the ears, making him purr. I scratch the gorilla behind the ears as well, but luckily he doesn't.

'Ready for bed, kiddo?' I say, looking down at Saul. He's staring at the TV screen as Bagheera and Baloo discuss Mowgli's future, but his eyes are glassy and tired. He's basically already asleep, he just doesn't know it yet.

I can sense an argument coming on, and steel myself for it by putting my hands on my hips – the no-nonsense-mummy stance. He stares at me and rubs his eyes with screwed-up fists, opening his mouth to say no. He doesn't throw many tantrums, but I can feel this one in the air – mainly because he's exhausted.

We're interrupted from escalating our minor disagreement by a knock at the door. I stand there, hands still on my hips, and really want to swear out loud. Saul stares at me, then back at the TV.

'You'd better answer the door, Mummy,' he says, grabbing hold of his gorilla and hugging it tight. I have been dismissed, it seems.

The knock comes again, and I roll my eyes in a very mature fashion. Just when I'd really like the whole world to piss right off, it decides to come and visit.

I stomp to the door, trying to get a hold of my bad mood, and swing it open.

Van is outside, leaning against the wall, peering at me as I finally materialise. He's wearing what looks like nineteen layers of clothing and his beanie, dusted with snow. His breath is gusting into clouds on the cold night air, and he looks freezing. I feel the usual little skitterry-skit when I see him, but even that is overruled by the fact that I don't want to talk to him. Not that it's personal – I don't want to talk to anyone.

'Hey,' he says, jamming his hands into the pockets of his body-warmer. 'You okay? How did today go? I tried calling but I couldn't get through . . .'

'It was fine,' I say, knowing I should invite him in but not really having the energy to follow through. 'There was something wrong with my phone.'

He takes in my positioning, the arms I realise I have crossed defensively across my chest, and the fact that I'm not budging, even though I'm letting the cold in. His eye twitches slightly, and his mouth twists into an almost-but-not-quite-amused grin.

'You're lying, aren't you? You never usually lie.'

I sigh, and admit: 'Yeah. I am. There's nothing wrong with my phone. Auburn said I needed to start telling fibs so I could be socially acceptable . . .'

'Ha!' he scoffs, looking at me intensely, as though he's trying to figure out what's wrong. 'Auburn is in no position to tell anybody how to be more socially acceptable. And you don't need to lie to me, Katie.'

'Don't I, though?' I ask, letting out a big breath from all the tension. 'I wouldn't have done, not so long ago. But now I'm worried about hurting your feelings, or saying the wrong thing. So here I am. Lying.'

'Well, stop lying. Tell me the truth.'

'The truth? Okay. Basically, Van, I'm exhausted. It's been a big day. It's been a big month. All I want to do is curl up in a ball in bed on my own and hope tomorrow's different. I can't deal with . . . people right now. Any of them.'

He doesn't reply for a while, and I see him trying to control what may very well be the first flash of anger I've ever seen from him. What can I say? I've still got the magic.

He backs off a few steps, and holds his hands up in the air in a gesture of surrender.

'No problem,' he says, his voice controlled. 'I understand. I'm sorry to have crowded you. And don't worry about hurting my feelings, Katie – I'm a big boy. I can handle it. You get some rest, and I'll see you soon.'

He doesn't give me the chance to reply, just turns on his heel and jogs over the road to his parked truck.

I feel terrible, as soon as he walks away, and know I should shout him back. Apologise. Explain. Invite him in. I try to, I really do – but all that comes out of my mouth is a whisper, his name murmured so quietly that even I can't hear it. I go back inside and close the door behind me, leaning back against it and shaking my head.

I listen to the sound of his engine starting up, and hear a slight squeal of tyres as he pulls away a lot faster than he usually does. Shit. I've been a complete cow to someone who really didn't deserve it.

I go back to the kitchen and get my phone out of my bag. I decide I'll bite the bullet and text him right away. Say I'm sorry and offer to meet him for a drink tomorrow after work. I really do need a night on my own – but there are far nicer ways of saying it. It's not like he wouldn't have understood – I just snapped at him without giving him the chance to.

All the fight's gone out of Saul now, and he's lying limp

and splayed across the sofa, one hand caressing the gorilla's furry head as he tries to stay awake. I watch him, my precious little boy, as I wait for my phone to switch back on.

When it does, I see that I have three new text messages. I'm ashamed of the way I behaved with Van, and don't want to read anything that's going to make me feel even worse.

I'm about to start tapping away on the keys when there's another knock at the door. I sigh and put the phone down. Maybe he's come back, I think. Maybe he's so annoyed with me, he's come to give me a piece of his mind. Maybe we'll end up screaming at each other on the doorstep – fast forwarding right past the honeymoon stage and into more familiar relationship territory. For me, at least.

Wearily, I trudge back through the living room and into the hallway. I take a deep breath, and open the door.

Waiting outside, complete with an uncharacteristic suntan and wearing a weird shirt with a mandarin collar, is my dad.

'Hi, love,' he says, sounding pretty exhausted himself. 'I've been doing some thinking, and I've decided you're right. I need to sort this out. Is your mother in?'

# Chapter 27

'No, she's not . . . come in, Dad. But be quiet, Saul's just gone to sleep and I'm going to try and put him down for the night.'

I feel exhausted in every way possible. If I have a tether, I think I've just reached the end of it. I tiptoe into the living room, and manage to hoist Saul up into my arms without really waking him.

It always amazes me how kids can sleep through things – when we were potty training, I used to be able to do the same late at night. I'd hold him on the loo on his special make-the-seat-smaller device, and he'd do his business, all the while his head lolling and his eyes closed.

I do the same tonight, before carrying him through to my bed. Looks like I've got a guest for the evening, and Saul is back to sleepovers.

I tuck him under the covers, and pause for a minute, stroking back his hair and giving his smooth forehead a kiss. He looks so peaceful when he's asleep, and I feel a wave of love wash over me. This, I remind myself, is what life is all about – the purity of the way this little person makes me feel. All the rest of the complications can bugger off.

I call into the bathroom to splash cold water on my face in an attempt to wake myself up, and go back downstairs with as much of a smile as I can muster.

I find Dad in the kitchen, making tea, looking weirdly exotic with his trendy shirt and his tan.

'Want a cuppa, love?' he asks, holding up a mug and waving it at me. I nod, and get the milk out of the fridge for him.

'What's with the new look, Dad?' I ask, watching as he stirs the tea bag. He likes his tea strong, my dad, and always spends a good minute pressing the tea bag against the side of the cup with a spoon until every last drop of flavour's been squeezed out.

'Oh . . . you mean the shirt? It was a gift from Miguel, who was leading our course. We all got them, in different colours. To match our auras.'

He at least has the good grace to look a bit embarrassed by that last sentence, which makes me laugh. They're at this weird stage in their lives, my parents – both of them changing; like they're starting to emerge from cocoons as different people.

'What's your aura like, then?' I ask, taking the tea he offers and gesturing for him to follow me through to the living room.

He glances down at the shirt and replies: 'Apparently, it's turquoise.'

I gaze at the sofa with something approaching adoration, put my tea on the table, and immediately collapse down onto its lovely squishy softness. I'm next to the gorilla, and remind myself to take it upstairs when I finally get to bed – maybe Saul can practise Beauty Parlour on it in the morning. Tinkerbell has disappeared off somewhere, which he tends to do when he meets new people – he's probably watching us from a corner, doing a feline risk assessment.

Dad sits in the armchair, and we're both silent for a moment. I'm too tired to start a conversation, and he doesn't look too perky himself.

'I did text you, honest. I dropped my stuff at home and drove straight down,' he says eventually. 'Were you there? While I was gone?'

'Yeah, I stayed there last night,' I reply, wondering how he knew.

'Right. Makes sense. Saul left me a picture on the fridge door – looked like a penguin, but could have been a panda. Maybe in space, there were stars all around it.'

'That sounds about right – he's currently obsessed with both animals and becoming an astronaut. We were . . . there because we met Jason. And his wife, Jo. She's having a baby.'

Dad leans forward in the chair, and looks me over, as though checking for damage.

'How was that? Was it all right?' he asks. He sounds genuinely concerned, and for a moment I let myself bask in it. No matter what problems I had growing up, he's still my dad – and every now and then, it's nice to still feel like a little girl.

'It was fine. Nice for Saul. Jason seems good. He's given up booze, sees a therapist – right up your street, Dad. Jo's lovely too. Everyone was on their very best behaviour. I'm just . . . well, I'm secretly glad they live so far away. Probably makes me a terrible person, doesn't it?'

'Course not, love. It's completely natural. You've done a great job with Saul on your own – better than me and your mum did together. I know you'll always do what's right for him.'

I nod, and hope he's right. I'm feeling a bit off kilter tonight, and don't trust myself quite as much as I should. I was mean to Van, and that's still bothering me.

'So, where's your mother, then?' he asks, looking around the room, a bit like he expects her to leap out of a cupboard dressed as a pantomime villain.

'She's moved out. Got herself a new job and a new place.'

His eyebrows shoot up into his forehead, and he seems temporarily thrown by the whole idea.

'What did you expect, Dad?' I ask, half amused by his reaction, half annoyed on Mum's behalf. 'Did you think she'd be here waiting for you, like a good little woman, all apologetic and submissive?'

'God, no,' he says quickly, shaking his head. 'I'd never expect that of your mother! But the way you were talking about her last time, it seemed like she wasn't doing so well.'

'People change, don't they?' I say, pointing a finger at him. 'When you least expect it. They run off with the ice cream woman, and start wearing turquoise shirts, and going on mindfulness retreats.'

'Fair point,' he concedes, grinning. 'And . . . well, I'm happy for her, then. I think we both needed to realise there was a life out there for us that didn't involve battle stations at the breakfast table. I just got there a bit earlier, that's all. What's she doing, then?'

'She's working at the café – you know, the one I told you about? She's living there as well. One of the staff is pregnant and they needed an extra pair of hands. There's a flat she's using. She's . . . happy about it. She feels useful again. So, lovely as it is to see you, Dad, I have to ask – why are you here? Are you going to mess it all up?'

'No, love, I'm not. I just thought I owed it to her to talk about everything. Explain about Fiona. Whatever our faults, we loved each other once. We built a life together. We've been married for a long time, even though if we're honest most of it fell into the "worse" category, not the "better". And we had you – we did at least one thing right.'

He sounds so genuine when he says that, so emotional, that it makes me realise that I'm his Saul. I might be all grown up, with a child of my own, but to him, I'm the equivalent of that magical little boy I was gazing at in his sleep.

I stand up, yawning, and walk over to him to give him a hug. He looks like he needs a hug.

'All right, Dad. Look, I'm knackered. I need to go to bed. Saul's in with me, so you can take his room. We'll sort it all out in the morning, okay?'

'Okay, Katie,' he says, holding on to the hug for as long as he can. 'And I promise, I won't mess anything up.'

*Those*, I think, as I trudge up the stairs yet again, *sound suspiciously like famous last words.*

# Chapter 28

I leave Dad in bed the next morning, despite the fact that Saul is desperate to see him. In particular, he wants to jump on his head making gorilla noises.

I channel his enthusiasm away from that concept, by telling him he can take his toy gorilla – now named Marmaduke for some unfathomable reason – into pre-school, along with the map of the zoo we brought home as a keepsake.

'And,' he says excitedly as we make our way on the bus, 'I can tell them about my daddy too!'

*Great*, I think, gritting my teeth. I will now officially be the Jeremy Kyle mother of Applechurch pre-school. Just another day in paradise.

I promise Saul that his granddad will still be there when he gets home, and try not to think about the alternative – that he goes to the café unannounced, Mum skewers him with one of Laura's posh chopping knives, and disposes of the evidence by feeding his body into the smoothie blender.

They're grown-ups, I tell myself. I can't control them or

their lives, and I shouldn't even want to. I have enough problems of my own.

I called Van early this morning, because I know he's always up at the crack of dawn, but he didn't answer. It feels weird, being potentially at odds with Van. It throws everything off balance, and I hate it. I hate the fact that I'm worried about him, I hate the fact that I might not even see him for days to sort this out, and I hate the fact that he's not answering his phone.

The fact that I did exactly the same to him the day before does very little to make me feel better about the situation.

I try and put it out of my mind and concentrate on what I can do – go to work, after getting Saul safely dropped off at nursery. It's his last few days in before they break up for the Christmas holidays, and both the staff and the kids seem to be going giddy with excitement about it. Possibly for different reasons. I don't have any more classes at college until the New Year either, which also feels like something of a Christmas miracle.

As I push open the door of the pharmacy, setting off the tinkling bell, Auburn leaps up from the giant red lipstick chair and rushes towards me. She seems to have been lying in wait, which is slightly terrifying. Her red hair is loose and flowing behind her as she makes her dash, and she looks a bit like some kind of super villain in her white coat – one of those beautiful but mad scientists who's trying to create a mega-virus to wipe out the human race because she was bullied at school.

Before I even have the chance to take my coat off, she throws her arms around me and physically lifts me up off the floor, spinning me around like a child. Did I mention how tall the Longville sisters are? And how short I am?

I splutter and protest and struggle to breathe, and she eventually puts me down again, where I wobble slightly on unsteady feet and feel confused.

'What the hell, Auburn? What was that all about?' I ask, backing away from her slightly in case she tries to do it again. You never know with Auburn. She can be strange and unpredictable, it's all part of her offbeat charm.

'I just wanted to say thank you!'

'What for? And since when did spinning someone until they're dizzy constitute an accepted way of showing gratitude? I would have preferred flowers, or cake, or a diamond necklace!'

'Well, I'll get you all of those as well,' she replies, grinning at me. 'Or being realistic, maybe a cubic zirconia necklace off the shopping channel . . .'

'Okay. I'll look forward to it. But what have I done that's made you all thankful? If it's for sorting out that new delivery of Gaviscon, then don't worry, it's all part of my job . . .'

She frowns and perches her head on one side, like some kind of exotic parrot.

'I thought you'd heard?' she says mysteriously. 'Didn't Van come over last night?'

'He did,' I reply, biting my lip in shame at the memory. 'But I was tired, and he left, and we didn't really get a chance to talk properly.'

Her lips form into a small 'oh' at that, and I can tell she's picked up on the fact that there's something wrong from my tone. I'd never make it as a Russian spy.

'Right. Well. I'm sure you'll sort it out,' she says eventually. 'But I wanted to thank you because of Mum. You know we were taking her for her health checks because she's been so off recently?'

'I do. Wasn't that a few days ago?'

'It was, and because of your suggestion, I basically insisted they check her bowels as well. It was all pretty hideous – you've not met hideous until you try explaining a camera up the bum to an Alzheimer's patient. Anyway, they found something, and they took a biopsy, and the results came in yesterday. Bowel cancer.'

I stare at her, blinking rapidly as I try and digest this news.

'What . . . why is that good news? Why are you thanking me? How is she? What happens next?' I splutter.

'Well, it's good news because we've caught it really early. It's only stage one, and the docs are sure they can sort it out. She'll need surgery, which will be another barrel load of laughs obviously, but hopefully that'll be all. They'll know more after some CT scans, but fingers crossed it's a small op—'

'A local resection?' I ask.

'Yes. Forgot how clever you are. Hopefully one of those, yes. And if the margins are clear and the lymph node tests come back okay, she won't need any chemo or radiotherapy. So that's why I'm thanking you – because of you saying we should get it checked, we've found it now. While it's just a teeny-tiny bastard tumour, rather than a ginormous flesh-eating bastard tumour.'

This isn't a funny subject, but I have to laugh at her language. I wonder if she used terms like that when she was sitting her pharmacist's exams.

'You're welcome – although I really did nothing. I don't like this new trend for treating me like I'm a hero just for doing normal things. Promise me you won't throw me a party and make me a cardboard medal?'

'I make no promises,' she replies, punching me in the arm. 'But probably not – it's going to be a bit busy anyway. We'll know more soon, once the other scans are done. Sorry to ambush you – I genuinely thought Van had told you. I heard him come home last night, but he just disappeared off into his new man cave straight away.'

'His new man cave?'

'Yeah. His new man cave on wheels.'

'Oh! Tom's camper van? It's arrived?'

She nods enthusiastically, and replies: 'It has, and it's a

thing of beauty. I wish I'd thought of it to be honest. I'm hoping he'll let me have a turn. I might just move in when he's out at work one day, and cover all available surface space with bras and knickers and tampon boxes so he can't face the thought of stepping foot inside ever again . . .'

She's gazing off into the middle distance, and I recognise the signs that she's gone off into some kind of mindscape known only to herself. Auburn World. She's tapping one toe, and chewing a fingernail, and tugging at her hair – never still, always hyper.

It does, at least, give me the chance to scuttle off to the back of the shop, and put the kettle on. I fill it up with water without even thinking about it, then realise that I don't actually want a cup of tea. All I seem to have done for days is drink hot beverages.

I'm doing it because I'm on auto-pilot. I'm looking for something to do with my hands while my mind is busy elsewhere. My mind is busy making me feel awful.

I put the still-empty mug down, and notice that Auburn has tacked up some tinsel along the stock shelves, along with some mistletoe. I better watch myself.

I wash up the mug – which is still clean – and realise that no matter how busy I try and keep myself, I'm going to carry on feeling awful.

Van was standing there, on my doorstep last night, knowing that his mother has cancer. He'd been calling me all afternoon, knowing that his mother has cancer. He got sent packing by a selfish cow he was foolish enough to think of as a friend (that would be me), knowing that his mother has cancer.

Van's mother has cancer. As well as Alzheimer's. And I didn't even give him the chance to tell me – I assumed he was there to find out about my day, and didn't even engage with the concept of his day. I shrivel up inside a bit more each time I remember our non-conversation. The tone of my voice. My body language. The fact that I kept him on the step. That I gave him the impression he was a burden, that he was crowding me.

Even if he had only come there to check up on me, it would have been unforgivable. What a nasty way to behave. But under the circumstances I've just been made aware of, it's even worse. He probably needed someone to talk to who wasn't a member of his family. He probably needed some space, away from the cottage. He probably wanted someone with a medical background to talk to. He probably just wanted a hug, and for me to tell him it was all going to be all right.

Instead, I rejected him – because I was tired. Because I was stressed. Because I'm probably fundamentally evil.

*No, not evil*, I tell myself – but I definitely have issues. Van was getting too close, on a day when being around Jason and Jo had rattled my cage already. I shut him out, and it wasn't right, and it's especially not right now I know about Lynnie.

'Are you going to wash that mug again?' asks Auburn, jolting me out of my self-hatred meltdown. 'You've already done it three times . . .'

I stare at the sink; at the mug, still in my hands, submerged in soapy water. I pull the plug out, and grab a towel to dry myself with.

'You okay?' she says, leaning in the doorway, watching me while she sucks on a whistle pop.

'Hmmm . . . I don't know. Would you be all right without me for a bit?'

She glances back in to the shop. Mrs Newton from the local butcher's shop is browsing hand cream.

'Not sure. The rush might kill me . . . of course I can. Where are you off to?'

That, I realise as I get my coat from the hook, is actually a very good question. Where am I off to? There are any number of places.

'I don't have a clue, but maybe you can help me. Where's Van working today?'

She screws up her face, trying to remember, then replies: 'Briarwood. I remember because we had a conversation about it yesterday. I was there for some Star Lord interviews in the morning, before we had our appointment. And he said he was there today, fixing a whatsit with a whoojit. Or possibly something more technical than that. Why?'

'I was a complete bitch to him when he called around last night, and I want to apologise.'

She pulls a face, and says: 'You? A bitch? It seems unlikely.'

'It was likely. So . . . I need to get to Briarwood. That'll take ages to walk, won't it?'

'Yes. Can you teleport?' she asks.

'Not as far as I know.'

'Maybe if you think about it really, really hard?'

'It's okay . . . I'll walk.'

I remember how cold it is outside, and the fact that Briarwood's nickname with the locals is the House on the Hill. And I remember exactly how steep that hill is. Arrrgh.

'You can use my bike if you like?' she suggests, shrugging her shoulders in a 'this is a crazy idea but it might just work' way. 'I cycled in today. New fitness regime and all. It's out back. Not sure I'll do it again; too hard to hold a fag and control a bike at the same time.'

I am not the world's greatest cyclist, even when I'm not holding a fag. In fact, I'm pretty awful, unless I'm going in a straight line. Still, it seems like a plan – and it's the only one I've got.

I nod, and tell her I'll be back as soon as I can.

Just as I'm about to leave, she shouts: 'You could just call him, you know?'

I shake my head, give her a wave, and go back out into a freezing cold winter's day, to cycle up a steep hill. It doesn't sound like fun, but it has to be done. I was a bitch to his face, so I need to say I'm sorry to his face as well.

# Chapter 29

I gracefully arrive at Briarwood by skidding to a halt on the circular gravel driveway that leads up to the house.

Unfortunately, I skid to a bit too much of a halt, a bit too quickly, braking so hard the whole bike wobbles and judders and inevitably throws me so much off balance that I end up on the ground, a tangle of legs and feet and swear words.

This bike is pure evil. It absolutely hates me. I decided this on the way here, which was a journey fraught with peril. Seriously, it was like something out of *The Hobbit* – scary trees at the side of the road, tangled roots jutting out into my path, overflowing brooks, crows flying inches past my face, evil wizards. Well, okay, not evil wizards as such – but van drivers who overtook me with inches to spare. The Saurons of the Highway.

By the time I actually make it to the House on the Hill, I'm not only out of puff – that is one supremely steep hill – I'm a jibbering wreck. Every nerve I possess is frayed, which might explain my not-exactly-proficient braking technique.

I lie on the ground for a moment, looking up at a vivid blue sky and catching my breath. I'm not injured precisely – maybe some chunks of gravel in the palms of my hands, maybe a bruised coccyx. Most definitely a wounded sense of dignity.

I kick my way out of the bike, and climb to my feet. By this time, I seem to have an audience, which is a new kind of wonderful.

Several of Tom's budding geniuses have emerged from the house to see what's going on, which leads me to believe that I made a lot more noise than I thought I did. It was probably the swearing that attracted them.

They stand in small groups, staring at me like I'm a member of an alien species, in various stages of surprise and fascination. None of them have put on outdoor clothes, and most of them are dressed in variations of T-shirt and jeans. Some of them are even barefoot, or wearing flip-flops. They all look cold, as they stand shivering around the fountain that's in front of the big old Gothic building, but it doesn't seem to occur to them to go back inside.

They all look curious about who I am and why I've been rolling around on the floor, but none of them asks who I might be or what I'm there for.

Suddenly, I understand why Tom is looking for a Star Lord. These are not practical people we're dealing with. Clever, but also stupid, if you know what I mean.

I dust myself down, brushing gravel off my legs, and

then put the bike upright again. It's basically way too big for me, as well as being evil and hating me. I'm wheeling it away to the bike stands at the side of the house when the spell seems to break, and the geniuses finally realise that I am actually a real human being, not something conjured up by brains way too mashed on caffeine drinks and science all-nighters.

'Are you okay?' a henna-haired girl asks as I walk by. She's one of the barefoot ones, I notice.

'I'm fine, thanks,' I reply. 'But you really should get back inside before your toes get frostbite.'

She stares at her own feet as though surprised to see them there, and nods.

'Yeah. Good call. See ya!'

She turns to go back inside, where presumably she can continue her world-changing research without the need for socks or shoes. All the others follow her, as though they have one hive mind, trailing back in through the big wooden front door.

I notice as I walk past the fountain that the cherub-style figure in the middle of it has been decorated for Christmas, and is wearing a Santa hat on its head and has tinsel draped around its chubby midriff. Frankly, it looks terrifying.

I lodge the bike in the rack, and grimace as I stand up straight. My back has been in a weird position for the whole cycle ride, and the fall didn't help anything. This, I decide, was not one of my more brilliant ideas. I glance around, and have no clue where Van might be, which makes it an even less brilliant idea.

He does maintenance and gardening for Tom here, which means he could be anywhere. He could be in the house, fixing a leaky tap, or he could be miles away, in the deepest, darkest jungle of the Briarwood grounds. It's a bit of a dilemma.

I walk away from the bike, and into the hallway of the house. I never saw it when it was a children's home, where Tom spent part of his childhood, and I never saw it when he bought it earlier in the year, when it was neglected and abandoned.

Now, though, it's clean and bright and filled with light. The impressive staircase and original wood panelling are polished and shining, and I can hear the sounds of music coming from deep within the building. I follow the sound towards what used to be the ballroom, where Edie had her birthday party last time around. The one I chickened out of.

It's a grand room, with high ceilings and intricate plasterwork and dado rails and a huge, ornate fireplace. The bay windows are massive, the frames restored, the curtains thick red velvet drapes. If you screw your eyes up and only concentrate on those parts, you can totally imagine this place hosting dances during Victorian times and beyond.

If you don't screw your eyes up, though, it's harder – because then you get to see lots of young people with weird hair and flannel shirts and beards and bare feet, working in small teams at their work stations. The work stations contain various things I don't recognise, like machine parts and computer casings and tools that look like torture devices, and various things I do, like soldering irons and laptops and spirit levels.

I have no idea what they're doing, and decide it's probably better not to ask. I glance around the room, eardrums throbbing from the bass beat of the music, and hone in on the henna girl from earlier – the one who actually spoke.

She's staring at her laptop screen, chewing the end of a pencil, her face frowning in concentration. I walk over, and wave my hand in front of her eyes to get her attention. I have some nasty scrapes on my palm from my plummet from the bike, I notice, and probably should get them cleaned up. Soon.

'Hi!' I say, once she's torn her gaze from the screen.

'Hi?' she says, staring at me like she's never seen me before in her life.

'We just met, outside . . . I fell off my bike?'

'Oh yeah!' she says, grinning and pointing at me. 'That was funny! Are you all right, though?'

She adds the last part in quickly, as though she feels guilty for laughing at my misfortune, and continues to look slightly confused by the whole exchange.

'Yes, I'm fine. I was just wondering if you could help me

– I'm looking for Van? You might know him, he comes and does work in the house and gardens?'

She nods and smiles, and taps out a message on her screen: 'Anyone know the location of Van the Man?' She presses a button, and it must ping around the whole room on some kind of internal system, because I notice everyone else looking at their screens as well.

Within a few seconds, she gets a reply from someone called LostInSpace666, who says: 'Van the Man was heading to the second floor living area. He had his Toolbox of Justice.'

Henna girl points at the words to make sure I've read them, and I nod in thanks.

'Cheers,' I reply, pausing before I leave. 'Erm . . . wouldn't it have been quicker to just ask out loud?'

'Nah,' she says, raising her voice slightly. 'Then we'd have had to turn the music down.'

Okay. Well. I am clearly about 108 years old and living on a different planet to these guys. I leave the former ballroom, wondering what Ye Olde Dancers of Yore would have made of its current inhabitants, and head back to the staircase.

I make my way up, admiring the way Tom's managed to bring the place back to life, combining the character of the old with the functionality of the new. On the second floor, I find a row of individual rooms, and at the end of the corridor, a big communal living room and kitchen.

I find Van – or at least part of him – in the kitchen. He's lying on his back on the floor, with his head and chest beneath the sink. I can hear the clanging of tools, and assume that he's fixing something – loudly.

His legs are bent, his body twisted with the effort, and he's wearing cargo pants and thick work-boots that look like they have steel caps in the toes. Plus, I can't help but notice, one of those tool belts that automatically makes a man look macho and sexy. At least to me.

I'm quite keen on not surprising him so he jumps and bangs his head, so I cough a little, clearing my throat in the time-honoured manner of warning someone you're in the room. Naturally enough, it makes him jump, and he bangs his head.

He scoots himself out from the space under the sink, and emerges rubbing his scalp with one hand, holding a wrench with the other. He stays there for a moment, like he's doing a weird stomach crunch, staring at me, before getting to his feet.

'Sorry!' I say immediately. 'I didn't want you to bang your head . . .'

'No worries. My head's tough enough to take a few knocks. Just trying to get a plastic Yoda figure out of the drainage pipe. Apparently it's quite valuable.'

'Really?' I ask, surprised. 'How did Yoda end up down the drain?'

'Have you met any of the residents?'

'I have . . . and yes, well. Fair enough. Look, Van, I just wanted to say that—'

'Are you all right? What did you do to your hands?' he interrupts, taking hold of my wrists and examining the gravel-scraped skin.

'Oh, nothing . . . well, I kind of fell off Auburn's bike. In front of all the geniuses. That was fun.'

He shakes his head, wearing one of those expressions that people get when they decide not to even ask. He leads me off to the next door along, which turns out to be a bathroom, and waits while I give my hands a scrub.

He produces a first aid kit from a cupboard by the fire extinguisher – clearly essential items at Briarwood these days – and leads me back through into the kitchen.

'Sit down,' he says, firmly, 'and don't argue. I know you're a nurse, but you have grit in both hands, and nobody is good enough to do that on their own.'

His tone is stern, and I don't know exactly what he's annoyed at – me for last night, me for today, the unfairness of his mum's situation, of life in general. Whichever it is, I'm sure me disagreeing with him isn't going to help.

I sit on one of the chairs, and he drags one next to me. He reaches out and takes hold of one of my hands, spreading it out on the table so my palms are facing upwards. He picks up the tweezers he's just cleaned with a sterile wipe, and very, very gently begins to pluck out the biggest lumps of gravel.

I force myself to relax, because I know that will make this all so much easier, and look on as he works. At the broad hunch of his shoulders as he leans in; at the still-tanned face with its tiny white laughter lines; at the big hands that hold mine so delicately.

Watching him now, under the strip lighting, I can see the strain on his face. His usual smile has faded; his eyes look tired and dull, and he seems half asleep still, concentrating hard on what he's doing.

I reach out with the hand he's not treating, and gently run it over his hair. It's short and soft and lovely, and I let my fingers briefly caress his cheek before I say: 'I'm really sorry about last night, Van. I was a complete dick, to use a technical term. I took all my frustrations out on you, and didn't even give you the chance to tell me the news about Lynnie. I was selfish, and rude, and I hope you can forgive me.'

He tenses slightly – at the touch or at the words, I don't know – and pauses in his work to look up at me. He raises his eyebrows, staring at me as though he's trying to weigh something up.

'Are you just saying this because you feel bad about my mum?' he asks. 'Because I didn't expect you to be psychic and somehow know.'

'No! Well, of course I feel bad about your mum – but even if that wasn't part of it, I'd still be apologising. I wanted to apologise as soon as you'd gone. I felt awful, and was going to text you right away . . .'

'Why didn't you, then?'

'Well, my dad turned up on the doorstep, fresh from becoming Mr Mindfulness 2018 – so I couldn't. As soon as I found out where you were this morning, I quite literally got on my bike and came to find you. And I am honestly a really shitty cyclist. '

This, at least, does make him laugh, and I feel some of the tension fizz out of the room.

'I can see that,' he says, taking hold of my hand again. 'Now try and keep still and be quiet until I've done this, all right?'

I nod, and do as he asks. He's good at it – I'm guessing all those travels abroad and working in a school have taught him a few first aid lessons the hard way. He's gentle and steady, and somehow, even though 'picking gravel out of your bloody hand' isn't on anyone's list of Top 10 romantic occasions, the physical contact with him still makes me feel alive.

'Okay . . .' he says eventually, turning both my hands up to inspect them. 'I think we're all done. You've been a good patient. I'll give you a lollipop and a sticker on the way out.'

'Thank you. And I'm sorry,' I say, 'please believe me.'

He nods, and leans back in his chair and yawns and stretches at the same time.

'Katie,' he says, evenly, 'it's okay. I get it. I know you're sorry. Anyway, you're perfectly entitled to keep the riff-raff standing on the doorstep whenever you want to. Don't worry about it, apology accepted. Was your day all right then? With the ex?'

'It was fine. Just left me with a bad case of crazy bitch-itis afterwards. How are you, more importantly?'

He shrugs and gazes off into the distance, as though he'll find some answers there.

'I don't know. All right, I suppose. Can't quite reach Auburn's giddy heights of enthusiasm, and Willow's pretty bummed too, but . . . well, I keep getting told how lucky we are it was caught early. All I keep thinking is that "lucky" isn't a word easily used in association with Lynnie these days. Still, we shall overcome and all that – no use moping about it or complaining.'

The words sound a bit rehearsed – as though this is what he's been telling himself. That he shouldn't mope, shouldn't moan, shouldn't make a fuss.

'You have every right to mope, and to complain,' I say firmly. 'And if you don't want to bring your sisters or your mum down, you can mope and complain to me. I'll be your mope mopper-upper.'

Just a day or so ago, he'd have found that amusing. He'd have made a suggestive comment, and we'd have flirted a bit, but also known it was true – that we could confide in each other.

Today, he just nods and smiles – perfectly pleasant, perfectly civil, perfectly contained in his own headspace.

Despite him telling me that all is forgiven, things still feel slightly strained. I'm probably overreacting, and making everything about me when it's actually about him and his mum, but I get the sense that he's keeping his distance. That he still seems a bit wary of me.

That makes me feel even worse than I did before I came here. I've always seen this budding thing with Van from my own perspective – I've measured it in terms of what *I* have to lose, what I'm risking, what could go wrong for me and Saul.

Now I'm starting to realise that Van has opened himself up to risk as well, and that maybe right now he's decided to err on the side of caution.

He has no idea how much I want to fix that. How much I want him to trust me, to see me as an ally in life at a time when he needs one. To be honest, I didn't have any idea how much I wanted that until just this minute.

'So, Auburn tells me you have your camper van all set up,' I say, trying to lighten the mood. 'She seems very jealous.'

'Yep, she is,' he replies, grinning. 'But it's mine, all mine . . .'

I pause, and wonder if he'll invite me round. If we'll go ahead with our scheme, and sneak off for the night together. If everything we planned will actually happen. He stays silent, and I don't know quite how to interpret it.

'I can't wait to come and see it,' I say, mustering all my courage.

He doesn't quite meet my eyes, and is tapping the table top with his fingertips.

'Or not,' I add quietly. 'No pressure. Whatever you need, Van.'

I realise that I need to get out of there pretty quickly, or I might start crying. That I'm starting to feel overwhelmed by emotions I don't quite understand, and don't want to drag him down with me. He's got enough on his plate without me turning into a wailing woman at his workplace.

I stand up, and start bleating on about needing to get back to work, and then to pick Saul up from pre-school, and how first I have to do battle with evil road wizards and low-flying crows.

He gets up from his seat, and puts the palm of his hand gently over my mouth to stop me from bleating any further. Thank God for small mercies.

I look up at him, and nod. He lets his hand drop, and twines his fingers into mine.

'It's all a bloody mess, isn't it? Our timing?' he asks, leaning into me as my head rests against his chest. He smells of oil and manliness and Fairy Liquid.

'I guess so,' I reply, nodding against his T-shirt. 'And I'm really sorry about last night. And about Lynnie. And I would like to come and see your camper van.'

He nods, and wraps his arms around me. When he speaks, I can feel his lips moving against my hair.

'I think I'm probably breaking some kind of man code

here, Katie, but I'm not sure the whole no-strings sex thing is a good idea right now. I'm not sure either of us is capable of it . . . not physically, I mean. I am capable of that, honest. But last night, I was upset – no, please don't apologise again! It's not necessary. I know you're sorry, and it wasn't that big a deal – but it did make me realise that I'm maybe already in a bit deeper than I thought I was. And that's okay – but I know you're not. Not yet, at least. I think maybe we need to figure it out a bit more before we get even deeper.'

I slip my arms around his waist, and listen to his heart thudding quietly away through the soft fabric of his T-shirt.

I want to tell him I'm in as deep as he is – or at least that I'd like to be. I want to tell him we should wade out together, and see just how deep we get. I want to tell him all kinds of things – but none of them would be fair, because he's right.

We need to figure things out a bit more. We need to make sure we'll float, and not drag each other down.

'Now come on,' he says, pulling away from me. 'Let's get Auburn's bike in the back of the truck, and you back to the village. I'm not sure you'd survive the return route.'

# Chapter 30

We just about manage horrendous small talk on the blessedly brief journey back to the village. It feels so odd, all of this – so different to the way I usually feel when I'm with Van. He hasn't said it, not out loud, but I recognise when somebody has put their defences up. I should do – I'm a world expert at hiding behind my own.

He pulls up outside the pharmacy, and I turn to him before he gets out to retrieve the bike.

'Are we all right, Van?' I ask, quietly. 'Are we still . . . friends?'

He stares out of the windscreen for a moment, then turns to face me with a smile.

'Of course we are, Katie. That won't change, I promise. If you need me, let me know – I'll be there.'

'And what about you? What about if you need me? You know it applies in reverse, don't you?'

He nods, and swipes his hands over his hair, as though brushing off dust.

'I do. I promise, I do. I'm not trying to be an arsehole

324

here – I'm just tired. Didn't get much sleep, and my brain feels like some kind of black hole, sucking all logical thought out of my head. Look, don't worry about it. It's all good. Come on, I need to get back to Briarwood before Yoda makes it to the great sewer in the sky . . .'

He gets out of the truck, and I watch as he lugs the evil bike out of the bed. He hands it over to me, and I stand holding it steady as he gives me a quick kiss on the cheek, climbs back into the driver's seat, and toots his horn as he starts the engine.

I watch the truck pull away onto the road, knowing he'll do a U-turn at the car park by the café and come back up again. Part of me wants to stay there, rooted to the spot, so I can wave at him again as he drives past for the second time.

Luckily I realise this would be an insane and counter-productive thing to do. He's exhausted, and needs a bit of space, and it's probably a sensible choice to ditch the crazy lady and her complications and lose himself in some mindless plumbing tasks. It might just keep his head from exploding.

I wheel the bike down the entryway and through the gate into the back yard at the pharmacy. I half expect to see Auburn there, smoking, but she's inside. Only the big pink shell she uses as an ashtray remains.

I lean the bike against the wall, and resist the urge to kick it. I'd probably get my ankle trapped – that bike is definitely the boss of me.

I make my way inside, shedding my coat and scarf, and wonder if I should make some tea. Because, you know, I haven't had enough of that recently.

I glance through to the shop floor and see that there is, by Budbury standards, a rush going on. Two people are sitting on the lipstick sofa, presumably waiting for the prescriptions I can see Auburn working on, and there's a man standing at the till holding a packet of corn plasters and a roll of wrapping paper. I hope the two aren't connected, or someone's in for a big disappointment on Christmas morning.

I dash right through and serve him, then go and help Auburn with the prescriptions. I hand them out to the waiting ladies, checking their addresses first, while she carries on getting together some asthma medication that needs delivering later in the day.

We're busy for a solid hour, with customers and preparing scripts and taking a delivery that needs to go straight into the fridge, and by the time the coast is finally clear, it's nearing the end of my shift. I have to go and collect Saul, and then go home to see my dad, and then possibly referee a meeting between him and my mum. Even without the bedrock of anxiety about Van, it wouldn't be a vintage day.

'Cor blimey,' says Auburn, her eyes wide and slightly manic. 'That was intense! I think we should get more Christmas stuff in . . . we're almost out of the scented candles and snowman mugs, did you notice?'

'I did. I'll order some. Plus maybe some more gift wrap and tags. Might as well make hay while the sun shines.'

She nods, and glances out of the window.

'Or while the snow falls . . .' she says, as I follow her gaze. It is snowing, she's right – but not heavily, just a gentle dusting that probably won't settle. At least I hope not, or the buses might not be running.

She leans back against the counter, and I see her reach for a whistle pop, then think better of it and shove her hand into her pocket instead. Must be that health kick she's on. She'll probably have a fag instead, replacing sugar with nicotine – her whole life seems to be one big juggle between potentially harmful substances.

'So, did you find him?' she asks, staring at me, as though daring me to try and avoid the subject. 'And are you coming to the big bash at the café on Christmas Day?'

There are two questions there, but delivered in one rush of words. This is often the way with Auburn – her mind moves so fast that her lips can barely keep up.

'I did find him,' I reply, chewing my lip and wondering how much to tell her. I decide on 'not very much', as she is, after all, his sister.

'Everything okay?'

'Yeah. Fine. All sorted. Thanks for the loan of the bike. And as for the café . . . when was this decided?'

'I got a text from Cherie a bit ago. You might have done as well, have you checked your phone?'

I haven't, not since I did my last 'making-sure-Saul-is-okay' surveillance for missed calls from his pre-school. I look now, and see a couple of messages. One from my dad, saying he's okay to go and pick up Saul if I let him know the address of the nursery, and one from Cherie.

First I answer my dad, telling him I'll be home in five and will drive there with him. It takes a lot of pressure off, knowing our journey will be so much quicker. I really must learn to drive; I'm sick of relying on favours to get through the basics of my day. And if I learn to drive, I'll never have to cycle again.

Cherie's text is simple and to the point: 'Your presence is requested at the Comfort Food Café for a Christmas feast, in thanks and celebration for all we have. Fancy dress optional, from noon onwards. Bring nothing but your Christmas spirit xxx'

I slide my phone back into my pocket, and try not to feel stressed. It's an invitation to a party – one that will undoubtedly be splendid, which Saul will love, and which will surely do away with the need for me to overcook a turkey and peel parsnips.

But as I chat to Auburn, and gather my coat and belongings, I can't quite shake off the feeling that maybe a party at the café might be a step too far for me right now. That maybe I'd prefer to be at home, on my own with Saul, the same way I have the last couple of years.

That maybe I'd even prefer to be somewhere else entirely,

like on a last-minute flight to the Caribbean. Or, being realistic, somewhere cheap and cheerful in Spain.

I had a brief spell, I realise, where everything was settled. A brief spell where I happily sat with the café ladies and gossiped; where I started to relish my place in their lives, and feel safe and secure in the home I'd built for Saul and me in this community. A brief spell where I even began to open up to the idea that Van could be something more to me than the friend I flirt with.

Now, it feels like that brief spell is over. Like things have changed up again, just when I least wanted them to.

There's been drama, and hospitals, and illness, and exes coming back on the scene. There's been the reappearance of my parents, inserting themselves into my life with their usual carelessness. There's been Van, basically rejecting me when I feel like I offered myself to him. Not that simple, I know – but that's how it feels right now.

No matter how much I understand what he's saying, and even partly agree with it, the rejection still feels raw. It still stings. I'd almost forgotten how bad it does sting, as I've not been rejected for so long – keeping my emotions under bubble wrap has its advantages.

Now, I feel like the walls are closing in, and I might get crushed. I might suffocate. I'm trapped in a web of other people, and suddenly need to get out. It's irrational, I know, and I'm going to try and ride out the storm. Take things one step at a time, and not overreact. Not go into shut-down mode at the first sign of trouble – or, to be fair, approximately the first ten signs of trouble.

It's a party. At the café. It will be splendid.

Auburn is looking at me with some concern, as I faff around getting ready to leave.

'You might want to take a few deep breaths,' she says, placing a hand on my arm. 'You've gone super-pale, and you look like you're about to fall over. Do you want a whistle pop? Is your blood sugar messed up? Is anything messed up?'

Pretty much everything feels in some way or another a bit messed up right now – but Auburn has enough to deal with without adding my pathetic personal crises to the list.

'Nope, I'm fine, honest – just having a moment. It's probably a delayed reaction to the shock of riding your bike! Anyway, I'm off – let me know if you get any more news about Lynnie, all right?'

'Aye aye, captain,' she says, saluting me as I leave.

# Chapter 31

I've tried calling my mum to warn her we're coming, but there was no answer. I texted as well, but got no reply. I should have done it last night really, or at the very least earlier this morning, but . . . well, I had other things on my mind. Way too many other things.

So now, as Dad pulls up in the little car park by the bay, I have no idea how this is going to work out. Saul is incredibly excited, clutching his gorilla by its arm with one hand, holding his granddad with the other.

'That's our beach, Granddad!' he says, pointing down at the shoreline. 'And our sea!'

'It's lovely, Saul,' my dad replies enthusiastically. He's been here before, to the beach at least, but it was when we first moved, and Saul doesn't remember it.

'And that's the path to our café,' he adds, pointing upwards. 'And our snowflakes.'

Dad takes in the hill, and the café perched on top of it, and the snowflakes, and smiles.

'That looks even lovelier. Do you think they'll have cake?'

'They have ALL the cake! Every cake in the world! Come on, come on . . . they'll be waiting for me!'

My dad and I share a look over Saul's bobble hat as he dashes off, scrambling up the path like a baby goat. If you can't be an egomaniac when you're three, when can you?

We follow on a bit more slowly, Dad grimacing at the sharp slap of sea air on his tanned face. It's still beautiful here, but climate-wise, it's not quite the Canary Islands.

'So, how is this going to play out, do you think?' I ask, as we trudge upwards. We're both taking our time. Probably both a bit nervous. 'And are you sure we should even be doing it? Why don't we just arrange to meet her somewhere else, later? This is all a bit . . . public.'

'I know, love,' he says, grinning at me. 'That's why I chose it. She won't stab me in public, will she?'

'I don't know, Dad. Maybe she will. And if she does, it'll be your own fault. I don't feel comfortable with this at all.'

'I can understand that, Katie, and you don't have to come with me, you know? Feel free to give it a miss. Leave it to the grown-ups to sort out.'

I make an involuntary snorting noise at that. *The grown-ups*. Ha. He might have changed, but it'll take more than a few weeks to convince me that he's not the same dad I've always known – the dad with a temper, who's quick to anger, who can be loud and hurtful and just as up for a fight as my mum.

He glances at me, and I know he heard me. That he

knows what I'm thinking. That he wisely chooses not to engage with a debate about his newfound maturity as we finally emerge through the wrought-iron Comfort Food Café sign and into the garden.

The garden is, understandably on a day like this, deserted. The dog crèche field is empty, and only the inflatable Santa greets us, his tiny arms wobbling in the wind like a festive T-Rex, his flowing red hat dusted with snow.

Saul has already run ahead and gone inside, and I can see him through the windows, giving Laura a big hug. We follow him in, and I immediately cast my eyes around, searching for my mum. I have my phone in my hand, in case I need to call 999, and have already planned to take Saul for a rapid walk down to the beach if things look as though they're going to turn nasty.

I don't want to see them fighting – and I'm determined that he won't.

Laura straightens up, tucking her curls behind her ears as she smiles at us both. There's a question in her gaze, and I say: 'Laura, this is my dad. Colin. Is Mum around?'

She blinks rapidly, and chews her lip as she nods, and looks basically as nervous as I feel. I haven't seen Mum for a few days, not since she moved in here – I've been busy, and felt like we both needed some space to decompress from our enforced house-sharing. I didn't even tell her about meeting Jason, because I knew she'd have some strong opinion or another on it, and I needed to stick with my own.

I can tell from the expression Laura's currently wearing, though, that Mum has clearly filled them all in on her domestic situation, and probably painted Dad as some kind of evil philandering monster who broke her heart.

'Nice to meet you, Colin,' she manages, staring at him as though searching for the devil horns. 'And yes, Sandy's around – she's was just out back getting some fresh milk from the fridge . . . she should be through in a minute. Come on, Saul, let's go and get you and Marmaduke a snack, shall we?'

She leads him away by his hand, and I mouth a quick 'thank you' to her.

Dad hasn't really noticed Laura's cool reaction. I don't suppose he even realises it was cool, as he doesn't know how warm Laura usually is.

Mainly, though, he's too busy doing what most people do when they come into the café for the first time, and looking around at the decor. It's especially glorious with its Christmas clothes on, and he seems completely bemused by it.

As Laura disappears off with Saul in tow, he looks at me and says: 'Nice place. Great atmosphere. And since when did your mother become Sandy?'

'Gosh, Dad, let me think – probably about the same time you were sitting in Fiona's front room discussing your feelings with a bunch of strangers? Change isn't a one-way street, you know.'

As my mother wanders out from behind the counter, I realise that I have never spoken truer words. My mother has changed – into some kind of chameleon, who adapts her colours to her surroundings. Living here, in Cherie's rock chick lair, has clearly had an effect.

The garish make-up has gone; her hair is free of its usual sheen of lacquer, and she's wearing a tie-dyed T-shirt she's obviously filched from Cherie's wardrobe. It's way too big, and she's cinched it in at the waist with a belt made of seashells. Matching shell earrings drape down from her lobes, and she's completed the ensemble with open-toed Birkenstocks she'd never previously have been seen dead in. In summary, she looks exactly like the kind of woman who would go on a mindfulness retreat in the Canary Islands.

She stops dead still when she spots us, and I look on in horror as she lets go of the plastic milk bottle she's carrying. It seems to happen in slow motion – her look of shock; her fingers loosening; the bottle upending and falling to the floor, milk cascading in a river of white all over her feet.

Nobody reacts for what feels like forever, but is probably only a few seconds. Frank, who was sitting at his usual table in the corner reading a newspaper, jumps to his feet and grabs the bottle from the ground, stopping any more milk spilling out. Cherie, who was making cappuccinos at the machine, grabs the towel that lives next to it and spreads it over the liquid, stamping on it to mop the worst of it up.

Laura joins in, unspooling what looks like a whole tube of kitchen roll around the edges, and swiping it over the rest of the milk.

My mum seems to suddenly notice that she's in the middle of a hive of activity, and jumps, holding her hands to her face and bursting into tears.

Cherie abandons her cleaning duties, and puts her arms around her, squeezing her in tight. I have no idea what she's saying, but I'd be surprised if it doesn't include the words 'crying', 'spilt milk', and 'no use'.

Whatever it is, it seems to do the trick, and Mum emerges from their huddle blinking and pale but looking more together.

I take a few steps towards her, but am deterred from getting any closer by a combination of the still squishy floor, and the look on her face. It's a look that says she feels betrayed, and it makes me feel terrible. Like I've let her down.

I glance back at my dad, and he's equally horrified, although at what I'm not sure. In fact, only Saul seems to be all right, and is using Marmaduke's feet to soak up some stray milk splatter. Gorilla in the washer tonight, then.

'Hi, Mum,' I say, hearing the waver in my own voice. 'I'm sorry we surprised you. I did call, and text, and . . .'

'It's not her fault, Sandra,' says my dad, stepping forward. 'Don't blame Katie. I insisted on coming. I'm sorry I did . . . I didn't want to upset you . . .'

Mum stares at him, and I'm actually relieved to see some anger flash across her face. Anger is good. Anger I'm used to. Pale and weak and betrayed? Not so much.

'Well, how did you expect me to react, Colin?' she snaps, pointing one shaking finger at him. 'I've not seen you for an age, and then you turn up out of the blue like this? Were you expecting a red carpet?'

Cherie, Frank and Laura are watching this exchange with curious expressions, sensing the momentous shifts in mood, the emotions that are swirling across the surface of the words. Laura meets my eyes, and gives me a small, sympathetic smile.

'Saul – do you want to come and help me make sponge cake?' she says, holding out her hand to him.

'Can I crack the eggs?' he asks in delight.

'Course you can . . .' she replies, pulling a face at me over her shoulder. Laura knows as well as I do that letting a 3-year-old crack eggs is going to end in one almighty mess of yolk. Still, it gets him away, and keeps him amused, and distracts him from whatever might happen next.

It also, I realise immediately, takes away my excuse to make a sharp exit as well. There are a couple of tables' worth of customers in the café, all of whom are pretending not to be fascinated by the unfolding drama, and Cherie starts towards them, undoubtedly to offer them free top-ups on their drinks. Frank looks at me, raising his eyebrows in a question, and I nod.

'You know where I am if you need me,' he says quietly, heading off to his table and his hastily abandoned tea.

Eventually, the mood settles, and it's just the three of us. Standing there surrounded by damp towels and wads of kitchen roll and stray rivulets of spilled milk.

'Can we just sit down, and talk?' my dad says, holding his hands out in a gesture of surrender. 'I need to explain some things to you. And apologise.'

Mum is holding on to her glare, but I can tell it's waning. It's probably his timely use of the word 'apologise' that does the trick. That or she's planning on pushing him off the cliff.

She nods abruptly, and stomps off to the furthest table away from everyone else. Normally, new visitors to the café get swamped with cake and creamy beverages and a hearty welcome. Not today – everyone's far too sensible to get involved in this powder keg.

And, as my dad gestures to me to follow him, I decide that includes me as well.

'No, Dad,' I say firmly. 'You got yourself into this mess. You need to get yourself out of it. I'm going to do like you suggested, and leave it to the grown-ups to sort out.'

The look on his face as I stay still, arms folded across my chest in determination, is an absolute picture. I almost feel sorry for him.

I glance around, and notice the way everyone is very deliberately not looking at us. Very deliberately trying not to make an already embarrassing situation any worse.

I don't actually feel embarrassed, although I know I should. I feel annoyed, and exasperated, and trapped. Trapped in a situation I don't like, surrounded by drama I don't enjoy, in a cauldron of emotion that feels all too familiar.

I need to draw a line between their lives and mine, but I'm not entirely sure how to do that, as they seem to have followed me here. Part of me would like to scoop up Saul, and leave immediately. I could change the locks, or move house, or use my savings to buy us false identities and begin a new life in rural Canada. A fresh start, away from my mum and dad and Jason and Jo and even Van. Away from all the complications.

As my savings would probably only stretch to starting a new life in Wales, and I have no clue how to get us false identities, I stay put.

Besides, running right now wouldn't be fair on several different levels. Especially not to Saul, who I can hear chuckling away as he bangs eggs against the side of Laura's mixing bowl.

I turn my back on my parents – I don't want to be staring at them, analysing their body language, listening for the raised voices and changes in posture I recognise as familiar warning signs. I don't want to be a teenager again, sitting at the kitchen table, trying to gauge if it was safe to stay or if I needed to bunker down in my room with my headphones on.

Instead, I walk over to Frank's table. He looks up from his reading, and gives me a welcoming nod. He peels off a section of his paper – travel and leisure, very nice – and hands it to me. Then he chops the cherry scone Cherie's delivered to him in half, and pushes it towards me.

He straightens the crease out of the sports pages, and gives me a wink over the paper, blue eyes twinkling.

'Just leave 'em to it, love,' he says, before going back to his reading.

That, I think as I start an article about eco-friendly northern lights tours, sounds like great advice.

# Chapter 32

A very strange thing happens with my parents after that initial showdown at the Comfort Food Café.

They actually talk. And talk. And talk some more. It strikes me as an odd and serendipitous thing that via different routes, and for very different reasons, they've both ended up at a place in their lives where they seem open to change.

Dad stays at mine, and Mum stays at the café, but they meet often and apparently without bloodshed.

I'm wary about crossing the line I've drawn for myself and getting further involved, but today, as Dad helps me to wrap Christmas presents, I finally feel able to ask.

'So,' I say, biting off Sellotape while holding together edges of paper around Saul's new gardening set, 'what's going on, then, with you and Mum?'

He smiles at me, and carries on encasing a set of plastic zoo animals in paper decorated with bright red Santa heads.

'I thought you didn't want to know,' he replies. 'I thought you were leaving it to the grown-ups to sort out.'

'I am. And it looks like you have been. And now I'm . . . surprised?'

He nods, and finishes his wrapping, adding it to the ever-growing pile on the floor between us. Saul is over at the cottage with Willow and Lynnie, at Willow's request. They've had their scan results, which were as positive as they could be, and she's due to go in for her op in the New Year. Now they've pinpointed what the problem is and got her on pain meds, her mood has improved, and she asked if 'that little boy who looks like Angel' could come around and help them bake mince pies.

We're making the most of it to get ready for the Big Day, filling up the two red Santa Sacks that Saul will find under the tree in a few mornings' time.

'That's a shame, isn't it?' he says, sounding genuinely sad. 'That we've surprised you by acting like civilised human beings?'

'Well, yes . . . but better late than never, I suppose?' I reply, patting him on the hand. 'Do you think you'll . . . you know . . . get back together?'

He ponders this, leaning back against the chair, staring at the purple curtains.

'I don't know, love. Long way to go. We need to be apart for a bit, I think, see what happens. See if any of this is just skin deep. What do you think anyway? Should we get back together?'

I have to confess that my first instinct is to scream 'No!'

in his face. But that instinct comes from the cowardly part of me that struggles to trust them and their newfound behaviour. The part of me that thinks the same as I did when I was a teenager and old enough to understand what was going on: *you two should never even be in the same room as each other, never mind married – please get a divorce, for all our sakes!*

I manage not to say it out loud, but my lack of an immediate response doesn't go unnoticed.

'You don't think we should,' he says, resigned. 'And I don't suppose I blame you. You've seen too much, heard too much. Can't expect to undo years' worth of damage with a few days, can we?'

He's right, but I feel mean about it. Like I'm somehow dismissing them and their futures, either together or apart.

'Well, whatever happens, I'm glad something did,' I reply, moving on to wrapping a set of picture books about astronauts. 'And don't listen to me – I'm just a worry wart.'

I expect him to laugh, or tell me I'm not, or make a joke. Instead, he looks serious, and says: 'Yes, you are. And that's what upsets me most about all of this. About the way we've affected you. Your mum says you were close to Willow's brother, Van. She thought maybe you'd even get together. But you've not mentioned him since I've been here, and I hope that's not because you think all relationships are doomed to take the same turn as mine and your mother's did.'

I bite off some Sellotape with way too much enthusiasm, and hammer it over the astronaut books. I don't want to talk to my dad about Van. I don't want to talk to anyone about Van. I don't even really want to think about Van. It still confuses me, and hurts me, and stings like a patch of skin when you've burned it on a hot pan.

I've seen him, a few times. At the cottage, when I've called around to see Lynnie. In the pharmacy, when he's dropped Auburn off and called in for a cuppa. At the café, obviously, where everyone sees everyone.

We've chatted, and laughed, and shared news. He's been around, being useful as always. He fixed Edie's window, in advance of her coming home in the New Year. He fitted me a cat-flap in the back door, with Saul's invaluable help, so Tinkerbell can come and go as he pleases. Obviously, with usual cat-like contrariness, he's not been out since.

We've talked about his mum and what happens next. We've talked about my mum and what happens next. We've talked about Christmas, and the weather, and Saul, and about the new Star Lord Tom's taken on for Briarwood.

We've met. We've talked. But we've never gone back to the way we were. I don't just mean the kissing and cuddling and the excitement of anticipating what might happen next. I mean the casual intimacy I suppose I'd only just started to accept, only just started to appreciate, before we lost it.

We're both making a big effort to appear normal – but we're not. I know we're not, and it's painful.

'Earth to Katie . . . Earth calling Katie!' my dad says, prodding me back into the here and now. I look up at him, and smile.

'Sorry! Got lost in space . . . I think we're done here, don't you? I can't face another single gift-wrapping challenge.'

He smiles back, and replies: 'Sore subject?'

'No,' I say, getting to my feet in a way that I hope looks decisive. 'Just nothing to discuss.'

Nothing to discuss, I tell myself again. Nothing to cry about. Nothing to mourn. Nothing to regret. Just life, going on as normal.

I'm not at all unhappy. I'm not at all lonely. I'm not at all missing him.

I'm not at all telling the truth, even to myself.

# Chapter 33

By Christmas Eve, Saul's excitement levels have reached a fever pitch. He engages me in numerous conversations about the logistics of Santa's action-packed schedule, and I need all my wits about me to at least try and answer them. It's not long, though, before I am forced to revert to replies that involve frequent use of the words 'because he's magic'.

We've got a programme on the iPad that shows us Santa's route that night, tracking his whereabouts in 'real time', and that's got him even more hyper. He tells me he thinks maybe Father Christmas is an astronaut, and spends a good few minutes wondering how Rudolph gets his antlers into a space helmet, and is generally obsessing in the way that all little people do at this time of year.

I've taken him on a massive walk along the beach, where we used big sticks to write our names in the snow-covered sand. I've taken him to see Edie, who is out of hospital and recuperating at her niece's farmhouse. I've taken him to the café, where he was delighted to find both Tom's dog,

Rick Grimes, and Willow's border terrier, Bella Swan, in residence.

I've taken him to the pharmacy, where Auburn had him helping to wrap her gifts. When I say helping, I do of course mean hindering, but in such an adorable fashion that all is forgiven.

I've taken him on an adventure through the village, snapping photos on my phone of everybody's Christmas decorations so we can print them out and make a collage.

I've taken him to Matt's surgery, where Lizzie has Midegbo dressed up in a Santa hat and a tinsel collar for a festive photoshoot.

I've taken him, basically, everywhere I can possibly think of – and he's still on some kind of insane Christmas high. It's way worse than sugar.

I'm now insisting he sits still for at least two minutes, while he eats a bowl of grapes and crackers and drinks some juice and watches *Elf* in the living room.

By the time he's accepted this, and is happily giggling away with Buddy and his friends, I am in a state of near catatonia in the kitchen. I make myself a coffee and slump down into the chair, resting my head on the table top and wondering what time it's going to be feasible to get him to bed.

Personally, I'm ready for sleep right now – but it's actually only just after six. I need to get him to decompress, and feed and water him, before even considering calling an end to the day.

I glance through at him, and see him curled up in a ball, wearing his T-shirt that has a picture of a Christmas-hat-wearing T-Rex on it. Tinkerbell's next to him, and he looks so cosy and happy.

It makes me smile, despite my fatigue levels. Isn't this what I wanted for him? This kind of Christmas – crammed with magic and friendship and excitement and ginger cat hair? He lives in a little world that is full of laughter and fun and anticipation, and I created that world for him. I kept away the nasties, and I cocooned him in comfort, and I made his life jolly and safe. I did good.

Now, though, I just have to navigate my way through the tricky next level – maintaining it. That, over the last few days, has been getting even trickier.

First, there's the stuff I can talk myself out of. The stuff I know is bound up with my own issues, and which I work hard to overrule. Stuff like wanting to dodge tomorrow's big Christmas bash at the café, because I feel a bit overwhelmed by it. Stuff like me booking driving lessons for the new year, purely so I can always have a quick escape route if I need it. Stuff like me feeling as though someone is punching me in the chest every time they mention Van.

I never had anything with Van, not really. Not in reality – nothing actually happened. But things don't have to be real to hurt, do they? And maybe the thing I now realise I did have with Van was hope. Hope that I could change, hope that I could reach out to someone, and take a different path.

Having that hope taken away – in fact, being such a coward that I've agreed to let it go, been complicit in it all – is dragging me down. I've toyed with the idea of calling him, arranging to meet. Telling him how I feel. Telling him I've done like he asked, and figured stuff out – that I'm ready to plunge right in and see what happens.

I don't, though. Because I'm not. I'm stuck somewhere in between – suffering without him, not convinced I should be with him. And seeing Van, if I'm honest with myself, is a big part of what's stressing me out about tomorrow. Christmas. At the Café.

That, and my mum and dad. After a frankly befuddling period of calm, the cracks are starting to show again with my parents. I don't think they ever went away – they just both managed to paper over them for a while. A kind of honeymoon period.

They've been going for walks, nights out in the pub, talking. She's cooked him dinner in Cherie's flat, and he was smiling when he came back to mine afterwards. I even saw them holding hands once, as they strolled down from the café to the bay. I didn't know quite what to make of it, so chose to pretend it hadn't happened.

Most children would probably be delighted at the prospect of their estranged parents getting back together. But then again, most children probably hadn't put 'Mum and Dad getting a divorce' on the top of their secret Christmas wish list ever since they'd been old enough to know what a divorce was.

Today, though, when Saul and I arrived at the café, things seemed different. As we walked through the door, I saw Mum leaning back in her chair, arms crushed across her chest, nostrils flared and eyes narrowed. Dad was banging the salt and pepper pots together so hard I could hear them clanging, and he was staring out of the window, deliberately avoiding making eye contact with her.

The moment Saul ran towards them, they both seemed to snap out of it, making an effort to shake away whatever was causing the tension. I know them too well, though; I know the signs too well – I can sense the simmering resentment, the slow build-up of anger. I know where that usually leads, and it's nowhere good.

I suspect it's because my dad has told her he's heading back to Bristol on Christmas Day. He's agreed to pop in to the do at the café, but then go for a late lunch with Fiona and her girlfriend. He probably assumed that once he'd explained the situation to Mum – that there was no romance, and that he definitely hadn't dumped her for Jeff Goldblum – that she'd be chilled about it.

What can I say? He's clearly developed a blind spot about how evolved Mum's newfound sense of self actually is. I knew she wouldn't be happy about it, but I guess he didn't.

At least they do put whatever it is they're fighting about on hold while we're there – and hopefully they'll continue to do that tonight, when they're both due to come here for dinner. It'll be the first time I'm alone with them since their not-quite-reunion, and frankly I'm not looking forward to it. There are far too many ways for this to go sideways.

My parents aren't the only ones stressing me out right now. Jo sent me a friend request on Facebook, and I kind of had to accept it. So we're now just one big, happy cyber family. I could have lived with that – but the message she sent this morning wasn't so easy to dismiss. Partly it was just to wish us a happy Christmas, and ask if it would be okay to chat to Saul once he'd opened his presents. Which, you know, it will be – that's not unreasonable.

Less joyful was the second suggestion – that Saul maybe spends a weekend with them at some point in the New Year. Perhaps somewhere in between our homes, she thinks – somewhere in the middle. I can either drop Saul off, or I can come too, if I want to.

Neither option is appealing. The idea of spending a weekend with my ex, his pregnant wife, and Saul isn't enticing. But the whole concept of leaving him with them is even less so. It's a bit of a conundrum, and it's messing with my head. In the end, I just send a non-committal reply saying we'll talk about it after Christmas. Maybe, I think, they'll have decided to emigrate to Australia by then.

For Saul's sake, I keep smiling. I keep on keeping on. It's Christmas. He's three. There should be no downside to this.

I drag myself to my feet, and open the fridge door. Laura

called round with a scan photo yesterday – the generic blobs of black and white that still make you go 'aaah' even though they look like a Rorschach test – and as is her way, didn't come empty handed. She also brought a chicken casserole, which has been waiting to get heated up ever since.

Today, I decide, knowing that my parents will be here soon, is that chicken casserole's chance to shine.

I stick it in the oven, and spend the next hour finishing my wrapping. Saul is starting to crash, slowly but surely, fighting against it but losing the battle. He's rubbing his eyes, and hugging his now-washed gorilla, and generally displaying the signs of a toddler who needs to go to sleep but really, really doesn't want to.

I parcel up a few bits and bobs for my parents, glad that Cherie and the rest have instigated a no-gift rule. Money isn't exactly free flowing, and neither is time – not having to search for the perfect present for the café bunch has simplified everything.

I do, however, have a gift for Van. I had to get it handmade, so I'd ordered it weeks ago. I give it a shake, then set it on the kitchen table. It's a snow globe – of Tanzania. The snowflakes that I assume would never actually fall there in the real world are sparkly and glittering, landing on the backs of tiny zebra and lions.

It seemed quirky and fun at the time I ordered it – but now it makes me feel sad. I pick it up, and put it in a gift bag. I don't want to look at it, and I don't want to think about Van, and I don't want to feel sad.

I put the presents and all the gift-wrapping paraphernalia away and walk through to the living room. The casserole is smelling divine, and Saul is barely awake, and Tinkerbell has given up his latest fight with the Christmas tree. All is relatively calm.

I slump down into the armchair, and watch Saul for a few minutes. He looks so sleepy and content, and I try and focus on that – at how excited he's going to be in the morning.

I'm just about managing to escalate my mood from 'somewhere in the region of doldrums' to 'passable' when I hear the front door opening, and the sound of my parents arriving. There's a couple of minutes where they are obviously taking off coats and boots and dusting snow from their heads before they join us in the lounge.

I can tell, immediately, that things are going badly. I am like a fine-tuned receptor for their vibes, and the one they're giving off now puts me straight onto high alert.

Dad nods at me, and stomps straight off into the kitchen. He starts slamming cupboard doors and is somehow managing to even transform making tea into an act of aggression.

Mum says hello, and glances at Saul. He sleepily waves at her, and she stands with hands on hips, looking down at him. I can feel her tension, but she does at least dredge up a smile for his sake.

'I like your gorilla,' she says, reaching down to pat the furry toy clutched under Saul's arm.

'My dad got him for me,' replies Saul quietly, not even taking his eyes away from the TV screen. He's almost zonked.

'Yes,' she replies, turning to look at me. 'I heard about that. From your granddad.'

Her hands are lodged on her hips, and her eyes are narrowed, and she's looking at me as though I'm a small mouse and she's a hungry boa constrictor. Anyone else might think she's mad at me, for not filling her in on the Jason situation.

I, however, know her too well. I know she'll be annoyed and possibly hurt that I didn't confide in her. But this is more than that – this is the kind of mood that somehow makes the air around her crackle with the anticipation of a great big screaming row. I'm just the nearest target – I suspect the one she really wants to aim it towards is in the kitchen, abusing my kettle.

In the meantime, it seems, I'll do. I'm really not up for that, and I glance at my watch, seeing that it's now getting on towards half seven. Time, I decide, for the little man to go to bed.

He starts to argue when I scoop him up to take him upstairs, but it's half-hearted. He winds his arms around my neck, and I feel his tiny fingers twine into my hair, the way they do when he's really tired.

I feel his warm breath on my neck, and think again how big he's getting as I trudge up the stairs. I can still carry him at the moment, but he's not a baby any more. It's all so fleeting – it feels simultaneously like yesterday and like several lifetimes ago that he was so tiny I could hold him in one arm.

He's so wiped out he lets me undress him without any protest, raising his arms in the air for me to take his jumper off, holding onto my hair as I fasten up the buttons on his tartan pyjamas. He looks very Christmassy, decked out in his black and red.

I muss up his hair and give him a kiss, and draw the covers of his bed up to his chin.

He stifles a yawn, and holds my hand.

'Mummy,' he says, dozily, 'when will Santa be here? Can we check?'

'Course we can, sweetie,' I say, getting my phone out and finding the page with the Santa-finding device. I lie down next to him, snuggling in while we both gaze at the screen.

We see that Father Christmas isn't too far away now – heading in our direction.

'He'll be here soon,' murmurs Saul, sighing with content-ment.

'He will, my love,' I reply, stroking his hair from his forehead. I decide I'll stay here for a few minutes, with this precious boy, making the most of every moment of inno-cence he has to spare. Before I know it he'll be drinking cider in the park and choosing his Christmas swag from the Argos catalogue instead of doing this.

I lay my head next to his on the pillow, and watch as he tries to keep his eyes open and fails. His lids close, and his breathing steadies, and his face goes slack in that way that tells me he's in the Land of Nod.

And then I hear the first raised voice from downstairs that tells me my parents are in the Land of Arguments. I bite my lip and close my own eyes, and fight the tension that starts to sweep through me.

Maybe, if I just stay here and stay quiet and stay still, it'll all go away. I know, from too many years of experience, that it won't – but it's Christmas. I can but hope.

# PART 3 – GO?

# Chapter 34

I've had enough. My head is pounding, and my eyes are sore, and every inch of my body from my scalp to my toes feels like it's clenched up in protest.

All I can hear is the screaming, rising in shrieks and peaks above the sound of festive music, a playlist of carols I have on my phone to try and drown it all out. The mix is horrendous: the sublime choruses of 'Hark the Herald Angels Sing' alternating with yells of abuse.

Saul is sleeping, but restlessly, in that way that children will – I can see his eyes moving around under his lids, and his little fists are clenched, and every now and then his legs jerk, like a dreaming dog. It's the night before Christmas – maybe he's thinking about Santa, flying over the rooftops in his sleigh. I hope so, anyway. I hope he's not about to wake up, and hear all the rowing, and the banging, and voices. I worked hard to protect him from this, but it's chased me down, rooted me out.

I'm in my own little house, but I don't feel safe here any more. I'm in my own little house, and there are too many voices. Too much conflict. I'm in my own little house, and I'm hiding up the stairs, cowering beneath the bed sheets, paralysed by it all.

I'm in my own little house, and I have to get out. I have to get away. I have to run.

The problem is, I have nowhere to go – and no way of getting there. I'm barricaded into this room, with Saul, by my own emotions – just as securely as if I'd moved the wardrobe in front of the door.

It's been going on for almost two hours now. I only make out the occasional word from down the stairs, and none of those words are kind. None of them are mindful, or progressive, or belong in the mouths of people who have changed.

I want to just go down and tell them to shut the eff up. I want to kick them out. I want to scream at them myself, and tell them how much I despise this, how angry I am that they've brought their drama into my home on this night of all nights.

I want to do all of this, but somehow, I just can't. Maybe I'm a coward. Maybe I'm exhausted. Maybe I have no resources left.

Maybe hiding away and drowning it out with music is just too engrained in my behavioural DNA for me to do anything different.

I glance at Saul, and see that he's fine. I know he's fine. He sleeps deeply, and neither the racket from below nor the sound of the carols has roused him. He's fine – it's me who isn't.

I tiptoe out of his room, and into my own. I sit on my bed, and stare at the window. I get a rucksack from the cupboard, and I start to fill it. I place a few items of clothing inside, mine and Saul's. I put the framed photo of my nan I keep by my bed inside. I put the bag down on the floor, and kick it, several times, careful to aim at the clothes and not the photo.

There's a lull downstairs, and part of me wonders if it might be safe to come out. To creep down and take a peek into the living room. But I know better than that – I've been here too many times. I know it's only temporary, while they both catch their breath.

The door creaks and opens, and Tinkerbell leaps up onto my bed. He curls his face into the giant ginger fluffball that is his tail, and looks at me. I swear to God he looks sad, but I'm probably projecting.

I get up, open the wardrobe door. The two big red sacks are in there – Saul's presents. I want to take them out and carry them downstairs, and somehow get hold of Saul and run for the hills. I want this so badly it's like a craving.

I've done it before, and I'm starting to think that maybe I should do it again. I have a cat and friends and a job here. But now, I also have psychopathic parents and a man who somehow has become my ex without ever being my boyfriend. I have complications and ties and responsibilities.

I'm not sure I want any of it any more. It all feels sour, and joyless, and I decide I'm a fool for ever thinking it could be any different. For thinking I could escape the fate of the now-resumed screaming match below me.

I hear the familiar sound of my mum's high-pitched screech, the one I always think of as her war cry, and wait, head cocked to one side, for what I know will follow soon after – the sound of something breaking.

Sure enough, seconds later, I hear a crash and a thud. No shattering, so my plates and glasses are probably safe. It might be a book, or even the wooden fruit bowl, and I picture all the apples and tangerines scattering over the carpet.

I want to run, but I'm not sure I can. The logistics are challenging. It's Christmas Eve, it's snowing, and I have nowhere to go. I have the keys to the pharmacy, and I could set up camp there. I have the phone number for a taxi firm in Dorchester, who might charge me double-time but would at least get me out of here. I could go to Bristol as the first stop, to my parents' house. I could leave them to it, and decide what fresh start to make tomorrow.

I could wrap Saul up warm, and load those Santa sacks into some stranger's boot, and disappear. It's not like my parents would notice my leaving – I've learned this much by now. Everything else, including their own daughter and grandchild, is invisible to them when they're this deep into it.

Tinkberbell would be fine, I tell myself. I could text Matt, and ask him to get him. Auburn could find someone else to do what I do at work – it's not like it's rocket science. People might be surprised. Laura might cry. But eventually, nobody would really care – they'd all get used to my absence. They have each other, and their own busy lives, and after a while, it'd be like I'd never even lived here.

And maybe, I think, feeling a self-indulgent tear slip down my cheek, Van would even be relieved. He's trying to be a friend. He's trying to be steady. But wouldn't it, just possibly, be better for both of us if we made a fresh start? Whatever we might have had, we've messed it up. It might be my fault. It might be his. It might just be a great big enormous dollop of bad timing. But it's gone now – it was barely even there.

Better to go now, before it all gets worse.

I haul the present bags out of the wardrobe, and stare at them. Imagine how all of this would affect Saul. If there is any way I could sugar-coat this one – pretend it was a game, an adventure, an exciting piece of Christmas fun.

I slump back down on the bed, and feel like screaming in frustration. No. Of course there isn't. Waking him up on Christmas Eve, loading him into a cab on a freezing cold night? Taking him away from everything he loves, everything he's used to?

That wouldn't be fair. It wouldn't be okay, not even a tiny bit. There's another burst of vicious yelling from downstairs, and a bellow from my dad, and yes, right on cue, the sound of something actually smashing. Maybe my plates and glasses aren't so safe any more.

When I was a kid, I used to find ways to pass the time while I was exiled upstairs. Listening to music, texting my friends, reading magazines, even doing homework. A lot of the time, I even managed to sleep – with my headphones in, to drown out the cacophony from the floor below.

Now, I can't risk the headphones. I can't risk not hearing Saul. I'm trapped up here, with nothing to do.

I pick up the rucksack again, and for some reason hold it to me, like it's a baby I'm cuddling. I wander to the window, and look outside. The snow is falling more heavily now, piling up on rooftops and pavements and the swinging pharmacy sign. Under other circumstances, it might even look pretty. Christmassy, in that way that English Christmases are always portrayed in American films.

I notice the usual lights on in the usual homes; see the silhouettes of movement in bright windows. If I strain my ears, and turn off the phone carols for a minute, I can almost hear – or maybe just imagine – the sounds of laughter and companionship coming from the pub. It'll be busy in there, the log fire blazing and hissing, every table full, bar staff wearing their traditional elf and snowman hats.

I notice a car parked by the pharmacy, and realise that it's Auburn's. I frown, and squint so I can see better, and realise that a light has just gone off in the pharmacy. Weird.

I hadn't even noticed the light was on until it all went dark again.

I watch, in my dimly lit bedroom, wondering who's there. It's a lot better than wondering how long the screaming downstairs will go on for. It could be almost over. It could go on all night. They're certainly showing no signs of letting up so far – I suppose they have months' worth of steam to blow off, after all.

The pharmacy door opens and closes, and I watch as a figure emerges. Tall, broad, dressed in dark clothes. It's Van, although I have no idea what he's doing. I look on as he locks up, and turns to walk back to the car. He pauses, beneath the yellow light of a lamppost, frozen in a circle of shining shadow.

The snow is flurrying around him, and he's holding a box of some kind. His beanie hat is pulled down over his ears, and he's wearing his body-warmer.

He stands still, and looks across towards my house. I feel momentarily guilty, standing here spying on him, and wonder what he's thinking. Whether he knows where I am, or even cares. Whether he'd miss me if I left. How long it would take him to even notice.

I realise that I'm crying as I stand there, staring down at him, and wish so hard that I could be the kind of person who could reach out. Tell him how much I appreciate him. Tell him how much he's come to mean to me, and how much I need a friend right now.

But I'm not that kind of person. I'm not strong enough to be that weak.

I wipe the silent tears from my eyes, and at that moment, he looks upwards. He sees me. He waves, once, hesitantly.

I wave back, and close the curtains, and collapse onto my bed, too sad to even care about my parents any more.

# Chapter 35

I'm tangled in my sheets, eyes red and stinging and barely open, as my phone rings. I ignore it, but it's enough to wake me up – or at least drag me even more into consciousness.

I've not exactly been asleep. Not properly. I've just drifted in and out of a restless and traumatised state, and now I feel disjointed and bewildered. I blink my eyes open and shut a few times, and look at my watch. It should be four in the morning, but I see it's only just after eleven.

I can still hear my mum and dad hard at it – they obviously have a lot to sort out. I sit up, and slap myself in the face. I need to wake up properly, go and check on Saul.

Before I can mobilise – my body really doesn't want to cooperate – my phone rings again. I snatch it up from the pillow, where it had been playing carols to me, and look at the display. Van.

I want to ignore it again – I feel too compromised to add my feelings about Van into the mix tonight – but something tells me he'll just keep calling. And anyway, it could be something urgent.

I answer it, and say nervously: 'Hi? Is everything all right? Is your mum okay?'

'Everything's fine. She's at home with Willow and Auburn and the dog.'

'Oh. So, where are you then?'

'Look out your window,' he says, sounding amused.

I stand up, and walk my wobbling legs over to the window. I tug the curtain aside and see him there, in the street, holding his phone in one hand, waving at me with the other.

He's standing beside what I assume is Tom's camper van, and the camper van is decorated as brightly and colourfully as the Father Christmas sleigh that the Rotary Club used to ride around our estate every December.

The VW is draped in strings of fairy lights, in pink and yellow and blue, twinkling on and off in a frenetic spasm up and down the body of the van. Their brilliant blinks are swallowed up in the snow, shining through the flakes and making them multi-coloured.

Against the odds, it makes me smile – the first smile I've managed for some time now.

'I've come to rescue you,' he says simply, looking up at me from the street. It's weird, watching his lips move in real time out there, and hearing his voice in my ear. 'I was outside earlier, and I heard your parents. To be honest I think people in Applechurch heard your parents. I . . . well, you'd told me about it, what they were like, but I don't

368

think anything could have prepared me for those kinds of sound levels. Jesus. Is Saul managing to sleep through it?'

'He is, thank God,' I reply, still groggy and still confused by what he's doing here.

'Well, get your stuff together. Get his presents. Get him. And come to me. We're going to run away together, just for the night. I'm going to hang up now, so you can't say no. If you don't come out, I'll just stay here, and sleep in the van all night.'

He promptly does exactly what he said he would, and hangs up. I stare at the phone. I stare at him. I stare at the decked-out camper van taking up most of the road.

Then, I do exactly as he says. I do it quickly, because I know that if I pause – if I let myself think about it – I'll talk my way out of it. I'll persuade myself that this is a terrible idea. I'll come up with a million and one reasons why this is wrong.

First, I make two journeys up and down the stairs with the Santa sacks and my bag. Then I put on my trainers and a coat and a hat, ready to go out into what I know will be a freezing cold night.

I make my way into Saul's room, and wake him up. Kind of. He's still asleep, really, clinging on to me as I plunge his head into the neck of a chunky sweater and encase his feet in thick socks. He clings onto my neck as we creep downstairs, whispering into my ear as we go past the living room door.

I pause for a moment, and hear my mum's high-pitched voice telling my dad he's 'a useless lying piece of shit', and him replying gruffly that he wouldn't need to lie, if she wasn't an evil bitch with no soul.

If ever I needed any further prodding, that was it.

Tinkerbell has padded down the stairs after me, and is sitting on the bottom step, his green eyes glittering as he watches us sneak away. I hold the door open for a few seconds, as if inviting him to join us, but he starts licking his front paws instead. I take it that he's decided to stay where the radiators are, and I leave him to it. He's a cat. He'll be fine.

Van's waiting outside for us, rubbing his hands together in the cold. His face breaks out into a huge smile when he sees us, and I gesture to the bags in the hallway.

I carry Saul up into the van, and he follows, hefting all three bags at once, like a super-human Santa.

Inside, the van is even more Christmassy. There's a small fake tree set up on the fold-down table, decorated with tartan bows and glittering angels, and all the windows have tinsel tacked up around them.

There's a double bed, which again I assume can possibly be folded up, and I gently lay Saul down on top of it. The heaters have obviously been working overtime, and it's warm and cosy in here – warm and cosy and quiet.

Saul stirs as I tuck him in, looking up at me with big blue eyes.

'Is he here?' he murmurs, grabbing hold of my hand. 'Is Santa here?'

'Not yet, sweetie,' I reply, smoothing down his hair and soothing him. 'But we saw on the Santa tracker that he's very near . . . and . . . Van came round, to see if we'd like to go and find him. How does that sound?'

'Nice. Wake me up when we find him . . .'

Van's in the driver's seat, and all the doors are closed. He glances back at me, tugs off his beanie hat, and grins.

'Ready to go Santa hunting?' he asks.

I nod, and grin back. This is crazy. This is insane. This is probably completely wrong.

'I really, really am,' I say.

# Chapter 36

Van drives us to Briarwood. The snow is still coming down, and he knows the path into the clearing where Tom had the camper parked up for months.

It's tucked away in a wooded glade, the boughs of the trees heavy with snow, the moonlight filtering through them to dapple on the ground. It's dark and quiet, the only sounds the occasional hoot of an owl, cry of a fox, or snow slithering from the branches. I peer out of the window, curious, and it all looks unbelievably magical – like he's actually brought us to some kind of fairy glen.

Any worries I had about Saul being upset at not waking up at home disappear – this is so much better. This actually looks like somewhere a Santa hunter might do a stake-out.

Saul himself is out for the count, curled up beneath the blankets, looking so much more peaceful than he did back at the house, where the noise of background arguments must have been filtering through into his dreams.

Van clambers through to the back, and perches on the

edge of the bed next to me. There's a dim light on in the cabin, enough for me to see his smile, and to give one in return. He reaches out, and gently strokes my face. I lean in, and kiss the skin of his palm.

I feel so much better now. Whether that's because I've escaped my parents, or because I'm with him, I don't know. And I'm not planning on spoiling the moment by trying to figure it all out. Some things are beyond my control.

'He looks happy enough,' Van says, glancing at Saul.

'He does. Thank you. For coming to get us. I would never have asked that of you.'

He grins and raises his eyebrows.

'I know that!' he replies, taking hold of my hand and keeping it. 'You'd probably rather chop off your own limbs than ask for help. But when I saw you . . . standing there, in the window, clutching that rucksack . . . well, you looked like you needed to get away. In fact I thought you might be gone by the time I got back – you were holding onto it for dear life; it reminded me of those go-bags that spies have in movies? You know, the ones that contain wads of different currencies and a gun and a fake passport?'

I nod, because I know exactly what he means. I've often yearned for one of those.

'Sadly, mine only contained some clean socks. But . . . yes. I needed to go – I just didn't know how. I didn't know how I could leave, and not wreck Christmas for Saul, and not spend the night on the lipstick couch in the pharmacy. Mum and Dad . . . well, they were really going for it.'

He shakes his head, looking befuddled by it all.

'I noticed,' he says, squeezing my hand. 'I've never heard human voices that loud, or that nasty. I'm so sorry you grew up with that. Have you ever considered . . . I don't know . . . telling them to fuck off?'

I laugh out loud at the uncharacteristic swearing, holding my hand to my mouth to dull the sound in case we wake Saul up.

'I have considered it. And I think, tomorrow, I actually need to do it. Tonight, I just didn't have the strength. There's been too much else going on, and I turned into the world's biggest wuss.'

'Why?' he asks. 'What else has been going on?'

I look at him, with his bright eyes and chestnut hair and his kind smile. I look at him, and realise how much better I feel when I'm with him than when we're apart. I realise that leaving here would mean leaving him – and that might break me. This isn't about Saul, or my parents, or Jason and Jo, or my own supremely screwed-up attitude to life. This is about a simple choice: I need to take a risk and try to be happy, or I don't.

'Mainly,' I reply, quietly, 'you. And me. And it being all screwed up. I don't know how it all went wrong so quickly . . . before we'd even given it a chance to go right. I've been an idiot, and I'm sorry. You told me we needed to figure things out. You told me you I needed to figure things out. That you were already in deeper than you thought.'

'I did tell you those things, yes,' he replies, gazing through the window into the moonlit clearing, as though preparing himself to hear bad news.

'Okay. You were right to. And I have. I won't lie – I wanted to run. I wanted to grab my sub-standard go-bag, and leave. Some of that was because of my parents, and the new situation with Saul's dad. Some of that was just me being a coward, and feeling like I was getting too tangled up in other people's lives. In this place.

'But mainly, I think, it was because of you. You called me out, Van – you made me think about us, and what we were to each other, even if I didn't want to. You pushed me away, and that made me realise how much I wanted you. How much I needed you. I'm not proud of it, but it's the way I'm built – contrary, I suppose.'

He turns his gaze back to my face, and his eyes meet mine. His hand is still holding mine, but his expression is unreadable. I feel my breath hitch in my throat, and wonder if I've blown it. If I've left it all too late. If he's decided I'm more trouble than I'm worth. If he's got back together with the blonde one from Abba.

'So,' he replies eventually. 'Refusing to sleep with you made you realise what . . . that you wanted to sleep with me?'

'I already knew I wanted to do that, Van,' I answer,

nudging him. 'I thought I'd made that clear enough. But now . . . well, I also know that this is more than that. This isn't just physical, is it?'

He laughs, and wraps me in his arms, and kisses the top of my head.

'Duh. Of course it isn't. That's what I was trying to say. Took you long enough to cotton on, though, didn't it?'

I smile, and slide my hands around his waist, and stay exactly where I am for a few moments. Because – well, why wouldn't I?

'I know. What can I say? I'm a slow learner. Thank you for tolerating me.'

'S'okay,' he replies, holding me tighter. 'Nobody's perfect. So. Where does this leave us, then? Not that I'm expecting a life plan and a marriage proposal, Katie – I just want to know that I'm not going to wake up one day and find a note saying you're relocating to Vatican City or anything.'

'I'd never do that,' I say. 'Maybe Cardiff. But . . . well, I suppose it leaves us here. Me, and you, and Saul. In a camper van in the woods. Spending Christmas together. That's step one.'

'I'll settle for that,' he says, reluctantly pulling away from me. 'And on that note, we'd better get our Christmas act together. There's a little man here who's going to wake up expecting all manner of merriment. I dressed the van up for him, and you've got the presents – do you think he'll be okay with it? Will it be magical enough for him?'

I look around, at the little Christmas tree and the tinsel and the beautiful snow-bound woods outside. I look at Van, and recognise how special he is – that even now, after our big grown-up discussion, he's still thinking about Saul. He is, to put it simply, pretty much the best person I think I've ever met.

'It'll be magical enough,' I reply, leaning forward to kiss him. 'For all of us.'

# Chapter 37

We wake up at the same time as Saul. This is unsurprising, as Saul is bouncing around on the bed, accidentally kicking us in the face and screeching with excitement.

We spent the night lying either side of him, our hands meeting in the middle, a cosy trio of humanity curled up together like a litter of puppies.

Now, what feels like approximately one hour later, we're up again. Saul is screaming, 'He's been, he's been!', and scampering to the end of the bed to reach the two bulging sacks of presents. He pauses at the end, and turns around to look at us in confusion.

'Where are we?' he says, apparently noticing that he's not in Kansas any more for the first time. 'And why are you here, Van?'

Van yawns, and stretches, and drags himself out from beneath the covers.

'We're in the woods. We saw on the Santa tracker that he was coming here first. And I'm here because I didn't want to miss seeing you open all your presents. Is that okay?'

I realise I'm holding my breath at this point, watching Saul for any signs of distress, hoping he's not going to have a meltdown. I needn't have worried. He nods and jumps off the bed, and plunges right into the sacks. Little people are so much more sensible than big people.

We spend the next hour or so in a flurry of discarded wrapping paper, as Saul undoes all that time and effort I put into the gifts with ruthless efficiency. It takes a while, because he wants to play with everything as he opens it, and we let him. He's operating on around 700 per cent more energy than we are, so we're not in a position to argue.

Once that's done, Van makes us all some toast, and we eat it outside, in the snow. I'd brought Saul's wellies from the hallway, and he blows off even more steam by running around, making footprints and snowballs and shaking low-lying branches and laughing as the snow comes flying off.

Eventually, once he's calm enough to sit still for more than two seconds, he comes back inside and curls up on the bed with one of his astronaut books.

I make the most of the lull in the proceedings to give Van his Tanzania snow globe. He loves it, which is nice. I'm not expecting anything from him, but he produces a white envelope containing a card.

'Got this for you a little while ago,' he says sheepishly, handing it to me. I open the sealed envelope, expecting to find some kind of Christmas confection inside, but am confused to come up with a colourful card featuring a picture of Herbie, the VW Beetle from the movies. I open it up, and inside there's a piece of paper that's clearly been printed off from a computer at home. I scan the page, and start to laugh.

'Driving lessons?' I say, grinning. 'Are you trying to get rid of me?'

He smiles – one of those slow, lazy smiles that makes me feel warm inside. The kind of smile that promises so much more than I ever thought I'd deserve.

'No,' he replies, 'the opposite. I thought if you learned to drive, you wouldn't feel as trapped. And then you'd be more likely to stay.'

'Ah. I see. Reverse psychology . . . very clever. Thank you. I wanted to do this anyway, so it's perfect. Though now I feel bad, because this cost a lot more than a snow globe.'

'Not that much more,' he says, laughing. 'I'm not rich. If you don't crack it in ten lessons, you're on your own. Anyway . . . I'm glad you're pleased.'

I am pleased. Pleased with all of this. With being here, in this place, with these people. At the way my originally horrific Christmas has shaped up. With the idea of what the future might hold for us. All of the problems still exist – my parents are still psychopaths. Jason and Jo still want to be in Saul's life. Lynnie is still ill. But while those problems might still exist, they exist somewhere else. They don't live here, with us, in this place and this moment.

I want to kiss him, so badly. I want to throw my arms around him, and tell him how much he means to me. But there's a young boy lying on the bed, flat on his tummy, legs waving in the air, planning his first trip into space.

I settle for taking Van's hands in mine and kissing his fingers.

Saul gazes over his shoulder at us, and his eyes go wide.

'Are Van's fingers cold?' he asks, when he sees what I'm doing. I always kiss Saul's little hands to warm them up, so it must seem logical to him.

'Yes, love. That's exactly it,' I reply lightly. 'All that snow.'

'Okay. We have to go soon,' he says. 'To the café. They'll be waiting for me.'

He goes back to his book, and I think he's probably right. They will be waiting for him. For me. And that is absolutely fine.

# Chapter 38

The café is postcard pretty in the snow, the path up the side of the hill glistening in the weak sunlight that's filtering down through the clouds.

The sea is grey and white, rolling in to snow-dusted sand, the bay quiet apart from a few dog-walkers and desperate parents trying to wear out their kids.

We arrive together, leaving the camper van in the small car park, making the walk up to the Comfort Food Café sign in a row of three. Saul is between us, his small hands in ours, swinging and jumping and laughing. For him, this is just another lovely day with his mummy and his Van. For me, it feels different – like the start of something. Something wonderful.

Van has one of the Santa sacks hoisted over his shoulder, so Saul can show off his gifts, and I am carrying a box of whistle pops.

That's what he was at the pharmacy for the night before – Willow and Lynnie had made mince pies and snowman cupcakes to take to the party, and Auburn didn't want to go empty-handed. Not being as much of a domestic goddess, she'd sent Van to collect the lollies instead.

Once she'd heard about his plans to come and rescue me from my dysfunctional Christmas Eve fun, she'd put them in the camper van for Saul, after helping Van quickly decorate it before he left. We didn't get around to any whistle pop shenanigans the night before, so the box is still unopened.

We pause outside the café doors, Saul clinging on to our hands and trying to drag us through, and Van's eyes meet mine.

'Are you ready?' he asks, his tone serious.

I know what he's asking. Am I ready to walk through these doors, and become part of all of this? Am I ready to let the world see us together? Am I ready to see my parents again? Am I ready for whatever the heck it is that might happen next?

I nod, and smile, and say: 'Yes. For anything.'

He smiles back, and we go inside. Saul immediately disentangles himself from us, and makes a beeline for Laura. He barrels into her arms and snuggles up on her lap, and I see him starting to tell her all about his magical Christmas in the woods. I can tell exactly when it is that he mentions Van being there when he woke up, because Laura looks up at me, her eyebrows lost beneath her curls, her eyes wide, and a big 'oh!' forming on her mouth.

I nod and make a thumbs-up sign, and she reciprocates.

Looks like we just went public – because if Laura knows something, she's constitutionally incapable of keeping it quiet.

Everyone is there already. The teenagers are in a corner on their own, playing what looks suspiciously like rock, paper, scissors. Matt is talking to Frank, a can of Guinness in his hand. Cherie is bustling around serving up ginger snaps, Willow behind her with a jug of what looks like orange juice but is undoubtedly Buck's Fizz.

Tom is with Lynnie and Auburn, Rick Grimes curled up at their feet with the love of his life, Bella Swan. Midgebo is here, following Cherie and Willow, hoping for a tragic tray accident that might see all of the ginger snaps fall at his paws.

Zoe and Cal are dancing to The Pogues singing 'Fairytale of New York', yelling all the words in each other's faces as they jig. Scrumpy Joe is arranging bottles of his cider on a trestle table, a length of green tinsel tied around his head like a bandana.

Over in the corner, by the bookshelves, I see Edie, set up like a queen on a throne of cushions, a tartan blanket over her lap and a glass of sherry in her hand. Becca is with her, and I feel my heart soar at the sight. Edie is back, and she looks frail but all right, and for the first time I am convinced that she's going to be okay. She spots me across the crowd, and raises her glass in my direction. I wave back at her, and continue to scan the room.

Eventually, I spot them – sitting together at a table for two near the window. Nobody is near them, even in this packed room. It's as though they're emitting some kind of forcefield of bad energy that's keeping people away. Mum is leaning forward, fingertips drumming on the table, lips moving rapidly. I can't tell what she's saying, but I'm guessing it's not 'happy Christmas and peace to all men'.

Dad is on the opposite side of the table, leaning back, arms crossed over his chest, as though he's trying to be physically as far removed from her as he can. I can see the effort he's making not to respond, but I'm not convinced it'll last. He's like a ticking time bomb waiting to go boom.

I stride towards them, determined to sort this out once and for all. I've had enough of tolerating this bullshit, and now is as good a time as any to make that clear.

I drag a chair over to their table and plonk myself down. They both stare at me, as though I'm an alien visiting from another planet. Eventually, Dad speaks: 'Katie! Where were you? We got your text saying you were fine, but we didn't have a clue where you'd disappeared off to . . .'

'No, we didn't,' adds Mum, pulling a face at me. 'That was very selfish of you – taking Saul off when we'd been looking forward to Christmas with him!'

I shake my head and let out a sigh, and hold up my hands to shut her up. She's in that kind of mood, I can tell, where I could tell her she had beautiful eyes and she'd somehow manage to turn it into an argument because she felt I'd insulted her ears.

'No, Mum – just stop,' I say, before she can regroup. 'Both of you, just stop. At exactly what time was it that you even noticed we'd gone?'

There's a silence from both of them. Mum suddenly finds the view from the window fascinating, and Dad starts to rearrange the salt and pepper pots. Yep. Thought so.

'I'll take it from your silence that it was either very late last night, or this morning. I'll also assume that you carried on your slanging match without even hearing us leave.'

'That's not fair!' pipes up Mum angrily. 'It wasn't a slanging match . . . we have a lot to sort out . . . it was—'

'She's right,' interrupts Dad, reaching out and placing his hand over hers. 'It was a slanging match, love. And we didn't sort anything out, did we?'

Mum looks as though she wants to disagree, and I decide that I'm not going to let her.

'Look, Mum, Dad – I really don't care what you want to call it, okay? All I care about is that it doesn't happen again, anywhere near me, or Saul. If you want to have a slanging match, or punch each other in the face, or kill each other with a million paper cuts, that's your business. It's not mine, and I'm not going to let you make it mine.'

They're both silent for a while, and then Mum replies: 'But Katie, don't you want us to sort it out? Don't you want us to get back together?'

I look at her – at the sad eyes, and the new flower-power vibe, and the face that only seems to come alive when she's angry – and wonder what the answer to that is. Do I want them to get back together? In all honesty, no. I think they've been making each other miserable for way too long, and they should probably go their separate ways and find whatever pleasure and fulfilment they can in life while they're both still young enough and healthy enough to do it.

I don't say that, though – because that's not my place. Marriage counselling is not part of the job description of 'daughter', or at least it shouldn't be.

'I don't know, Mum. I can't say what you should do, or how you should do it. I can't live your lives for you. All I can say is this: keep it away from me, and Saul. I will not – ever again – put up with your drama. If it means not seeing you, then so be it. I hope it doesn't, because I love you both very much – but I've had enough. From now on, I'm concentrating on my own life. I'd suggest you do the same with yours.'

Dad nods, and looks sad but resigned. Mum bites her lip, and I can see her fighting the urge to answer back. She can't agree with me, but at least she's not arguing – which I suppose is a step in the right direction.

Before she can take a step in the wrong direction, I stand up.

'Right. I've said my piece. Now I'm going to spend some time with my friends, and my son, and enjoy my day. Happy Christmas.'

I walk away from their table, and into the crowd of people. I walk through the laughter and the chatter and the exuberance of a room full of my friends. I give Cherie an unrequested hug as I pass, which leaves her speechless. I tell Edie how fantastic she looks. I find the box of whistle pops, and I give them all to Auburn. I see Laura, reading an astronaut book to Saul on her lap, and give them both a peck on the cheek.

I walk all the way to Van, who is drinking a bottle of Joe's cider and chatting to Frank.

I take the cider bottle out of his hand, and I kiss him – properly. He looks down at me afterwards, both confused and delighted.

'What was that for?' he asks, laughing. 'Not that I'm complaining.'

'That was a thank you,' I reply, 'for the best Christmas ever.'

I'm aware that I've caused quite a stir, and hear Cherie whooping and cheering in the background, and Edie cackling, and Auburn blowing relentlessly on her whistle pop. Then, in a voice I'm biologically programmed to recognise over any other noise, I hear Saul.

'Mummy,' he says, sounding happy. 'Are Van's lips cold?'

'Yes, love,' I reply, as Van slips his arm around my shoulders and pulls me closer. 'That's exactly it.'

# Stay in touch with
# Debbie
# JOHNSON

Chat with Debbie and get to know the other fans
of the Comfort Food Café series:

 /Debbie Johnson Author

 /@debbiemjohnson

You can also pop over to Debbie's website and sign up to
her newsletter for all the latest gossip from the café,
book news and exclusive competitions.

www.debbiejohnsonauthor.com

# Look out for
# the next book in the
# Comfort Food Café series

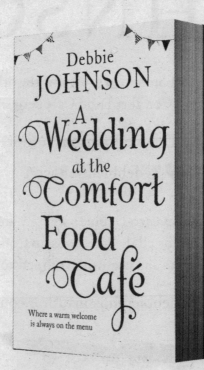

*Where a hearty welcome
is always on the menu*

OUT SPRING 2019